# ALONE
# IN
# ONASEGO

ALSO BY FORREST BACHNER

*The Colour of the Times:*
*Margaret Shippen Arnold and the American Revolution*
*A Novel of Treason*

# ALONE IN ONASEGO

*A Novel*

FORREST BACHNER

Library of Congress Control Number:2019916660

ISBN: 978-0-9972897-2-5

Published by

Illume Writers & Artists
PO Box 86, Gilbertsville, NY 13776

*Cover design, cover photograph and interior design by*
*Cynthia Dunne, Blue Farm Graphic Design*

Printed in the United States

*For KMB*

*"Life is too short to not be yourself."*

—Claire Wineland, CNN interview, 7/5/17

## 1 • EN ROUTE

MOST PEOPLE HAVE no idea of the beauty of upstate New York, or how a person can be shaped and claimed by living there. In the late 1990s, Anna Lawson was one of these people.

Leaving a smoggy, humid Manhattan soon after lunch, Anna and her husband, Paul, drove north, first on the Henry Hudson and then onto the Cross Bronx Expressway bound for the small, upstate town of Onasego, where Paul had a job interview the next day. Around two o'clock they turned onto the Taconic State Parkway, with foot-high grass shimmering in all directions, cloudless blue skies, and a quiet that city people are hard pressed to remember. With a wink from Paul, the sunroof on the rental car slid open filling the car with the heady scent of May while the river sparkled to the west.

Maybe I should take this seriously, Anna thought, looking out on the open fields and low hills of the Hudson River Valley. Nostalgic memories of long, sun-filled days at summer camp slipped into her thinking. Maybe if we lived out here, we would buy a house in the country, watch the sunset, and hear owls at night. Maybe we would go canoeing, hiking, and I could start a book at last. And maybe away from the Manhattan crowd, she stole a glance at her husband, Paul would keep his promise, never cheat on me again, and be happy.

Wispy clouds darted over the sun as the Lawsons crossed the quaint Rip Van Winkle Bridge to the Hudson's west side and entered the Catskill Mountains. Maybe her children would do well outside the pushy and materialistic world of New York City, she mused. Surely in Onasego children would stay children longer than on Fifth Avenue and Times Square. Molly, at thirteen, craved more freedom. A little town could give her that. And Joe. Wouldn't a smaller than average boy with few social instincts have a better chance in a slower, less complicated place? There might even be time for the swimming lessons he wanted so badly. At the very least, the children, the entire family, would be inestimably safer in the confines of a small, rural college town than among the streets, buses, subways, and skyscrapers of Manhattan. Onasego. Maybe.

Densely wooded mountains rose up around them as they passed through the Catskill towns of Cairo, Acra, and Windham. Towns that had seen better days and now needed a burst of tourism, a wealthy native philanthropist, at least a coat of paint. But by the same token, she noted the near absence of strip malls, strips at all in fact. She liked that. It seemed development had passed the area by leaving most villages intact, unmarred by Walmart, Home Depot, or Office Max. Instead, she saw signs for Chauncey's Ladies and Men's Clothes, The Wally Mart, and best of all, the Bun and Cone. Maybe while Paul interviewed at the college, she would find the public schools, call the realtor she had been trying to reach.

Coming out of the high mountains, farms, Currier and Ivish, dotted the countryside under a sky now gone gray. While cows munched and meandered in velvety green pastures, horses with their colts played in the light spring air. High overhead hawks wheeled slowly, methodically searching for unsuspecting prey below. About five miles outside of Onasego, Anna opened her purse and, flipping the mirror down on the sun visor, ran a comb through her hair. They had reservations at a place called Kitt's Lodge, courtesy of Catskill, the college interviewing Paul. She would enjoy a lodge experience—a place a few miles from town where they could walk, sit in rockers on the porch overlooking the countryside, and perhaps Mr. And Mrs. Kitt, or just plain Kitt as the case might be, would regale them with local lore over a glass of wine.

Deciding against lipstick, she snapped the visor back in place. Where her reflection had hovered just seconds earlier, a state trooper now stood waving traffic to a stop on the shoulder. With a slight shrug in her direction, Paul pulled in behind two other cars and a pickup. At the head of the line, two more troopers, one on either side of the car, appeared to be talking to the passengers. The process continued with each vehicle until it was Paul and Anna's turn.

A trooper who looked to be about fourteen asked to see Paul's license. "We're checking traffic on all the major highways, sir."

Anna looked out on the two-lane road where the one other car going in the opposite direction was also stopped. Safety Awareness Month, she bet to herself. So many people still wouldn't use their seat belts. The trooper on her side talked into a cell phone with his back to her. But he wasn't a trooper at all, she realized. Not in chinos, a battered oxford cloth with rolled-up sleeves, and blue black hair like Gregory Peck. The cell still at his ear, he turned toward her. Chiseled cheekbones, hazel eyes, the lines and creases of a forty-something smiling faintly—at her. She caught her breath.

"William, here," he said into the phone and turned away.

"Now yours, ma'am."

The young trooper was handing back Paul's license.

She fumbled for her wallet. "Ma'am." This kid was so polite. Probably the upstate influence. She handed the license to him. He looked from the card to her and back. "What brings you to the area?"

Paul took off his sunglasses. "An appointment at Catskill College tomorrow."

"Catskill," the trooper handed back the license. "Big soccer school. Really big. I'll need to see inside the trunk, please."

Paul pushed the button for the trunk to open.

The trooper walked to the rear of the car, paused briefly, and then was back at Paul's window. "You're clear."

Anna glanced at William, now standing on the side of the highway, then stretched across to look out Paul's window. "Excuse me, officer, is this a safety check?"

She saw the young man's eyes go dark. "No, ma'am, not hardly. A killer's loose in Onasego. Some guy with long blond hair shot an off-duty cop last night at the Big Save grocery store."

"A killer in Onasego," she repeated slowly.

The young trooper looked back at the car behind them. "Cold blooded, yes ma'am." He waved them on.

## 2 • ARRIVAL

MOMENTS LATER ANNA and Paul arrived at Kitt's Lodge, not one but two dark brown shanty-like structures set about fifty feet back from Route 23. The first building, a low-slung restaurant with neon beer signs in the front windows, lay underneath a massive set of inflatable, orange crab claws. Next door, the two-story hotel featured balconies overlooking the highway, carved bears at a picnic table in the front parking lot, and a sign reading BEST RATE $59.99. Across the four-lane service road, another sign rising from an empty meadow announced the future home of Shopbest.

"Paul?"

Her husband, boyishly blond, tanned from hours sailing on the Hudson, lean from more hours jogging in Central Park, grinned. The grin she loved. The grin too many women loved. "Not quite what we had in mind."

"You mean a murderer on the loose—or this?"

He shrugged. "Maybe the other motels are full, Parents' Weekend, something like that."

"It's Tuesday."

Paul unfastened his seatbelt. "I'll check us in, okay?"

Anna sat for a moment scanning the parking lot and wondered when would be the best time to call Molly and Joe. Perhaps after dinner, when both of them would be badgering the sitter for either extra TV time or an impromptu trip to the video store. But maybe before dinner, so she wouldn't have to weigh in. Molly's father, her ex, Jed, was supposed to have taken Molly for dessert after school. She wondered if, as usual, he'd bailed on the outing.

A battered Chevy pulled in beside her. The driver, late thirtyish with shoulder-length sandy hair and a muscle shirt, cut the engine and lit a cigarette. Beneath his sleeve a tattooed cobra coiled over bulging biceps. A dagger, its point red with blood, ran down the forearm. Holding the cigarette between his thumb and index finger, the man took a couple of slow drags before looking her way. His eyes were edgy, angry.

"Paul!" she yelled, yanking the car door open. "Wait!"

🙷

The short, somewhat portly clerk at the counter wore a denim shirt with snap buttons over navy blue shorts. Vaguely western, Anna noted. His name tag read, Ray, and there were no visible tattoos mixed in with a full head of medium brown hair, beard, and dark, inquiring eyes. Good. She was still somewhat shaken from the encounter in the parking lot despite the intervention of common sense, Paul's that was. The murderer wouldn't drive into a public parking lot in broad daylight and just sit there. "Local color," her husband called him.

"So, up from New York City," Ray said looking at their reservation, "coming to Catskill. Hope you like soccer."

"Huge fan." Paul answered. "Can't get enough of it."

Anna wondered if he was practicing for his interview.

"That your Camry out there?"

"A rental. You need the license number?"

Ray thought about it, then smiled. "No. I'll remember. You know I went to New York once. Couldn't wait to get back up here."

Paul cranked up his grin. "Now come on. The City's not so bad."

"Not if you like a lot of traffic, noise, and crazy people killing each other on the street."

What about in the grocery store? Anna wondered.

Ray eyed them over the computer printout. "This your first time in Onasego?"

Anna and Paul nodded.

"You know anything about the area?"

Anna and Paul nodded the other way.

"I tell you what, then." He handed them their keys. "Let's find some coffee and I'll get you started. Nothing worse than not knowing where you're going."

Their room was worse. While Paul unloaded the car, Anna walked up the outdoor stairs to the second story, found their room number and, using the coded key, let herself in. Into a hunting lodge. A deer's head hung over the door. Faux wooden beams covered the walls in log cabin style. Antlers twined about a chandelier hanging in the center of the room, and from the closed doors of the armoire, a moose looked out on deer grazing in a mountain valley mural. Anna threw her purse on the zebra-striped bedspread, then turned on the carved standing-bear, bedside lamp. She eyed the closed bathroom door. Could the murderer be in there? Should she wait for Paul?

Crossing from the bed, she opened the door cautiously and switched on the light. No Mr. Murderer. Surprisingly, there were also neither animals nor animal hides. Just bright pink towels and washcloths, a pink shag bath mat and toilet seat cover, pink toilet paper, and from floor to ceiling, except for the shower tile, a Whitman Candy wall paper of deep red hearts and brilliant blue ribbons. She caught herself in the mirror: kind of short, dark hair, wide eyes. A bunny rabbit sort of person her mother said. Right now a bunny in hell. How could she have thought about moving here?

The room door swung open.

"What the—!"

Anna turned to the doorway where Paul stood, open-mouthed, with the suitcases.

## 3 • THE NEXT DAY

THE NEXT DAY dawned sunny and blue for the appointment at Catskill. After leaving the hotel half an hour early to accommodate rush hour traffic and a spin through Onasego's mid-1800s, ("check out the brick mosaics," Ray had urged), pink-petunia- festooned-for-spring, eight-block downtown, Anna and Paul found themselves, ten minutes later, in a guest parking spot in front of Hardy Hall, the site of Paul's day-long interview. Nestled high against College Hill, the school echoed the red brick, back-in-time vibe of downtown but with an astounding view of the Susquehanna Valley and surrounding mountains.

Anna lowered the complimentary copy of *The Onasegon* from Kitt's. "The killer was robbing the grocery store while it was full of customers. The policeman, a local man, just happened to be there shopping with his wife, saw what he was doing and tried to break it up. They fought, the policeman ended up on the ground, and the killer pulled out a sawed-off shotgun and point-blank shot him in the chest." She reached for her Styrofoam cup of coffee. "I can't imagine anyone being that brave. I bet his wife wanted to kill him."

"Um-hum." Paul had his planner out making notes.

"Paul?" He looked over at her. "I don't think I can see us up here. It's pretty and all, but just so different."

Paul sighed and closed the planner. "Open mind. Remember?"

"What would I do?"

"You could still write."

"For *Manhattan Living*? I'm an urban freelancer, Paul."

He checked his watch. "Gotta go. Got your cell phone? Ray's map?"

Anna peered out over the valley. "With x's for the schools, the realtor's, Burger Max, Cooperstown and the Hall of Fame if I get really bored."

"Remember, you've got a tour of Catskill at four. See you then." He kissed her on the cheek.

Anna glanced down at the folded newspaper and the article about the policeman. "I hope so."

Three hours, a bacon, egg, and cheese, and two schools later, Anna stood in the reception area to the Onasego-Catskills Realty office waiting for Angie Wingo, a realtor recommended by the college to Paul. For weeks she had been leaving messages for Ms. Wingo, with none of them answered. So while she wanted to be able to tell Paul in good faith that she had, indeed, checked out the Onasego housing market, she was also curious to meet a realtor who didn't return phone calls. And finally she was there for a decisive sign from heaven after the school visits. A vote maker or breaker on this whole moving idea.

From the Onasego website, they already determined schooling would be public. The only private school was Catholic, an impossibility for Paul, and boarding schools were a nonstarter for her. Consequently, she began her day at Onasego Elementary School and continued on to the Onasego Middle School, home of the Falcons. Not that the schools weren't fine. In the big scheme of things they probably were. It was just that both—the tall, cozy brick elementary school and the flat institutional middle school—were almost carbon copies of schools she attended thirty years earlier. The school secretaries even had an eerie, toothy similarity to a Mrs. Penderbanks she remembered from third grade as they handed her copies of school calendars, outdated newsletters, and the state-mandated curriculums. Coming from art classes at the Met, immersion tracks in Japanese, and spring trips to walk sections of the Oregon Trail, all offerings of Molly and Joe's current schools, Onasego felt stuck in an old episode of *Saved by the Bell*. Yet she and Paul were products of the American public school system. Their parents never considered paying tens of thousands of dollars for the specialness of private education. But what did she, Anna, believe? Did Molly and Joe's school offer eighteen thousand dollars, the current annual price tag, more in quality than the free, hallowed academic halls of Onasego?

"You must be Ms. Lawson." A slight, fiftyish brunette beckoned to Anna. "I'm Angie Wingo. Come right this way."

Anna followed Ms. Wingo into a small office furnished with a desk, two chairs, telephone and Rolodex. In the corner on a card table, a collection of GI Joe dolls stood posed in a variety of battle positions around toy tanks and trucks. A handwritten SOA—NO! legal sheet was scotch taped to the table.

"S-O-A?"

"School of Assassins at Fort Benning. I'm thinking about a protest." Angie Wingo waved her toward one of the empty chairs. "But! Welcome to Onasego. How are you finding things?"

Now there was a question, and the realtor wasn't helping. Anna fought the urge to walk out. "This murder thing was sort of a surprise. You know, small town and all."

Angie Wingo nodded. "Awful, I know. A cop killer with absolutely nothing left to lose, out wandering around Onasego. I swear, the way people die around here, I've never seen anything like it."

Having no idea what to do with that, Anna moved on. "I left several messages. I was surprised not to hear back from you."

Angie Wingo leaned forward, slapping the desk with the palms of her hands. "No reason to call. There isn't anything."

"But I've got *The Onasegon* right here with the housing listings." Anna took the paper from under her arm and spread it out on the desk. "I circled the ones I'd like to see."

Angie ran her fingers down the column. She stopped at a four-bedroom center hall colonial Anna had not only circled but also starred and put smiley faces beside. "Ought to be illegal to even list that house. Lead paint in every room." She continued down Anna's circles. "The cape, radon. This

Victorian? Cold, cold as a witch's teat in every corner of that house. And, oh my God, here's the Brawleigh house again. Hope does indeed spring eternal—just like the springs that run right under it. A downstater," she paused to look up at Anna, "almost bought it last year." Her finger zipped over the remaining listings. "Nope, nope, and nope. As I said, nothing."

Anna stood, stunned. Never in her life had the possibility of "nothing" occurred to her. When people in Manhattan said "nothing," it really meant nothing at your income, or nothing that a co-op board will let you into, or nothing that you might want, but this woman was saying "nothing" to mean nothing.

"What if my husband gets a job here? What would we do?"

Angie stood and ambled over to the GI Joes in thought. "You'll have to rent 'til something decent comes on the market. But right now I don't know of anything there either." She picked up one young man and dusted off his fatigues. "You know what I'd do? I'd take out an ad in *The Onasegon*. Three lines for three dollars. Family needs house to rent. Moving to town in August. Contact us at blah, blah, blah. Something like that."

Anna took a deep breath. Heaven had spoken. Nothing to buy, nothing to rent. Surely that combined with Mrs. Penderbanks constituted a sign. She wanted to kiss Angie Wingo right there.

Angie leaned the GI Joe back against a model tank and squinted at the tableau of fighting dolls. "Or, you could try Cooperstown."

## 4 • THE LAST OF...

AT ELEVEN THIRTY-FIVE Anna headed off to Cooperstown according to Ray's directions. Cooperstown, the Otsego County seat, home of the Baseball Hall of Fame, and at eighteen miles away, the closest, next-biggest town to Catskill College. Reasoning that as she had canvassed the school and real estate market in Onasego, this was her last obligatory box to check before reporting to Paul, gathering her belongings from the lair, and returning to her rightful home in the city. Eighteen thousand was once again sounding reasonable. She couldn't wait to see their doorman, and as for the haunting sounds of owls, she'd buy a tape.

Barely two minutes from Onasego's center, Anna was in the country. Bearing right at the clearly marked Y on North Street, she felt bold and adventuresome passing by a blood red barn, farms with laundry fluttering in the wind, and dark green, sweet smelling fields for as far as the eye could see. Behind her a cloud of dust from a fellow traveler marred the otherwise pastoral view.

Soon trees arched over the road and the pavement became a lane of composition, dirt, potholes, and ruts. State park land to the left and right was demarcated by official signs and in a blur, a grouse jumped from a low road-side brush. She thought it was a grouse anyway. It looked like the one on the scotch bottle. She dug her new Nokia cell phone out of her purse to leave a message for Joe at home. She wanted him to know she had thought of him at her first grouse sighting. And if he said anything smart, she could tell him not to grouse about it, Ha! She pressed the phone to her ear for the familiar ring and his little boy voice on the family answering machine, "You've reached the Lawsons. We'll call you back if you leave your exact number." That was her boy. Everything had to be exact. But no ring. She glanced in the rear-view mirror. The vehicle behind her was kicking up a huge cloud of dust. So stupid, speeding on a two-lane country road. She slowed down to let it pass.

The woods were thicker now, broken occasionally by dirt roads ending in a trailer or shack but mostly just disappearing into the heavy brush. She would have thought she'd be in Cooperstown by now. Cooperstown, according to Ray, settled by the father of James Fenimore Cooper, the author of *The Last of the Mohicans*. She wondered if the movie had been accurate. Did the daughter taken by the Indians really just jump off a cliff? Did the Indians actually just shrug and walk on? And, didn't Daniel Day Lewis look something like William on the highway? The car behind her slid closer. The car... a beaten up Chevy.

She floored the gas but the Chevy roared closer; the guy from Kitt's parking lot, the same hair, the same edgy eyes, filling her rear-view mirror. Jabbing at Paul's speed dial, she pled, bargained, begged God to live. "NOT NOW! PLEASE, NOT NOW! I'LL DO ANYTHING!" Corn fields, forests, deer whizzed by as she tried to keep the car steady, the cell phone to her ear. Behind her the Chevy's horn blared, headlights blinking on and off.

"I'LL NEVER DOUBT YOU! I'LL TREASURE EVERY MOMENT, PAUL, GODDAMIT, WHERE ARE YOU?" Too late she saw the limb, crashing over it, the cell phone flying from her hand, ricocheting off the dashboard. "I'LL TAKE MOLLY AND JOE TO CHURCH. I'LL DO UNTO OTHERS." Hot tears cascaded down her face as the Camry pulled violently to the right. She heard an explosion, and the car spun to a stop.

## 5 • THE MURDERER

JERKING UP THE edge of the floor mat, Anna searched frantically for the cell phone. The Chevy had pulled in behind her. She felt under the gas pedal, the brake pedal, under her seat and the passenger seat. The driver's side door on the Chevy swung open. She ran her hand along the seat and console and then between the seat and the door. There! The oblong case met her fingertips. She punched in the speed dial for her husband. "Paul! Paul!" she yelled. Nothing. Was his phone turned off? What the hell was he doing? She jammed in 911. The murderer was out of his car now and walking toward her. The black muscle shirt, the huge arms, the confident sneer. She had to do something. "Officer," she screamed into the dead phone. "I'm in terrible danger. Terrible danger. A white Camry between Onasego and Cooperstown. Right now. You have to hurry. Yes, I'll stay on the line."

The murderer walked slowly around the Toyota, stopped in front of the car, and then came around to her side. He bent from the waist, folded his arms and laid them on her open window. Just inches away she could see the hood on the cobra was extended, ready for the death strike.

He flipped a strand of hair behind his shoulder. "Got a cigarette?"

Anna could feel his breath. "Didn't you hear me? The police are on the phone right now."

"Lady, I asked you if you got a cigarette. I'm about to lose it here."

Anna took a deep breath. "The police are on their way this very moment. You should leave." Then for effect she added into the phone, "Yes, officer, I'm still here."

The murdered squatted. He looked her directly in the face. "Those things don't work out here."

"Of course they do."

The murderer's mouth curled downward. He rested his chin on his forearm. "No towers."

She collapsed over the steering wheel. "Please don't kill me. I've got a daughter, a little boy; I'll give you money, anything you want."

The murderer stood up. "Kill you? Right now all I want is a cigarette."

Right now. What about later? Was it like sex? Was smoking somehow part of the act? "Please don't kill me, please." The tears were pouring down Anna's face again. The world was so beautiful, she had seen a grouse, she didn't want to die.

"Lady, you got to quit that crying; you're making me mad."

With that Anna hit the lock button. At least he couldn't drag her off into the woods somewhere.

"Why did you follow me out here? Why me?"

The murderer looked agitated. "Ray told me about you and your husband."

Ray! The murderer's accomplice! The map!

"But why us? Me?"

"Ray said you'd never been up here before. Didn't know nobody."

She'd played right into their hands. No one would miss her until she didn't show up to the tour. No one would even know where to look.

"Open the trunk."

What was this? Was he going to stuff her body in there? Take her somewhere else to torture her?

"No! I won't!"

The murderer shrugged. "There's no getting out of here with that flat."

He was right. Anna sat and smelled the freshness of the woods around her. She closed her eyes and saw Molly and Joe's faces. Why had it all come to this? A cop killer with nothing left to lose. This precious life over at forty-four. She felt strangely calm.

"Hello, Ellis. What have we here?"

Anna opened her eyes as a short, muscular man crunched his bicycle to a stop beside the car. Dressed in black spandex from throat to knee, an aerodynamic helmet, wraparound sunglasses, and a stubby two-day growth, he would have fit in seamlessly with the packs of bikers swooping down Riverside Drive. His accent was Southern. Also, pompous.

"Derek." Her tormentor stood and swatted the stranger on the back. "You got a cigarette? I'm trying to cut down but it's killing me."

Derek climbed off his bike and zipped open his biker's bag. "I shouldn't be aiding and abetting, you know, but here." He handed the murderer a pack of Marlboro Lights and turned to Anna. "I see this is your lucky day. Having Ellis out here to lend a hand."

Anna could barely speak. "My lucky day? He..." she waved toward the man she now knew as Ellis, "... he followed me out here. He knew I didn't know anyone."

"That's right," Ellis interrupted, "Ray told me about these new people in town. I saw her turn down from North and wondered what the hell was she doing out here. I mean, holy shit, why drive out here?"

"Cooperstown," Anna murmured. "I'm going to Cooperstown to look at houses." She reached into the glove compartment and took out Ray's map. She handed it to the two men.

"Aha," Derek said to Ellis. "Our Ray is no dummy. He sent her the back way, so she'd go by that farm he's trying to sell. Smart move."

Anna looked at Ellis. "You came to help me." She burst into tears again.

"Look Lady, nothing's going to hurt you out here." Ellis stuck the cigarette in his mouth, reached in his back pocket and handed her a perfectly folded bandana. "Now I swear if you don't wipe away those tears I will."

"My name is Anna," she announced miserably.

"Well, Anna," Ellis blew three perfect smoke rings, "stop whining and pop the trunk. Derek and me, we got to change that flat."

## 6 • DEGANAWIDAH

ANNA SAT ON a surprisingly comfortable bench in the slanting rays of the afternoon sun in front of the college library, her tour of Catskill, with its renowned elevations, mercifully completed. As the motley group of prospective students, parents, and herself had trudged through the two-hour upward, always upward, tour of the college's classrooms, laboratories, dorms, lounges, and athletic facilities, the young student guide's repetitive "Remember! You're building your thighs!" had grown increasingly old. Heidi would have been challenged by the place. Probably even Heidi's goats. But, Anna thought, looking over the mountains and valley, while Catskill struck her as a fairly traditional, small, northeastern college, it was also set apart, very far apart, by one of the most majestic natural settings she could imagine. The only improvements she could think of would be more landscaping to soften the bricks. And on tour days, a van service. Perhaps Paul, who'd sent word to meet him here, could pass that suggestion along.

Below her two chipmunks were waging a territorial war over a set of steps. One apparently owned the top and the bushes there that the second was trying to ascend. Chip would run up to about the middle step then Dale would chase him down. Over and over and over. How would they ever resolve this? When had she last seen chipmunks?

To her left two Catskill students, one male, one female, discussed their plans for the evening that apparently included bar hopping followed by more bar hopping. Her Molly was just a short five years from SATs, college, leaving home, going to bars. Her Molly whom only hours before she despaired of ever seeing again. Her Molly whom she called like a crazy woman as soon as she got back to Onasego. Her Molly, her Joe, her Paul. What an idiot she had been on that road to Cooperstown. Yet still, she felt as though she received a second chance. But, for what? She fingered Ellis's bandana in her jacket pocket and vividly remembered making a great many promises to God. Doing unto others. Never doubting.

Across the quad she saw Paul walking toward her carrying his briefcase and a plastic shopping bag. With his jacket slung across his shoulder, and the wind ruffling his hair, her husband looked happier than she had seen him in ages. He climbed up Chip and Dale's steps and sat down on the bench beside her.

"What did you buy me?"

Paul pulled out two green and white tee shirts emblazoned with the Catskill logo. "Sorry. These are for the kids. Think they'll fit?"

Both shirts looked huge to Anna. "Sure. How was your day?"

"Great." Paul stuffed the shirts back in the bag and loosened his tie. "Kind of astounding actually. They offered me the VP for Development job."

"But," she squinted up at him, "the interview was for assistant VP."

"True. But their development guy quit out of the blue last week so they offered it to me."

Anna patted his shoulder. "You must feel very complimented. Guess we've got some thinking to do."

Paul placed the briefcase at his feet. "They need my decision tonight."

Anna stared at him. "That's ridiculous. There's an enormous amount to think about. Talk to the kids about."

"Anna, I want the job."

"But," she tried to calm a mounting panic, "it's a family decision. Not just you."

Paul looked up at her, his eyes deep with conviction. "This is the kind of chance I've dreamed about: to be in charge, show people what I can really do. We could try it for a year. The kids would be okay, they might even like it better up here."

She glanced around the balcony for an escape. Time to think. "But, what about that murderer running around here?"

"They got him. Arrested him out west somewhere."

Anna should have felt relieved but she didn't. "Still, there was a murderer right here just a couple of days ago."

"What about the few hundred in the five boroughs right now? Look, Anna, I've made mistakes. This could be a fresh start for us, too."

She felt stupid, dense. "This is too fast. We don't really know anything about Onasego."

He reached for her hand. "I know this is an incredible opportunity. Sort of a miracle. And I know I want it."

She shook his hand away. "What about what I want?"

"All right, Anna," Paul bent forward, resting his elbows on his knees, "tell me, what do you want?"

After the floods of the morning, it surprised Anna that she was capable of tearing up again. She pulled the bandanna from her pocket.

"Damn it, I don't know…"

Standing, she turned away from Paul, and looked out at the view of the valley. It was beautiful. Joe would think it was beautiful too. Molly? Who knew what Molly thought these days. Why couldn't she and Paul take a week to sort this out? Just hours earlier she'd been euphoric, experienced a second chance at life, made promises she wanted to keep.

Anna turned back toward the front wall of the library. Having entered from a side door she had not really noticed the stately facade of the building. Six large panels covered the front of the library. Three on either side of the massive double doors opening to the lobby. The panels offered ancient adages, words of wisdom. The first read, *The mark you make upon the world, is measured by God.* Chilam Balam, the *Book of the Maya.* But it was the words cut into the white stone of the fourth panel that left her stunned:

*I wipe away the tears from your face*
*I make it daylight for thee*
*I beautify the sky*
*The land shall be beautiful*
*The river shall have no more waves*
*One may go everywhere without fear*

Deganawidah

The extraordinary trip to Cooperstown played in her mind like a movie.

*I wipe the tears from your face.*
"If you don't wipe those tears away, lady, then I will."

*I beautify the sky, The land shall be beautiful*
A blood red barn, farms with laundry fluttering in the wind, dark green, sweet smelling fields, and above it all, the intense, vast blue.

*One may go everywhere without fear*
"I'll never doubt you!"

She stared down at the bandana, then turned back to Paul. "One year. I'll try it for one year."

*Editor@manhattanliving.com*

*Dear Marty,*

*How do you think a series of articles about life UPSTATE would go over in Manhattan Living?*

    *We know a lot of people in the city think about making the move.*

*In other words, Paul took the job.*

*Best,*

*Anna*

## 7 • THREE MONTHS LATER

*Moose Moves from Otsego to Delaware County.*

*August 22. East Meredith. Yesterday, Angus Lynch, an organic meat and dairy farmer in East Meredith sighted a moose on his property around 3:00 pm. Lynch believes that the moose is the same animal whose meanderings have intrigued local residents for a month now and led to an informal "moose watch and reporting group" much like the hawk counters on nearby Franklin Mountain. "I'm sure he just wants to get home," Lynch observed. He also reported that his herd was not unduly excited by the intruder.*

Anna dropped the paper in her lap and looked across the stacked cartons and bare walls to where Paul was folding his tie in front of the only unpacked mirror in the house. "Middle East peace talks are revving up again, Clinton could get impeached, and two of our embassies have just been bombed, but the headline in *The Onasegon* is about a moose wandering around the countryside. How can that be?"

Paul glanced back at her in the mirror. "Because *The Onasegon* isn't competing with *The New York Times*. Small town, remember?"

"But the front-page headline..."

He pushed the knot into place and turned around to face her. "Hey, neighbors dropped in on us last night, our first night here. And kids barged in—just like they're supposed to. After six years in our co-op we knew what, one other couple on our floor?"

"Those people were checking us out, Paul."

"Not so unusual. The wife, Deedee, is going to be working for me in alumni affairs."

"Yeah, well, Deedee was all over this house. All she talked about was how Victorians fascinate her; how we were so lucky someone answered our ad. And did she have to take her husband upstairs for a look around?"

"Look, she read about us in the email that everyone at the college got, knew we decided to put our kids in the public schools, and then saw the moving van. She's got a daughter Molly's age. I think she was just being friendly."

"Maybe. But it's kind of creepy. All those people know about us and we don't know anything about anybody."

Paul took his wallet, keys, and PalmPilot from the mantel. "I better be off."

Anna looked around the room in dismay. Despite directing the movers for most of the previous day, the rental house was, at best, only half unpacked, and that was the big stuff.

"Can't you go say hello and come back? We've got all this work to do here. And opening dinner isn't 'til tomorrow night."

Paul reached for his jacket slung over a floor lamp. "An audit team is going over Catskill from top to bottom and I need to meet them. The kids can help."

Anna stood tightening the belt of her robe. The children help organize the house? "You know I'd like to get my office set up too. The magazine is going to expect something from me sometime soon."

He didn't take the bait. "Any ideas yet?" he asked instead.

She really didn't want to pick a fight. Treasure every moment, that was one of those things she was supposed to be working on. She patted his tie. "No. I'm still amazed a magazine called *Manhattan Living* is letting me do a column from upstate New York."

Paul put his arm around her. "Take it as a compliment." He smelled good. He looked good. It was seven o'clock in the morning, Molly and Joe were asleep. Why was he leaving? "Maybe I'll write about the moose."

He kissed her lightly. "Hey, what was Deedee's last name?"

Anna felt the familiar clinch "Why?"

Paul took her face between his hands. "Don't go there. She works at the college. I should remember her name."

A few minutes later, the doorbell rang. She was back.

"Deedee," Anna opened the front door, bewildered, and still in her robe, "come in."

Deedee's smile was workmanlike as she entered from the porch. With henna-colored hair razored to no more than an inch, tanned, rippling biceps, black lycra tank top and shorts, and a clipboard, she was clearly ready. But, for what? Standing amidst the chaos of the unpacked and half packed cartons, Deedee looked like a slightly punkish military officer sent to impose order.

"You've got a skunk under your porch."

Anna pulled her robe tighter. "Now?"

"Yeah," Deedee pointed to the south side of the house, "just went in by the lilac. But don't worry, he'll sleep all day."

Anna was pretty sure a lilac was a shrub. "What do I do?"

"Call the city," with a flurry of her pen, Deedee scribbled a number on the clipboard, "ask for animal control. Here." Using a burgundy nail to crease the paper, Deedee ripped off the number and handed it to Anna.

"Thanks," Anna mumbled, eyeing the flimsy front door screen. "Want some coffee?"

"You know," Deedee began, ignoring the offer, "with school starting next week you've got to get ready for soccer season. I'll give you the number to get Joe in a league, but Molly will want to go out for one of the middle school teams. 'Course we all pitch in with transportation, overnights when they travel, you know..." She paused and looked at Anna expectantly.

"I'll ask the kids about it," Anna hedged. Transportation, overnights, leagues. Grinding torture. Was she going to have to buy a station wagon?

Deedee raised a perfectly arched eyebrow. "They do play soccer?" It was a question, but barely.

"Sure. But mostly indoors, you know, because of the city."

"Hmmm."

Anna sensed that wasn't the right answer. "Sure you don't want some coffee?"

The flat smile again as Deedee scribbled on her clipboard. "Did that a couple of hours ago; just stopped by on the way back from the Y. Here's the number to call about Joe."

With another perfectly executed shred, she held out another sheet of paper then pulled open the front door.

For the first time Anna noticed the black Suburban with its motor running by the curb. With a quick look left and right, she followed Deedee onto the porch.

"Hey," Deedee called from the driver's seat, "Jen and I are going blueberry picking this afternoon. Want to come?"

Anna pulled her robe together at the throat and peered cautiously over the porch rail. Nothing furry peered back. "Thanks, I'll ask the childr—"

"Great," Deedee yelled back. "Out front at 2:00. Bring bags." And with a lurch she was gone.


"So, those kids you went out with last night, how were they?" Across from Anna, Molly and Joe sat cross-legged having bagels and juice on the living room floor, the only place cleared enough for the three of them to sit down together.

Molly lifted the juice bottle and pointed it at her mother. "It's like they don't know anything. Did you see their clothes? I wore that stuff in fourth grade." Molly had recently acquired the teenage art of doing a really good disgusted. Beautiful, with long white blonde hair pulled back loosely in a scrunchy, she also had her grandmother's huge indigo eyes. Anna hated to see those eyes go narrow, even cynical, as they were now.

Joe burped.

"Mom, do something!"

Anna tried to look askance at Joe. "Come on, you know better."

Joe laughed his "hey, hey, hey" halting, artificial laugh. With the recent buzz cut he'd insisted on, he looked like an elfin skin head. Why did laughing have to be so hard for this boy?

"What don't they know?"

"Like, besides the clothes, did you see their hair? They all had on those hair band things that jocks wear. And that one girl, Jen, all she could talk about was taking lessons to get certified to babysit. Gross! One of them, Caroline, is okay. At least she's been to the city."

Anna knew better than to take on clothes and hair. "Hey, speaking of jocks, Jen's mother stopped by this morning. She asked if you two want to play soccer."

"NO!" Joe announced into his juice bottle, the words reverberating against the glass.

Anna nodded. On his team that played in Central Park, Joe's coach, Eddy, always saw to it that Joe got into the game. And that no one kidded him. He'd also confided to Anna that team sports might not be a fit for Joe.

"Molly? You like soccer."

"I don't like anything up here. Besides, I'll be traveling a lot to see Dad."

Whenever he works you in, Anna thought. "And hey, I know last night was kind of weird, but I don't think you asked about going with those kids for pizza."

"And I don't remember you asking me if I wanted to come up here."

Anna felt suddenly weary. Jed had refused to even consider Molly moving in with him for a year. But could she tell her daughter that? No way in this world. "You know this is a huge opportunity for Paul. We said if things don't work out in a year or so we'll go back—or make some kind of arrangements. Now... how about if we all unpack this morning, then take the afternoon off. We've been invited to go blueberry picking."

"Blue berry picking with who?" Molly asked, a flicker of interest lighting her face.

"Jen and her mother, Deedee." Anna said brightly and watched the flicker die.

## 8 • DEEDEE

"HI," ANNA HELD the back door of the Suburban for Joe. "Joe, say hello to Mrs. Molina and Jen."

"Hello, Mrs. Molina and Jen."

Jen waved. Deedee spoke into the rear-view mirror. "Hello, Joe. Where's Molly?"

Anna stepped up onto the running board and pulled herself onto the passenger seat. "She already had plans with Caroline. They're walking downtown, I think."

Deedee's eyes flashed back to the rear-view mirror and Jen.

"She hopes for a rain check," Anna offered feebly pulling the seatbelt over her shoulder.

"Umhumm," Deedee murmured as she backed out of the driveway. "Got everything?"

Anna looked at her quizzically.

"Bags and everything," Deedee explained heading down Summit Avenue.

Anna held up her canvas tote. "Bags and everything."

Deedee squinted at the bag and adjusted the visor while they waited their turn at the blinking light at Summit and Green. A pert, turquoise Honda idled in front of them, and about six feet down. When the car turned Anna saw it was Ray.

"And, animal control, did you get that lined up?"

Anna felt like saluting. "I did. I got Deb somebody at City Hall who said she would send someone out in the next week or so."

"Good," Deedee grunted, taking the left onto Green. With the animal control and bag issues under control, she seemed to relax into the drive. "So, Anna, I hear you're a writer. Tell me about that."

Anna looked back at Joe who was punching the overhead light panel. Between Joe and Deedee it was going to be a long afternoon. "Joe, honey, leave those alone." She turned back to Deedee. "I freelance. Mostly for a magazine called *Manhattan Living*."

Deedee shot Anna a quizzical glance. "But what does that mean exactly?"

Anna pushed her bangs back from her forehead. Did Deedee really not know what a freelance writer was?

"Well, first I research then I write and hopefully sell articles on topics I think other people might think are interesting. For the magazine, it would be some aspect of life in the city. Something like trying to find someone to fix your vacuum cleaner in Manhattan. You can't imagine how hard that is. Or, well, my most recent column was on all the ways borax can just be magic for apartment dwellers. I'm going to try to keep it going from up here."

Deedee wheeled the Suburban onto a four lane. She seemed to be think-ing. A QuikGo station flashed by, The Pantry House Diner, and a mall where Anna noticed the huge 'FOR RENT' sign hung in front of the Big Save. Mr. Murderer had done in that too. Next they passed several building supply companies, car dealerships, a working farm sandwiched between an Agway and a fleet of snowmobiles, before coming to open country and a sign read-ing, The Susquehanna River Valley. Long ago she had read in Michener's book, *Chesapeake*, that someone started at the Chesapeake Bay and followed it inland to find its origin. On and on they walked, as the bay became the Susquehanna River, then a stream, then at last, they'd encountered the head-waters at Lake Otsego, in Cooperstown. Would *Manhattan Living* readers be interested? Suddenly the word estuary came to mind. Wonder what that was?

"But," Deedee said, turning off the highway toward East Meredith, "what do you do the rest of the time?"

Anna spied Joe two rows of blueberry bushes over. How did one treasure every moment when one was terrified? For the third time since their arrival at the Windy Knob Farm, Joe had just meandered off, out of sight, and scared her to death. The farm, four acres of dense, head high blueberry bushes, stood surrounded by thick, dark woods. "Not somewhere to get lost in," Deedee had said as they pulled into the parking lot, adding breezily, "and, you know, every so often, bears."

Anna looked around to make sure Deedee and Jen were out of earshot, then walked over to Joe and hissed in her son's ear, "If you can't stay where I can see you you'll have to wait in the car. Do you understand?"

He looked up at her, frustration written all over his face. "But Mrs. Molina said you only take the real, real blue ones. I have to find the real, real blue ones." He dug in the bag looped over the string around his waist. "See?" He opened his palm where four sapphire-colored berries lay.

She sighed. After an hour and a half of blueberry picking, Joe had four blueberries. Only Joe could make an exact science out of blueberry picking.

"Well, honey, those sure are blue. But you could wander away and get lost out here. Now stay near me."

He dropped the berries back in the bag. "Can I get my juice from the car?"

"I suppose, but come right back." She added a smile as Deedee approached, adjusting her sunglasses. Even in the afternoon heat Deedee was still the picture of crisp efficiency, right down to the slash of blood red lipstick that worked surprisingly well with the bristly hair and black tank. For the afternoon, she had slipped a loose pair of white, drawstring pajama-type pants over her shorts and handed a second pair to Jen. Anna knew she must have looked mystified as Deedee said simply, "ticks," as though that explained it all.

"Everything going all right here?"

"We're okay, I think."

"I still feel bad about the belts."

Anna fingered the string at her waist where, just like Joe's, it ran through the handles of a plastic grocery bag and tied in the back.

"Hey, you said bags and... everything." She smiled again but with less force. Like everyone knew that as white pants were to ticks, bags tied onto belts were to blueberry picking. "And you did have twine in the car."

Deedee started working some of the upper limbs of the bush adjacent to Anna's.

"Such a shame Molly couldn't join us."

Anna brushed a bee away. She had felt this coming. "I know. She's really missing out."

Deedee gave Anna a sideways glance. "A word of caution: Caroline dropped out of soccer last year. She just couldn't dedicate herself."

Anna tried to look concerned. What would Deedee think of Joe, who wouldn't even play? Joe—who should be back by now. "Deedee, I need to find Joe."

She walked back down the path to the parking area, Deedee's footsteps echoing after her. The big black Suburban stood alone. She peered in the window. No little boy sitting with his juice. Where the hell was he? She felt the first edges of panic. "Joe! Joe Lawson, where are you?" No answer.

She scanned down the row. Many of the bushes were way over her head. Above the bushes at the perimeter were the woods. Do not let him get into the woods, she prayed.

"Deedee—"

Deedee smiled, "Anna, I'm sure—"

Anna held up her hand. "Please, just go that way and look for him." She pointed toward the parking lot. "Yell, if you find him. Wait at the car." For herself, she turned and raced across the rows, swiveling to look up and down each one, and simultaneously wondering if she shouldn't be organizing the four or five other pickers to search.

"Need help, ma'am?" asked one of the pickers, a heavy-set woman with frizzled blonde hair.

"My son," she snapped.

Something tugged at the back of her shirt. She wheeled around.

Joe, his eyes wide, pressed his index finger over his mouth and shook his head furiously. No talking. She knew these moods. Giving him a piece of her mind would have to wait awhile. He grabbed her hand, pulling her behind him. She looked back at the frizzled blonde and mouthed "My son." Twenty feet deeper in the woods Joe stopped behind a huge pine and pointed solemnly. Gasping, she bent with her hands on her thighs, and followed the slightly blue stained index finger to the colossus chewing languidly on a white birch near a ribbon of stream. Standing at least six feet high at the muzzle, the creature grazed slowly from limb to limb. Antlers with a four or five foot spread hovered over soft eyes and long, horse like muzzle.

She dropped to one knee with her arms around Joe. Despite the moose's enormity, he didn't exude the dignity that she would have expected of an animal this size. Something about the sloping back, long skinny legs, and "who me?" look about the eyes and muzzle, robbed him of all that. Instead, he seemed like the sweet but goofy type, the one who would never get the joke. The one who could never imagine being loved just for himself. While she watched, the great animal lumbered to the stream, and in a gesture she could never have imagined, went down on his front knees, and drank.

Twigs rustled behind them, cameras snapped, flashes crackled. The massive creature lifted its head, nostrils flared, and seemed to Anna to eye her and Joe. More camera din and the beast was pulling itself up, charging straight toward them. She grabbed the twine about Joe's waist and yanked him to the far side of the tree. The moose, its hooves shaking the ground, pounded past.

## 9 • OPENING DINNER

"THE MOOSE AND I *did* have a close encounter," Anna said to Erika and Tom Blake, another couple new to the college and to Development, from Boston. "So many people have asked me about it tonight, it's kind of embarrassing."

Erika, a kittenish Melanie Griffith type, elbowed her husband. "Tommy, where have you brought me? I paint still life, not wildlife."

Anna pushed her plate to the side. Before dinner, Paul had asked her very specifically to chat up Erika, make her feel welcome. "Erika, I could show you where the blueberry farm is. We could make a day of it."

"Sounds great," Erika answered, "but I'm heading back to Boston to get ready for a show. Maybe we can have lunch or something when I get back." She glanced at her husband. "Let's get some dessert before the president starts talking again."

With a wave to Erika and Tom, Anna looked out on the cavernous room, The Great Hall, as it was called on the invitation, and the five or six hundred people chatting over the end of their meals while student waiters and waitresses roamed among the tables serving coffee and tea or clearing empty plates. The opening dinner, again according to the invitation, was to kick off the beginning of another academic year as well as to welcome staff and faculty back from their summer sojourns. The fallacy with all this, according to Paul at the dessert table himself, was that the staff at these institutions had no summer sojourns, a point the academics seemed to repeatedly miss. Although these opening dinners were nothing new for her, this was one of the few she could remember actually enjoying.

Dinner had been surprisingly good for this large an institutional affair, a chicken, mushroom, leek, and rice mix. The cocktail hour worked as well. Kendall Jackson, no less. With barely two days under her belt as a resident of Onasego she felt unexpectedly at ease, replaying the near moose incident with Deedee, spotting Angie Wingo in the crowd and finding out that Derek of the flat tire incident was her husband as well as the chairman of the Future Studies Department and a poet. The last bit of information had been offered by Derek himself with a somewhat wearied intensity. A stocky blonde in blue jeans completely threw her, however, when she asked after Joe, or rather "your son." Even Molly contributed to the evening by offering to babysit Joe as long as Caroline came over. The two girls were taking him to the park. Now would that be happening in Manhattan? All in all a better than expected evening except that in a black linen cocktail dress, she was somewhat over dressed. Also, a bit mystified by a surprising homogeneity. In the entire room, she'd seen maybe four people of color.

"Just in time," Paul announced, taking his seat beside her. "Looks like Pug will introduce the new people soon."

Anna looked toward the dais where Russell "Pug" Wenley stood organizing note cards. Pug, introduced earlier by Paul, was a former long-term administrator of the school, now its president, and to Anna, a system failure of her normally reliable antennae. First, she was struck by the impression that he was almost a caricature of a funeral director; slight, swooped hair, bushy brows over owlish eyes, and a soviet era gray suit. Yet, after an avuncular welcome back to the college community, his assessment of the school's challenging financial picture bore all the trademarks of a brash, tough talking hedge fund manager. Then there was the intriguing detail that Angie shared about how he was slavishly devoted to his much younger girlfriend, Denise, or as she was called behind her back, The Niece. Finally, Paul referred, twice now, to the fact that Pug Wenley was nobody's dummy.

"Introducing the new people… like us?" She grabbed her purse. "I'll be right back."

The ladies' room next to the Great Hall was blessedly empty. Anna checked her hair and perked up her lipstick. Then thinking of the long speech yet to come, she entered the first stall just ahead of the heels and chatter of several other women entering the room. Their tones were crisp and clear.

"She says she's a writer."

Anna knew that voice. She slowly sat down on the john lid and pulled her feet up and out of sight.

"What do you mean, she says?"

"Well, would you call someone who doesn't work for anybody and writes about where to get a vacuum cleaner fixed, and, get this, amazing uses for borax, a writer?"

Through the slit between the door and the side of the stall Anna could see Deedee spiking up her hair in front of one of the mirrors.

"I heard she and her husband got the Victorian on Summit." This comment came from a woman she didn't know drawing in lip liner. "Can't believe anyone would pay that kind of rent."

"You know how these outsiders get paid," a third voice chimed in over water running, "like they're gods coming to save us."

The second woman pressed her mouth on a paper towel. "What's with the moose thing?"

Deedee swiveled in front of the mirror. "A near-death experience according to her."

"It wasn't?"

"God, no."

The lights blinked twice. The heels clacked toward the door.

Anna sat quietly through Pug's introduction of each of the new employees along with their spouse or partner followed by two or three lines about where each new hire had previously worked and what they would do for the college.

After about thirty minutes, it was their turn.

"And now we come to Paul Lawson. Stand up, Paul."

Paul pulled Anna to her feet beside him. So many faces turned staring at them; she forced herself to smile.

"Paul comes to us from CUNY Hunter and as our new head of development will be a very important man around here. So, everyone, please, give a nice round of applause for Paul and his lovely wife," Pug held his hands aloft to lead the clapping, "Alma."

It was three in the morning by the time Anna finished her first column. With stinging eyes and a dull, thudding headache, she pushed the send button. Vacuum cleaners and borax be dammed.

*"Alone in Onasego"*

*As some of the readers of this column are aware, our family recently moved from Manhattan to the small, upstate college town of Onasego. Onasego is located at the northern edge of the Catskills, between Albany and Binghamton, and eighteen miles from its better known neighbor, Cooperstown. (For the unini-*

tiated, Cooperstown is to baseball as Mecca is to Muslims.) Nestled amid rolling farms, very few restaurants, and almost no shopping opportunities, Onasego
is about as far from Manhattan as, shall we say again, Mecca. Having lived
my adult life in the greatest city in the world, this move to upstate life seems
part cross-cultural experience and part adventure. An experience and adventure that I hope you will join.

In my first week here I was surprised to see that the headlines in the local
paper focused on a lone moose traversing the nearby countryside rather than
say, the Middle East, embassy bombings in Africa, or even a celebrity divorce.
That was relegated to page 14 (out of 18). But, determined to enter into the
spirit of my new place, I read on. According to a dairy farmer by the name of
Angus Lynch (is that a name or what?) who had seen the beast passing near
his farm, his herd was not much disturbed. I was relieved. By the way, according to www.mooseworld.com, the word "moose" is derived from the Algonkian
term "mon" or "moz", depending on the dialect, meaning "twig eater." (Surely
that piece of trivia is worth reading this column.)

The moose, who is obviously far from his native woods in Maine, has attracted folk status among some of the locals and is followed daily by a crowd
of thirty to forty, all wide-eyed, camera wielding, and note taking, called the
Moose Watch and Reporting Group. (And when do these people work?) I know
this as I ran into, or to be more precise, was almost run into by, Mr. Moose and
company during an afternoon of blueberry picking. (Note: next week's column
will focus on the dos, don'ts, and must haves when you are out among the
bushes; another note: blueberries do grow on bushes.)

Anyway, perhaps because of our close encounter and similar circumstance
of having unexpectedly arrived in upstate New York, I got to wondering about
that moose. Does he feel as lost as I do? These woods and streams must look
as generically familiar to him as the grocery stores, post office, and school
schedules do to me. But, as the moose surely knows, these woods and grocery
stores are foreign—no more like Maine woods than the RiteMarket resembles
Dean and Deluca.

My husband believes that the primary value of travel is having the opportunity to see yourself without the insulation of familiar customs, routines,
friends, and enemies. You're bare and therefore, exposed. Perhaps this move will
provide that personal insight. Perhaps not. We'll see in time. But right now, I

*feel as I suppose that moose does, adrift, a little scared, and most of all, alone in Onasego.*


## 10 • TREASURE EVERY MOMENT? (1)

ANNA HUNG UP the phone and leaned back in her new rolling and swiveling desk chair, a gift from Paul for her office. Marty liked the moose article, "a good beginning," he'd said. "Dig in deep with the community," he'd said. "Keep the 'Alone in Onasego' columns," Marty's headline decision, "coming." But about what? She spun herself in a circle. Getting her license renewed at the DMV and being the only person in line? The 300 page Onasego telephone book including white and yellow pages? Finding Ray the hotel clerk and farm seller show up at the door as their Ward 2 alderman? Joe getting class assignments through the Christmas break with the hyper-organized Mrs. Wimbish? Or Molly? Refusing on the first day of school, to be dropped off much less picked up by mother. No, not that one. She probably wouldn't publicize the "call me, Alma" moment, or being maligned for being afraid of a stampeding moose either. However, her shock at finding her column on line for anyone, anywhere, to see at the new *ManhattanLiving.com* site might find its way into print one day.

She gazed around her semblance of an office still mostly in boxes. She had her chair, her desk, and to keep the motivation going, she'd even bought a wood-trimmed bulletin board to which she had tacked a legal sheet with TREASURE EVERY MOMENT written in a thick red marker. Underneath she had entered NEVER DOUBTING, TAKE MOLLY AND JOE TO CHURCH, DO UNTO OTHERS. That was the list as best as she could remember it. That her list had nothing to do with *Manhattan Living* was beside the point. This was her place.

"Mom, I'm going downtown with Caroline," Molly yelled from downstairs, "and somebody's at the door."

"Okay, I'll be right down." Anna rose from her chair. "Be home by five."

At least there was very good news on the Molly front. Caroline and Molly had overnight become thick as thieves. They talked on the phone incessantly, spent the two weekends since school started together, and walked to the Lawsons every afternoon after soccer practice, which Caroline had conveniently rejoined.

Moreover, Caroline's parents, Jamie and Gwendolyn, were treating Molly as one of their own. Suddenly it was Jamie this and Gwendolyn that, horseback riding at their farm out North Street, tarot readings from a psychic in Woodstock, a free Siamese kitten (immediately returned due to Paul's aversion to animals in the house), and the *pièce de résistance*, a promised rock concert in Manhattan over Christmas with reservations at the Plaza. According to Paul, who knew Jamie's background as a Catskill trustee, the Vans were swimming in cash, Jamie from banks, restaurants, as well as oblique, far-flung interests, and Gwen, old Oklahoma oil money. The couple were also, each in their own way, strikingly attractive; Jamie, sort of Alex Baldwiny and Gwen, a Grace Kelly type but with red hair. What thirteen-year-old girl wouldn't be captivated?

Downstairs Anna found the front door open but no person. She walked into the living room where Joe sat fixated in front of the TV. She tapped him on the top of the head. "Did you see somebody at the door?" Joe, in game world, grunted noncommittally.

"Looking for me, Anna? Or was it, Alma?"

The never-to-be-forgotten voice, slightly slurred, came from the back of the house. Spinning around, she saw Ellis lounging against the doorframe between the living room and the hallway. "Scared you, didn't I?"

Joe stared up at Ellis, either in fear or fascination. Anna wasn't sure. Like the day on the road to Cooperstown, Ellis was dressed in black tee shirt, jeans, the cobra and bloody knife as threatening as before. But today he also had a cigarette pack tucked in a turned up sleeve and he reeked of alcohol.

She put herself between Joe and Ellis. "What do you want?"

"Nothin'," Ellis drawled, "you wanted me."

Jesus, she had been right about this guy the first time. He'd come up with that helper story for Derek's benefit. Ellis folded his arms over massive pecs.

"I don't want anything," she said.

"I think you do." An Elvis type sneer crossed his face. "I think you want it bad."

She glanced down at Joe. "You are quite mistaken. There is not one thing I want from you."

"Well, hell's bells, Alma," his gaze bore down on her, "Why'd you call animal control?"

Ellis pointed to the broken framing on the side of the porch. "That where he went in?"

Anna shrugged. Standing in the side yard of her house with the combination of the Branch Street and sidewalk traffic passing by, she felt on stage, wary of being seen with the clearly inebriated Ellis, particularly as the idea that the city would hire such a person seemed moment by moment more dubious. Someone obviously had told him about the Alma slip up from opening night. Deedee could just as easily have mentioned the skunk around town. All of Onasego could be having a good laugh right now. Joe, video game forgotten, hung cautiously at her side.

"I was told beside the lilac."

"That's a lilac," Ellis pointed to a shoulder height shrub.

Anna wasn't going to give him that one. Since there was only one plant beside the hole, it would have to be the lilac. "What do you do? Exterminate them?"

Ellis gave her an exaggerated sideways glance. "Think, Alma. Dead skunks under your porch. Not good." He pulled a Winston from his sleeve and clanked open a zippo. "You don't kill them cause they eat bad stuff." He lit the cigarette, "Bugs, rats."

"Cool," Joe whispered moving to get a better view of the opening.

Anna studied the trim. If Ellis was who he said he was, shouldn't he have a name tag reading Animal Control Officer or at least be driving one of the city vehicles with the Indian on the side? From somewhere in the neighborhood the recorded strains of the Yellow Rose of Texas wafted toward her. "Can't you just put up new wood so it can't get under there?"

Ellis took a deep drag, the cigarette between his thumb and forefinger. "You could do that. Keep one out, keep maybe a slew more in. This house on South Street, it had like twenty skunks under one porch."

Anna had a vision of twenty skunks navigating the traffic on Branch and Summit. "I think we would know if we had twenty skunks under the porch. Actually, I think we'd know if we had one."

"I'd say for sure there's been one." Ellis pointed his cigarette hand to a series of coin size indentations Anna had never noticed before. "See those round holes—that's the skunk looking for grubs. They love grubs. Course they like peanut butter too. But then he might have moved on."

"Mister," Joe raised his hand, "if I lie down on the ground, could I see it?"

"NO!" Anna grabbed his shoulder. "Heavens, Joe. It could bite."

Ellis exhaled in a series of perfectly formed Os. "Unless they got rabies, they ain't going to bite nobody. Besides, daytime's when they sleep."

She could ask who his supervisor was. Get a phone number. "But, Joe, he might wake up and spray you." The music was coming closer, punctuated with periodic honking.

Ellis tapped the ash off his cigarette onto the grass. "Nope. First they hiss, or growl, or stamp their feet. Some even walk on their front feet with their tails way up in the air. Then, spray, maybe. I heard accurate up to about ten feet."

Skunks walking on their front feet. Was this a kind of small town hazing for the new people? But what if it wasn't? She soldiered on trying to ignore the two young mothers with their baby carriages walking slowly on the other side of the street. Four children on scooters joined them. "Okay, so what are you going to do?"

"Me, nothing. We don't know if you still got one."

Anna felt as though she were standing in a haze of gin. She took a deep, Lamaze-style, breath. "How do I find out?" A car honked. Angie Wingo waved from a Subaru Forester. Anna waved back. She wasn't sure if Ellis did. He lit a second Winston off the first.

"Pour some flour around the spot. After it gets real dark see if he walked through it."

"Tracks," Joe interrupted sagely.

Ellis nodded.

"And if he or she did? What then?"

Two youngish women joggers stopped to join the mothers and children across the street. One was The Niece in lavender running shorts and a matching bra.

"Couple of things," Ellis said staring at the twosome. "Stuff some bags with mothballs and throw them under there. Skunks hate that. You got the time?"

"What else." Anna checked her watch. "Three forty-five."

Painfully, reluctantly, it seemed, he turned back to her. "A new thing at the Feed and More store called Skunk Skrammer. Sprinkle it around the hole. People say it works."

A crowd of about fifteen now milled about directly across the street. Why were they there? She turned back to Ellis. "What's in the powder?"

Ellis pulled a folded up brochure out of his jeans. "Well, if you just got to know... fox pee. Scares em into thinking there's a fox around."

Fox pee. That was it.

"Look, I got to go. Parole officer don't like it if I'm late."

Flour tracks, fox pee, and now a parole officer. Anna decided the chain yanking had gone about far enough. "And why have you got a parole officer, Ellis?" A bright yellow truck, the source of the music, turned from Branch onto Summit.

Ellis handed her the brochure. On the front was a striped skunk under the words RABIES: IF YOU GET BITTEN. The seal of New York graced the back along with an inserted stamp, Ellis Utt, Certified Animal Control Officer. "I got a couple of DUI's."

That she could believe.

"And one of those restraining orders." He winked at her, "I told this cop I really wanted to kill somebody."

One last yank. "Oh, sure, Ellis. Who?"

The yellow Mr. Ding-A-Ling ice cream van pulled up to the curb. Ellis ground the butt out in the grass. "My old man. That's who."

## 11 • *THE ONASEGON*: LETTERS TO THE EDITOR: A PARTIAL LIST: OCTOBER 1998

*INANE IN ONASEGO*

*I know it's not hunting season yet but there is something I just have to shoot down. Heads up, Anna Lawson, from wherever yours is. You might not like to feel alone, but moose sure do. Ants come in colonies, wolves in packs, geese in gaggles, but moose—nearly never in multitudes. I know you're in the sticks now but even WAY OUT HERE we've heard of fact checkers.*

*William "Bill" Floyd, Pindars Corners*

ODE TO ALCES, ALCES,
Alces, Alces in our wood
You are **fearless**, strong, and good
Ancestors guide you,
you're **never lost or adrift**
Just proud and determined
With every hoof you **lift**

Britney Burbank, age 12, Milford

Editor's note: Alces, Alces is the Latin nomenclature for moose. Miss Burbank is
the president of the newly formed Latin club at Milford Central School.

A SOPHISTICATED CERVID
"But as the moose surely knows, these (woods and) grocery stores are foreign."
quote from "Alone in Onasego", (Manhattan Living, 1998, September 28, page 2)

Derek Wingo, Onasego

Editor's Note: The moose is a member of the cervid (deer) family.

SOME MOOSE FUN FACTS FOR KIDS
Moose are members of the deer family but are about the size of a big horse
Moose hair is hollow; it helps keep them warm during long winters
Moose like their veggies, adults eat between 40 to 60 pounds of plant food a day
Moose babies (or calves) will stand and walk the same day they are born
Moose are good swimmers and good runners
Moose are solitary creatures who only join with other moose to feed or mate
What else can you find out about moose?

Stephanie Mills, Grade 4 Teacher, Laurens Central School

FIND SOLACE IN THE LORD
The recent "Alone in Onasego" column, Manhattan Living, (ibid), is but one
more example of the pervasive sense of loss and isolation so common in our
modern world. Yet, I believe, actually I know, that the Biblical adage, "Seek
and Ye Shall Find" offers the solution for Mrs. Lawson and all others in her

*condition. She must simply learn to seek her comfort in the arms of our Lord and King, rather than among the aisles and shelves of Dean and Deluca.*

*Penny Gleason, Morris*

*Editors Note: Due to the high volume of inquiries pertaining to the moose mentioned in the "Alone in Onasego" column (Manhattan Living, 1998, September 28), Friday's Outdoors Column will feature a past article by nature writer, Rick Brockway. "WE CAN HELP THE MOOSE MAKE A TRIUMPHANT RETURN TO NEW YORK."*

## 12 • PLEASURES

FROM HER SEAT in the back row of the Onasego All Paths Church, Anna checked her watch and hoped that Angie Wingo seated beside her hadn't noticed. The speaker for the day, Tim Denny, a lanky, guffawing kind of guy, was describing the role of stewardship in the life of an All Paths Church and the needs specifically, for the building surrounding them. A second, younger man, standing alongside, wore overalls, a hard hat, and was holding what looked to be a blow torch. According to the order of service, following this homily there would be the offering with piano accompaniment, something called Pleasures and Problems, a final hymn, and announcements which she could surely skip—If, that is, the mystery of the blow torch could be solved.

Of all Sundays to begin the exploration for a religious venue for herself and her children, she'd chosen the kick-off Sunday of the All Paths Church, APC for short, pledge drive. Actually, she'd only picked the Sunday; her daughter had chosen the All Paths. Or Caroline's family did some years ago, and that was how she, Molly, and Joe had ended up here today. She had rather liked church as a child until the Episcopalians (a.k.a. Frozen Chosen) adopted the excruciating practice called "the peace" wherein everyone, on cue, was to gaze with love at their nearby fellow parishioners and wish them "peace." The less frozen among the congregation would go beyond smiles to hugging and kissing. The more frozen like her family would mumble, "hi," or "good morning," and study the bulletin. Before today, she had been under the impression the All Paths were a garden variety Protestant group, just sort of New Englandish, and so, therefore, she'd reasoned, there wouldn't be any of that "peace" kind of foolishness.

Also mindful of New Englandish punctuality, she had gotten her little flock of Molly and Joe (Paul escaping due to a prearranged golf match with a prominent alumnus) to the church punctually at ten-fifteen, declined the offer of a bright yellow GUEST button, and taken up position on the back row for the ten-thirty service. By ten twenty-three, Molly was chatting with her father in New York on Anna's cell phone and Joe was on his second visit to the bathroom. At ten forty, all those under eighteen scampered out to their Sunday school classes, but Joe, with terror in his eyes, refused to budge. Molly, by contrast, joined Caroline and the middle school group without even a semblance of a look back, and Angie Wingo, arriving late with brief case and *New York Times*, took Molly's seat beside her. Yet, for all this, she was being treated to a litany of the structural defects of the church from two guys with a blowtorch.

Giving into boredom she let her eyes roam about the cavernous sanctuary. The place really could do with some sprucing up. Of course not much could be done to change the glint of the industrial gray metal folding chairs providing seating for her and the other sixty or so worshipers gathered that morning. Moreover, she supposed, a replacement for the teal indoor/outdoor carpet would not be high on the budget list for an obviously not so prosperous congregation. But a few little things would go a long way. Like some Lemon Pledge for the dowdy paneling at the front of the sanctuary. Maybe a wash coat of paint, she was thinking a sunny yellow, over the mashed potatoes-with-the-skins-mixed-in colored walls. And candelabra, flowers, murals, anything, anything at all, to relieve the yawning blandness of the place. With her heretofore religious life passed amid gleaming crosses, crisp choir robes, and satin altar hangings, the visual banality of the All Paths Church felt like a parking lot. And with no prayers, no gospel, and not a smidgen of awe for a mysterious other, the service so far had felt like the fall opener for the League of Women Voters—except for the blow torch. She glanced at Angie beside her rifling through the *Times*. Maybe Angie could clue her in on Ellis. What to believe. What not to.

A piano fanfare brought Anna's attention back to the front of the church where Tim seemed to be winding down. "So, for now, and for the weeks to come," Tim looked around the room, "we ask that you give particular thought to increasing your contribution to All Paths right here in Onasego." He motioned to the man standing beside him, "Ready for the grand finale, Peter?" Peter nodded.

"Here we go." He dug a book of matches from his pocket. "OK."

The two male voices recited in unison:

*If we raise a lot of money*
*our church will sure be neat*
*so dig deeply in your wallets, friends,*

They paused while Tim struck a match and yellow blue flames hissed into the air...

*Cause we're turning up the heat!*

Joe, his face lit with wonder, threw his arms around her.

## 13 • MORE PLEASURES

"PEG, HERE. MY particular pleasure this morning came to me when I saw the bright red maple bough on the corner of Summit and Branch. The very first color of fall. My problem is that many of you may have missed it." The silver-haired speaker lowered herself gingerly back to her seat. Twenty hands shot up immediately.

Anna no longer cared. She pushed her sleeve back with drama, eleven-forty. Would these people never shut up? Beside her, she noticed Joe staring up at the ceiling, picking his nose. She elbowed him and handed him her copy of the order of service and a pencil.

Peter, still in his hard hat, stood up next with a RiteMarket bag. "First, how about that Tim and the blow torch for a pleasure?" The room burst into applause as Peter took off the helmet and, after fishing around in the plastic bag, replaced it with a doo rag. She took him to be mid-thirties, but his eyes were a dark soulful brown, like a young boy's.

"Second, as director of the APC Youth, I want to remind everyone of the concert Friday night, October fifteenth. Seven to twelve, right here. And, last," Peter slipped the scarf off, and again, reaching into the bag, came up with a beret, taking precious seconds to make the proper fold over one eye, "but certainly not least, Derek asked me to announce that after the much-needed summer hiatus, the APC poetry slams will resume its first Sunday of every month schedule in October."

"When and where?" a deep voice from across the room called out.

Peter shrugged. "Same old drill. Two to four, Sunday afternoons at Nora's. As usual, Derek will be MCing and leading off with his new poem, 'After Dark.'"

The next speaker introduced her daughter from out of town, a joy having her here, a joy above all others.

"Want me to introduce you?" Angie whispered in Anna's ear.

Right, Anna thought. Then I can sign up for the poetry slam. She shook her head.

A short, sort of Native American man stood up, "My name is Victor, I have a problem."

At least Victor had the good sense to look ill at ease, Anna observed, as he stammered his way through a plea for contributions to a proposed slaughter house for rural residents. Surely he couldn't mean that the way it came out—the idea blinking on for a *Manhattan Living* column.

Beside her, Angie suddenly rose. "Good morning, everyone."

Chairs scraped while faces and bodies swiveled their way.

"I have a pleasure and a problem this morning, actually a couple. My first problem is that we only have ten computers to take to Cuba. Now if I'm going to prison to get those computers into Cuba, I think there should be a few more than ten."

Anna looked up at Angie, the realtor. Angie, the prisoner?

"My second problem is that Sam and Penny Poindexter's first grandchild is due early, around mid-November, so we need subs for our protest delegation to THE SCHOOL OF THE AMERICAS. Anyone interested should speak to me over coffee hour. And, the pleasure? Friday I was named to the Susquehanna Million Dollar Sales Club."

Whoops and whistles rippled across the hall while Angie curtsied. The sound of coffee being ground whirred behind them. Angie, the protester, sat down.

A woman of indeterminate age took the floor. She was dressed in a floor length dirndl skirt, long sleeve turtleneck, and her hair, a braid, was wound into a bun.

"Laurel Loomis for Country Coven."

"Coven?" Anna mouthed to Angie.

With the hymnal in front of her face, Angie whispered. "Used to be. No real members anymore."

Laurel Loomis began in a low, measured voice. "I meant to speak to you today about our upcoming, very exciting equinox and Samhain activities but instead, I must address the recent assault."

The room was silent now except for muffled sounds of clinking china coming from behind the accordion door partitioning the rear of the hall from the kitchen. Even Joe put down his pencil and sat straight against the hard metal seat. Ah yes, Anna thought, the assault within our community, a vicious murder committed in a crowded grocery store. Coven or not, this was a problem she agreed with.

Laurel grasped the back of the chair in front of her, her voice rising. "While just one incident, this assault affects all of us on so many levels. First," Laurel raised her index finger shoulder height, "the assault threatens our sense of community, so vital for a small town."

Anna felt herself nodding right along. She remembered how she hadn't let Joe and Molly go in the hall alone for weeks after the co-op's board concluded that Mrs. Hardy's mugging outside 3A had to have been an inside job. How much worse for a small town to have a murderer.

"Second," two fingers now hovered in the air, "the assault threatens our personal priorities, our choices for how we pass each and every day, knowing that we could be being watched and followed by someone with a malicious agenda."

Amen, Anna thought. Even though months had passed since the murder, bouts of icy terror still seized her, particularly when she was alone. If a random murder could happen at a grocery store, then why not anywhere else? Just a few days earlier she'd lost her car in the Walmart parking lot after a late night grocery run for snacks Molly suddenly remembered she

HAD to bring to school the next day. She'd wandered among the rows of vans, pickups, and SUVs, many with their engines running, for almost twenty minutes—so obviously on her own, so obviously vulnerable. By the time she'd found her car, she'd broken down and sobbed against the steering wheel.

"Third," now Laurel held up the index finger on her left hand, "the assault targeted selfless commitment to the protection of the weaker among us."

Anna wished she could get the pencil away from Joe, who had started scribbling again. She should be taking some of this down. That was exactly what that young officer had done, he selflessly risked himself for others at the Big Save, and for that he'd been shot dead in cold blood.

"Protection especially for our fellow travelers on this earth, those without a voice, that is without a voice that we can understand, those with wings, scales, and four legs instead of two."

Wings, scales, four legs? Anna felt Angie's eyes on her.

Laurel was back to one finger now. "Yes, our community has been assaulted publicly, as a poor cousin to a baseball haven, as a place to have a cross-cultural experience."

Angie's arm crept along the back of Anna's shoulders.

Two fingers. "And yes, our personal priorities and choices, also. The perpetrator has noted and publicly ridiculed the most essential issue of existence, the search for our true way home. A search vividly brought to mind by *The Onasegon's* allegorical coverage of the plight of a lone moose lost in these upstate hills and valleys over the soul killing stuff of embassy bombings in Africa and mayhem in the Middle East."

Anna pulled Joe onto her lap. Jesus Christ, she'd never write "mayhem in the Middle East." Angie disappeared down the aisle.

"And finally," Laurel's voice was now pure ice, and all ten fingers were in the air as though she was about to grab something, "even commitment to the protection of the weaker among us has been compromised by the slandering of the Moose Watch and Reporting Group, for which I proudly serve as recording secretary. Our group, referred to in the pages of the widely read *Manhattan Living* as 'wide-eyed,' and with questionable employment, was founded out of selfless commitment to one certainly qualifying as the weaker among us, and a totem of our—"

The church chimes pealed in shuddering succession, heels clacked on the kitchen linoleum and the accordion door, with Angie yanking it along its metal tracks, snapped open. Waves of cinnamon, lemon, and coffee instantly suffused the room. Within seconds, children's squeals echoed up the stairway signaling the end of Sunday School, and Molly and Caroline, along with four or five other teenagers, all red-cheeked and windblown, strolled in from the foyer. Yet Laurel Loomis remained standing until Peter, rising to her aid, called out for quiet and respect for the speaker. With some already standing, others adjusting their jackets, the room came quickly to a hush.

Holding her hands primly at her waist, the right cupped into the left, she began again, "And because of this article-cum-assault, and despite its cutesily alliterative title, 'Alone in Onasego,'" she paused, allowing time for the dramatic beat, "not only is murder with us, ladies and gentlemen," her gaze bore in on Anna and Joe, "but now rape has arrived as well." After one more slow scan over the congregation, Laurel dipped into her seat.

Joe, still on Anna's lap, waved both hands overhead. "I've got one!"

"Joe, not now!" she hissed, mortified.

"One what?" Peter answered wearily.

"A pleasure and a problem; listen," Joe held the order or service in front of his face with both hands:

*I like this church*
*It's cool as can be*
*But you all sure talk a lot*
*And I've got to pee.*

With that, Joe nestled back against his mother.

## 14 • SOC-HER (1)

"MAYBE YOU SHOULD join something," Paul had said over breakfast. "You know, something civic, help us get a foothold around here."

Anna stepped out of the Lawson's new car onto the parking lot in front of the Onasego High School/Middle School complex. The car, a BMW, was white and a mistake.

"It's a German car for Christ's sake; of course it will work upstate."

"The safety record—you just can't beat that safety record."

"Thirty-five thousand miles, not even broken in."

"It's been leased, still under warranty, good discount."

With those pithy sayings in their ears, she and Paul signed on the dotted line at Paul's brother's dealership in Suffern, played with buttons and dials for two hours back to Onasego, familiarized themselves with the owner's manual, and proudly parked in the driveway. Two weeks later, in a blazing flash of consciousness brought on by a gas smell permeating the car, a terrible problem occurred to them: If there was no BMW dealership in Onasego, and there wasn't, then how many BMW mechanics could there be?

She looked around the smooth green soccer fields surrounding the schools. Girls and boys in Onasego's now familiar crimson and black uniforms darted up and down four of the fields while parents splayed in lawn chairs and chaises, hovered near the sidelines. Deer grazed not fifty yards away at the base of the hill leading into Veterans Park. Molly, playing the first game of the season for the girls' middle school team, was somewhere out there. At least it was a home game. The idea of traipsing around mostly two-lane roads looking for middle school soccer fields, new BMW, or not, was worrying. The early trip to Cooperstown remained vivid.

"Anna!"

Anna turned to see Deedee, carrying a playmate cooler and a black fold-out chair in a bag, striding toward her. This Deedee in work clothes radiated the exact same vibration as Deedee the blueberry picker. In stilettos, form fitting emerald green suit, trademark spiky hair, and tomato red lipstick, she was READY.

"Wow, that your car?'

Anna seriously considered lying. If the ladies of the ladies' room thought their rent was extravagant, what would they make of a BMW? She fumbled for an answer. "Yeah, we only had rentals in the city, so we had to get something for up here. Paul's brother is a dealer. Gave us a good price."

"You mind if I have a look?" Deedee asked, setting the cooler and chair on the ground.

A roar erupted from one of the fields. "No. Course not. Wonder which one of those is our girls' game?"

Deedee reached for the door handle. "Different games. Jen's an A. Molly's a B." She swiveled herself into the driver's seat, then ran her hand across the faux wooden dashboard. "Must be nice."

Anna handed her the keys. "Trade in the Suburban—get one."

Deedee flashed Anna a sideways glance. "Right. People from the outside," the sunroof slid open, "they get all the money. The natives, the ones who really need that school," the passenger seat automatically eased down into a horizontal position, "we don't count, except when things get tight. Then..." the seat eased back up.

A Windstar pulled up. The driver's side door opened and a woman with frizzy blonde hair wearing a Catskill tee shirt and jeans stepped out. A beagle jumped out behind her, biting at its leash. With the dog pulling badly, the woman pulled a canvas bag from the back seat and headed off toward the rear of the building.

"Then, what?"

"Then some of us get fired. Or contracted out like the grounds crew last year. The out-of-towners never take a hit. If things get bad, they just leave."

Anna shielded her eyes against the afternoon sun. Did Deedee know Paul's salary? Did everybody? Did Deedee not wonder that Anna might repeat all this to Paul, and that Paul might repeat it to Pug Wenley? Is that what Deedee wanted to happen?

Another roar. Anna saw delicate elongated legs and flippy white tails bounding up the hillside. "Guess I better go find those B's." She reached for the blanket from the back seat, her bottled water, and Molly's warm-up jacket that she'd left at home. "Why an A and a B team? Too many kids?"

Deedee stepped out of the car, smoothing down the tight green skirt. "The A's made the cut. They'll be our varsity in a couple of years. Then most of them will move on to scholarships, good schools, perks."

"There's a cut in the seventh grade?"

Deedee stooped to gather up the playmate and chair. "Of course, there has to be."

Anna couldn't help herself. "What happens to the B's?"

Deedee shrugged. "They get to play." She held out the keys to Anna. "They get that."

## 15 • SOC-HER (2)

THE GAME APPEARED to be in full swing by the time Anna got to the B girls' field. Once she knew where to look, it was pretty simple. The A teams, girls and boys, played on the fields at the side of the school while the B's played behind the gym and up a little hill. The field was surrounded by a respectable, composition track, and several joggers plus a few walkers were taking advantage of the opportunity to get some exercise and watch the game. Parents, like those on the fields below, sat in groups of twos and threes with thermoses and carryout coffee cups. A few heads turned in her direction but only for a second.

She studied the field for Molly, searching first the players on the field, then the girls doing warm ups on the sidelines. In a way, they all looked so similar. Beyond shirts, shorts, socks, and cleats, the uniform included severely tied back pony tails and braids, narrow elastic bands worn an inch back from the hairline, hefty thighs, and steely eyed determination. As she watched, two girls near center field crashed into one another, eyes closed, shoulder to shoulder, both rising into the air, as if pulled up on the same hook, for the ball. When an Onasego player trapped the rebound, guttural commands of "Look Right! Find Erin! Set it up! Watch the corner!" spewed from her fellow spectators. She needed a manual on this stuff.

As the players moved down field, she spotted Molly sitting on the bench hugging herself against the afternoon chill. She debated walking the jacket across to her, but not wanting to be seen as a hovering mother decided not to. Instead, wishing for a lawn chair like the others, she walked over to an open spot, spread the blanket, pulled out her water bottle, and tried to get comfortable on the lumpy grass. Anna wished Joe could have come with her but a stomach ache had him at home watching a video. Paul said he'd make it if he could. Maybe he'd bring *The Times*.

"You must have one out there."

Anna looked over her shoulder to see the blonde woman walking toward her with the beagle. The woman was holding a plastic bag by the knot at the top. "Mind holding Ralphie for a sec?" She threw the leash at Anna and held up the bag. "Be right back."

Ralphie lay down on the blanket, sides bellowing in and out, panting wildly. Anna picked up the red canvas strap. Was she supposed to know Ralphie's owner? Did she look like someone who adored dogs? Her best friend's family growing up owned a mostly beagle named Beautiful, about the homeliest dog she had ever seen but also the sweetest. Together she and her friend Estelle tried to talk Anna's mother into letting her get a beagle also so they could name him Beastly, and Beautiful and Beastly could go on walks together. But, as with so many things with her mother, Beastly was never seriously considered.

"Mission accomplished." The blonde woman sat on the ground catty cornered to Anna and took the leash back. "This dog is going to be the death of me. Supposed to be my daughter's dog, but I'm afraid she's allergic." Ralphie's mother looked out over the field. "So which one is your daughter?"

Anna was on the verge of asking if they had met but then backed off. "Mine? She's the one sitting on the bench in the blanket. And yours?"

The woman nodded. "Dawn, she's on the bench, too. At the other end, the chunky one holding the bag with the extra balls. She's real excited about this first game, I tell you. Wanted to sleep in her uniform last night."

Ralphie, mouth still open, crept over to the water bottle and began to lick the sides.

"Hey, where's that cute little guy of yours?" Ralphie's owner picked up the water bottle and handed it to Anna. "I thought I would just fall out of my chair when he piped up in church the other day—'cause you all talk a lot, and I gotta pee.'"

Anna tried not to stare. How could this woman have been in church and she hadn't noticed her?

"I mean everybody in the church was thinking the exact same thing— Laurel Loomis, we all have to pee so just sit down and shut up. When I first saw your little boy at the blueberry farm, I just knew he was something special."

The blueberry patch, church, and now soccer. Anna was thinking of best friends in Manhattan who didn't see each four times in a year much less in a month. A column?

"Aren't you nice. He's at home with a bad stomach. Okay if I give your dog some water?"

"Sure. Should have thought of that myself. What I wanted to talk to you about, Alma, was about trying to raise some money for the church. I was thinking of organizing a booth at the Fun and Fabulous. Maybe you could take a shift."

Anna poured some of the Poland Springs water into her cupped hand and held it out to Ralphie. Alma. That's right, she had been at the opening dinner. Alone. Another Catskill employee. "The Fun and Fabulous?"

"It's a big flea market downtown in October. Tons of people sell things. Main Street is closed off."

Ralphie finished up the water and stared at Anna 'til she poured some more.

"You know, I'd really like to help, but I'm trying to protect my time this year, not get over committed. Can I just write a check? And," she tried to look apologetic, "my name is Anna, not Alma."

"Anna! And here everybody called you Alma. Love that name, my grand-mother's name, means soul." Ralphie's owner took a clipboard out of her canvas bag and made a note. "Sure, just make a check to me, Libby Holmes. Of course you're busy getting settled—with that big house and all." She pointed to the field with her pencil. "Hey, look. Our girls are going in. What did you say your daughter's name is?"

"Molly, Molly Parish. She's from my first marriage."

"Your daughter is Molly Parish?"

Anna smiled. "Yeah, her real name is Maria but we've always called her Molly."

Libby nodded. "Dawn's mentioned her." Then, for the first time in the conversation, the woman had nothing to say.


## 16 • VISIONARY FIELDS

"Joe, this cliff we're standing on is from the Devonian Rock age and is at least 359 million years old. I learned that at a lecture this morning."

Joe, with his hand gripped in hers, stared up at the two squirrels bicker-ing down at them from a blue spruce to their rear. Other than the spits and snorts of the squirrels, the woods and rock formations surrounding them on three sides were hushed in the dappled glow of the midafternoon sun. Before them, the river and Catskill foothills lay splayed, like a partially opened fan. Anna, unsure if Joe was listening to a word she said, decided to try again.

"And, then, just about fifteen thousand years ago, a glacier came right through here, pushing a whole bunch of dirt in front of it. It stopped, don't ask me why, the weather got warmer, and it started going the other way. What do you think of that?"

Joe swung around. "I want to see a grouse like you did."

Apparently neither their three hundred fifty-nine million-year-old perch overlooking the Susquehanna River Valley nor the idea of the entire area being covered by a gigantic glacier piqued his interest. But then again her version lacked the majesty and drama of the morning's speaker, a member of the geology department, to the Catskill Board of Directors in town for their fall meeting. Standing at this very spot, holding a battered fedora, the professor eloquently attempted to educate the college's overseers, certain staff, and lucky staff spouses like her, as to the ice age founding of Onasego. Rocks, ridges, and streams that to the uneducated eye were merely rocks, ridges, and streams, became in this story the evidence of an immense glacial juggernaut grinding its way over centuries into the Susquehanna valley, slid-ing first west, then east, depositing great heaps of gravely sediment about the valley, sculpting lakes, shaping the present day earth beneath the direc-tors' largely wing tipped feet. But, enchanting as the talk was, a box lunch and the budget for the directors were like a grouse for Joe—where their minds were. Minds she would spend a long evening with that night at her first Catskill Board dinner.

Sounds from one of Catskill's many teams echoed from the hills over-head, reminding Anna of the steep road supposedly leading from the upper parking lot through the woods to the summit of College Hill, actually a mountain, that Catskill was built on. The mountain a glacier slid down.

"The grouse I saw was at the edge of some woods. Is your stomach all right?" Joe had come home from school complaining of a stomach ache.

"Fine," he burped. Juice stains she hadn't noticed before dotted his tee shirt, brand new from Penny's.

"Okay, we don't have to pick up Molly at soccer for another hour. Come on."

Anna stepped out of the BMW and into a scene that would have caused Julie Andrews to fling her arms wide and burst into song. After a winding, root-filled drive up the side of College Hill, Anna and Joe stood at the very roof of Onasego where soccer fields and yellowing meadows lay carved from a ridgeline of dense pine forests some hundred yards away. If she had her bearings straight, that ridge would wind west toward Otego and Unadilla and east to the hills above Veterans Park. To her right, lavender asters and goldenrod banked the slopes overlooking Onasego and the rolling Susquehanna River Valley extending east into the horizon. The spring view she had first noticed from the library balcony that fateful afternoon with Paul had now turned into fall. The land shall be beautiful. Deganawidah had that right.

"Is this like Yonahlossee, Mom?"

She gazed down at her little skinhead. He had caught the beauty as well. "In a way."

"What way?"

She reached for his hand and started across the mown trail to the woods. Since their birth, Molly and Joe had been hearing stories of her summers, from age eight to eighteen, at Camp Yonahlossee in North Carolina. Stories of crippling trail rides, snakes sunning on canoe docks, stately pow-wows; she'd even made them learn all the verses to Oh Yonahlossee set to the tune of O Solo Mio and the Sunday night favorite, Follow the Grail. Though she had never told them that for one month out of a year, for ten years, the world was as it ought to be—somehow they'd gotten it.

"It is like Yonahlossee," she pointed to a doe and her fawn that had meandered into the meadow, "because you just know, you can't really explain it, that it's a perfectly special place."

"Hey look, there's Dad in the golf cart. And Tim, the guy with the blowtorch."

It was true. Coming out of the woods on their same path was a small convoy of three golf carts painted in Catskill's green and white. Paul, with sleeves rolled up and tie loosened, drove the first, with Tim as passenger. Behind him Pug Wenley rode with a board member she had been introduced to that morning but whose name she couldn't remember. The same with the occupants of the third cart. Paul pulled off into the grass beside them, waving the two other carts on.

"Tim, this is my wife, Anna, and son, Joe."

Tim Denny, in shorts, polo shirt and Catskill baseball cap, stepped out of the cart. "Saw you two at church, but nice to be introduced. And congrats on the column. It got people talking." He crouched in front of Joe. "What are you doing up here, buddy?"

"Looking for grouses," Joe answered, peering at the cart and his father, "but we could look better from that thing. Take me for a ride?"

Tim squinted up at Paul. "I'd just as soon walk back down to campus, too pretty not to."

"Okay with me," Anna added. "Meet you at the parking lot."

Paul shrugged. "If you're sure." He motioned to Joe who clambered into Tim's seat. "We'll just be a minute. Got a bunch of emails to get off before the social hour." Then turning the tiny vehicle back onto the path, Paul and Joe disappeared into the woods.

Anna fell into step with Tim. "I'll walk back to my car with you. You weren't looking for grouse up here I don't think."

Tim, flushed, pulled a handkerchief from his shorts' pocket and ran it over his face. "I'm president of the Friends of Catskill College, local people who try to help the school. Anyway, Jamie Van is looking all over for places to lease land and put in baseball camps. He thought this could be a good spot."

"Baseball camps?"

"Yeah, twelve and under teams come play each other. Big deal because it's near Cooperstown. Big money maker, too."

"What do you think?"

Thirty feet away the doe stopped grazing, eying them over her shoulder.

Tim took a breath. "Not for the column, right?"

She nodded. "Right."

"Hate it. But, hey, I read meters for a living. I figure these corporate types on the board know what they're doing. Hope they do anyway."

At the BMW, Tim said goodbye and set off down a trail leading from the dirt road she had come up on. That's what I'll do the next time, Anna thought looking back out over the valley. As Tim had said, too pretty not to.

Just because she now owned a car for the first time in her life didn't mean she had to use it. She leaned against the hood and watched as the golf cart emerged from the woods and trundled toward her, weaving in and out of the meadow then back to the path, Joe now sitting on Paul's lap and driving.

Paul pulled up beside the BMW and high fived Joe before shooing him out of the cart. "Remember, drinks at six."

Anna unlocked the car. "What's this about a baseball camp up here?" She glanced at Joe doing his duck walk around the golf cart.

Paul reached out and caught the waistband of Joe's jeans as he waddled by, dangling him in the air. It was an old game, but one Joe never tired of.

"It's not going to happen; too inaccessible up here. This little foray was just to show the other board members that. Get Jamie to look into other property." He dropped Joe the six inches to the ground then whacked him on the behind and revved the gas. "Later."

Watching him maneuver the golf cart down the trail Tim had taken, Anna thought how hard Paul had to work at these board events, at once Mr. Personality, Mr. Professional, Mr. Care and Concern. He hadn't been home for dinner in a week what with Pug calling one late night meeting after another. She held the back door open for Joe.

"Mom, is this Visionary Fields?"

"Yeah, how come?"

Anna swung Joe's door closed and got in herself. The deer had disappeared, perhaps spooked by Joe's screaming or the runner cutting through the meadow. A runner in a gray tee shirt and black shorts. A man with a black hair, olive skin, the same man from the highway.

"Caroline and Molly were talking about Visionary Fields."

She clicked in her seat belt. The runner paused, hands on his knees to catch his breath.

"Oh yeah, let me hear that seat belt," she waited for the click. "What did they say?"

"Caroline said lots of people go there."

The man glanced their way, lifted a hand, and waved.

"Why, Joe, to hike? Play soccer?'

The runner set off again, this time toward the woods.

"Nope," Joe's feet banged lightly against the back of her seat. "To get hot."

## 17 • BOARD GAMES

ANNA STARED AT the wedge of grilled chicken breast on her plate. Positioned Gibraltar-like over waves of Minnesota wild rice and a medley of locally grown broccoli and cauliflower, according to the menu, she wasn't sure if she should cut into it as it was, preserving the "presentation" for as long as possible—or just flip it on its side and have at it. The owners of the other five entrees on the table, Angie and Derek, the golf coach and his wife, The Thompsons, and Sharon, the manager of the bookstore, seemed to share her quandary, eyeing their plates and readying attacks. By contrast, Paul, across the table, sat over an untouched salad, while a student waiter reset the empty seat next to him with fresh china, silver, and napkin for the next revolving board member who would descend upon the table.

"The Revolving Board—Not A Merry Go Round." She couldn't help herself. The title came to her as Pug explained the mechanics of the evening during the social hour. This innovation, a lightning bolt in the night as he'd explained it, had individual board members moving at each course to a new table. With three courses, and seven people to a table, each board member would share ideas and perspectives with at least twenty-one members of the college community. Therefore, with twenty board members, the evening presented the opportunity for four hundred and twenty new relationships. So touchy, the cocktail hour buzz ran, so feely, so not Pug. The consensus was that it had to be the brainchild of The Niece—especially as the inspiration arrived in bed. In any event, while the rest of the table crunched baby spinach with orange slices in an almond vinaigrette, Paul dutifully took notes from Mrs. Woltz, of the Curriculum Committee, and her desire to incorporate debate into the general ed requirement. Now with Paul continuing to scribble away, and everyone else locked in a conversation about the upcoming opening of Shopbest, Anna gazed out at the assembled twenty or so tables. As at the opening dinner, invited community members like Tim, Ray, and, her own personal wacko, Laurel Loomis, dotted the assorted staff, faculty, and students chosen to embody Catskill to its Board of Directors. Two tables over, Erika and Tom sat captured with their own version of Mrs. Woltz. Despite Anna's repeated invitations, Erika's studio and trips back to Boston schedule seemed to preclude lunch, or a walk, or even a glass of wine. After Erika's last thanks but no thanks, she decided to take the hint.

Her gaze returned to the quickly cooling dinner before her. Over the salad course she'd resolved to ask Gwen about the Visionary Fields issue. Over the entrée she could toy with some comeback to all the letters to the paper about her metaphor with the wandering moose. For a moment she considered calling home but decided she was being paranoid. Molly and Caroline were babysitting Joe, they were stocked with pizza and videos, and she could be home if need be in five minutes.

A remarkably tall, trim, sixtyish man with a head full of silver hair pulled out the chair beside Paul. Whipping a linen napkin from under newly laid flatware, he nodded to the table, "Phil Coxe, here. Eat, everyone, eat." Between the greeting and what could only be a several-thousand-dollar black on black pinstripe suit complete with red silk tie, the man emanated China deep pockets and a hefty *noblesse oblige* to match. Paul held up his notepad, obviously prepared to show obeisance to the great one. Anna tumbled her chicken onto its side.

"I thought we'd go around the table and talk about what Catskill could be doing better," Coxe announced, stopping six forks in midair. Paul clicked his pen perfunctorily. Angie winked at Anna. Board games.

Coxe studied the golf coach's name tag. "Coach Thompson, what do you think Catskill could do better?"

Coach Thompson, in a creased French blue shirt and gold tie, glanced wide eyed around the table for help. This whole conversational gambit by Coxe was outside the Coach's play book, Anna guessed. After a few very quiet moments, however, Thompson finally came up with the need for more training funds to get the golf team to Florida. While Thompson elaborated on the need for snow-free practice courses it occurred to Anna that her tentative title "Apologies to a Wandering Moose" or "Pardon, Tamoose Latrec" ... might be trying too hard. Maybe she should just do something like, "Onasego Believes Moose Metaphor Misapplied" or "My Many Moose Mistakes." She reached for her menu and the pen in her skirt pocket. Derek was up next. She heard something about the need for cross disciplinary education. Team teaching. Then Angie picked up the thread. More volunteerism. These kids should experience the third world, see how the bulk of humanity really lives. Cuba, maybe. Over the very nice broccoli and cauliflower Anna got it. So simple. She wrote carefully, "Mea Culpa, Mr. Moose."

The table was still again. She looked toward the bookstore manager whose name she couldn't remember. The bookstore manager looked back, silent.

"Anna, isn't it?" Coxe's reading glasses were halfway down his nose. "Read us your notes."

Anna smiled and folded the paper. "Oh, I'm sorry. This is... about something else. I don't really have any ideas for you. We're new—and I'm not a college employee."

Phil Coxe leaned toward her. "Maybe so. But you're here eating college food and drinking college wine." He took off his glasses. "You owe us."

Anna glanced at Paul, still writing away. How in the hell was she supposed to know what Catskill College needed? Suddenly a memory of the campus surfaced from the day of watching Chip and Dale. "Well, there is one thing. Maybe you could do something with the landscaping—you know, soften the brick look."

Coxe looked around the table with a 'now see what I mean' expression. He returned to Anna. "And what are you going to do about that idea?"

And what are you going to do about being a complete and total jackass, she thought, peering at his name tag. "As I said, Phil, we're new. I don't know who to share this idea with—other than yourself, of course."

Coxe leaned toward Paul. "Isn't there some kind of Friends' Association?"

Paul nodded. "The Friends of Catskill."

"The Friends of Catskill," Angie repeated.

"So there you have it, Anna. Now, get involved."

Anna reviewed her options: cry, leave the table, or throw something—at him. Instead, she simply stared back at Coxe. She hated this man.

"Phil," Paul broke in too loudly, making a show of pushing his plate away and folding his arms on the table, "you've had a long association with the school. Your father, your son, yourself. You've been so very generous with the school—serving on the board, funding the Philip Coxe scholarship. What direction do you think the school should head in?"

Coxe fiddled with the end of his tie. "You really want to know?"

"I really do." Paul said.

Despite herself, Anna had to give Paul points for segue control.

Coxe dropped his tie, folding his hands on the table instead. "Okay, I'll tell you what I think. I think the world is changing and Catskill should too. What these kids need is to get out of here, go out in the real world." Coxe spoke slowly and deliberately, eyeing each person in turn, Anna noted, around the table.

"I say we should jump on this internet distance learning. Lots of schools are thinking about it, even Cornell and Duke. Everything here should go on line with kids coming up for a few concentrated weekends. Then we'd cut the staff, cut the residence requirements, cut the sports..." he gave a withering look at Coach Thompson, "I mean why would a school in upstate New York spend good money on a golf team? You're right. They should be playing in Florida. And, my God, division one soccer. Sheer insanity." Coxe paused apparently taking note of the coach's ashen face, "You asked me. I told you."

"Next course," Pug boomed into a microphone.

Coxe pushed his chair back, the meal untouched. "Good talking to you folks. Enjoy your dessert."

The table sat in silence until Derek spoke. "I think he meant it."

A young waiter appeared with fresh linen, silver, coffee cup and a tray with eight pieces of cheesecake. As the waiter unloaded the tray, Anna leaned toward Paul. "Insufferable man. Totally insufferable."

Paul shrugged. He'd probably heard it all before, several times.

"I bet he's a member at Augusta," Coach Thompson said loosening his tie. His wife folded her arm around him.

"And he named a scholarship after himself," Angie added.

"No, he didn't," a low, steady voice cut in. Dressed in an open-necked white oxford cloth shirt and gray herringbone jacket, the man from the highway and the woods stood at the empty chair. He pushed the blue black hair away from his face. "Sorry I'm late. The scholarship is named for his son who died of meningitis. He was a student here at Catskill."

Anna felt sick; the man had lost a son. And, hating herself, wondered if she had broccoli in her teeth.

Paul rose to his feet. "William, hello. Have a seat."

## 18 • WILLIAM

"YOU CERTAINLY GOT quiet over dessert." With his arm stretched along the ridge of Anna's seat, Paul backed the BMW out of the space near the Great Hall. Nearly the last to leave the dinner, they'd found the parking lot almost empty. "You barely said a word. Not rude but close."

Anna fingered the collar of her dress, a three or four-year-old sheath. Not a bad dress but not a great dress. "That Phil Coxe thing just got to me. I'm very sorry his son died, but he really is a jerk." The ability to lie was one of her few reliable talents.

"A jerk, but a very wealthy and influential jerk. A honcho jerk actually, with CDG industries, a multinational food outfit." Paul turned to look out the front windshield and slide the gearshift into drive. "And, according to Pug, somebody who pours an unbelievable amount of time into the school." He laughed. "Coxe sure ripped into you though."

She really should have worn her long sleeve black knit. The one that made her look thinner. More sophisticated. Paul turned onto West Street, avoiding a group of students walking toward downtown.

"So what did you think of William Johnson?"

She rolled the window down a couple of inches to give herself a little time. Over dessert he had made small talk with the table, quizzing in the most low key way the golf team's record from the previous spring, Derek on his new course: The Future of Foresight, Paul's comparison of Catskill to other small northeast schools and, as he rose to leave, a quick "hope you aren't still feeling so 'Alone in Onasego,' Mrs. Lawson," to her. Courtly, enigmatic, incredibly attractive. She couldn't wait to go home, get in the shower, and, well, contemplate. "He seemed okay."

Paul slowed at the blinking light at the intersection of Summit and Green. "You know, somebody's going to get killed here." On the Summit side, the light blinked red and on the Green side, yellow. Their first day in Onasego, thinking that it was red on all sides, they almost plowed into an oncoming Subaru. "It was a real struggle to get him on the board. He's famously private. Almost always has a different agenda."

She knew that already. She knew from the way he had stood on the highway talking on his phone. She knew from the way he ran in Visionary Field.

She knew from the way he didn't give out one detail about himself tonight while completely charming the table.

"Did you meet him before this week?" Anna tried to focus on the students streaming down Summit toward downtown.

Paul blasted the car horn at a kid riding a bike the wrong way up the street. "I've called on him in the city. You ought to see his house. It's fabulous. Up in the East Seventies."

The East Seventies. She liked the East Seventies.

"What does he do?"

"Real estate. Apparently he's got that sixth sense about what will be the next new hot spot."

"Didn't he say he's got family around here?"

"Yeah, he did. And, of course, he is an alum." An alum. She'd go to the library tomorrow. Immerse herself in yearbooks.

A car sat idling in front of their house. For a second, she had the wild idea that William Johnson would step out. But it was Ray who rolled down his window as they approached after turning into the driveway and parking.

"Get the board all squared away?"

Paul put his arm around Anna. One of those "we're home now and want to go inside" type of gestures. "Yeah, I think so. What did you think of the evening?"

Ray punched the air with his fist. "Great. All those executive types coming up here to pitch in. We need them."

Paul pulled Anna a little closer. "Come in for some coffee?"

Ray started his car. "No. I was just waiting for you two to get home. I picked up your daughter and her friend. I didn't think they should be out walking alone so late."

Anna ducked down to Ray's window. "Out walking?"

"Crossing Main Street, headed back up here, I think."

Anna looked back toward the intersection of Summit and Green. On both sides of the streets college kids swarmed, several obviously drunk.

"I guess we better go attend to this," she heard Paul say. "Thanks so much."

Ray checked the rear-view mirror, "Hey, no problem, just glad I happened by." Then with no wave, no look back, and no farewell, he eased into the traffic.

## 19 • YOUNG GIRLS

"Okay," Molly began, her voice breaking, "We made a mistake. I know that." Dressed in jeans, an old turtleneck sweater, flip flops, and her hair in braids, she looked like she needed a babysitter herself. Anna wasn't sure if she had ever seen her daughter in such abject misery.

Anna and Paul had decided their strategy outside on the sidewalk. Because Paul was home for once, he would be the primary talker. First, he would ask the girls what they had been doing walking downtown and, second, why, as Joe's babysitters, they thought they could leave Joe alone and asleep in the house. Whatever was said, Anna believed Caroline should be taken home and they would deal with consequences for Molly later. Paul felt that decision should be made once they heard what the girls had to say. They would confer in the kitchen or upstairs, out of the girls' hearing. Reluctantly, Anna agreed. So, while she checked on Joe, Paul called Molly and Caroline downstairs to the living room to explain themselves. Now, both girls sat side by side on the sofa while she and Paul sat in the two armchairs facing them. Paul crossed one leg over the other. "Go on."

"Mr. Lawson, please, can I say something?"

Caroline, with her hands balled up in a corduroy barn jacket that Anna bet was straight from Abercrombie's, gazed between her and Paul.

Paul loosened his tie. "All right."

"Don't get mad at Molly; this is my fault. I wanted to get ice cream, and I talked her into it."

"Where'd you go?" Anna asked, ignoring Paul's glare. She couldn't get the Summit and Green Street intersection out of her mind. Much less Visionary Fields.

"The Green Street Market. And, I swear, we weren't gone fifteen minutes."

"But Mr. Rubino said he picked you up coming back from downtown on Summit."

Caroline clicked the heels of her cowboy boots together, a token from some place named Barnett in Texas ("Dad goes there all the time, he'll get you some.") and a source of great admiration from Molly. "No, we were coming back from the Deli. He probably just thought we had been downtown. Really, this is all my fault. You know I live out in the country and we can't walk places like you can here. Molly didn't even want to go. Did you, Molly?"

Despite herself, Anna admired Caroline's cool, blunt candor.

Molly's hands sank between her knees. "It doesn't matter. I shouldn't have let you talk me into anything. I should never have left Joe." She looked at her parents, lips trembling. "You won't ever trust me again, will you? You shouldn't!" Then she burst into tears.

Paul looked at Anna. "Why don't you girls give us a minute?"

"Look," Paul said reaching into the liquor cabinet, "they're teenagers, they admitted making a mistake. I say we tell them we appreciate their honesty and forget it. Wasn't there some vodka in here?"

Anna leaned back against the kitchen counter. "I thought so. Absolut." She looked around the kitchen. The girls had cleaned up really well: no crumbs, no pizza box, everything put away, the garbage tied up to take out in the morning. "I still think Molly should have some time alone to think over what she will and will not do for her friends."

"You mean send Caroline home?" He pulled out the Tanqueray. "Guess I'll have a gin and tonic. You want one?"

"Wine, please."

While Anna retrieved a wine glass for herself, Paul pulled out an open bottle of Chardonnay from the refrigerator door. "The thing is, if we take Caroline home it's going to turn into a huge deal, we'll have to explain to her parents, hell, we don't even know if Jamie and Gwen are home yet. They may have gone out after the dinner with some of the other board people." She held the glass up while he poured. "And to be real honest, it would be a damned awkward conversation."

"True," Anna murmured, "but this is a trust issue. The girls need to know that."

Paul unscrewed the cap from the tonic, then poured it over the gin and ice. After the long buildup to the board meeting, this was his first chance to kick back in a couple of weeks. He tilted the glass in her direction. "You tell someone you don't trust them… frees them right up to do whatever. Tell the same person you do trust them; they're almost obligated to behave."

Anna swirled the Chardonnay. This was probably not the most opportune time to go into "that whole trust thing" with Paul. "Maybe you're right. Would you have this talk with the girls? I'm afraid of what I might say." She started down the hall.

"Going to read?" he asked.

She was pretty sure where that might be going. "No, a little computer work... a shower."

"See you in a bit then."

Trust indeed, she thought, climbing the stairs.

Apparently William Johnson's famous privacy extended to the web. After half an hour searching on AltaVista all she learned was that he was an alum of Onasego High School and Catskill, earned an MBA from Columbia, solely owned a company in Manhattan, and, that an engagement to a Catherine Weisen (no picture) appeared in *The Times* three years earlier. Anna tapped the keyboard. There had to be more.

Squeals of laughter came from Molly's room. The time on her screen read midnight. Tomorrow, Saturday, the girls were playing soccer, Paul had an all-day board follow up to attend to, and Joe's first class at the Y with the beginning pollywogs was set for two o'clock. With luck, she could get a half an hour to check out the yearbooks at the Catskill library. She stood and walked down the hall to Molly's for lights out. She knocked lightly then pushed the door open a few inches and peered into the pitch dark room. "Time to settle down, girls. You've got a big day tomorrow."

"Okay, Mom, goodnight. I love you."

"Night, Mrs. Lawson, sleep well."

Anna shut the door softly.

"Check this out."

Paul stood in the doorway to their bedroom holding an empty Absolut bottle. She looked at him blankly.

"It was buried in the trash."

The very tidy kitchen came to mind. "Did you put it there?"

He switched off the hall light. "I really can't remember."

## 20 • MORE BOARD GAMES

ANNA THREADED HER way to the bar set up outside the Catskill library. Rather than the usual clusters of students and staff sitting at the picnic tables smoking, a hundred or more Onasegons filled the library balcony, steps, and adjacent field for the fall kickoff of the Friends of Catskill. Coming one week after the Catskill Board of Directors meeting, she supposed the idea was to get the locals on message. Or to use up the leftover wine and cheese. In any event, she was here out of obligation. "Get involved," Marty said. "Join something," Paul said. "Tell the Friends your idea," Phil Coxe said. So, here she was, waiting in line for a glass of wine, wondering if this was all there was to Friends' membership.

As on the fateful day when she'd thrown her fate to the heavens, the view of the Susquehanna Valley, surrounding mountains, and late afternoon sky was crystalline. Even the panels on the front of the library gleamed alabaster white in the slanting sun, probably washed for the beginning of the school year. Outside of the college people, Pug, The Niece, Paul, Tom, Erika, and Deedee, and community regulars like Tim, Ray, and Angie, and of course, Laurel Loomis, the crowd was largely a bank of unfamiliar faces, mostly middle-aged or older, better dressed than the opening dinner, and enthusiastic from the conversational timbre. While a few students dotted the crowd, there was not a faculty member in sight. There was also no William Johnson, a vague hope that she tried to ignore while spending over an hour pulling clothes from her closet. In the end, black slacks and a black-and-white striped sweater had won out as more slimming than a red coatdress.

"Ma'am?"

"Shiraz, please."

Tim, in chinos and a polo shirt, looked up from the beer cooler. "What brings you here?"

She reached for the glass of wine from the student bartender. "First off, I'd like to join Friends of Catskill. And I had an idea about sprucing up the campus, maybe with some ivy or something. Angie said to bring it here."

Tim twisted the cap from a Saranac Pale Ale. "Well, maybe. But mostly we do fundraisers. This year it's Catskill: Forget Me Not, a spring thing that we hope will coincide with the forget-me-nots coming out."

Static buzz from a microphone shot through the assembly. "Everyone, please, could I have your attention?"

Anna and Tim turned toward Deedee standing at a lectern by the balcony wall. Dressed in a plum-colored silk pantsuit, she held a mic in one hand and a clipboard in the other. A sailor's cap rested on the lectern. Conversation gave way to an attentive silence.

Deedee licked her lips painted the same color as the pantsuit and began again. "I want to welcome you, the Friends of Catskill College, to your home away from home. Is everyone having a good time?" She raised the hand holding the mic to her ear. "Come on, let me hear you." A fairly robust "YES" rose from the crowd. She continued. "And we couldn't have a more beautiful afternoon, could we?" Cued, the audience looked out over the valley with appreciative nods and smiles. "Finally, does everyone have a drink?" Tim grinned at Anna, clinking his beer can against her wineglass.

Looking over the crowd, Deedee continued. "I have the distinct privilege of introducing our leader, visionary, and," she held up the sailor's cap, "the captain of our ship. Captain Wenley! Captain Wenley, we need you on deck." With this invitation, Deedee positioned the sailor's cap amid the spikes and gazed up toward the entrance to the building. Recalling Peter's hat routine from her first Sunday with the APCs, Anna wondered if Deedee wasn't plagiarizing. If nothing else she was laying it on a little thick.

Amid the applause, the staffers in attendance donned their own sailors' caps, and with shouts of "Aye, Aye," formed an *Onasegon*-ready photo op. Paul, standing beside Erika at the cheese and fruit tray, joined in, combining weary shrugs with a wicked grin while getting hat to head. He seemed to Anna to be genuinely enjoying himself. Something of a surprise, she thought, given his resentment over Pug's last-minute mandatory attendance decree. For weeks he'd had a dinner scheduled for tonight with a big-time donor in Albany.

Low laughter rippled up from the gathering as Pug emerged through the library doors. Instead of the very Pug-like attire he'd had on earlier, navy sports jacket, pink shirt, ivory pants, no socks, he was now all heavy weather: slicker, overalls, boots, and a life ring. As he passed by The Niece, she poured a glass of what looked like water over his head. With the crowd now whooping appropriately, Deedee handed Pug the mic.

"Good evening," Pug began, "or should I say, Welcome Aboard." Pushing the hood of his dripping slicker back, he leaned against the podium. "You know a college is a lot like a ship. It takes many hands to stay afloat." Pug's tone had that Doctor Phil, state the obvious and sound astounded, quality. His eyes swept across the crowd. "Also, like ships, we have to venture out into rough weather, steering our way through economic turmoil, ever changing technology, and demographics that defy our best long-term planning. And despite our Board of Directors," he pointed to two local trustees, "composed of some of the best business minds in the country, we may still lose our wind, become stalled, and even find ourselves in danger of being pushed onto rocks." Deedee, hugging her clipboard, had the rapt attentive gaze that Anna was used to seeing on the faces of TV evangelicals. Studying her former blueberry co-picker, Anna also had a good idea of where this speech might have come from.

"But," Pug continued, "as ships have lighthouses to help them stay on course, so to do we." His tone turned from endangered to exultant. "As captain of the Catskill ship I sleep easier every night knowing that from Onasego's shores, your bright light beckons out to us," Pug raised the life ring overhead, "and, that with your lantern continually shining, you, the all important Friends of Catskill," the float dropped to his shoulders, "will guide us safely home."

The tears on Deedee's cheeks, remarkably free of any mascara residue, glistened in the setting sun.

Pug unsnapped the slicker. "And now an announcement. Tim Denny, will you come forward?"

With a shy smile, Tim handed Anna his beer to hold and stepped up beside the podium. The Forget Me Not fundraiser, Anna speculated. Time to whip up the crowd.

"When I speak of bright lights," Pug intoned, "I surely speak of Tim Denny, president of the Friends of Catskill, Onasego native, and son of Timothy Denny, a long-time local dairy farmer with a keen interest in preserving our natural resources."

Anna watched Deedee, suddenly back on the job, wave two cheerleaders, one male, one female, down the library steps to stand beside her. Maybe not the Forget Me Not. Maybe Pug was going to recognize Tim for his role with the Friends?

Pug continued. "When Tim Denny senior died two years ago, he left our Tim his farm, one thousand acres of pastures, forests, and streams that all of us pass regularly and, I'm sure, reflect on the beauty of the spot." Perhaps to reinforce the beauty of the spot, Pug took a second to squint out in the direction of the valley. Anna followed his squint. Maybe the fundraiser would be held at Tim's farm?

"However, fearing that same beauty and access would one day find their way into the hands of developers, Tim approached Catskill last summer with a vision that would honor his father's ecological interests, protect the land from the onslaught of bulldozers, and provide Catskill with a new educational venue.

"Yes, Ladies and Gentlemen, Tim's vision, now realized," Pug pointed at the male cheerleader who knelt for the female to climb onto his shoulders, "is the gift of his father's land, valued at a one and six big zeroes, to our college FOR..." the female cheerleader held her arms aloft in a V while Pug grasped Tim's shoulder with one hand and pointed back out to the valley with the other. "THE DENNY CENTER FOR SUSTAINABILITY STUDIES!"

While Tim sheepishly stood during a long round of applause, Anna first wondered about the relative crowd appeal of sailor outfits versus cheerleaders versus blow torches. And, as an aside, how she should never volunteer to be in charge of an event in Onasego. The second thing she wondered about, and knew that she would wonder about for a very long time, was how a man whose job it was to read meters door to door, all day, every day, would give away an inheritance worth a one and six big zeroes.

Anna handed Tim his beer. "That's incredibly cool setting up that center with your father's land."

Tim knocked back the rest of his Pale Ale while Deedee introduced the next speaker, Jason Flannagan of the Greek Life Society. "Dad would be happy. That land meant everything to him."

"Captain Pug seemed mighty pleased as well."

"Captain Pug, that calls for another beer."

Anna tried to keep a straight face while she and Tim walked back to the packed bar. If Pug had made his metaphor comparing the Friends' to a tugboat instead of a lighthouse, she could have named a column "Pug's Tug." Maybe she would do it, anyway. She reached for a club soda while Tim picked up another Pale Ale.

"Okay, let's get you signed up. Laurel, hey, Laurel, get over here."

To Anna's horror, Laurel Loomis, chatting a few feet away with Ray, looked up. Did Tim not remember Laurel's attack during that first Pleasures and Problems? Did he not care? Then, from some crevice in her brain, she dimly remembered Tim slipping from the sanctuary through the side exit with the blow torch as "Peg, here" waxed eloquent on the red maple. "Hey," Tim continued, "something I meant to mention, have you heard about the pumpkin regatta? If there was ever a natural for your column, that would be it."

"Pumpkin regatta?" That fell in the "think about later" category, kind of like Captain Pug and Deedee, because Laurel Loomis, swathed in a black linen, ankle-length dress with no waist and long sleeves, was headed toward them. The gray braid, hanging loose today, reached almost to her knees. A beaten silver pentacle dangled from a black leather string at her throat. At the podium a preppy six footer enumerated the economic impacts of the student population within the Onasego community over the murmuring of numerous intra-group conversations.

Laurel pulled Tim in for a kiss on both cheeks. "Well done! Such an extraordinary gift to our community. Your father would be so proud." Then, with a brief glimpse over Tim's shoulder. "Miss Lawson."

Anna smiled demurely. "Anna, please." Although the women had attended Sunday services for several weeks at the same time, they also successfully avoided each other. Until now.

Laurel turned to Tim. "What can I do for you?"

A henna-haired waitress holding a tray of canapés joined their circle, offering the appetizers first to Laurel, who declined with a slight shake of her head. Anna followed suit although she was starving. By contrast, Tim stuck his beer under his arm and loaded four of the tiny sandwiches onto a napkin. "Anna wants to join the Friends of Catskill. Would you add her to the mailing list?"

Sliding the pentacle back and forth along the leather, Laurel peered at Anna. "Are you trying to further infiltrate our little community, Miss Lawson? Perhaps find new subject matter for your column? Or are you just fond of attending cocktail parties like the majority of people here?"

Nail on the head time, Anna thought. "Actually, Miss Loomis, while I *do* enjoy a cocktail party and I *do* write a column about life in upstate New York, I *am* trying to become more involved in the community. I'd like to help out. The Friends seem like a worthy organization."

Laurel smiled. "Oh, is it now?"

Tim speared a Swedish meatball with an orange plastic toothpick from the tray. "And she wants to put some ivy around on the buildings."

Laurel gazed up at the library. "And the variety you have in mind?" At the podium, the student speaker thanked Pug and the Friends, then handed the mic back to Pug against a smattering of applause.

Anna shrugged. People were drifting in twos and threes toward the parking lot. If she could find Paul, she could make her excuses. "There's more than one kind?"

A smile played around Laurel's mouth. "Yes, Miss Lawson, and some varieties are, how shall I say this… *wicked* to buildings." The waitress laughed. "But if you *really* want to help, I think we may have a job for you, since, as you said, you are a writer."

Anna saw Paul walking into the library behind Erika, the sailor cap crammed in his pocket. She couldn't wait to tell him about wicked ivy. "I believe you know I am."

"Then, you'll do for our opening, don't you agree Tim?"

Tim, working on his fourth sandwich, nodded enthusiastically.

Visions of newsletters, grant applications, membership notices, and brochure design crowded Anna's imagination. A professional writer on call to the Friends of Catskill College? They would soak her dry. "But you should know that I don't have a great deal of time."

Laurel let go of the pentagram, smiled at the waitress and, with a sigh, selected a puffed shrimp from the tray. "Not a problem. It's only minutes once a month."

Anna checked the waitress's jewelry. No pentagrams that she could see. "Well, sure, I have time for that. But what only takes minutes?"

"Taking minutes," Tim said, grabbing two more sandwiches. "Laurel's leaving the secretary's job next month to take over the gala committee. You'll be her replacement."

Laurel demurely took a bite of the shrimp, then cocking her head to the side, eyed Anna. "Quite a delicious thought, don't you think, Ms Lawson?"


## 21 • EQUINOX

ANNA LOWERED THE car window as Paul backed out of the driveway. The Sunday afternoon was startlingly clear with the sky an intense blue she usually associated with Sierra Club calendars. The car thermometer read fifty-five. Here and there neighbors were working in their yards, cutting down dead plants, raking out beds, taking advantage of the weather for last clean ups before the cold weather. In a way she felt guilty for being in the car, even if she, Paul, and Joe were on their way to Cooperstown to have lunch, poke around a bit, and, she couldn't get her mind around this, watch the pumpkin regatta Tim had mentioned. What would that be? Pumpkins bobbing around Lake Otsego? The first to hit shore the winner?

And, to be honest, she was curious about Cooperstown. From Angie's description, Cooperstown was in a totally different league from Onasego—that being rich, no covenants exactly, but no fast foods either. According to Angie, one young woman with an old family fortune was a sort of patron to the village, underwriting everything from hospitals, museums, and schools to the fresh flowers hanging from street poles. She also knew from Paul that a number of wealthy donors to Catskill either lived in Cooperstown or summered there. For that reason she hadn't changed out of her church clothes while Paul, in khakis, a long sleeve tee shirt, and windbreaker, probably looked a lot more like a pumpkin race.

She glanced back at Joe. Although immersed in his Game Boy, impervious to everything around him, he did have his seat belt on. Molly, in a huff over her father's canceling a planned trip to the Hamptons for the weekend, had elected to stay in Onasego and play tennis at the park with Caroline, maybe work on a poem for the slam.

"So," Paul began, "What was up with the APCs today?"

"Well, the APCs are quite excited about the upcoming equinox." A football sailing over the hood of the car stopped her. Two guys in baggy shorts, no shirts, one on either side of the street, grinned and waved.

She propped her elbow on the window ledge. "Now, you and I might not think that day and night being of equal length is exactly news to write home about but, for those of certain persuasions, this is big. Very big. Don't we have to get the car inspected soon?"

"Why?"

"For the warranty."

"Why is the equal length thing a big deal?" He reached across the car and punched the glove compartment button. "I think it's 40,000 miles. Check the manual."

Anna reached for the pile of papers, dark glasses and debris spilling out over the compartment door. "We are supposed to think of the harvest, give thanks, prepare ourselves for the upcoming darkness. How did we get so much stuff in here already?" She separated out the owner's manual, then began to sort through the rest. "There was also something about sacrifice because soon there will be more darkness than light, but I didn't get that. Angie was explaining the essence of it during coffee hour, but it was kind of hard to hear."

Paul paused for two cars to pass before taking the left onto the county highway. Today, rather than the infamous back way of Anna's first trip, they were taking the main road to Cooperstown, a two-lane, paved county highway. "There is an essence of it?"

Anna gave him a quick sideways glance. "Angie says that, whereas Judaism, Christianity, and Islam are linear, Wicca is nonlinear because its traditions are based on nature's cycles. And that's because of the core belief that the earth is sacred."

The Gun N Bow slid by. Mason's Farm Supply. "Do you get that? Linear, nonlinear?"

"Not really. You didn't tell me you went to La Taverna." She held up a receipt from the upscale Italian restaurant in Onasego. "I thought we were going to try it for one of our birthdays."

Paul held out his hand. "It was one of Pug's meetings. Did that woman go after you again?"

"Laurel Loomis? No." Anna handed him the slip of paper, stowed the rest of the trash in the side pocket, and picked up the owner's manual again. On the cover, a BMW drenched in sunlight sat parked in front of an intricately scrolled wrought-iron gate covered in bougainvillea. The ivory portico of a villa beckoned in the distance above a row of cypress. Surely whoever designed that page wasn't into darkness and sacrifice. "But Laurel did announce that interested persons are invited to a Pagan Pride Day in New Mexico. I'm sort of amazed she hasn't started one here. Maybe next year."

Paul looked in the rear-view mirror after a gleeful "yes!" from the back seat. "So, what else went on today?"

"The building fund is behind. Fourteen computers have been donated for Cuba." She flipped through the table of contents first under W for warranty, then I for inspection. "No subs have been found for the trip to the School of the Americas, I signed up to make refreshments for the Youth Concert, and it seems the Poetry Slam is over subscribed. And, oh yes, Packy O'Connell is giving some early thought to Rosh Hashanah. Here it is." She scanned the inspections page. "Forty-five thousand miles."

The cars ahead of them began pulling out into the passing lane one by one. A tractor loomed ahead, its pale gray diesel smoke sending up an out-of-place plume in the open country air. Just past a vacant antique shop, a lonely billboard announced: Cooperstown Dream Fields Coming Soon.

Paul sped up, getting ready to pass. "I don't know why you go."

Anna looked out of the car window. Milford Center passed by. With the Susquehanna's shore so close to the hamlet, she couldn't imagine houses should be built there. "I go because thinking I was going to be murdered, I made promises to God, one of them being to take my children to church or somewhere, and for reasons beyond my control both my children really like this church."

The car lurched as Paul started out and then pulled back in. Anna braced herself against the dashboard. "God, I hate these two-lane roads. You could take them to synagogue, you know."

Paul checked the side mirror, flipped on the blinker, then pulled out again, this time rounding the sputtering tractor that they could now see was pulling a huge green igloo like object on a flat bed. "Anna, they're your promises."

The tractor driver in jeans and a short-sleeved gray tee shirt smiled as the white BMW sped by. William.

Entering Cooperstown, Anna abruptly put aside the very intriguing question of why William Johnson, real estate mogul, would be driving a tractor and pulling a green igloo. Angie's assessment of the village was right. Cooperstown was in a very different league from Onasego. It was perfect.

The first hint, at the outskirts of the village, was a dairy farm set high on a hillside overlooking the river valley. Framed by gleaming black rail fences and waves of sculpted boxwoods, a complex of champagne-colored barns and silos presided serenely over acres of verdant, windblown pasture land. Unlike most dairy farms, visual blots of raw wood, milking pens, and mud, this bovine abode exuded a cathedral-like gravitas—solid, massive, hushed. Who lived there? she wondered. Who could afford to maintain such a site? Even Paul raised an eyebrow.

The next hint was the parallel row of Victorian homes lining their entry into town. Some mansion-size, some one-family, some in between, but the crispness of these turquoise, rose, and emerald painted ladies along with their edged lawns and window boxes overflowing with pansies, mums, and cabbages, gave at least a local lie to the struggling upstate economy. By the time they had ridden through the circular drive of the Otesaga, an early 1900s resort conjuring images of raccoon coats, rustling silks, and steamer trunks, stepped out onto the hotel's Georgian veranda to swoon over the ten mile sapphire corridor of Lake Otsego, and had lunch alfresco by its shore at the nearby Blue Mingo, named for a character in a James Fenimore Cooper novel, Anna knew exactly where her next column was coming from—Cooperstown Bound? Otsego Odyssey? Baseball's Home: Surely Not Natty? She'd work out the title. And to think… they could have lived here. While Paul paid the bill, Anna called Molly to describe the incredible find, but with no answer, ended up leaving a message.

Spotting a parking place downtown, the trio strolled past the Baseball Hall of Fame, many, many baseball paraphernalia stores, and Christ Church, the burial spot of the Cooper family. Finally, following signs marked PUMPKIN REGATTA, they found themselves in Lake Front Park amid a crush of farm stands hawking everything from pumpkins and spinach to organic meats and cheeses as well as more typical craft show fare of tee shirts, jewelry, and dried flower arrangements. A Cooperstown Garden Club banner hung over a set of picnic tables advertising pumpkin carving contests on the half hour. Joe immediately begged to enter.

"I'm going to try Molly again," Anna announced buttoning her jacket against a mid afternoon breeze. "I'll meet you two in a sec. Hey, try to find out about the race. Maybe we've missed it."

With Joe tugging Paul to the garden club booth, Anna retreated toward a relatively empty corner of the park, leaned against an oak, and dialed her home phone. Once again, the phone went to message. What to do? There was no neighbor she knew to check on the girls, and Caroline's parents were out of town for the day. Clicking the phone off, she resolved to let Joe carve his pumpkin and head home. Maybe she'd pick up some produce in the meantime.

She screamed as claws raked the back of her legs.

"RAL-phie!"

A tiny female in wheat jeans and a coral jersey stormed toward Anna and the dog. "RAL-phie, horrible dog! Come here, now!" The heavily accented English was deep, commanding, Eastern European or Russian like in cold war spy movies. She reached down to pick up Ralphie's leash. "He escaped, this bad, bad boy. I was asked to hold him. I am so sorry."

The woman was not short so much as petite, the top of her head just reaching Anna's shoulder. Adding to the picture were chunky gold jewelry, thick, collar length charcoal hair swept back in tortoiseshell combs, and eyes that Anna usually associated with the likes of Georgia O'Keefe, Golda Meir, or Ruth Prawar Jhabvala. Huge, glittering black, and missing nothing. She was one of the most beautiful women Anna had ever seen.

"Think nothing of it." Anna held out her hand. In another age she would have surely bowed. How could Libby have approached this personage to take care of her dog? "I met Ralphie at a soccer match. I'm Anna Lawson."

The black eyes peered into Anna's. "Ah, I see." She paused, seeming to consider something, then looked back toward the lake. Apparently there was to be no explanation of the, "I see." She gazed at Anna again. "The race, it is beginning. You must call me Domnica."

## 22 • ALMOST DARK

FROM HER SPOT on the bank, Anna could make out three large motor boats along with a dozen or so canoes in the middle of the lake bunched around a floating dock. Several figures stood on the dock in sunglasses and life preservers. If that was where they were throwing the pumpkins in, she might as well set up a sleeping bag. They could take hours to drift in. She gave some thought to calling Molly again, but decided against it, not wanting to give her daughter the satisfaction. Anyway, Paul had overruled the plan to get back to Onasego before the race. How much trouble could you get into in Onasego on a Sunday afternoon, he'd said before heading back to the car to get his sunglasses. Joe, sitting beside her, cradled a small *cucurbita pepo*, Latin for pumpkin, according to an octogenarian garden clubber. He'd won a gold silk ribbon, the type bought at trophy shops, for his entry: a carving meant to resemble George on Seinfeld. The ribbon, now hooked around a shirt button, fluttered in the late afternoon breeze. Several race watchers asked to inspect George and the ribbon, but Joe, being Joe, refused, unwilling to part with either. How to convey what winning, winning anything, meant to her boy.

"Hey, look who I found."

Squinting into the sun, Anna saw Paul standing above her with Erika and Tom. Anna rose, brushing off the seat of her pants. "Hi. This must be the place to be—" Garbled speech from a bull horn cut her off. A woman on one of the motorboats appeared to be giving directions to the canoes.

Next, a gunshot ripped through the fall afternoon breaking the cluster of boats as effectively as a cue ball into a rack. In an instant, canoes scattered sideward, the crowd jumped to its feet, and Anna got her first glimpse of the pumpkins. Pumpkins at least five feet across, lopped off at the top, and hollowed out to make room for the people sitting in them. People with kayak paddles, smacking the water with short, choppy strokes, splashing and pushing off one another, wobbling drunkenly but somehow moving mostly toward shore. And one of the pumpkins was green, the igloo containing two females in hot pink sweats.

"Mom," Joe's upturned face was pure frustration. "I can't see."

She nodded, barely able to see herself. "It's okay. Go on up front."

He thrust George at her. "Hold him."

Stowing George under one arm, she squinted out at the other contestants: lots of teenagers in Cooperstown Central School tee shirts, a few obviously serious thirty- and forty-something jocks, a bearded guy in a pirate's hat, a platinum blonde with a lab puppy in her lap, and a white-haired man wearing fatigues—but no William Johnson. Paul wrapped his arm around her shoulder. "I'm going to get something to drink. You want anything?" She shook her head. Erika made a tipping gesture with her hand at Tom, then she too headed back toward the concession stands. Joe, she saw, was stationed about thirty feet away from the crowd on a cement dock. Sitting with his feet dangling over the edge, he seemed more intent on the tourist-savvy gray ducks congregating among the rocks below than the giant pumpkin race.

Gasps rose up from the crowd. One of the two pink sweatshirts was now beside the green pumpkin, not in it. Anna watched as the dunked sweatshirt grabbed onto the other sweatshirt's paddle, trying to pull herself back in. Something about the woman in the pumpkin looked familiar... Libby? Could it be Libby in William Johnson's pumpkin? Libby, if it was Libby, leaned way over to pull her partner in. Suddenly the pumpkin listed heavily toward the swimmer and, with a lazy roll, flipped over. Two canoes darted from the sidelines for the rescue. Cheers ricocheted around the park.

Anna held her hand up over her eyes to block the glare: Joe would be loving this drama. Her eyes roamed from the capsized pumpkin across the water to the ducks to Joe. Joe standing now, not looking out at the regatta but pulling at his shirt, looking behind, then down at the rocks. In a moment of horror, she saw Joe jump into the lake and begin doggy paddling away from the dock. Joe, a beginning pollywog! Pitching George and her purse to one side, she ran down the bank and into the water.

Paul strode out of the comfort area, a tent with folding chairs and a cot inside, just as an organizer entered carrying a tray of drinks. Anna stuck a hand out from her blanket for hot tea; holding it gingerly to one side, afraid of spilling. Joe, with his head in her lap, lay across two of the folding chairs, not quite in the fetal position but almost. With her free hand, she tucked his blanket in around his feet.

"We can get hot chocolate," the volunteer offered.

"Joe, hot chocolate?" Anna asked. Joe's only response was to squeeze his eyes tighter shut. Across from her Libby and Libby's daughter, whose name she couldn't remember, accepted hot tea also. Where Libby was pasty and blonde, the daughter was darker with caramel pigtails and thick arching eyebrows reminding her of someone. She could feel their eyes on herself and Joe.

"You, okay?" Libby asked finally. "We didn't see much but water there for a while."

Anna could see herself pushing through the crowd, racing into the lake, and looking up to see a canoe plucking Joe out of the water before she'd swum ten feet. One of the very kind motorboat operators took over from there, depositing Joe back on shore about the time Anna waded out. "I'm feeling very, very stupid, but fine."

"What about the guy who makes rhymes in church?"

Anna smoothed Joe's hair. "He's extremely upset about losing a ribbon he won. It blew into the lake and he went in after it." She could feel Joe stiffen against her. "And he's mad because I was holding the pumpkin he carved and I accidentally smashed it." She looked up, wishing they could all just be quiet. "What about you?"

Libby and her daughter exchanged a glance. "We feel dumb too, don't we, Dawn? We capsized a 785-pound pumpkin."

Dawn, that was her name.

"I'm not dumb." Dawn's words were uttered in a halting monotone, a space between each word.

The look on Libby's face told the true story. "No, Dawnie, not for a minute."

An awkward silence filled the tent. Anna glanced outside, hoping to see Paul hurrying back to them. He'd gone to try to find the canoeist who pulled Joe out of the lake to thank him. But now the sun was getting low, and they had yet to hear from Molly.

"Did he find the ribbon?" Dawn asked, her face expressionless.

"No, he didn't," Anna answered, trying to sound light.

"Did the pumpkin look like a cat?"

"George, on Seinfeld," the bundle in her lap whimpered.

Dawn threw off her blanket and stood over Joe, holding her hand out stiffly. "Come. Mumma has the ribbons. I'll get you one."

Libby stood and arched her back in a stretch. "I'll go too." She piled their blankets on the bench. "I've got to get to work. Dawn, you're eating at Mumma's tonight."

Anna gazed down at her boy. "I think he probably just wants to stay here."

"No, I don't," Joe said, sliding off her lap and grabbing Dawn's hand. "I want a ribbon. Now."

Paul checked his watch. "Where did they go?"

Anna shrugged. "I don't know. Off to get Joe a new ribbon from somebody named Mumma. Libby has to get to work so they can't be too long."

The park was mostly empty now except for the volunteers taking down tents and picking up trash. A few concessionaires lingered by their stands, chatting with one another, slowly packing up, hoping for a few last sales she supposed. Her eyes ran over a banner with a familiar name, Angus Lynch—Organic Turkeys. The stand beneath the banner was vacant. Mr. Lynch must have stepped away.

"You know, Paul," she said sliding first her right and then her left arm into her husband's windbreaker, "it started out as such a great day. Cooperstown, the race. Then Joe lost his ribbon. And Molly," she sank her hands down into the cottony pockets, "why won't she call us? She's got to know we're worried."

He pulled her to him. "You've got to be cold."

"Not so much. I'm too nervous." She pressed her face into his chest, willing herself to think of something besides murderers and water closing in over Joe's head. "What does Libby do at Catskill, anyway? She doesn't seem like the academic type."

He kissed her forehead. "Maintenance, cleans Hardy and Nold Halls at night. Does my office, actually, and does a damn good job."

She tensed, unable to tamp down a priggish cringe. "Libby's a janitor?"

"Yeah, I've run into her a few times when she's finishing up."

Right, she thought. The green tee shirt with CATSKILL in large white letters that Libby wore to the soccer match was not the sign of a huge fan. But work clothes. A uniform.

"Mom! See what I got!"

Anna looked over Paul's shoulder to see Joe racing toward her, followed by Libby and Dawn. A gold ribbon dangling from his shirt once more, but this time attached by a two inch safety pin. In his arms he cradled two pumpkins along with several ears of Indian corn. "Look," he said, pulling up in front of her. The words came out in little puffs. "Libby... even gave me... a pumpkin... for Molly."

Anna bent down and wrapped her arms around him.. "Speaking of which," she looked back at Paul, "maybe you could try Molly one more time?"

Paul's tone was cynical. "If you want. While I'm at it, I'll get the car."

Joe wriggled in her arms. No stomach ache. An abundance of treasure. A good day. She rubbed her cheek on the stubbly hair. "Dawn, Libby, you have made this boy very, very happy. Do you need a ride back or anything?"

"Mumma's taking us," Dawn said, the words again slow and flat. "She's over there." Her arm swept around to point out the red Windstar, with a minuscule figure at the wheel, idling across the street.

Libby slipped an arm around Dawn. Behind them, dying rays of sunlight glinted off satiny waves. "Yeah, work calls. Goodnight."

Anna watched as Libby, with her arm still firmly around Dawn, strolled to the pedestrian crossing and waited for the light to change. Libby, who in just a few hours would be pushing a janitor's cart down shadowy corridors, emptying people's trash, scraping gum off tables and desks, and brushing out spattered toilets—all through a long, Onasego night. Libby with Dawn to look after every single day after that. Libby who had understood completely why Anna couldn't pitch in for a flea market. First thing tomorrow she'd call to volunteer.

The BMW's headlights raked the pavement as Paul pulled into the lot. She opened the back door for Joe, then got in herself. One look at Paul's face told her the news wasn't good. "Molly's at the house. Said she forgot to check the message machine."

Anna switched on the heater. "She's lying."

"I know. Oh, and the girls quit soccer today, too. Too much work." Paul leaned across the console. "Should we stop? Pick up something to eat on the way?"

She felt for the seatbelt then watched as the sun slid silently below the western hills surrounding Lake Otsego. "It's almost dark, Paul. I just want to go home."

## 23 • FUN AND FABULOUS

FROM HER LAWN chair situated behind the All Paths Church table, Anna studied the burly bald man standing in front of the Otsego County Democrats booth eating a knish. She had seen him on and off over the morning wandering slowly amid the hundreds of eager shoppers and sellers crowding downtown Onasego. She knew him. But how? Not from Onasego. And not from the city. It was driving her crazy.

Her gaze swept down Main Street at the extravaganza consuming downtown. A garage sale Libby called it, failing to explain that the Fun and Fabulous, the official name, involved closing all downtown to traffic for the day not only to accommodate a half block long sound stage with continuous entertainment, but also the twenty to thirty vendors making up the Saturday morning farmer's market, as well as and above all, the vast chaotic profusion of wares being offered by individuals, families, groups of families, charities, and civic organizations lining both sides of Main Street.

Baby clothes, ab rollers, lathes, 1960s Motown records, ice skates, crock pots, crocheted afghans, futons, encyclopedia sets, glassware, linens, macramé plant holders, all the usual characters from garage sales everywhere spilled out of cartons, jammed tables, hung off rolling racks, and lay strewn about on blankets. It was enough collected junk to either make you never want to purchase anything, anywhere, ever again, she thought, or drive you to sift through every box in certainty that a Waterford bowl was out there somewhere for a dime.

Joe, a "helper" for the day, decided early on the latter. His stash underneath the table already included a chess set, roller blades, a bamboo fishing pole, and all twelve issues of *Orienteering Today*, from 1995. With two dollars remaining he was still on the hunt as just moments earlier Dawn had appeared with Ralphie in tow, announcing that she knew where the really cool stuff was.

Paul should be here too, she thought, as a man carrying two shovels pushed past the table. He could be searching for yard tools, gardening implements, things she didn't even know the right name for since falling leaves, heretofore, had been more song title than logistical detail in the Lawson household. But just yesterday Pug called a meeting of the Catskill finance committee along with the Cabinet for this morning to review the long-awaited audit report. So much for weekends. Likewise, Molly was unavailable for foraging, hunkered down as she was putting the finishing touches on a poem for the upcoming slam. Anna wondered if she was working on an homage to childhood by the kid's books she was poring over. Old, old favorites like *Good Night Moon, Home for a Bunny,* and *The Cat in the Hat* lay stacked beside Molly's bed as research or inspiration, she wasn't sure. But God forbid that she should ask a detail of Molly. Right now Anna couldn't peel a carrot correctly in her daughter's eyes. However, just yesterday, Molly made her promise to attend the slam. That seemed like a good thing; she still wanted her mother watching when she performed.

Forcing her mind away from Molly and Mr. Knish, Anna went back to work. The ancient masking tape peeled easily from the box in her lap, one of several boxes of clothes she was donating to the sale. This one held her mother's cocktail dresses from the sixties, dresses she always thought she might have an occasion to wear but never did. Cocktail dresses of the type no longer made. All of them black, but cut variously from silk, satin, or matte jersey, and decorated with jet, slinky gauze, slits, rhinestones, and sequins, statements every one of them. She remembered her mother being happy in those dresses, giggling, rustling out the front door ahead of her father on Saturday nights as soon as the babysitter arrived. Later, over scrambled eggs and toast, her parents would talk and talk until she fell asleep listening to their voices below. The next day, after church and lunch, the family females—herself, sister, Barbara, and mother, Sybil—would carry her father's suitcases to the company car, a tri-state sales territory taking him away Sunday through Friday. The trio would stand on the sidewalk, waving until the Buick was out of sight, then her mother would ask what she and her sister could do to entertain themselves—quietly—because she would be lying down.

Anna pulled the top dress from the box, a black and silver metallic sheath. Crazy how you could bring back childhood so vividly and not remember what you ate for breakfast. Sybil had this dress on the night she came home from a party to find the babysitter with her boyfriend on the living room floor—not sitting. Anna could still feel afraid just recalling her mother rip into that young girl. "What the hell are you doing? You're just a whore! Get out of here, you hear me?"

She gave the dress a long look, relieved in a way to see tiny rust spots. For fifteen years she had been carting these clothes around; time to make the break. Slipping each one onto a hanger, she picked up the bunch and found room for them on the clothes rack Libby had dropped off. Then, sitting back down, she opened a second box, her own maternity clothes from the eighties.

The bald man was finished with the knish now and investigating Angie's stand where a bright, shiny TREK mountain bike stood propped against a lamppost. Computers for Cuba, the raffle sign read. One dollar a ticket. The mystery man took out his wallet. Damn it, how did she know this man? She even knew what his voice would sound like, New Jersey, thick, dull sounding. Suddenly she had it. She turned to Deedee, her shift mate, who had barely looked up from her cell phone all morning. Something must be up at the Molina household, or somewhere, Anna thought after hearing several distinctive "oh, shit"s and "Mother of God"s slipping from the toffee-colored lips.

"Deedee, check out the Computers for Cuba raffle, the guy talking to Angie. Is he a ringer for Tony Soprano or what? Who's the actor? James somebody?"

Deedee held a perfectly manicured nail aloft. "James Gandolfino."

"Right. Looks just like him."

"Because," Deedee's eyes narrowed at something on the screen, "it *is* him. He owns a restaurant near here." Deedee scanned the crowd, "You know, celebrities aren't just in *the city*. That's Yoko Ono buying eggs from Angus Lynch. Parker Posey came through earlier."

Anna put the elastic-fronted pants and tunic tops she was unfolding aside. "Maybe I could get a quote for the column. Can you watch things by yourself for a moment?"

Deedee pressed in another number. "Of course I can."

Yoko Ono lifted her opaque dark glasses, peered into Anna's eyes, dropped the glasses, and walked away. At least she'd gotten a guttural "uh, don't think so" from James Gandolfino.

Anna turned to face Angus Lynch's farm stand. The same banner she had seen in Cooperstown adorned the front of the white canopy shielding, she assumed, Angus Lynch, the medium height man with thick gray hair and a mischievous grin standing behind a table laden with cheeses, homemade fudge, egg cartons, and a sign-up sheet with RESERVE YOUR THANKSGIVING TURKEY TODAY printed at the top. An erasable board tied to the roof of the canopy listed cuts of meat and prices per pound that she guessed filled the coolers underneath the table. One cooler was marked beef, one chicken, and the third pork.

"Mr. Lynch?"

"Mrs. Lawson?"

Anna held out a hand. "How did you know?"

Angus Lynch extended his hand in return, a worn, callused hand that trembled slightly on its route to hers. "Your dramatic entrance to the pumpkin regatta was much remarked upon." The perfunctory shake completed, Lynch raised a tray of sample cheeses for her inspection. "Tell me, will your swim be noted in a future 'Alone in Onasego?'"

His tone had a Spencer Tracy quality to it. Open, plain, mischievous. Was he asking for her to apologize for that first column when she cited him? She reached for a slice of the cannonbear.

"Sure you want to talk to her, Angus?" Ellis's unmistakable voice called from behind her.

Tim, Ellis, and Ray clustered about the table, forearms resting on guitars hanging across their middles. All three wore matching flannel shirts and baseball caps with RNM stitched across the rims. Against the melee of the garage sale, the ensemble kind of worked.

"You might be next week's column," Tim continued.

Ellis shoved a plastic bag crammed with sale loot under the table. "Yeah… 'Alone with Angus's Stinkin' Cheese' or something."

Lynch surveyed the group. "You boys signing up for your Thanksgiving turkeys?"

Tim draped an arm around the farmer. "What we want is something to eat."

"Real hungry, Angus," Ray added, eyeing the squares of plastic-wrapped fudge.

Lynch made a show of looking up and down Main Street. "The possibilities abound, gentlemen."

The PA system crackled overhead. "Red Neck Mothers, five minutes."

Angus Lynch held out a plate of fudge in one hand and cheese in the other. "My dear mothers, as time is of the essence, have at it."

The crowd near the sound stage pleaded for a third encore but the RNMs, after deep bows to the crowd and one another, were done. The hometown favorites for sure, Anna concluded, although Al Gallodoro, the world famous jazz musician, who at 90 was still composing and performing, had come a mighty close second. But, for sheer audience participation, the RNM's had it. The swell on the chorus after every verse of UP AGAINST THE WALL RED NECK MOTHER blasted the downtown. Anna joined in the wild applause. She turned to Angus Lynch. "Wow, did they write that?"

"No, Ray Wylie Hubbard did. But Jerry Jeff Walker, who grew up near here, sang it a lot. Only then he was Ronald Clyde Cosby."

Anna watched the three men still tipping their hats to the crowd. "They're really good!"

"Should be," Lynch said, "they've been playing together since they were kids. The three of them found each other in kindergarten, and they've been together, one way or another, ever since." He reached for the cheddar tray with a shaking hand. Then set it back down.

"How do you know them?" Anna picked up the tray and held it for him.

"The same way you get to know everyone in Onasego. And my sister's child used to play in a band with them. But that was a long time ago." As he talked, Lynch consolidated the remnants of the cheddar, camembert, and goat cheese onto Anna's tray.

She decided to take a chance. "Ellis, he kind of scares me. Told me he's on probation. That he threatened his father."

"Well, his father deserves it." Lynch turned to the sales board and slashed through most of the beef items, the whole chicken, and bacon. "And don't you concern yourself about the Parkinson's," he added. "I don't, modern medicine and all."

She left his stand utterly charmed and, with a map to his farm for the turkey she had reserved, to be picked up at noon on the Tuesday prior to Thanksgiving.

"A date I shall look forward to with the utmost pleasure, Ms. Lawson."

"Anna, please, Mr. Lynch."

"Then we shall be Anna and Angus to one another."

A swoon at that very moment, she reflected later, would have been very much in order.


Joe pulled at her hand. "Mom, come see. It's only a dollar. Please?"

Dawn, with Ralphie's leash doubled around her wrist, nodded solemnly in agreement.

Anna turned to Deedee. "It seems like I just keep running off."

Deedee looked up from her phone. "We're done here and I need to get up to the college. I'll just throw the stuff in a box... take it to Sal's later."

It was true. All their cookies were gone, the coffee urn long emptied, only a few limp sweaters and slacks remained hanging from the clothes rack. Her mother's dresses sold while she was chasing Yoko Ono, her own maternity clothes not long after.

"Thanks. Hey, if you see Paul, would you ask him to call me? Let me know if there's another Pug meeting tonight or if he's coming home for dinner."

Deedee's face scrunched in confusion. "Pug meetings?"

"You know, all those dinner meetings Pug calls."

Deedee reached under the table for an empty box. "Oh, those Pug meetings. Sure."

"Mom!"

Sliding her purse over her arm, Anna let Joe, followed closely by Dawn and Ralphie, pull her to the far end of Main Street and into the lot beside

City Hall. A lot, she realized quickly, dedicated solely to charitable and civic services. Tim waved from behind the Friends of Catskill College table: the Onasego Multiple Sclerosis Chapter appeared to be raffling off a gleaming yellow and black late 1960s Mustang; and an athletic blonde sold daffodils for the American Cancer Society. The State University was represented by a chicken barbeque stand alongside pizza by the slice to benefit the Catholic Charities of Otsego County. In the far corner of the lot, a cabana covered shelves of paperbacks under a Dollars for Scholars banner. So many people out working for their causes, she thought, almost tripping over Ralphie's leash. People without a lot of money or a lot of time themselves.

Joe's destination turned out to be the Otsego County Greens booth, sharing a table with the Country Coven exhibit on organic gardening and alternative energy sources manned by, she should have known, Laurel Loomis. The two women locked eyes, Anna turned away first.

"Look!" Joe commanded, pointing to a poster entitled Endangered Species of New York. Anna gazed at the cardboard—a plethora of wildlife stared back at her. "Mom, grouses! Grouses are endangered! You can give a dollar and help it."

Victor from the church stepped around from the back of the table. Victor who she now knew to be a geology professor at Catskill with wide-ranging interests. Most recently, during Pleasures and Problems he had added "declaration of the city as a nuclear-free zone" to his campaign for mobile slaughter houses. "To be exact, it is the spruce grouse that is endangered in New York—not the ruffled. The boreal woods, its habitat here in New York, have been severely damaged by acid rain. Contributions go toward protection of endangered species breeding grounds."

"But I saw one here. On the road to Cooperstown." She fished in her purse for her wallet.

Victor picked up the glass jar marked "contributions" from the table. "Possible, but not likely."

Anna took another look at the picture then opened her wallet to see a lonely ten-dollar bill. She could have sworn she had a twenty the day before. "That's what I saw, I'm sure." She handed him the ten.

"Did you hear the big Catskill news?" Joe slouched back against her, his head pressing into her stomach. Laurel Loomis fanned herself slowly with a brochure. "The audit report came in."

"I know, Paul's up there now for a meeting on it."

Victor stuck the jar back on the table. "Seems the budget's worse than anyone knew. Combination of things. Freshman class smaller than expected, the roof over Hardy Hall about to cave in, a lot of pledges that Paul's predecessor reported weren't really in the bag, probably why he cut and ran, anyway, the bond rating got lowered yesterday. A lot of people are going to have a hard time sleeping tonight."

Anna knew she wasn't getting something. "What do you mean exactly?"

"Somehow the college has to find twenty million dollars—"

Laurel Loomis's brochure hovered in mid wave.

"Or?"

"Or," Victor rounded the table behind the Endangered Species of New York sign and pointed down at the exhibit, "Catskill College... right here."

## 24 • NEVER DOUBTING (1)

"Hi."

Anna looked up from the pile of bills on the kitchen table to see a worn out and harried Paul. Since hearing the Catskill news from Victor, she'd hovered somewhere between terrified and dying to hear the gory details. Did Paul still have a job and who were the screw ups?

"Where are Joe and Molly?"

"Joe's upstairs organizing stuff he bought at the sale. Molly's practicing for the slam tomorrow at Caroline's." She watched as Paul headed straight for the liquor cabinet. "How are you?"

"In need of a drink."

She stuffed the five-hundred-dollar Geico bill for the BMW back in its envelope. "Is it all true? About the audit report?"

He pulled the doors open studying the possibilities. "What did you hear?"

"That lots of the campaign pledges your predecessor reported weren't real, that maintenance costs and enrollment are bad, and that Catskill is like twenty million in the hole."

"That pretty much sums it up. Who told you?"

"Victor, but I think a lot of people on Main Street knew." Paul seemed to be weighing a scotch versus vodka option. "Any heads going to roll?" she asked lightly, slipping what she knew was going to be a humongous Visa statement to the bottom of the pile.

"Not mine, at least right now, if that's what you're asking." He pulled out the scotch bottle and reached for a glass.

"So what will happen?"

Paul twisted off the cap and poured; took a drink; then poured some more before leaning back against the counter. "Right now I pack a suitcase and get on the road. Try to turn some of those wishful pledges into the real thing. And while I'm out there, I call on every major donor Catskill has had in the past ten years. Meanwhile, there will be a lot of scrambling by Pug, conference calls with board members, and then the whole board will take up the problem at the December meeting. See what the options are. For us it means I won't be around very much."

Anna tried to process this scenario. Paul always traveled with his job so for him to say to he wouldn't be around very much was enormous. She opened the AAA bill to their new account while Paul poured another drink.

"At least you still have a job."

"Very much. That may be the silver lining."

Cars. AAA. Auto Insurance. Her new life in Onasego. She reached for the NYSEG bill. "What do you mean?"

"If I can pull this out, I really will be able to write my own ticket. Paul Lawson saves school. I can see the headline in the *Chronicle of Higher Education* right now."

"And if you don't?"

Paul rolled the glass against his forehead. "Kind of obvious isn't it? No school, no need for a development officer."

She pulled out the four-page energy bill. One hundred and fifty dollars. And it was only October.

"Paul, have we made a terrible mistake?"

## 25 • SLAMMED

NORA'S BISTRO WAS jammed, jammed for the slam Anna thought, observing the capacity crowd. And she didn't even know what a poetry slam was.

Nora's, as the restaurant was fondly known around Onasego, intrigued her. It combined the conflicted food heart of its founder with a stylishly, if eclectically decorated (men's and women's work boots, worn but gleaming, lined the shelf above the bar), dining and music venue. While the set menu leaned heavily toward stuffed-squash- and-sprouts oriented fare, the specials were nothing short of gastronomical grandeur, like grilled baby back ribs over polenta with a side spinach and goat cheese salad (from local organic growers), poached sea bass with sweet potato wedges, and pumpkin, sage, chestnut, and pancetta risotto. On selected Friday and Saturday nights, by some sleight of hand, tables would be shoved aside, a stage assembled, and Nora's transformed to not quite a night club but darned close to a pub. Local, regional, and a fair number of music groups from the City included Nora's on their touring schedules. Anna's favorites so far were a Cajun group, Rubber Band, from nearby Jefferson, and an Irish singer who made his way to the stage by walking not over but across the bar—joined by the Lawsons' new insurance agent. She hadn't seen that much nightlife in twenty years. On Sunday afternoons, however, after the busy mid-day brunch and before the restaurant closed for a much-deserved thirty-six hours of rest, the owners often hosted special community events with dessert and coffee. Thus far she had attended a lecture there on "The Underappreciated James Madison," a terrifying presentation on the implications of the peak oil crisis for the country, and a silent auction fundraiser for a recently burned-out family. Yet as packed as she'd seen Nora's, especially with the Irish guy, this Sunday afternoon event was even more of a standing room only event.

Looking ruefully into an empty coffee cup, she tried to catch the lone waitress's attention. Beside her, Angie mouthed the words to her poem silently, checking a legal pad from time to time, apparently oblivious to the hubbub all about them.

She waved to the waitress again, this time catching her eye. The Poetry Slam was already half an hour late in starting and with twenty some participants signed up not to recite but to "perform," according to Molly, "Mom, it's SPOKEN WORD, not just poetry. You get points for your poem, but also for how you *perform*. God, Mom…" So with twenty people signed up, three minutes a person, time for the judges to judge, Anna was looking at a shot afternoon rather than a few quality hours with her next "Alone in Onasego" column. One working title, Just Call Me Alma, sounded all right but the issue, people confusing knowing who a person was with actual knowledge of a person, felt iffy. Too philosophical. Her other thought, tentatively titled Soc-Her, would be a column on Onasego's cradle to grave obsession with soccer. In it she envisioned picking up on the early education craze with a mother-to-be playing not foreign languages or arias for the fetus but tapes from the women's 1991 Women's World Cup win.

The waitress, less pierced than most, held up both decaf and caffeinated carafes. With the roar in the room, Anna pointed to the caffeinated; a defense against the coming hours.

Anna looked across to the booth where Molly sat with Caroline, Jamie, Gwendolyn, and Peter. From Angie she now knew that Peter supported himself by giving guitar lessons, bartending sporadically, and had recently split up with a Catskill professor tired of supporting an "aspiring musician." Anna checked her watch. Two forty-five.

"Angie," she hissed, "can you make Derek start this thing?"

Angie nodded obediently, stood, then cut through the mass of tables to the front row where Derek was holding court with his five volunteer judges, and pointed to the clock over the bar. Derek, conveying an appropriately poet-like air in baggy corduroys and a turtleneck shirt, kissed Angie on the forehead and swung around behind the improvised podium, a bar stool supporting a hand-held microphone. Picking up the mic, he tested it with a couple of taps. Talk in the room promptly subsided.

"Ladies and gentlemen, my lovely wife believes we need to get started. And, as with all things, she is right." While Angie wove her way back to the bar, Derek explained the rules for any newcomers. The rules were brief. "Each poem must have been written by the performing poet; there will be no props, music, or costumes; the high and low scores for each poet will be dropped and the remaining scores averaged. I will be the sacrificial goat and get us started. My score will not count." He looked around the restaurant. "Any questions?"

With no takers, Derek took a deep breath, held a hand to his chest, and began. "My poem is entitled, 'After Dark.' The poem came to me one evening last summer while sitting on a bench right outside on Main Street. It was a warm evening and downtown was packed with teenagers. Watching that parade of passers-by, I was suddenly hit with the wonder of young girls, the beauty, the *joie de vivre*, the self awareness just around the corner. So, here is what came to me that evening."

**AFTER DARK**

Young girls walking after dark
With silk spun hair
Skin so bare
Far too young to care
And I, so aware,
Of all the young girls... Walking
After dark.

Anna studied her coffee. She didn't dare look at Angie. Applause, scattered at first, then becoming respectful, met Derek's bow. What the hell had that been about? The clapping died down and the judges flashed their scores. Two eights, one nine, one six, and one five. Throwing out the five and the nine, Derek's poem was a 7+ something. Boy, did she have a lot to learn about poetry.

"Caroline Van, Caroline, you're next."

Caroline glanced at her parents and Molly with an exaggerated grin and stood, hesitating for a second as the spotlight found her. With her ebony hair swept up into a messy bun and tight black tank/skinny jeans combination showcasing remarkably upright assets, she all but screamed nubile.

"My poem," Caroline announced while walking to the front, "well, my poem comes from the fact that I always think I should get what I want. And because I'm in the seventh grade, I think about boys a lot. And my favorite movie when I was little was *Snow White and the Seven Dwarfs*." She picked up the mic from the barstool and took a seat. "So, the poem is," her voice vaulted across the room, "'Hey There Happy and Dopey.'" Caroline drew herself upright with one shoulder slightly forward, raised her chin, and looked down at the audience, just like a snotty, entitled little princess, Anna noted, fascinated.

> Hey there Happy and Dopey
> Sneezy and Doc

Caroline's hand rose to her chest.

> While I lie here in my coffin
> You need to comb my hair
> Straighten my silk gown
> And, please, I beg you,

She licked her lips.

> Bring this princess a prince.

One nine, two eights, and two sevens flashed almost immediately. Caroline curtsied to whistles, foot stamping, and screams, then ran back to the booth and collapsed against her father. Anna hoped that Molly wasn't next. The princess was a tough act to follow. However, the next sequence of poets turned out to be dreary enough to make Anna wish for espresso. A double. By the time Peter rose to take the mic, she had come up with, and thrown out, three new column titles. In ripped jeans and a Dave Matthews Band tee shirt, he greeted the audience with a low, "Hi Guys." A murmured "Hi Peter" came back at him like a twelve-step program. "You all know I write songs, not poems, but then what is a song?"

Peter paused, allowing the audience time to ponder. Then, after a practiced gaze about the room, he continued. "Okay, people, here we go with an acappella, 'My Love.'" Peter closed his eyes, threw his head back, tilting the mic back to meet his lips.

> Almost every morning
> I rise from bed about three or four

Wondering if I heard her
Was there movement at my door

The wait is always anxious
Could it be that she'll resist
There's only one reason for living
This chance I cannot miss

Angie turned a pained expression to Anna. She flipped the page of her legal pad and scribbled, *Heard this one a million times.* Across the room, Molly and Caroline crept between tables, then made seats for themselves on the floor in front of the barstool as Peter went into crescendo mode on the chorus.

My love she comes on tiptoe
And never hurries in
She takes her time before she's mine
Before the hymn begins
Yes, she takes her time before she's mine
Before the hymn begins

Angie pushed over a drawing of a stick figure with a noose around his neck. Crooning into the mic, Peter smiled down at the girls.

I feel her coming to me
Soft footsteps in the night
The barriers begin to open
From black to gray to white
And then we lie together
Creating heaven from the Sun
She sings her song, I sing along
She sings into my heart

The girls, knees drawn up under their chins, appeared on the brink of tears. But, Anna thought, in the big picture, what could be more naturally teenage than a crush. She could still remember pining over a married coun-selor at camp who had to have been ten or twelve years older. Peter repeated the chorus, and the very long song was finally over. Peter got a ten, a five, two sevens, and an eight. Angie emitted faint gagging sounds. Anna smiled. Who cared? Molly was having a good day. She was with a friend, acting like a normal teenager, participating in a community event. I needed this, Anna thought. Next, Derek called a short intermission, followed by Angie and her composition titled "Thoughts for Americans from Ho Chi Minh." Her poem was a loser with the crowd, reaping two fives, two sixes, and an eight. Too much included, Anna decided, Viet Nam, voting rights.

"Well I liked it," Derek yelled. Then, "All right, Molly Parrish, you're up. Molly will read 'My Own Stone.'"

Molly pushed herself up to standing and rubbed her hands on her jeans. In a sage tee, her hair tied up in a ponytail, she was the nexus of breathtak-ing and tom boy. Anna felt a glow of parental pride. At that age, she would never have entertained the idea of performing publicly in front of a packed audience. Particularly performing her own composition.

"'My Own Stone,'" Molly began, her eyes fixed squarely on her mother.

> I remember a book about a bunny
> Looking for a home of his own
> I remember that bunny went looking
> Under a rock, a log, and a stone

Molly, her golden girl, spoke with practiced, chilling confidence.

> But Margaret Wise Brown never told me
> Why that bunny looked under a stone
> Maybe Margaret Wise Brown never knew
> Why that bunny wanted a home of his own

> Maybe Margaret Wise Brown
> Was always happy, writing little bunny stories to sell
> Maybe Margaret Wise Brown
> Was never thirteen, and sentenced by psychopaths to hell

⤚

Angie caught up with her about midway home, between Beech and Haven Avenues. "Ah, these teenagers. All Sturm und Drang, pathos, and melodrama."

"Right."

"Molly won. Squeaked past Caroline and Peter. Got the gift certificate to Penny's."

This time Anna decided on a "Yeah."

"Derek thinks she's got real talent—the alliteration, the way she lined up Margaret Wise Brown with thirteen-year-old angst. He offered to help her with phrasing."

Baskets, pots, and planters filled with yellow, white, maroon, and orange chrysanthemums called out from nearly every house along Summit Avenue. A happy, comforting look. The landscaping around the rented house amounted to some patchy periwinkle with a few left over marigolds planted by the previous tenant. No window boxes or planters. "Is Molly still down there?"

Angie stopped, shifting the ever present canvas bags to her other shoulder. "She left with the Vans. I heard something about a sip of champagne." Angie's black clad arm slipped through Anna's. "Don't worry. She's just doing the mandatory teenage bullshit thing."

Anna checked her watch. Four thirty. She was fairly sure about a nursery that stayed open 'til six on Sundays. She could be away by herself for almost two full hours buying flowers. Angie's expectant expression reminded her she should say something.

"Yeah. Right."

## 26 • UP AGAINST THE WALL

THE OVEN TIMER pinged from downstairs alerting Anna that the sheet cake for the Youth Concert tonight had ten more minutes. A yellow cake that would be iced with mocha fudge straight from RiteMarket: explicit instructions from the poetry princess, Molly's new name around the house.

Psychopaths, teenage bullshit, whatever. She was sick of thinking about it. Both Angie and Paul chalked up Molly's little stunt at the slam the previous weekend to the utter drama of the early teen years. Both advised her not to take it personally. Just drop it they said. "How?" her bludgeoned self worth asked over and over.

She propped an elbow on her desk. The previous night's work glared back at her from the laptop screen ready for the next day test. Very good? (Spine tingling) Good? (Needs some editing) Blah? (Needs a lot of work; maybe not salvageable) Really bad? (Job at Barnes and Noble.). She took a sip of coffee and began.

*It Takes a ... Coven*

*Hello Manhattan Living Readers. It's fall here in Onasego, I know, I know, it is in Manhattan too, but fall takes a slightly different form here. Before we go into that, however, let's take a moment and review what we've learned so far about living in an upstate college town.*

*First, moose can and do walk through the neighborhood; the same goes for deer, groundhogs, lots of skunks, and many, many roving bands of drunk college students. Blueberries grow on bushes and are best harvested with plastic bags tied at the waist. Picking up broken beer bottles on Sunday morning left by the roving bands is also best done with plastic bags at the waist. In addition, you now know that glaciers were the early developers of upstate, carving up land helter-skelter, also scary and slithery. And, you have learned about the ubiquity of soccer here (when a fetus kicks a lot in utero up here it is an especially good sign), the gift of goldenrod and purple asters, people who go out of their way to help you, not rob you, and, a grouse.*

*But back to fall in upstate, today's lesson involves a unique community event that happens here the first Saturday of every October. We Manhattanites have our own community events, the Macy's parade, the St. Patrick's Day parade, the summer exodus to the Hamptons, and, let me think, oh, yes, the annual transit or trash strike. But have we, living as we do in the epicenter of trade and commerce, ever considered an all-island... drum roll, please... FLEA MARKET ?!?! In this era of recycling, going green, volunteer service, thinking globally but acting locally, and targeted charitable giving, a community garage sale is the ultimate win-win, no brainer, and in corporate and basketball parlance, a slam dunk. Why did it take the Red Neck Mothers, Country Coven, (both are real names I swear), and the Onasego Common Council to figure this out instead of those geniuses on Madison Avenue and Wall Street? Is it because we New Yorkers aren't materialistic? Don't like shopping? Wouldn't enjoy getting paid for junk? But I say if Onasego can use a crisp autumn day to pull off the Fun and Fabulous Flea Market on Main Street as it did last Saturday, then we can too. (Consider Fifth Avenue closed off from Washington Square to Central Park.) From my catbird seat behind the All Paths Church table where we sold donated women's and children's clothing at pretty much "whatever you wanted to pay prices," I was both observer and participant. Let me paint the picture for you.*

Anna sat back in her chair. She'd give it between a good and a very good, but Marty would love it. Every now and again, and this was one of those moments she thought, things seemed to be coming together professionally for her. While Paul's professional life was now officially in turmoil, she felt solidly optimistic. The column was being well received and, for the first time in her life, she had her own office. A place completely specified for writing. The ground floor of the Victorian might be drafty, but upstairs in the fourth tiny bedroom where she had set up her desk, computer, fax, writing references, photos of the family, and all the accoutrements of a freelance writer, she could count on being toasty and oddly content. Just as soon as she was sure "Alone in Onasego" was established and had a few months of columns in the hopper, she would finally start her book, a nonfiction on the early settlement of Manhattan. Most people had an idea but she would do details (introduce the Manhattans, pry apart the Dutch, follow Peter Stuyvesant hobbling out of town, watch the village grow, burn, then grow and grow again). As a writer for *Manhattan Living*, what could be more of a natural extension? Maybe, she'd thought, the magazine would even serialize parts. But, she pulled herself back to the present, today at least until three, was for the column. With Paul out of town for the weekend, this would be it until Monday morning. From downstairs, the timer pinged once again. She pressed save, then pushed her chair back.

The phone jangled just as she got the cake out onto a burner. No cracks, no wedges, no crumbs on the fork. Perfect.

"Hello."

A business-like female voice said, "This is Onasego Elementary calling. Could I speak with Mr. or Mrs. Lawson?"

Joe's class was at a fall picnic at Veterans Park. Did Paul forget to drop off the oatmeal raisin cookies on his way out of town?

"Yes."

The voice continued, "Mrs. Lawson, we need you to come over here right away." An instant clench spread through her gut. "Is Joe all right?"

The voice had the decency to falter. "We're just not sure."

Joe, soaked and sobbing, stood with his face literally pressed into a corner in Mrs. Wimbish's fourth-grade classroom. Anna, wrapping a towel around him, tried to make her voice sound calm. Except for Mrs. Wimbish, herself, and Joe, the room was empty, the rest of the class still on the day-long picnic. "What happened?"

Mrs. Wimbish, mid-thirties and apparently bewildered, just shrugged. "The children finished a snack, then started playing dodge ball. We did our count, realized we were one short, and couldn't find Joe. After we got everyone sitting on the ground, we spread out and found him in the middle of the creek, pretty much as you see him now. We don't know what happened. He wouldn't tell us."

Anna dragged a desk chair behind Joe, sat down, and pulled him onto her lap. He buried his face in her shoulder. "JoJo?" JoJo, his baby name had been off limits for a couple of years, but she couldn't help herself. "Please tell us, how did you get so wet? What's wrong?"

Joe just laid his cheek on her shoulder, still sobbing but beyond tears.

"JoJo, I've brought dry clothes. I brought your new plaid shirt, the one you and Dawn bought at the Fun and Fabulous. You know how much you like it." She felt the little head nod on her shoulder. "And I've got your jeans, the ones with all the pockets. If you change your clothes, we can go to The Pantry for lunch."

She felt a sigh pass through him. "All by ourselves?"

"All by ourselves," she promised. After a few minutes, she continued. "If Mrs. Wimbish and I go out in the hall will you change clothes?"

His arms grabbed around her neck.

"You can have pancakes for lunch."

No answer.

"How about pancakes and bacon?"

"All by ourselves?"

"All by ourselves."

Anna reached for her tote bag for the clothes. "We'll be right outside."

Joe stood, still wrapped in the towel as the two women left the room.

Once in the corridor, Anna gestured for Mrs. Wimbish to follow her a few steps from the door. "Please. You must know something. Or one of the children knows something. Maybe somebody got into the park..." She couldn't finish that thought.

Mrs. Wimbish leaned against the wall. "The class was all in one area. I'm just about positive some outsider didn't bother him."

"Well, do you have any ideas?"

The teacher looked troubled and very tired. "Of course I'm going to ask the other children. We just wanted to get him out of the park as soon as possible. All I know is—" She paused.

"What?"

"Well, Joe's little. He's not that interested in fourth grade ideas of 'cool.' Sometimes he doesn't show the best judgment about not annoying other kids."

Anna didn't like the sound of this. "So?"

"To be honest, Mrs. Lawson, Joe is kind of a target."

The lunchtime traffic at The Pantry was brisk. Anna, feeling the need to join her son, however she could, toyed with an English muffin and coffee while Joe, a large paper napkin stuffed in the collar of his new shirt, concentrated on the platter of pancakes, side order of bacon, and orange juice in front of him. He had been quiet on the ride over, answering her attempts at conversation with an uhuh or an unhuh.

"Well, JoJo, now that you have a day off, what do you want to do this afternoon?"

Joe poured more syrup on the stack. "Go home."

"Go home and do what?"

He crammed in a forkful she wouldn't have believed could fit into his mouth. "Just go home."

Anna picked up a muffin half and slowly buttered it. "You want to tell me what happened today?"

All she got was a quick shake of Joe's head.

"But, Joe, something happened that made you get wet and cry. I don't like to see my boy unhappy."

His eyes remained fixed on the plate.

"Hi, guys, didn't see you over here." Libby and Dawn stood by their booth. "Playing hooky?" Libby continued.

"Kind of," Anna answered quickly. Libby had on the ever present CATSKILL tee shirt while Dawn was dressed in a flowered skirt, pale blue blouse, with a red purse strap crossed over her chest, bandoleer style. "What about you?"

"I took an allergy test," Dawn offered in her slow monotone. "But I don't have to go back to school. Later on I'm going to watch *Home Alone*, one AND two."

Libby winked at Anna and Joe. "She loves that little boy, what he does to the bad guys."

For the first time Anna saw Dawn smile. A smile that became a gleam in her eye and a giggle behind her hand.

"I like those movies," Joe said, dunking a strip of bacon in the leftover syrup.

Dawn rocked back and forth, gripping the red purse. "You want to watch them with me?"

Joe tipped his head like a robin eying a worm. "Mom?"

The invitation seemed to Anna like a shaft of sun breaking through very dense, gray skies. While the hustle and bustle of The Pantry swirling about them had temporarily muted the morning's sadness, she knew the pancakes and bacon effect would wear off soon enough.

Anna looked at Libby. "Would that be all right?"

"Fine with me." Libby said. "In fact, it's better than fine." She made a face at Dawn. "It'll keep her from bugging me to watch them with her."

Joe took his napkin out of his collar. "I'm done. Can we play with Ralphie?"

Anna balled up her napkin and scraped syrup off Joe's face. "Libby, would you call me when you get home?" Anna hoped the mother-to-mother element was coming through in her voice. The "call me because I need to explain something but don't want the children to know." The "call me because I'm very worried about my little boy." The "call me because I'm about to lose it here." "We could talk about logistics. How to get to your house to pick up Joe." She dropped the dirty napkin on the plate with the uneaten, unwanted English muffin. "We could talk about—you know—those sorts of things."

The night was clear and pleasantly warm even though it was almost eleven o'clock. The white and burnt-orange chrysanthemums she'd found at the nursery might last another week or two, Anna thought as she locked the front door behind her and began walking down Summit to pick up Molly from the Youth Concert. The princess had argued hard to walk home alone, or at least with friends. The parenting books talked about this, the paradox of teenagers constantly challenging yet in reality seeking limits. But why did they have to be so nasty about it?

Being outdoors felt liberating. She probably should have taken a long walk earlier, maybe she could have walked off the headache that had been with her all afternoon. Instead, she'd stayed by the phone hoping to hear from Mrs. Wimbish. But the only calls all afternoon had come from Libby, first for the "logistics" talk where Anna had explained the little she knew about Joe's meltdown; and later to ask if Joe could spend the night. He and Dawn had gotten so involved outside playing in the leaves and with Ralphie that the movies were forgotten, that is until they came in tired and hungry. Anna wasn't sure if Libby was being the nicest person on the earth today or if, as reported, the schedule just ran over.

A furry shape slunk into the shrubbery one house up from where Anna walked. Maybe it was a cat, but the way it ambled so low to the ground she thought it more likely a skunk. But it was just too dark to tell. Even with porch lights, street lights, car lights, and the lights from Catskill shining down from College Hill, the darkness of an Onasego night still caught Anna by surprise. The clarity of it. The depth. She wondered what it would be like to camp a couple of miles out in the country. She wondered but knew she'd never try it. Out there lots and lots of skunks would be slinking around.

A convertible whizzed past. A convertible with Peter driving and Molly in the front seat.

"I told you not to come to the church!" Molly screamed. "I told you!"

Anna stood in the upstairs hallway outside Molly's bedroom. The door locked shut. Anna could hear glass breaking, and something, maybe CDs, being thrown against the walls.

"Open the door, Molly. Open that door right this minute."

"Make me!" Another explosion against the wall.

Anna pressed then rubbed her temples. Why the hell couldn't Paul be here? Arriving at the church, she'd had to push her way through at least twenty teenagers smoking on the sidewalk and steps to get inside. Once in, she found one hapless chaperone in the kitchen and fifty or sixty kids filling the barely lit parish hall with a skull-shattering heavy metal band. But not her daughter. So when Molly and Peter pulled up in the convertible ten or fifteen minutes later, she met them on the sidewalk. Molly stepped from the car, all laughter and blown hair, and flatly refused to come home. The concert went until twelve. Peter, jovial and expansive, offered to bring her home. But no, that was not the agreement, Anna said. Eleven was the curfew. And, by the way, what was she doing out riding around when she had promised to stay inside the church throughout the concert. Then the screaming started outside the church, up Summit Avenue, and onto the front porch until Molly ran into the house and locked herself in her room.

"Molly, I told you to open that door. We have to deal with this."

The door opened six inches. Molly's swollen, blotched face stared at her. "I told you not to come down there, and you came anyway. Peter was just showing me his new car, and you act like I murdered somebody—in front of all those people." She caught her breath, "I hate you! I hate you so much!"

Anna glanced at the open windows. "You don't mean that. And keep your voice down. The whole neighborhood can hear you."

Molly shook her head slowly. "You think I don't hate you? Then you are so stupid. And as soon as you go to sleep I'm going right back out there."

Anna studied her daughter. "You do that, and you'll be in such a world of trouble, you won't even want to think about it."

Molly laughed, licking up tears with the tip of her tongue. "Oh yeah, what are you going to do? Stay up all night and watch me?" She slammed the door shut again. Seconds later angry, rasping lyrics reverberated from inside the bedroom.

Anna closed her eyes, grateful for the closed door between herself and Molly. There was probably something correct she was supposed to do now, something known to all other parents but her. Call Paul? Call the police? With a vision of her daughter out in that black, black night, she walked downstairs to the living room. Lights needed to be turned off. Windows closed. Chain bolts put on; chain bolts that could be taken right back off. She paused at the front door. Why would a thirteen-year-old not expect their mother to pick them up at a church youth concert at eleven o'clock at night? Why would a thirteen-year-old scream and curse at their mother for that? And then there was the enormously fuzzy piece of Peter driving with Molly during a youth concert. Anna dragged up the steps. The horrid noise was gone. No light showed under her door. "Molly?"

No answer. She crossed into her study where the dark screen saver rather than the good to very good column waited on her computer alongside the rhythmic blinking message light of the phone. She pressed the play button. A message from Libby from ten-fifty-five. "Anna, hi, I think I have some news for you. Not good. I heard Joe telling Dawn that two boys, Casey and Daniel, said they were going to beat him up and then they chased him into the creek. And I heard him ask her what a faggot meant. That all the children called him that. Sorry. But I thought you would want to know."

Anna held the phone to her chest. A faggot. Fourth graders. Switching off the light, she walked into her bedroom for a pillow and quilt, then returned to the hall, guided by the neon glow shining from the laptop. She dug her foot into the runner in front of Molly's room, thick pile, a little shaggy, definitely in need of vacuuming. Maybe a job for tomorrow—after she'd figured out a plan for Joe and when Molly might be herself again. Dropping to the floor, she doubled the pillow over and wrapped herself in the quilt. Then, doing the only thing that seemed possible at the moment to safeguard her daughter, she lay down in front of the door.

## 27 • EAST MEREDITH

"THAT WILL BE fourteen dollars even." Pops, the hunched, seventyish owner of the usually empty Exxon, looked in at Anna through the driver's window. "How are you, today?"

Anna handed him her credit card. "I'm okay. And you?"

The old man swiped the card, gave it back to her, then leaned an elbow on the roof of the BMW. "Blessed. You wake up in the morning, you look out at those mountains, you got to feel blessed."

"I'm jealous," she admitted. But also not up to much small talk. The night on the floor and a breakfast encounter with Molly had about tapped out any reservoir of patience. After wrestling most of the night with the issue of Molly's extreme acting out, she'd decided to give Molly a choice: grounded into infinity or therapy. A few more broken CDs later, she got her answer. A note: "Quack for me, no infinity." The poetry princess was back at work. "You think my tires are okay? I'll be on dirt roads today."

Pops pulled a gauge from his pocket. "I'll see. Won't take a minute."

While Pops made his way around the car checking the tire pressure, Anna studied the directions to Libby's, about twenty miles from Onasego. She wanted to just get out there and get back. Going places down dirt roads made her edgy, going places down dirt roads with directions like "take the unmarked dirt road off the main road right after the village, go to the church, then look left, see the vacant seasonal home, go in the driveway, take the grass road to the left, don't worry you'll see the flags, go up through the trees to the top of the hill and there we'll be," as Libby had directed her to do today, had her stomach in knots.

"They're fine," Pop said, leaning on the car again. "Where you headed?'

"East Meredith." Anna answered, tightening her seat belt. "Got to pick up my son out there."

"Well, let me tell you, young lady," Pops pulled a handkerchief from his overalls and rubbed a spot off the windshield, "You watch out over that boy. I didn't watch out over my boy and he's a disgrace. A disgrace of a human being."

Anna glanced up at Pops. "I find that hard to believe."

Pop stood back from the car, a slow smile lighting his face. "Well, it's true.

You couldn't find one worse. But I just concentrate on all the other ways I been blessed. And I tell you something else, out in East Meredith, you'll feel blessed too."

The way to Libby's turned out to be the way to the blueberry patch. Only that day she had been pretty involved in trying to explain freelance writing to Deedee. Today she slipped easily from the main highway to the unmarked dirt road, raising a solid cloud of dust and some concern for the new car's finish. A few asters still marked the edges of the road, but the foliage and soft green hills were the real eye catchers. She slowed to twenty to take in the view: a huge groundhog frisking on the lawn in front of a two-story Greek Revival farmhouse; fields of soft grass flanking a narrow stream with a wooden bridge she bumped over; and cows grazing in groups of four or five on both sides of the road. Another mile on she found herself passing an immaculate, probably Congregational Church at a crossroads with a stop sign. No traffic but a stop sign. Across the road a hand-painted sign with an arrow pointing right read, *Angus Lynch: Organic Meats and Produce 3/4 Miles.* At least she had an idea now where to come for her turkey. A motorcycle somewhere behind her broke the country quiet.

Turning left, Anna saw a trailer with a brown dirt square to one side. Ruts cut through the grass to the left, and at the beginning of the ruts, a series of ragged pennants fluttered from an angled beam. Except for the trailer, open countryside fanned out as far as the eye could see. She thought for a moment before the directions clicked. Trailer; seasonal home; new euphemism. She turned into the dirt patch and paused before the grass ruts. The term "broken axle" flashed up from some misbegotten Drivers' Ed memory. She reached for the owner's manual—was this an application for those never-used mystery gears, first and second? A Harley turned into the plot beside her. The driver, ensconced in a full set of gleaming leathers, splayed booted feet out to either side of the motorcycle and unsnapped his helmet.

"Anna."

"Derek."

"Not another flat?"

She held up the manual. "No. Just trying to find out what gear to put the car into for," she pointed to the track through the trees, "that." She gazed at the Harley. "A new purchase?"

"A veritable elixir. Try second."

"Congratulations."

He held his hand to his chest, the same dramatic gesture she remembered from the poetry slam. "I heed the siren's song for the call of the open road."

And she thought the weekend couldn't get any worse.

"Well, thanks for stopping by to check on me," she chirped. "But I better go. I'm late to pick up Joe."

Derek narrowed his eyes, looking over the valley. "Anna, think on that. It really is so much later than we think, so much later." He revved the engine.

"So much bullshit," Anna thought, dropping the car into first and starting down the lane.

Joe's squeals met her as she rounded the corner to Libby's. Real squeals, not the usual he-he-he. The drive had not been all that terrible but she certainly wouldn't want to do it every day, much less in the winter with ice and snow. What if you flipped? Slid in a ditch? The spot was as secluded as any around Onasego. What if a Mr. Murderer happened by—a possibility she didn't even consider when Libby extended her invitation.

Set against a stand of sugar maples, the house was actually no more than a simple adobe square with a weathered wooden frame and door, currently wide open. One huge window mostly filled the single story front southern exposure. Landscaping consisted of the surrounding fields and woods. Though tiny, the rustic simplicity of the place seemed to Anna—dignified. She pulled in beside the Windstar. Her boy was lying on his back on the ground wriggling, laughing, pretending, but not really trying, to keep Ralphie from licking him on the face. Meanwhile, Dawn kicked leaves on both Ralphie and Joe. Sounds of a vacuum droned from the open front door.

"I don't wanna go home," Joe yelled as she approached them. "No, no, no."

"Well, good morning to you, too. Hi, Dawn."

Dawn, dressed in jeans and the regatta pink sweatshirt, ignored her. Ralphie, however, trotted right over to sniff her shoes. Ralphie, she had to admit, was a much better looking dog than Beautiful had ever thought about being. A compact little fellow with an industrious yet slightly vulnerable air about him. Kind of like Joe.

"You've got a little longer while I talk to Libby. But when I say we have to go—" She turned her back, heading to the front door. Dawn, armed with a fresh pile of leaves, resumed her attack.

Anna stuck her head in the open front door. Unlike the spare, clean lines of the outside, the interior was a riot of magazines, books, vitamin bottles, house plants, and CDs covering every surface in the one space that combined dining and living rooms. A coat tree next to the door stood laden with parkas, ski jackets, and inexplicably, a man's white cashmere polo coat, while the tiny kitchen overflowed with dishes, mugs, and pans stacked haphazardly. Even the stairs in the back ascending to a loft were lined with puzzles and board games. The chaos made her want to turn around and run. Libby, a bandanna tied over the curls and vacuum in hand, was busy trying to get under a couch. Anna had to yell to get her attention.

Libby flipped the canister switch with her foot. "Sorry. Didn't hear you. Dawn's doctor has me on an anti-allergen attack." She picked up a jacket from the armchair and threw it on the stairs. "Have a seat. You want some tea?"

Anna almost flinched. Nothing from that kitchen was passing her lips. "Better not, I've got to get back—for an appointment." Her eyes fell on the weathered trim around the window, at least one nice feature. "Quite a house."

Libby gazed around the room, running a hand over the burners of the wood stove. "I just rent. Got it when my uncle kicked Dawn and me out."

Kicked out by an uncle. Special needs child. Janitor. What next? "Why did your uncle do that?"

Libby stared off toward the woods. "He didn't take it well when I wouldn't tell him who Dawn's father is. Doesn't matter. Fuck him."

More squeals from the front yard broke the mood. Anna hefted her purse up on her arm. "Thanks so much for keeping Joe. Clearly he had a wonderful time."

"Dawn loved it, too," Libby said, looking out the front window at Dawn and Joe now buried in the leaf pile. "She doesn't have to pretend—she can be the little girl inside that teenage body."

Anna leaned against the door frame. "Joe's just a little boy and, in the fourth grade, he has kids calling him a faggot. Where do they get this stuff?"

Libby picked up a guitar from the sofa and flopped down. "Sure you don't want some tea?"

Anna's eyes went briefly to the stack of mugs and plates, the automatic lie expanding. "I'd really love to, but the thing is the dentist is working me in."

Libby plucked at the guitar. "With Dawn they started the name calling early too. Now she gets notes passed to her addressed to 'Retard.'"

Outside, Joe shrieked. He was carrying Ralphie and running from Dawn. Anna recalled how Dawn always sat on the end of the bench at practices and games. "Will she talk about it? Let you know who's doing it so you can get the school to... do something?"

"She tells me about it, but—" Libby hesitated, tightening a string. She doesn't want me to go to the school."

Anna knew something wasn't being said. "How come?"

"Might get worse."

Anna brushed at tears. Was this Joe's future too? A future of never fitting in. Being so alone. "What do you do?"

"Mostly," Libby pointed vaguely in the direction of the woods, "I talk to our friend, Mumma; she lives about a mile and a half up the road. Mumma knows everything about everything. She even raised the pumpkin for the regatta. She's at home today—canning, I think. Why don't you go talk to her?"

Anna remembered the tiny figure bent over the Windstar at the regatta. She couldn't quite see herself walking in on "Mumma" and her pressure cooker to get some psychological advice, much less driving another mile and a half on that road. "Wish I could. But I've got to get back—the tooth, it's abscessed. Really painful." Her eyes rested on the guitar. "Does Dawn like music? Is it helpful?"

Libby ran her thumb across the strings. "She couldn't care less. This is mine. I fool around with it sometimes, when I sing."

Anna could well imagine Libby fooling around with a lot of stuff given the contents of the house. "Good for you, I admire people trying new things." She looked at her watch, then felt in her pocket for her keys. "Better run."

"Wait a moment," Libby said, picking up a stack of CDs next to the couch. She rifled through them, then brought one over to Anna. "Here's a copy of a CD I made—tell me what you think."

Anna reached for the CD. Lots of would-be artists in these upstate hills. But if Libby could find enjoyment learning guitar and singing, then more power to her. Libby with her guitar, her fundraising, and her pumpkin regattas. "Great, thanks." She stopped just outside the door. "Hey, Libby, you know the day of the pumpkin regatta? We passed your pumpkin as it was being driven to Cooperstown. I keep seeing the man who was driving it. William, I believe. Do you know him?"

Libby giggled. "Of course I know him. William is Mumma's son. He's up there today." She straightened the overcoat on its peg. "Hey, hope that tooth feels better."

## 28 • *THE ONASEGON*: LETTERS TO THE EDITOR: OCTOBER 20, 1998

*ONASEGO UNDER ATTACK*

*In the most recent issue of Manhattan Living, Anna Lawson continues her attack on Onasego. For anyone who missed the column, Ms Lawson, under the guise of praising Onasego for the community effort in pulling off the Fun and Fabulous, actually accomplishes just the opposite. Rather than mentioning mainstream organizations, of which perhaps thirty participate in the F&F, she chose to focus her attention on Country Coven and the Red Neck Mothers. Why, Ms. Lawson? Could it be that Family Services, Catholic Charities, and the Girl Scouts (real names, I swear) are at odds with the eccentric caricature of Onasego you seem so intent on creating?*

*Richard 'Dick' Rogers*
*Tomorrow's Onasego Today.*
*www.tot.org*

*In a column entitled "It Takes a... Coven" (Manhattan Living) the writer Anna Lawson compares an ice age glacier to a land developer, scary and slippery. I feel the glacier deserves much better.*

*Angie Wingo*

*Anna Lawson entitled her last column for Manhattan Living, "It Takes a... Coven," hoping (I imagine) to snag readers with a sensational, for some lurid, title. If Mrs. Lawson would spare a moment for research, she would find that we are neither. In fact, we are a prosaic, if vocal, 501 (c)(3) registered educational nonprofit organization made up of community-minded witches and warlocks. Please visit us at www.countrycovens.org.*

*Laurel Loomis*
*Country Coven*

*Onasegons were probably surprised to see their fair city in the most recent column of "Alone in Onasego" compared to a coven ... two weeks early. The real event for all our witches and goblins is the annual Halloween parade down Main Street at seven pm on October thirty-first. Lineup for all participants will begin at six-thirty p.m. on Holly in the St. Teresa's parking lot. See you there.*

*Althea Betford*
*Chair, Onasego Halloween Parade Organizer*

*In a recent installment of the ongoing column, "Alone in Onasego," the writer refers to many, many roving bands of drunken college students wandering through city neighborhoods. We believe this to be an inaccurate and unfair assertion. Far from being bottle breaking, marauding bacchanalians, we students ENRICH Onasego as contributing scholars, athletes, artists, and consumers.*

*Jason Flannagan*
*President*
*Interfraternal Council of Catskill College*

## 29 • HELP

THE CENTRAL WAITING room at the United Upstate Health, or UU Health to locals, clinic was packed. Built as a square within a square, the central waiting area fed Onasegons into treatment and examining rooms lining the outer perimeter. X Ray patients were called by name to enter through one door, ob gyns and internal medicine patients through a second, a whole raft of assorted canes, wheelchairs and walkers through the third, and through the fourth—Anna didn't know who else went through that door but she knew people seeking therapy did because half an hour earlier she had—with Molly trailing a good three feet behind.

The other thing she had picked up from her time at the clinic was that one saw many familiar faces here. Pulling into the parking lot, she passed Deedee gunning her Suburban on the way back to work. At the registration counter she stood two people behind Ray and his daughter, Lisa, a senior at SUNY Purchase. Lisa, in town to get vaccinated for a spring semester in Ecuador, was all freckles and giggles, challenging her father to thumb fights while Ray gazed around the waiting room in mock desperation. Pug Wenley waved hello across the leather couches and chairs, and while searching for a cup of coffee, she'd run into Ellis coming out of the men's room.

Reluctantly, she put aside *People* magazine and picked up the October *Ladies Home Journal* sporting a subtitle of "Ten Easiest Halloween Costumes Ever." Joe wanted to be either the Catskill Bobcat, the school's mascot, or a black stallion, the horse not the boy, of the movie, neither one of which she had a clue how to make nor would she find on a shelf at Walmart, CVS, or Time to Play Toys. Whatever happened to children becoming pirates and cowboys?

Despite herself, Anna glanced back at Door 4. What would Molly be telling Dr. Young, one of two family therapists recommended by the Catskill medical center? Dr. Young won out on the sole factor that the other therapist, a Dr. Badescu, was located over a tattoo parlor downtown. The appointment was set up so that first, she and Molly met together with Dr. Young, followed by a private session for each of them with the therapist. Medical histories, both for immediate and extended family, had been filled out in advance of the visit. Paul, in Manhattan talking up donors and alumni, was scheduled for a separate meeting the next week. In her brief time with Dr. Young, he impressed her as friendly and accessible.

"Hi," Libby said, slipping into the seat beside her. "What did you find out about Joe?"

Anna took in a crisp, striped shirt with Catskill Maintenance embossed on the pocket. Was this the face of William Johnson's lover? Dawn's father. The polo coat she'd seen at Libby's was driving her crazy. "His teacher says she's on it. And she's scheduling a meeting with all the parents about name calling and bullying. How about you?"

Libby sighed. "Dawn's allergies, it's Ralphie. We're going to have to give him up—at least for a while."

"Who would you give him to?"

"I've been racking my brain. I mean we all know he has a mind of his own." She looked up at Anna. "Want a dog?"

"Anna Lawson." A large woman in a flowered smock held the door as Molly entered the waiting room and walked toward the foyer. Anna couldn't read anything from her daughter's expression.

"Paul's not an animal person. But if I think of anybody, I'll let you know. Okay?"

Anna gazed around the therapist's office. During her initial ten-minute introduction, she somehow missed the turtle motif. Stuffed turtles, turtle prints, a turtle pencil sharpener, turtles smiling from the wall paper trim. Dr. Young, balding but boyish, mid-thirties she guessed, sat at an angle between his desk and her. Never having visited a therapist before, she wondered if this was a form of inclusion, removing the barrier between practitioner and client.

"So, you and your daughter are mixing it up?"

"That," she tried to smile, "would be a vast understatement. Since we moved to Onasego, I can't open my mouth without getting screamed at—or ignored. She's in a rage all the time."

Dr. Young looked at his laptop screen. "Your family just moved here from the city, correct?"

"In August."

"Your daughter is thirteen?"

"Her birthday was in July."

"And her father lives in Manhattan?"

"Yes, and I know she wants to live with him. But he's too busy."

Dr. Young glared over the screen. "We're not here to talk about Molly's father. Did you ever move as a child, Mrs. Lawson?"

"No."

"Do you have clear memories of being thirteen?"

"Pretty clear."

"What do you recall?"

Anna saw herself, curlers and all, in her twin bed reading. "My sister went away to college that fall. I had the whole upstairs to myself. I remember reading a lot, listening to records, being with my friends."

Young swiveled toward his desk and began typing slowly. Tap... tap... tap. "Were you the rebellious sort, Mrs. Lawson?"

Anna suddenly had a feeling there was a right and a wrong answer to this. "What do you mean by that?"

He looked at her over the screen. "Did you like to break rules? Or at least challenge them?"

"Not really." Probably not the right answer. Tap... tap... tap.

"Why not?" With the question, Dr. Young's eyelids lowered to a squint.

She thought about squinting along with him. "For one thing, my mother was tough. And," she decided to go for broke, "I think rules can be good things, orderly, protective."

TAP. TAP. TAP. Whoops, wrong answer.

"What is your usual reaction when Molly pushes your buttons?"

Anna felt the age gap between herself and Dr. Young growing. Did the man even have children? "I'd say it is much more than pushing buttons, Dr. Young."

"How is that?"

Anna looked out the office window to the parking lot. What the hell was she doing in here? "It's hard to describe how vitriolic she becomes, how narcissistic."

No taps. Young lifted his hands from the keyboard like a pianist finishing a piece. "Mrs. Lawson, all teenagers are narcissistic and at times, vitriolic. Have you ever heard of the A team and B team categorization of teenagers?"

Outside, a groundhog clambered out from underneath a boxwood beside the parking lot. Goddamn teams, again. "No."

Dr. Young leaned back in his desk chair, hands clasped behind his head. She revised her opinion. Probably late twenties.

He continued. "The vast majority of teenagers can be classified as either A or B team. The other small percent, well, those are the tails of the curve, not part of our talk today." He rolled closer to her chair. The ground hog sat up on his haunches eying Libby walking toward her car. "The B team pretty much goes along with the status quo. Mostly easy kids, mostly okay grades, go with the flow types. But the A teamers, they test everything. They are just hardwired that way and hormones being the influence they are—well, you know about that."

"You know, I do." A bone thrown from the young, Dr. Young. Libby had caught sight of the groundhog and was making shooing motions with her hands.

"But," the doctor's voice dropped, taking on a portentous quality, "unless the A teamers' parents are very well clued in or on drugs, they are going to have a rugged several years, while their very smart children try out everything they can." He paused seeming to want a response.

She tried not to sigh. Libby, hands on her hips, seemed to be looking around for help.

Dr. Young did sigh. "Look, Mrs. Lawson, we can put you and your daughter on a schedule here, but I have to tell you that nothing jumps up from the medical background. And nothing strikes me as dangerous or even extreme from the talk I just had with Molly. My very strong hunch is that the only thing going on here is, well, that while you, yourself, were probably a solid B teamer, your daughter is one heck of a high-end A girl. A tough mix."

A tough mix—this was therapy? She saw Libby back away from the groundhog, then make a wide arc toward the parking lot. "My life is hell, what am I supposed to do?"

He rocked forward. "Two things. First, recognize times have changed since your day. Your daughter needs a lot more freedom than you're giving her."

She should send Molly over to his house. "And the second?"

Dr. Young picked up the stuffed turtle from his desk and held it against his chest. "You, Mrs. Lawson, must learn to relax."

## 30 • SAMHAIN

"AT FIRST I thought she was talking about something related to pork," Anna said, passing the potato chips to Paul. "It's that word you see all the time in old English novels, Samhain, that you think is pronounced SAM HANE like bug bane but, according to Laurel Loomis, is pronounced SOW IN. So for most of this long, long 'pleasure' about the opportunities and miracles of this time of year, I was trying to figure out how it all related to a pig. Then I saw the note in the order-of-service from the Country Coven about the whole thing, including the pronunciation and got it. Joe, could you quit just looking at your lunch and eat?"

"Stomach ache." Joe, still in church clothes, sat hunched in his chair, the sandwich and carrots on his plate remaining untouched.

Anna stole a sideways glance at Paul, who put his sandwich down and turned to Joe. "You want something else? I could make you—"

"You?" Molly interrupted with a half laugh. Molly still had on her church clothes as well, the same pair of jeans and one of the generic tee shirts she wore to school every day.

At least he gets laughs sometimes, Anna noted looking around the kitchen table at her family. For the past few days, since the meeting with Dr. Young and Paul's return from the city, Molly's mood seemed a tad improved. Still chilly but no major knock downs. Joe still wouldn't talk about the picnic, but did get enthusiastic about a hike with Paul to Visionary Fields. Too short a hike but, with the pressure on Paul to produce at work, she was glad he could take any time at all.

"How was church for you two?" Paul asked.

"Great, we went out for coffee," Molly said, taking the lettuce out of her turkey sandwich.

Paul did the obligatory disbelieving eye roll. "What about you, Joe?"

"We ate candy skeletons." He rested his chin on the table. "Mom, what about my bobcat outfit? Wednesday's Halloween and the parade."

How well she knew it. The shreds of brown felt, her last attempt to fashion a giant bobcat's head Joe could wear over jeans, and a brown sweatshirt were stuffed in the linen closet, a disaster. "Let's talk about it after lunch, honey."

"And we have to talk about my staying at Caroline's Halloween night,"

Molly added. "Jamie and Gwen especially want me to come because of their Halloween party. It goes 'til midnight."

"It's a school night."

"It's Halloween."

Paul intervened. "Hey, Joe, why did you eat candy skeletons?"

"I don't know. You tell him, Mom."

Anna poured herself some tea from the pitcher in the center of the table. "It was part of this church-wide recognition of the origins of Halloween. The young kids had a Day of the Dead celebration like they do in Mexico—"

"Yeah," Joe waved his napkin at Paul, "cause dead people come back for food they like."

Anna nodded. "And the middle school was supposed to talk about All Souls Day and what that has to do with Halloween—"

"That's why we went out for coffee," Molly inserted.

"Right," Anna acknowledged, "and that's why Laurel Loomis went on and on about Samhain, also October thirty-first. It's very big for her group."

Paul, sarcasm playing about his face, reached for a pickle. "Why?"

"Because," Anna looked at Molly and Joe trying to think how to broach the topic, "according to Laurel, some people believe that our deceased ancestors are very close to us at this time of year. That it is a good time to try to contact them and to honor their lives."

"What's a dis–dis–cestor?" Joe's face was twisted up in curiosity. Somehow, without eating, he had gotten mayonnaise on his cheek.

"A deceased ancestor is someone like a grandfather or grandmother who is dead. Laurel went on at some length that because it is the Wiccan New Year, it is also a good time to work on bad habits."

"Do I have one of those?"

Molly eyed Joe. "Try burping and farting."

"Not that." He stuck his tongue out at his sister. "Do I have one of those dead people?"

Anna stood and wet a paper towel. "My mother, your grandmother, Sybil. Here," she handed the towel to Joe, "wipe your face."

Molly shrugged and pushed her plate away. "I don't remember her—my grandmother."

"Your grandmother was lovely as a girl; she had lots of friends and did a great deal of volunteer work." She reached for Paul's plate, stacking it under her own. "Molly, why don't you bring the old photograph album in from the den, you know the brown leather one. I often think you look like my mother when she was young."

"Why can't Joe get it?"

Anna tried to keep her voice neutral as if asking her daughter to carry out a common task and having her daughter comply were normal, everyday occurrences—like they used to be. "Because he can't reach it and because I asked you to do it. Can you hand me your plate?"

A silence followed before Molly slowly rose from the table. A silence in which Anna turned her back, making a show of rinsing dishes and loading the dishwasher until she heard the scrape of Molly pulling her chair back in. Then she dried her hands and, trying not to look at Molly, sat back down and opened the album so everyone could see.

The first picture was of Sybil as a young girl sitting astride a chestnut mare, her hair pulled back in a loose ponytail, gloved hands clutching the reins. A few pages over, Sybil showed up as a college girl, in a sweater set and skirt carrying text books across a college green. A formal black and white eight-by-ten showed her just married in a long-sleeved satin gown standing beside her father in his military uniform.

"I think she's pretty," Molly said in a mildly surprised voice.

"She was." Anna flipped the page to baby pictures. "This was me and Aunt Barbara as babies. Aren't we cute? And here we are a little older, at Halloween with some neighborhood kids. We're the Indians." She pointed to a picture of four small children sitting on a front stoop, one cowboy, one princess, and Barbara and herself, Indian maidens with dresses fringed around the neck and sleeves. Pictures of suns, moon, and stick animals were drawn on Barbara's. Hers had flowers and vines. They both had red lines down their foreheads and wore moccasins.

"That's cool," Joe said. "Who made your costume?"

Anna smiled at the earnest little Indians staring back at her. She had absolutely no memory of that day. "I'm sure my mother did. That's the way it was when I was little." She lifted the picture from its jacket. Barbara would want a copy.

Joe squirmed around in his chair. "Mrs. Wimbish says there were lots of Indians near here."

Paul nodded. "She's right. The Six Nations of the Iroquois Confederation. You know over in Cooperstown there is a model of the kind of house those Indians used to live in. A Long House behind the Fenimore Museum. You can see what clothes they wore, the way they cooked, how they slept."

Anna flipped another page to a shot of herself in tee shirt and jodhpurs sitting astride a cream pony looking pensively into the camera for the Camp Yonahlossee brochure. On the lower half of the page, dressed in their Easter Sunday suits and hats, Barbara, her mother, and herself stood poised to eat the ears off of chocolate bunnies.

"Sybil also adored chocolate." She glanced up at Paul, "How did you hear about the place in Cooperstown?"

"Remember that board member, William Johnson? He told me all about it. Said we had to see it."

That board member. She looked back at the picture.

"Hey, Mom," Joe said, fingering the photograph album, "can I be an Indian—like one from Onasego?"

Relief forced William Johnson from her mind. Compared to a bobcat how hard could an Indian costume be? She turned the page back to herself and Barbara as Indians. "You bet. In fact, I know one," she struggled to get the syllables right, "Deganawidah. You know, let's run over to Cooperstown, see the Long House, see what he would have worn." Joe, wide eyed, nodded. "Run up and change, we've got to get moving."

Molly leaned against the sink as Joe ran out of the room. "What about me, Mom, can I go to Jamie and Gwen's party Wednesday night?"

The vision of Dr. Young cradling his turtle rose in Anna's mind. "You have to give her more freedom, Mrs. Lawson. You have to relax, Mrs. Lawson."

"How about a compromise? You can go to the party after trick or treating but we'll pick you up at eleven."

"Eleven?" Pained disbelief crossed the golden face.

Anna turned another page to junior high, braces and glasses, then high school, secretary of the student council, Barbara walking under arched swords on the arm of a cadet. "It's still a school night."

She felt Paul's arm come around her waist as Molly walked out, not happy to be sure, but not screaming either.

"Well done," he said. "But what was all that about your mother?"

She hesitated over a photo of her parents at the annual cotillion—her father still boyish into his fifties, her mother with a staged smile not evident in younger years. "What do you mean?"

Paul's chestnut eyes bore in. "Well, you told them how lovely she was, about her volunteer work, about her friends..."

Anna picked up the Indian picture. Two little girls squinting up at the camera. An incredible amount of work had to have gone into those outfits. "So?"

"So, when are you going to tell them," he pointed at the cotillion shot, her parents frozen in formal wear, "that she was crazy?"

## 31 • MOTHERS

THE BANK CLOCK flashed the temperature at thirty-four degrees. Beneath her witch's robe, Anna wore tights, jeans, Joe's Wigwam socks, a long sleeve turtle neck, wool sweater, down vest, and she was still freezing. Joe, huddled up against her, had the good fortune to be wrapped in a Hudson Bay blanket, ripped from the guest room bed, as part of his Deganawidah outfit. Joining them on Holly Street by St. Teresa's, scores of Harry Potters, Elvises, J Los, fairies, unicorns, Cookie Monsters, ghosts, ballerinas, black cats, NY Yankees, and goblins milled about waiting for the march down Main Street comprising the annual Onasego Halloween Parade.

Since the march was organized by age group and school, a bevy of decorated carriages and strollers from the Best Babies Preschool stood poised to lead the way with many parents as costumed as their children. The Onasego Elementary School came next, followed by the Onasego Middle School delegation, followed by the Onasego High School marching band. In between the school groups, a couple of convertibles, those of the mayor and the Otsego County Dairy Princess, idled while trucked floats from Family Services and Catholic Charities carried children practicing songs along with fire trucks, cherry pickers, and ambulances. Adults sans offspring pulled up the rear: a panoply of political figures, TV and movie characters, historical personages, as well as the more mundane Liberaces and chorus girls. The whole production reminded Anna of the movie "The Ten Commandments," when the giddy Israelites were heading out of Egypt to a tinkling symphonic percussive. But, unlike herself, those giddy Israelites (she read somewhere Cecil DeMille paid thousands of Egyptian soldiers to play the departing Jews) wouldn't be facing frostbite.

She looked back toward the Onasego Middle School banner near the rear of the procession. Somewhere in that mob, Molly and Caroline were marching as two Victorian-era vampires. Dressed in evening gowns and cloaks supplied by Gwendolyn, the two had spent the afternoon applying white stage paint and gobs of eye makeup and painting artful drops of blood dripping delicately from the corner of each mouth. A great costume that she wished she, rather than Gwen, had thought of. But, looking down at Joe's head swathed in turban and feathers, it was also true that no-body in the whole of Onasego could be happier with their costume than her boy.

The dash to the Long House in Cooperstown had been pure genius, Joe lapping up every moment of it: lying on the bunk-like beds, holding animal furs, having his picture taken by dugouts poised by the lake. And his costume cost exactly $3.56 not counting the shell necklace from a long ago trip to Hawaii. She'd caught a few of the other boys in Joe's class eyeing him—one firefighter, a martial artist, and the third in camo. Were two of these Casey and Daniel?

"Joe!" Mrs. Wimbish tramped toward them, the flower on her Mary Poppins hat bobbing appropriately above a chestnut wig, black suit, white blouse, and cameo. "I am so impressed. You're an Indian!"

Joe looked up at her arrogantly, playing the part. "I am a special Indian. I am Deganawidah."

Mrs. Wimbish giggled. "Well, maybe tomorrow during circle you can tell us all about De... him. Mrs. Lawson, can I have a word?"

Following the teacher's lead, Anna stepped a few feet away from Joe.

"I'm sorry," Mrs. Wimbish leaned on her umbrella, a carpet valise stuck under one arm, "but we have to postpone the class parents' meeting. I got a flood of calls and emails. Apparently, this is not a good time."

Anna pushed her hands up into the billowy sleeves of the witch's robe she'd bought at Walmart and leaned toward the teacher, the brim of her witch's hat grazing Mrs. Wimbish's boater. "So when were you thinking of having it? The next week?"

"We've got the teachers' planning days that week and the midterm parent meetings the one after that. I think we're probably looking at after Christmas."

"But," Anna groped for words, "my son, this is too important."

"Ms. Lawson," parallel lines furrowed between Mrs. Wimbish's eyebrows, "I can't make parents come. It's voluntary—so we have to wait for a time that suits."

Anna dropped her voice to a loud whisper. "What about those boys?"

Mrs. Wimbish, accommodating both hats, bent to speak in Anna's ear. "We brought the boys involved and their parents in. We talked to the boys and thoroughly explained the inappropriateness of what they did."

"Explained! How about punished?"

A siren wailed, followed by flashing police lights. Mrs. Wimbish extracted a long wooden measuring spoon from the valise and turned the umbrella parrot's head up. "Look, I think you and your husband should come in to see our principal. But I'm afraid we'll have to talk about this later."

Around them parents and children straightened costumes, pulled down masks, and shuffled forward.

"All right, JoJo, here we go." Anna grabbed for Joe's hand then wondered if perhaps she shouldn't. Joe didn't seem to mind, however, his fingers gripping hers. As the high school band struck up a familiar march, the procession wound a half block on Holly, then turned onto Main Street where crowds two and three people deep lined the sidewalk. Paul had called to say he couldn't march because of an emergency budget meeting but would try his best to meet them downtown. A yapping sound came from her right.

"Joe, look over there. It's Libby and Ralphie."

Joe stared down at the street instead. Stage fright? She checked out the crowds again, suddenly aware of being in a parade for the first time in her life.

"Joe, look up! There's Ms. Molina, and, wow, Indiana Jones." She pointed toward Deedee, completely done up as Sigourney Weaver in *Alien*, in front of the entrance to City Hall. Beside her, Herb, with drawn-on stubble, a battered bomber jacket, cords, and fedora, tipped his whip in their direction. Anna waved, relieved to know at least two people in the crowd. Ahead, Mrs. Wimbish, flourishing the spoon, directed the class to pick up their pace. After the parade, one way or another, she would have to corner her. Postponing the meeting just wasn't right—not right at all.

"Anna!"

Gwen, clad in what looked to be an authentic silver fox coat, sequined headband, and rope pearls, dashed out from the sidewalk, temporarily joining the parade. "I just saw the girls! Molly really, really wants to stay at our house tonight. She sent me to beg you."

Anna pasted on a smile and yelled back over the crowd clapping in tune with the march. "Molly also knows I said no. I can barely get her up for class when she's in bed by ten. But, thanks for thinking about her."

Gwen tapped her foot long cigarette holder against Anna's shoulder. "On my honor," she shouted against a flute interlude. "I'll have them in bed by eleven."

Anna stepped sideways to avoid trampling on a rosebud and lace bridal train. Would Molly and Caroline have come up with this scheme on their own? "Another time," she yelled back, "okay?"

"Come on—it's Halloween!"

The trumpet section kicked in. DAH, DAH, dah-dah, DAH. To her left, Anna saw Paul walking out of Nora's with Pug, Erika, and Tom. Emergency budget meeting? She took Gwen's arm. "It's not a good idea."

Gwen gazed out into the distance, shrugged, then peeled off toward the curb, leaving Anna with the certainty that her reputation as an uptight, prudish spoiler was set in stone. Words sung to the march suddenly came to her, something about web-footed friends. She took Joe's chilly fingers between her hands. Ahead, the judges at the reviewing stand were taking notes on children's costumes. "Hey, Deganawidah, look sharp there. We're almost at the judges."

An unexpected face turned up to her, swollen eyes, trembling mouth, war paint mostly rubbed off. She reached into her jeans and found some Kleenex. "Come on." They slipped out of the procession and into the empty hall leading to the parking garage. She swept off her witch's hat and bent down. "Honey?"

He shook his head.

"Tell me—please."

She waited while Joe made his decision. She could see it all. Yes, no, maybe. Then, just pure bewilderment. He stared into her eyes. "While you were talking to Mrs. Wimbish," the tiny frame shuddered, sending the turban and feathers over one ear, "those kids came up. They said I wasn't a special Indian. They said I was a *queer* Indian." He stuck a hand out from the striped blanket to right the headdress. She wasn't sure she had ever seen anyone look so weary in her life.

"Mom, why do they say that?"

Paul found them a couple of moments later watching the parade from the sidewalk in front of the parking garage access. Joe, somewhat better for one of the chocolate bars she'd cached in her ample witch's pocket, leaned against a street light watching the school groups go by. She was indulging as well. Semi-sweet with almonds.

"Hey, guys!" Paul paused, giving them a once over. "Why aren't you in the parade?"

Despite her slow blink sign not to pursue it, he cocked his head toward Joe. "What's up, Deganawidah?" Joe, the Hudson Bay blanket hanging listlessly from his shoulders, kept silent. "Come on, Big D, why aren't you showing your stuff?" Paul repeated a little too loudly. She knew the tone, a certain magnanimous tone Paul broke into after a few strong ones.

She crumpled up the candy wrapper. 'Where have you been?"

"I told you. Emergency meeting. The budget."

"Yeah?"

Jen and three other girls passed by carrying the Onasego Middle School banner. Anna stood on her tiptoes looking for Molly. She saw Dawn as Dorothy, carrying Ralphie as Toto, plenty of Goths, and then there at the back, Molly and Caroline walking arm and arm down Main street, sedately, importantly, clearly separating themselves from the rest of the thirteen-year-old hoi polloi. As the girls passed by, Molly flashed a sideways, uninterested glance in their direction.

Paul rested his elbow on her shoulder. "She looks great, doesn't she? Hey, I ran into Gwen in front of Nora's just now. She told me about Molly wanting to spend the night and I thought, what the hell? Who knew Halloween was such a big deal in Onasego? Gwen said she'd tell Molly."

"You told Gwen that Molly could spend the night?" Two Onasego fire engines crept by spewing hard candy, followed by the Dairy Princess, a utility truck from the Onasego Water Department, and the motley array of adult spooks pulling up the rear. She twisted out from under Paul's arm and leaned down in front of Joe. "Want another Kit Kat?" He nodded.

"Gwen invited us to the party, too. With as much as Jamie gives Catskill, we should probably drop by. What do you think?"

Anna thought a second dark chocolate for herself would be a grand idea. She reached in her pocket, took out a Special Dark bar for herself and a Kit Kat for Joe. A flash of sequins caught her eye. Several in the crowd took up a familiar lyric.

*And he's not responsible for what he's doing.*

Gwen and Jamie, Jamie also in fur, marched by with a banner reading Scott and Zelda—Together Forever.

*Cause his mother made him what he is.*

Denise, sporting a black wig and navy dress raced by, followed by Derek as Bill Clinton followed by Angie as Hillary. Anna wrapped an arm around the lamppost. Right after Marge and Homer Simpson, three visions of her mother sauntered down Main Street carried along on the bare, hairy arms and legs of Ray, Tim, and Ellis. Sybils' best cocktail dresses from the Fun and Fabulous. The heels were somebody else's. Score one for Laurel; her mother had come. With guitars twanging, she found herself joining in on the chorus.

*And it's up against the wall Redneck Mother*
*Mother, who has raised her son so well.*

She caught Joe's eye. Did he have a clue what this was about?

*He's thirty-four and drinking in a honky tonk.*
*Kicking hippies' asses and raising hell.*

After the third round, Ellis hoisted his guitar overhead, signaling the end of the song and sending the stuffing for his black, metallic chest onto the pavement. The Onasegons around her burst into applause, for the song or the stuffing, it was hard to tell.

"Wish I had a picture of that one," Paul yelled as the trio passed by. "Maybe *The Onasegon* got it. Great publicity for the town." He dug his car keys out of his pocket. "Hey, why don't you and Joe trick or treat a while and then we'll head to the party. Okay?"

Anna reached for Joe's candy wrapper, folded it neatly with her own, and threw them away. Then she bent down beside Joe. "Will you stay right here for a moment? I need to speak to Daddy."

Joe nodded, still watching the Red Neck Mothers make their way down Main Street. With a crooked index finger she beckoned her husband toward the glass doors of the entrance to the parking garage. "Paul."

He followed her. "Yeah, babe?"

She waited until the heavy automatic door had shut. "You asked me what I think."

"Right, about tonight."

She scratched her temple beneath the witch's hat. "You really want to know what I think?"

Paul grinned. "You know I do."

"Okay. Well, first, I think Mrs. Wimbish, that's Joe's teacher, in case you don't remember, doesn't know her ass from a hole in the ground. But you don't know why I think that because you were out at another budget cocktail party."

The grin vanished. "Hey, wait a min—".

Anna held up her hand. "Oh, and by the way, if you had been with us instead of the emergency tonight, you might have saved your little boy from getting savaged by those kids again. But that's another thing you don't know about, so I guess you don't know your ass from a hole in the ground either."

Paul eyed her warily. "What the hell's gotten into you—"

She shook her head. "Nope, still telling you what I think. Now, Gwen had already talked to me tonight about Molly spending the night and I said no, but then she went to you. So I think Gwen should remember whose daughter is whose and then she should, well, I'll leave that to your imagination." She tapped her chin.

"Hey, anyone could walk in here."

Anna gave an exaggerated look about the room before beginning again. "You said Molly could spend the night out although I had been real clear about that not being a good idea. So you can guess what you can do, too."

She paused. Outside, the crowds were beginning to thin. She should get Joe started on his trick or treating. That is if he still wanted to go.

"I've had about enough of this." Paul stepped toward the door.

"Just one more thing." Anna pulled out a third candy bar. White chocolate. "You should go to that party. Because you sure as hell better not come home."

## 32 • MORE HELP

THE NEXT MORNING was like waking up with a hangover—then Anna thought about it for a moment and realized it was a hangover. Vaguely she heard someone on the stairs, next the bang of chest doors from Molly's room, thumps back down the steps, and the slam of the screen door hitting against the frame. A car, Gwen's she supposed, backed out of the driveway. Next, silence. She reached for the bedside alarm clock. Seven fifteen. The other side of the bed was empty, made, and by the looks of it, never slept in. Probably to be expected, she thought, given her little oratory to Paul. She slid out of bed with a surprising sense of self satisfaction.

She had one arm in an old sweatshirt of Paul's when the odor hit her. Skunk? Maybe her skunk had come back, or maybe there was a new mephitis, mephitis scuttling alongside the house. She glanced reflexively at the eyebrow windows Paul always cracked at night, this morning shut tight in his absence. Then she got it right. Not skunk. Urine. The smell grew stronger and stronger as she walked down the hall to Joe's room where he slept, an inert little body tangled in soaking Batman sheets. The last thing he'd said before she tucked him the night before was that he had a very, very bad stomach ache. "Well, then, no school for you tomorrow," she answered, believing that with that particular terror banished both of them might get some sleep. Terror? Banished? How absolutely simple minded. Crossing to the large window overlooking the street, she threw it open, letting in a rush of brisk morning air. Joe, oblivious, muttered something in his sleep and turned over. She just had time to grab a shower. Dr. Young's office surely wouldn't open before eight.

Three hours later, Anna replayed the scene from the psychologist's office while Pop, having filled up the BMW's tank and squeegeed the wind shield to shining perfection, took Joe inside the service station for a free-for-good-boys ice cream of his choice.

"Very fortunate," the receptionist had said, "A cancellation at eleven thirty; we'll see you then." A ray of hope after being told that she couldn't see the principal at Joe's school until the following day and having heard nothing from Paul, much less Molly. Her only communication this morning had come in a call from Gwen, a breezy message on the answering machine assuring her that both girls had gotten a full night's sleep and seemed bright eyed and bushy tailed for school. "So you see, Anna, it all worked out just fine! Just fine!" The subtext being that she, Anna, was a paranoid neurotic. An opinion held also, apparently, by Dr. Young, or turtleman as she was coming to think of him.

"So, young man," he said, beginning the wrap-up to the session, "Walk with friends. Don't go places by yourself. Tell your mom and dad about anything that is bothering you, and," Dr. Young paused before an upbeat, "Remember our CALM exercise. Let's do it one more time. I'll be the bully. Give me a C!"

Joe puffed out his cheeks, then exhaled and yelled, "C! Cool down!"

Dr. Young made a lopsided A from the YMCA dance routine. "A?"

Joe put his hands on his hips and stuck out his chin. "Assert," his voice trailed off on the "yourself."

And that means? Anna thought to herself watching from a stool in the corner.

"L?" Dr. Young prompted with his index finger to his glasses as Joe leaned forward, glaring, for L. Look your bully in the eye.

"And, M?" Dr. Young raised his right foot.

Joe stamped down on the wooden floor, flapping his arms for emphasis or balance, as well. "Mean it!"

"By George, I think he's got it." Young swiveled around on his stool to Anna. "Okay, Mom, you've got all that too?"

She nodded too quickly, frantic that the "very fortunate" session had amounted to no more than bromides and talk show solutions. "I do. But I've got some other questions."

Dr. Young checked his watch and the printout on his desk. "Out of time, sorry. I do think," he paused and looked over at Joe, "that, after all, it might be good to get your sister and your father in here with the two of you, for all the Lawsons to come and talk, get into some whole family therapy."

"But," Anna fought to keep her voice businesslike, "Molly and Joe's issues have nothing to do with each other. Right now, what we need is very clear instruction on, you know, dealing with the school, the parents, stopping these bullies. I don't even know what we're doing tomorrow."

Dr. Young stood and opened the door, indicating the end of the appointment. "Family usually comes first, Mrs. Lawson. Remember my advice from our other visit." Young gave a sideways glance at Joe, smiled, then picked up a turtle and wagged him in Joe's face. "If one of these boys bothers you again, don't be like a turtle hiding in his shell, you be" he puffed out his cheeks waiting for Joe's response.

"CALM!" the two yelped in unison.

"You'll be just fine," the doctor said and handed Joe the turtle. "Here, this is for you."

"Mom," Joe hopped back in the car with a Nutty Buddy, breaking her fantasy mid flight of leaping over Dr. Young's desk, hands outstretched for his skinny throat, "what are we doing after this?"

Anna returned mentally, albeit reluctantly, to the gas station. "We could go on a hike or get out our bikes. Molly has her class with Derek this afternoon so we're on our own." Her column, a half-done article entitled Cooperstown Bound, surely wouldn't be on the agenda. "What would make you happy?"

Joe kicked the seat back in front of him. "Nothing."

Anna checked to make sure Joe's seat belt was buckled before starting the car.

"Come on, there has to be something." Anna turned out of the lot and onto Main. What indeed? No real friends outside of Dawn, no sports, just herself, video games, and movies. The last time she had seen Joe acting completely like a silly, happy little boy was lying in Libby's front yard with Ralphie bathing his face in dog spit. Ralphie.

"JoJo, I've got an idea."

Anna stepped tentatively into the foyer. A bucket of what looked like water sat in the middle of the hall. Joe, with a leash wrapped twice around his hand as Libby had shown him, was taking Ralphie on his inaugural walk to the corner. A dog bed, dish, and forty-pound bag of IAMs waited in the car.

The kitchen door swung open and Paul, with her witch's cape and hat, walked toward her. "There's the water. Let's go outside and you can throw it at me. I deserve it… melting or freezing."

It took her a minute. "Like in Oz?"

He nodded. "I was such a jerk. Forgive me?"

"Sure," she said lightly. Better enjoy this while it lasted.

Paul held her out at arm's length. "This thing with Joe. We've got a lot to talk about."

"Hey, Ma," Molly leaned over the upstairs railing, the white blonde curtain of hair pitched to one side. "You need to run me over to the mall. Derek thinks I need a really good thesaurus."

Anna smiled. "Yes, I'm fine, honey, thanks for asking."

She heard the door click open, Joe's insistent, "Come on, see your new house," followed by Ralphie's rasping pant straining against the leash. She felt Paul's and Molly's eyes on her.

"Anna, you didn't."

"Jesus, Mom, he gets a dog?"

Anna puffed out her cheeks, her backup needed much sooner than she'd imagined, then exhaled rapidly. C. She placed her hands on her hips, staring between her husband and daughter. A and L. Beside her she heard whining and giggling as Joe, with Ralphie zipped into his jacket, let the little dog chew on his ear.

She could have stamped... but didn't.

## 33 • TREASURE EVERY MOMENT (2)

MRS. WIMBISH WAS into displays. Though Anna had been in the classroom a number of times, she'd never noticed much beyond the generic small people's desks, blackboard, battered rug for circle time, and cubbies in the rear of the room. Now, however, from her seat on the front row beside Paul tapping on his PalmPilot, she felt bombarded. From the KENYA! LAND of the LION photo exhibit over the blackboard; to the twenty-five crayon drawings of, she assumed, squirrels hung in five rows between the door and the fish tank; to the wall of book jackets under a GET THE FORCE: READ! banner in the back of the room; to the tissue-paper-stained glass squares suspended from a clothesline over the street-side windows; to the food pyramid behind Mrs. Wimbish's desk; to the NOVEMBER: TURKEY MONTH themed bulletin board beside the pencil sharpener. Where did the woman find the time to produce all this?

The door swung open and Mrs. Wimbish, still in the Mary Poppins wig, a bit much Anna thought, entered the classroom accompanied by a short, heavily bearded man. He extended his hand, first to Paul, then to Anna. "Hi, Ric Anunzio, thanks for coming in." Anna had seen Mr. Anunzio at some of the school kick-off meetings but this was the first time she'd had any inter-action with him. The teacher and principal pulled two of the diminutive desks around to face Paul and Anna and sat.

Mr. Anunzio looked at Paul. "You're at Catskill, right?"

Paul nodded.

Next, Anna. "And you write a column?"

"Yes," she nodded, hoping he wasn't a member of TOT or the Moose Watch and Reporting Group..

"From home?"

"Yes."

"So," Mr. Anunzio began, "your son, how is he doing?"

Paul looked at Anna to start. She fingered the cuff of her suit jacket, a tweed suit she hoped screamed, "I demand action!" "He's hurt, scared, and confused. About what you'd think."

Shouts and whoops from the after-school class floated up from the playground outside. Mr. Anunzio continued. "Did Joe ever give any indication he was worried about anything?"

"The only thing was stomach aches. Several stomach aches. I put it down to new school jitters."

"Mr. Lawson, did you notice anything?"

"No more than my wife." Paul stuffed the PalmPilot in his jacket pocket. "What we really want to know is what the school is going to do about all this."

Mr. Anunzio leaned heavily against the arm of the desk. "I think Mrs. Wimbish told you that she called in the boys and their parents. We had a very strong conversation with all parties."

A whistle blew below. "Children," a voice called out, "form a line. Homework time."

Anna leaned forward. "The strong conversation with the boys and their parents doesn't seem to have stopped them from coming after Joe again at the parade. I need to know that something is in place to protect our son."

Mr. Anunzio stood and closed the classroom door against the tramp of footsteps on the stairs. "First of all, Mrs. Lawson, please remember that we operate under vastly different circumstances than I believe you were used to at Joe's school in Manhattan."

"I can appreciate that."

Mr. Anunzio and Mrs. Wimbish exchanged glances.

"I wonder if you do, Mrs. Lawson," Mrs. Wimbish said, her gaze casting about the classroom. "Along with all the things kids endure, a quarter of our children live at or below the poverty line. And a lot can come with that. We're not even sure some of them get enough to eat when they're not at school. We've got children here in so much trouble that I'm almost surprised more don't act out than do."

"But," she could feel "demanding" slipping away, "we still need assurance."

Ric Anunzio bent forward over the desk toward them. "That's what I'm trying to tell you, Mrs. Lawson. I can't promise full-time protection for Joe. We don't have the staff for that. And from what Mrs. Wimbish tells me, Joe, besides being small, is young for his age. Immature. He needs some time to catch up." The principal splayed his hands on the scarred desktop, a "take me seriously" gesture of his own. "After consulting with our school counselor, we think, if you possibly can, you should take Joe out of here. Some parents don't have that option. We think you do."

Paul broke the silence. "Exactly what are you suggesting?"

Mrs. Wimbish rose, pulled a manila folder from her desk drawer, and handed it to Paul. "As you know, I have all my assignments laid out for the year. Joe's certainly smart enough to handle them on his own. A couple of days a week, he can get a little private tutoring in reading and math with one of our tutors. It's just the social side he needs some time on."

"You mean home school him?" Paul asked, opening the folder and leafing through the first few pages.

Mrs. Wimbish nodded. "Just for a while and under our guidance."

Paul looked back at Anna. "What's your thinking?"

She looked up at the Land of the Lion display. Her thinking was that Joe would love this plan; Paul would barely be affected, and her life would be ruined. She groped for an out. "What about friends, after-school activities? I mean, how is he supposed to get this social maturity being at home all the time?"

"The same way lots of home-schooled kids do it," Mr. Anunzio offered. "Church groups, lessons at the Y, special interests, volunteering. Spending time with other homeschoolers. Does he have any friends, Mrs Lawson?"

"One." Her beautiful office. A classroom.

"Some special interests, Mrs. Lawson?"

The deep quiet time between eight-thirty and three. Gone. "A few. Swimming lessons, Native Americans, dogs."

"Right," Mrs. Wimbish chirped. "He was that Indian I couldn't pronounce for Halloween."

"And he has a new dog," Paul added dryly.

Mr. Anunzio settled back in his chair. "As long as Joe has one friend and some interests, he'll be fine. And he'll be safe, get some more confidence, and come back to us maybe next semester, maybe next year. I really think it's the right thing."

Anna couldn't stand it any longer. "But," the word came out in a whining non-Dr. Young approved whimper, "what about me?"

## 34 • MEPHITIS, MEPHITIS (LATIN: DOUBLE FOUL ODOR)

*Anna, great work. "It Takes a... Coven" was right out of the park and then, everybody's favorite, at least by the email we got, "Mea Culpa Mr. Moose." I think you're really onto something here. In fact, I'd like to talk to you in person about an idea I have about all this. Could you come to the city for a day? We'll put you up for a night and pay expenses. Let's make this happen soon. Marty.*

Anna stared at the email. Put her up for a night? Pay expenses? Marty never paid for anything. He was going to make some kind of offer. She was sure of it.

The skyline of the city from the GW Bridge hopped up in her mind. Barely three months in Onasego and she already felt like an outsider. She tried to envision herself window shopping up Fifth Avenue, pushing through the heavy glass doors of the Morrow Building, ascending in the elevator to the twenty-third floor of the chaotically cluttered *Manhattan Living* suite, and sweeping into Marty's corner office. Suddenly Joe walked into the daydream, gripping her hand in the elevator, his face tear stained and swollen like Halloween night. What in the world would she do with Joe?

She pulled her bathrobe from the back of the chair around her, blanket like. Tonight *The Onasegon* was calling for temperatures to drop into the low teens; one good reason not to be with Paul, Joe, and a reluctant Molly at the local community theatre's production of *Oliver*. She'd snagged four tickets from Ray and, to grease the skids of Molly's going, offered one to Caroline. From the back of the house, she could hear Ralphie's tough guy little barks from the newly installed trolley line in the backyard.

She turned back to the article she had been working on entitled, "Getting Darker."

*Out here in the country, I've come to appreciate light and dark in a way I never did in the city. In Manhattan, dark feels more like an absence of electricity than an absence of light. Onasego, at least to this writer's eye, looks like the maps we've all seen of North Korea from outer space. V-e-r-y dark and not much going on. Though having spent much of my adult life in NYC's incandescent environs, I have also taken notice of the fact that the days grow shorter this time of year. So, with shorter days and darker nights, my thoughts traveled to... Where do you think dear reader? Compact fluorescents? (Nope. Hard to find lamp shades.) Quilting? (Out of character.) Maybe bread making? (Then what are bread machines for?) Sex? (No comment.) Or... the Onasego Area Allied Arts Councils Association (try saying that five times really quickly) fall film festival? Fortunately, the Onasego Area Allied Arts Councils Association has the somewhat pronounceable acronym, OAAACA, which I will use in the rest of this column.*

*Should anyone imagine that rural cinematic interest would be dominated by regional classics like Drums Along the Mohawk or farm fare a la The River, they would be quite wrong, at least by the line extending over a quarter of a mile in twenty degree temperatures to see Winged Migration. In fact,...*

Her eyes fell on the post-it with Ric Anunzio's number beside her computer. In fact, she had to come up with some sort of schedule or plan for the JoJo dilemma. OAAACA would have to wait. She clicked on "save" then hit the minimize button on the keyboard.

After promising to call Ric Annunzio with some kind of decision, she and Paul drove to the bar at Kitt's to have a quiet glass of wine and try to figure things out. But she already knew in her heart that Mr. Annunzio and Mrs. Wimbish were right. "Small for his age. A target. Needs some time to catch up." All obvious bits of truth she knew but didn't want to acknowledge. Joe had been lost at the mainstream school in Manhattan and so, why would anyone figure it would be better in Onasego? At least the folks here were honest.

Paul had been just as honest. Before the Shiraz hit the table at Kitt's, he stated the obvious. Given his work day, heavy schedule of night-time entertaining, and on top of everything, this latest financial emergency the school was going through, there would be very little he could contribute to Joe's new situation. Perhaps they could hire someone to come to the house every day: a retired school teacher, a student majoring in education, someone who was already home schooling their kids, or, he added lamely, some combination of those people. Well... she clicked back on Marty's email and forwarded it to Paul; they just might have to. Outside, Ralphie snarled at a passerby.

She picked up her calendar and a tentative schedule for herself and Joe. According to Mrs. Wimbish, with one child, the school work could get done in a couple of hours. "*So what about the other twelve or so in the day?*" Not to worry, again according to Mrs. Wimbish. Let him sleep late. Sign up for lots of lessons. Play board games. Get him involved in a service project. "*Like what?*" Some kids are swimming for the Polar Plunge, so fun, people jump in Spruce Lake in February to raise money for sick kids. Joe could also. You said he's taking lessons. And you could do a "Where I Live" project. "*A What?*" At that one Mrs. Wimbish took her hand and explained in a soft voice, a series of short reports describing places and events around Onasego. Mrs. Wimbish made it all sound so easy. All those things school teachers knew how to do and got paid for. Right now she had Joe down for sleeping till eight-thirty, an hour and a half of language arts from nine 'til ten-thirty, and a tutor at the school from eleven to twelve. After lunch would be projects and lessons, like the five-day-a-week swimming lessons she might have coordinated at the Y instead of the single Saturday class he was currently enrolled in. A service project she had yet to figure out. To Mrs. Wimbish's Polar Plunge suggestion she barely pulled herself back from screaming, "*Are you nuts? Is that wig doing something to your head?*"

Opening the top drawer of her desk, she took out the number two reason for not going to see *Oliver*, a small cardboard box with Cottage Boutique stamped in silver on the lid. With Joe getting Ralphie, she thought a peace offering might be in order. Her plan was to hang them on the earring tree on Molly's chest tonight and wait to see how long it would take her to notice them. Sliding the earrings into her pocket, she stood, switched on the screen saver, and heard the yips from the yard go frenzied. She tore back the curtain.

Below, standing on hind legs, Ralphie pawed the air, struggling to get at something. What was it? A cat? A person? A MURDERER? All that was discernible were the scrubby little box bushes that lined the yard and the side of the garage. She shoved open the window and screamed, "Get the hell out of there!" Then, grabbing the cordless phone, she punched in 911 and raced down the stairs to the back porch door. Looking out the glass panels, she saw Ralphie, now on all fours, yelping, straining against the line trying to get inside.

"Onasego 911. What is the nature of your emergency?"

Anna scanned the backyard, "I don't know. Maybe an intruder." Ralphie stared up at her, terror written all over the little face.

"Where are you, ma'am?"

"In my house."

"Where in your house, ma'am?"

She flipped the deadbolt open. "By the kitchen door."

"All right, ma'am, stay in your house. Is the door locked?"

"No."

Dropping the phone on the kitchen counter, she stepped out onto the back porch. Behind her, the 911 operator's instructions turned stern. "Lock your door, ma'am, Lock your door. Did you lock your door?"

From the street side of the yard, branches cracked. A swirl of black crested in white disappeared around the corner of the garage. Anna bolted toward Ralphie, unsnapped the line, and ran with him, whimpering, into the house.

"Ma'am," the voice demanded from the counter, "are you all right? Answer me, are you all right?"

She collapsed into one of the kitchen chairs, Ralphie cradled in her arms. "Yes. I'm all right. I'm fine."

"Ma'am, is the intruder gone?"

She lowered her head so Ralphie could lick her chin. "Yes."

"Ma'am, did you know the intruder?"

"Yes."

The first edges of scent crept into the kitchen from the out of doors. She pushed Ralphie to the floor.

"Ma'am, was he or she armed or dangerous?"

"No, he or she wasn't!" she called to the phone on the counter, the "no" coming out in two syllables. She ran down the hall toward the steps and the open upstairs window. Would the FEDS swoop in to arrest her for abuse of public resources? Would *The Onasegon* report her in the police blotter for 911 fraud? She reached for the banister and forced herself to yell, "He… or, she… was a skunk!"

Two glasses of wine and one call to leave a heated message for Ellis, the ineffective animal control officer, later, Anna's fit of self hatred was spent. With Ralphie snoring in her lap, she marveled at the clarity of it all. Joe and Ralphie. Ralphie and Joe. Both vulnerable, precious, and much in need of protection. She brushed a tear away. Well, she could do that. Ralphie could be brought inside. And she would and could find a way to make Joe's home schooling work. With that resolved, she decided to have the fun part of her evening. She slid Molly's earrings from her pocket. *Oliver* should be over by now; the guys would be walking in the door any minute. First she'd regale them with the skunk story, then wait for the discovery.

Walking into her daughter's room was like entering a version of the big bang: CD's, books, soda cans littering the floor, sketchy posters on every wall, clothes covering the mattress, the mattress on the floor, even Benny Bear, Molly's favorite from toddlerhood, face down beside the trash can. At least the earring tree was in place, right next to a legal pad page filled with flowery cursive. Anna's curiosity was piqued. Kids didn't write on legal pads. She picked up the yellow sheet.

> *To my first thought on rising, my last, before sleep,*
> *and all that rises in dreams,*
> *Dearest Molly. Dearest protégé,*

Rises in dreams?
Dearest protégé?

> *I worship your mind, lithe, expansive.*
> *I worship your body, dew-kissed, taut.*
> *You are the exquisite elixir of youth, the unreachable love,*
> *Who calls to me like the siren…*

She whipped the paper over to the closing.

*You are with me, always,… and everywhere,*
*As I will be with you.*
*Derek*

꙾

The legal sheet lay on her desk like excrement. Anna's stomach caught at the mere sight of the flowing black lines. Paul walked in the room and pulled a chair up across from her. "What are you thinking?"

"I'm thinking I want a gun. How're the kids?"

"Joe's out like a light. Molly seems fine… downstairs watching a movie. She thought the note was kind of funny."

Anna glanced at Ralphie snoring in front of the radiator. The skunk seemed so long ago. Marty's email even longer. "Yeah, real funny. What do we do next?"

Paul leaned forward, rubbing his temples. "I don't know. I just don't know. Maybe I could speak to one of the Human Resource guys at Catskill."

Anna shoved the letter across to him. "How about the police! I mean look at this… *I worship your body, you are with me, always… everywhere, As I will be with you.* You didn't hear that poem he read at the slam. He talked about fantasies of young girls. That could be Molly."

Paul shook his head. "Don't go hysterical, Anna; he's a late middle-aged Future Studies professor with arthritis. The guy would need a cane. Besides, Molly said he's never done a thing, just slips her notes once in a while. And she was clear; she doesn't want anyone finding out about it either. We need to respect her wishes in this too."

Anna stared at her husband, incredulous. "Paul, get a grip. This is wrong. We're the adults here."

He extended his hands, palms up, toward her. "What do you want me to do?"

She looked out the window. "Go to the police. Get a restraining order. Something."

He sighed. "Look, it's been a long night; I think we have to give this more thought. If we go to the police… it could get publicized, open a big can of worms. Catskill could have some liability. Molly's name could be smeared around."

Anna slapped the desk. "I want to beat the shit out of this guy. Why don't you?"

Paul stood and pulled at his tie. "Cause I'm not a 'beat the shit out of him' kind of guy. Listen, let me talk to HR anonymously, no names. I'll do it tomorrow. Right now I've got to check some emails."

Check emails. Of course.

Paul walked to the door. "Molly's okay. She knows there will be no more tutoring. That's all we can do tonight."

She willed herself not to say anything as Paul left the room. Behind her Ralphie slept on his back, paws again in the air. She bet Ralphie was a "beat the shit of him" kind of guy. What to do? She turned back to her computer where the "Getting Darker" column, started eons ago, remained. She skimmed through the text, incandescent environs, OAAACA, rural farm fare, down to where she had stopped, *in twenty degree temperature to see Winged Migration. In fact.*

In fact, first, Joe, now, Molly. She stared at the screen. An hour later she had her thoughts together.

> As I've written, the land I am standing on here in Onasego is three hundred and fifty-nine million years old. Three hundred and fifty-nine million years. A great glacier swept the area way back then, pushed one way and then another, and created the hills, valleys, and flood plains I now walk on. One would think being able to simply stand in this place would impart such reverence that my life would be assured, calmed, and directed. But, instead, I find life can so terrify with the unimaginable for my children that despite the constancy of three hundred and fifty-nine million years, I find this same ground can sometimes shake, sometimes buckle, and on particularly bad days, just crack wide open beneath me.

She switched off the light. This one would not be for Marty.

## 35 • SOC-HER (3)

"So, what did the HR guy say we should do about Derek?"

Paul flipped up the collar on his sports jacket and leaned heavily on the steel mesh fence encircling the Catskill soccer field. He should be wearing a coat and hat, Anna thought. It was one thing to be the supportive head of Development and attend some of the school's sports events. It was another to catch pneumonia doing it.

Though the afternoon was just at thirty, and gray with intermittent snow flurries, students in flip flops and tee shirts handed out game programs and seat cushions beside the ticket booth while Catskill cheerleaders in tiny green and white skirts cavorted around the perimeter. Despite a strong drive by the opposing team, the Catskill goalie had just pulled off an improbable save. The score remained two to one, and the scanty, yet boisterous home crowd in the midfield bleachers stood clapping along with the Catskill band's rendition of the college fight song.

Paul blew on his hands. "As I suspected, he thinks we should downplay the whole thing. Not drag a lot of people into it. He'll speak to Derek."

Anna looked past Paul to the Friends' snack trailer where Joe, barely recognizable in a new Catskill green hooded sweatshirt, waited in line for cocoa. At least he was happy today. "I just don't understand. Why should a grown man writing highly suggestive notes to a young girl get downplayed? It's wrong. It's dead wrong."

On the field a whistle blew, flags dropped. "Get 'em Cats," rang out from the sidelines.

Paul put his arm around her. "It's not like he threatened her, Anna. It was really more sad than scary."

"Sad!" She lowered her voice. "I think writing, 'I will always be with you,' is pretty damn scary. I'm telling you, he could be a stalker. Like right now, she's at home alone. He could come right up to the door and she'd answer it!" She glanced at the snack line. No Joe. "Where the hell is Joe?"

Paul gripped her shoulder. "Don't get hysterical. Joe's right beside the gate, talking to the Bobcat."

She took another look. Paul was right. The Bobcat, down on one knee, had an arm around Joe. From Joe's gestures, the Bobcat was getting an earful of something. However, the next moment the Bobcat swung Joe up onto his shoulders and started kick dancing to the Catskill band.

"And as far as Derek's concerned," Paul continued, "think about the challenges of being a fifty-something stalking a teenager in Onasego. Now," he dropped his arm, "lighten up, here come Pug and Denise with the Vans."

Or, the beautiful people, Anna thought as the two couples approached. Today Pug was gentleman president in cords, suede jacket, and cashmere scarf, while The Niece was all about very tight jeans and paisley pashmina. Gwen, as usual, trumped everyone in a stunningly simple brown tweed coat over black wool trousers, while Jamie, looking every inch the banker, wore a camel overcoat, white oxford shirt, and regimental tie. Amazing, she thought, how great clothes, expensive haircuts, and confidence translated to good looks.

"Lawsons!" Pug boomed. "What are you standing out here for?"

Paul glanced toward the field. "Anna and Joe came up to catch some of the game. I'm just taking a break from the office."

Anna smiled her good spouse smile: like she would be here if Paul hadn't called her to come. The Bobcat settled Joe back on the ground then swept off his hood. Tim. She should have known.

Jamie looked over the rims of his dark glasses. "If you're trying to find that twenty million, as I trust you are, I'd like to see the latest numbers on the real estate. You could just fax them to my office."

Paul shrugged. "I'd prefer to drop them by. Not so public."

Gwen lifted a black leather gloved hand from her coat pocket and brushed a clump of snow from her husband's lapel. "Come on, Jamie, no shop talk, not here."

Behind them the Catskill base was back on its feet. A collective "NO" rose from the bleachers as a high, cross kick wafted over the goalie and into the far corner of the net. Jamie looked down at his wife. "My darling, there's always shop talk. And it's always everywhere. Paul understands that."

"Mrs. Lawson!"

Anna turned toward the familiar staccato voice. Standing by the ticket booth, Dawn and Libby, carrying stadium blankets and thermoses, stood in line to go in. Dawn leaned forward, insistent. "Where's Joe?" while Libby flipped the pages of her program.

Anna lifted an arm in the air and pointed at Joe and Tim walking back from the snack trailer. She saw Dawn pull on her mother's hand to join them, but Libby, with a nod to the ticket taker and an arm around her daughter, ushered her inside.

Whistles erupted again and the two teams parted for the half. With a trumpet blast the Catskill band began filing out onto the field. A dance corps followed. The Niece slipped her hand around Pug's arm and smiled sweetly. "I think Libby does so well with that girl. Can't be easy." She leaned in to snuggle against the suede shoulder. "It's the half, Hon, let's get seats."

"Yes, duty calls," Pug said looking back toward the bleachers. "Phil Coxe is waiting for us somewhere up there. He'll be whining about soccer like always." He tapped Denise's behind. "Paul, try to get out of that office some-time soon. You take care, Alma."

"Right," Anna murmured, "enjoy the game." She smiled this time in what she hoped was a folksy, "good to see ya at the soccer game" kind of way as the four headed off into the crowd, then turned to Paul. "Wish to hell I could figure out who Pug looks like." She stamped the ground. "My feet are freezing. I'm getting Joe and walking home."

Paul took his cell phone from his pocket. "Okay, hey, saw your email about Marty. We should talk…" He paused, staring down at the tiny screen. "Wait a minute. There's a message from home."

"Anna!"

Anna turned to see Gwen striding back down the concrete toward her, stopping a few feet away. "Almost forgot. The Saturday after Thanksgiving, our house at eight, casual, everybody comes, okay?" Without waiting for an answer, she turned and ran to rejoin the others.

"Mom!" Joe ran up, grabbing her around the waist. "Tim's says I can go meter-reading with him, all over for the 'Where I Live' project."

"Anna," Paul held up the phone. "Molly's locked in the bathroom at home. Someone's trying to break in."

Anna slapped her hands over Joe's ears. "Derek!"

Paul's voice was sharp. "No. The guy's screaming for you."

"Onasego 911, can you tell me the nature of your emergency?"

Tim slid his pickup out of the college onto West Street. Anna, using Tim's cell, tried to speak crisply "A break-in at 81 Summit. An intruder."

"All right, Miss. Did you say 81 Summit?"

"Yes, 81 Summit." Anna looked in the side mirror to see if Paul and Joe were anywhere behind them. With the BMW in the college's library lot, and the car keys locked in Paul's office, she'd jumped on a ride from Tim, whose truck sat parked beside the Snack Trailer. With Tim nimbly navigating the lines of half time revelers, they were out of the college complex and onto Green Street in minutes. One stop sign and one block later, however, the truck had been forced to a full stop before the lanes cleared and they could ease around Mr. Ding-A-Ling. "*Oh, give me a home,*" beep beep, "*where the buffalo roam,*" beep, beep, reverberated through the truck.

"This couldn't be that skunk again, could it, Miss?"

Anna gripped the phone. She was in hell. "Of course not! My daughter says it's a guy. A drunk, screaming guy!"

"You're not at the house, Miss?"

"Almost."

As soon as they turned onto Summit, she heard the bellowing between beep, beeps, "Anna Lawson..." beep, beep, "You get out..." beep, beep, "You good for..." beep, beep, "borax, moose idiot, person..." beep, beep.

Tim pulled up in front of the house where Ellis, screaming from atop an iron cage in the middle of the rhododendrons, stood with arms and legs splayed in a black X against the large right living room window. Black jeans, black beater shirt, black shoes. Neighbors, standing in clumps, watched warily from the sidewalk across the street. Molly looked down from the upstairs bathroom window.

"Are you at the house yet, Miss?"

"Yes," Anna whimpered.

"Shit," Tim pulled up the emergency brake and reached for the phone. "Hi, 911. False alarm. No problem. We're okay here. What?" He eyed Anna as he listened. "You've had other calls? Okay, I'll speak to the officers when they get here. Thanks." He threw the phone on the dashboard. "You know what this is about?"

Anna recalled her high-handed call from the night before. "Maybe. Last night I left a message on the city phone complaining about the animal control officer."

"Why?"

"A skunk I thought was gone came back."

"Look," Tim said, "roll up your window and keep the door locked. I've got to get him out of here." He eased his door open and slid out. "Hey, Ellis!"

Ellis turned toward the truck. In one leap he was off the cage and staggering across the yard. "There ya are, ya alone in an asshole, Anna Lawson. Did ya do any… any of the things I tol you?" He yanked at the door, then kicked it. "Moth balls, lots of moth balls. The Skunk Skrammer. Did ya see if he was comin' or goin' with the flour? Did ya do any of those things?"

Anna sat in the truck with her hands over her face. One bag. One crummy bag of moth balls she had thrown under the house. For a very drunk man, he was surprisingly eloquent. She lowered the window an inch.

"I did. I put out a bag of mothballs."

Ellis pressed his hands and nose flat against the passenger window and screamed. "One bag! Ya told people I didn't do my job. But ya didn't do your job. Now everybody is going to think Ellis is bad, bad, bad. But, ya know what? I'm not bad. Skunks aren't bad. See that cage over there? Ya ought to be in it."

Two Onasego cruisers parked across the street. Paul and Joe in the BMW pulled in behind them.

"Hey, buddy," Tim walked up behind Ellis and wheeled him around, "You gotta calm down. The police are here."

"Police? Fuck, shit, damn."

Tim draped his bobcat's paw around Ellis's shoulders. "Look, here they come. Put your hands in your pockets. Don't say anything. I'll talk."

Anna waited until she saw Paul get Joe into the house. Molly, standing on the porch, had the cordless phone and was probably relaying the scene to Caroline and who knew who else. She eased out of the car. "No, I'll talk."

Ellis held up his fist. "Ya, ya, skunk hater!"

The two officers joined them by the truck. Both seemed relaxed, but business-like. One was the young officer who pulled Anna and Paul over at the roadblock after the murder. Now, as then, he did the talking. "Hello,

Tim. Interesting outfit. Hi, Ellis." He turned to Anna. "I'm Officer Taylor. This is Officer Barber. We had a 911 for this address."

"I'm Anna Lawson. I called 911." The two officers exchanged a glance. Paul was back out with a coat on, walking toward them. Joe stood on the porch with Molly.

"You called 911 last night I believe," Officer Taylor bit his lower lip, "about a skunk."

Officer Barber focused on the roofline of the house.

"That's right, officer, but you see today…"

Tim held up his hand. "Look, Guys, I can cut through this. There's been a misunderstanding."

Drums and screaming erupted from the Catskill hill. Paul edged up beside Anna. Officer Barber looked at his phone for the text. "Still 2 to 2."

Tim began again. "In the heat of the skunk incident last night, Ms. Lawson felt that the animal control officer had not performed his job properly and phoned the city's help number. On reflection, however," he flicked his gaze toward Anna, "she realizes that was not the case. That there were further steps *she* should have taken. Now, Ellis, here," he tightened his grip on Ellis, "was understandably angered to be the object of what he believes is a false accusation."

"Thas egzatly right," Ellis agreed, flipping his hair behind his shoulder.

Officer Taylor looked over at the neighbors. "I can understand being angered by a false accusation, but you scared some people, Ellis. Let's go downtown, have a little talk. Maybe check in with your parole officer."

Anna kicked the truck tire, wondering what to say.

Ellis pointed at the Have A Heart cage in the bushes. "I was just gonna trap the little bugger. I'm not bad… did my job."

Tim looked at Anna, Officer Taylor, and then Ellis. "You did do your job, buddy. You sure did."

Paul was angry. She knew from the way he stood: still, but no give; from his gaze: steady, but no focus; and from his tone: about a minute and a half from assault and battery. "Anna. This is a small town. You have to use your brain. You left a message about someone we know to be somewhat unstable on a city machine. Did you ever stop to think that might not be a good idea?

That he might become very angry, as he did, or that he might also lose his job, as he may. And, of course, this all comes after you assumed he was a murderer when he was, in fact, trying to help you."

Paul paused. He was a practiced speaker. The audience needed breaks to absorb the message. Snowflakes, large and feathery, swept the sky.

"You dove into Lake Otsego because Joe was in waist deep water and made a huge spectacle of yourself. You fell apart in front of his principal and teacher because they suggested some temporary home schooling. On the Derek thing, you might have tried to get some details from Molly before deciding I should just go beat the shit out of the guy. You called 911 over a skunk. And, if I may," another pause, small but intentional, "you sounded just like your crazy mother when I couldn't make the Halloween parade at precisely the time you wanted."

The unfairness caught in the back of her throat. "Some of that is not quite accurate."

Cheering, horns, and the deep, indiscernible announcer's voice cut through the gray afternoon again. A score. Maybe someone won. Young Officer Barber was probably texting like mad. Paul's gaze hardened. "It's the way I see it. And I can't keep getting caught up in all this hysteria. I need a break."

Molly and Joe had gone inside now. The neighbors had drifted away also. "A break from me?"

Paul nodded. "Yeah. Go find out what Marty wants. Take Molly to see her father. I can figure out Joe."

She looked across at Ellis's Have A Heart cage. "I'll give it some thought."

Paul caught her arm. "It would also help me. Those numbers I have to get to Jamie, well, William Johnson's on the same committee. If you're in the city, you can take a copy to him." He glanced sideways at her. "Think you could do that?"

## 36 • JED AND AVA

SITTING ACROSS THE coffee shop booth from her ex husband, Jed, listening to him explain to Molly why he had bailed on their lunch and afternoon plans, Anna decided he was looking good. Not as good as his young Courtney Cox look-alike wife, Ava, but still, quite good. Though mostly bald since his thirties, he, or some pricy hair dresser, had taken a new approach to the wisps. A brush-it-straight-back tactic that lent a definitely cool touch. Sort of Ed Harris. With the new hair, no visible paunch, and dressed in what she was sure was at least a three-thousand-dollar suit, he looked every bit the successful, guy about town, go-to tax attorney, that he was.

Ditto for Ava. Her charcoal suit, paisley scarf, pearls, and Manolo Blahniks, were an exquisitely appropriate covering for the Wharton MBA, with distinction, and wild little overachiever that *she* was. While anyone could see in a heartbeat what Jed saw in Ava, it had taken Anna a little more time to figure out what Ava saw in Jed: twenty years older, kind of oblique, and damned hard to get out of his office in the Twin Towers. Then she got it. They both loved being *in* the office. Talking finance. Making deals. Getting the stratospheric professional high that New York City could offer. But, and she had to hand it to Ava for broadening Jed's horizons, if work was great at work, why not take it to the gym, to the newest, trendiest restaurants, to investing in a winery, to buying a loft in Tribeca, and of course, the requisite place in the Hamptons. For herself, after biding time during Jed's Shermanesque march through three years of law school, another year to get a Master's in Tax Law, then partner at Hardin and Hardin in seven years, and managing partner in ten, she was done. Done being a single parent when she wasn't. Done getting birthday presents for Jed's mother… and herself. And done with the possibility that that this was all there was. She divorced Jed when she was thirty-four, he was thirty-eight, Molly was three, and, after a Jewish, different from anyone she had ever known, fun-loving, party-going, openly affectionate new fundraiser, Paul Lawson, showed up in her writing class for professionals. A year later they married. Joe came eleven months after that.

Jed, on the other hand, power dated until Ava showed up three years ago, right out of business school, brandishing a new model of municipal bond fund behavior. The rest was history. Though initially uninterested in children, for the past year or so, Ava, like Gwen, had become a hipper than hip "best friend" to Molly. At least when time allowed. She wondered what Ava would have to say about the Derek letters. Jed's response had been limited to "the need for careful documentation."

"So you see, Molly, that's why when Thomas Anderson of Anderson and Wiley called I just had to rush right over to explain," Jed, looking down at Ava's empty cup, signaled for the waitress, "that this proposed change in the New York tax code would not," he paused again for the refill, "affect his company's exemptions. But I hope you had a nice lunch anyway."

Molly tossed back her hair. "Street vendor stuff. Mom had to get to her meeting. Then I just sat at that office. Really boring."

Anna held up her cup for the waitress. "Just a touch please, and can we have the bill now?" She was not going to let Molly ruin her trip. Molly was Jed and Ava's until eleven the next morning. Joe was Paul's. She was looking at almost eighteen hours to herself, plus a hotel room, in which to be self-indulgently out of Onasego. And there was the very slight chance that she might catch a glimpse of William Johnson within the hour.

Ava tore open a packet of raw cane sugar, pouring in half. "Molly, you poor baby. We have to make this up to you. Don't we, Jed?"

Jed stretched an arm around Ava. "We certainly do."

Molly leaned across the table toward her father. "Did I tell you Mom got completely lost driving here? I mean, it wasn't like the road wasn't right there. She just kept saying, 'never eat shredded wheat, never eat shredded wheat' and looking for the sun."

Anna pushed the cream toward Ava. C. Cool down. "SHE will be the first one to admit that SHE has no sense of direction and was totally relieved to find a little country store and ask directions. It was near Margaretville, out in the middle of nowhere except a reservoir, tons of woods, all these seasonal and country roads and the turnoff was barely marked. By the way I should add, that SHE's daughter was of no help whatsoever."

Molly folded her hands on the table, "Mom, you're not funny, so don't even try."

Capital C. Anna checked her watch. Four-thirty. "Well, you are almost free of me and my nonhumor. In fact, I better head out in a few minutes. I need to be somewhere at five." She looked up as the waitress scribbled out the check. "Thanks."

"Mine." Jed grabbed the check from the startled waitress and took out his wallet. "So, Anna, how did your meeting go?"

Anna folded her napkin on the table and picked her jacket up off the seat. Knowing Jed, he was probably angling for a cut in child support. "It went fine. He wants to make the column a weekly. Some of the staff gave me feedback on what they liked and what they didn't. Then we tossed around some ideas for upcoming columns."

Molly swirled her untouched coffee. "Probably something besides garage sales and skunks."

Anna, one arm in her coat, hesitated. "You read my column?"

Molly shrugged.

"Good for you, Anna," Ava looked over Jed's shoulder at the bill, "I think the way you've worked this little part-time gig is just fantastic. And probably fun for you, too." She patted Jed's hand. "I'd go thirty. And speaking of fun, I need to shop for the baby shower."

Jed slipped a twenty and a ten underneath the salt shaker and eased out of the booth, clearing the way for Ava behind him. "Ava's got to get a present before tomorrow and I need to swing by the office." He winked at Molly, "Won't take ten minutes. Can we drop you somewhere, Anna?"

Anna pulled the manila envelope Paul had given her out of her tote bag. "I just have to drop this off for Paul. It's close; Broadway and sixty-seventh. Thanks for the coffee."

"Broadway and sixty-seventh? That's a really hot property." Ava's gaze traveled to the name and address, then back to Anna. "W. Johnson? Anna, do you know what business he's in?"

Anna stood. "Real estate developer, I think."

Ava's eyes locked back on the envelope. "Oh, my god, Jed. She's going to see William Johnson."

## 37 • I (HEART) NY

"Paul, I can't hear you. Hold on, I'm going inside."

The doorman at Anna's hotel tipped his hat. "Good afternoon, Miss, let me get that for you."

"Thanks," Anna said walking through the heavy brass and glass door and into a brightly lit lobby. At almost six-thirty, the reception desk was a blur of travelers four and five deep waiting to check in, clerks in crisp black and white uniforms tapping out reservation slips, and porters ferrying racks of luggage over the gleaming checkerboard floor. A sandwich board by the concierge's office listed the current conventions with their respective meeting rooms. From the bar, faint piano strains blended with an end of the week happy hour buzz. Spying an empty corner on the far wall from the reception area, she wound her way through the clusters of conventioneers and dumped her suitcase, tote, and purse beside a vacant love seat. "Okay, Paul, this should be better."

"How's the hotel?"

Anna pulled off her coat with one hand, sat, and looked around at champagne walls, burgundy and green striped furnishings, and sisal rugs. "Generic. Probably gives a great corporate rate." A petite blonde holding a drink and a conference packet sidled up to a club chair opposite the love seat, pointed, and mouthed, "Okay?" Anna smiled and nodded.

"Well, Joe and I are off in a minute for his advanced pollywog test at the Y. I just wondered how it went with William Johnson."

"Paul, I didn't see him, I—"

"Hey, Joe," Paul's voice was muffled. "Wait for me in the living room, all right?" There was silence. Then Paul was back. "Anna, I asked you to do one thing. Just one."

Anna swiveled away from the woman studying Circle Line brochures. "Paul, I got to his office right at five. It was shut down tight as a drum. I waited for an hour. I don't know what else I could have done."

Paul sighed. "I'll try to find out what happened. Keep the phone with you, okay? I really don't need this. Bye."

Anna sat back in her seat. Where was the "thanks for trying." the "I'm sorry you waited an hour for nothing," or even, "how did it go with Marty and the column?" She looked over at the reception desk, still too busy to check in. The blonde leaned forward. "I'm here for the City Administrators' Conference. What about you?" Anna's phone rang. She held up her phone. "Excuse me. I have to take this." She turned away. "Yes, Paul."

"Is this Anna Lawson?" a slightly familiar female voice asked.

"Yes, it is." The city administrator pulled an I LOVE NEW YORK visor from her kit for Anna to see.

"Ms. Lawson, we're all here and ready to come to order. Where are you?"

"Where am I? Who is this?" Then she knew. Laurel Loomis. The Friends of Catskill meeting, Friday night, six-fifteen, sharp. The reminder was tacked to her bulletin board. "Ms. Loomis, I'm afraid I'm in Manhattan on business."

A pause. "Who, then, is taking minutes?"

Anna could tell the woman across from her wasn't reading the conference materials. "I'm so sorry. I forgot about the meeting... and the minutes."

"I see." Another pause. "Someone must take minutes, Ms. Lawson."

Anna's phone beeped for an incoming call. "I have another call coming in. Could you do it, please?"

Dead air. Was Laurel making hand signs to the Friends? Shrugging her shoulders? Clutching her pentagram for outside guidance?

"It seems I must." Click.

Anna waited, hoping the incoming call would go away. Meanwhile, the city administrator shoved the materials back in the envelope, fluttered her fingers at Anna, and rose to join two other women in I LOVE NEW YORK visors.

"Paul,"

"No, Anna, it's Jed."

"Hi. What's up?"

"Molly says her stomach feels weird. She thinks it's the vendor food you made her eat. What should I do?"

Made her eat? "I don't know. Try some ginger ale."

"Maybe I should bring her back to you."

*Back to you?* Not on his life. "Now, Jed, it's probably just excitement, and... this is your night with Molly." She heard another incoming call. "I'm here at the hotel. Call me if it gets worse. I've got another call. Bye."

"Paul,"

"No, Ms. Lawson, it's William Johnson."

William Johnson. She took a death breath. Paul must have found him. "Hello."

At the piano the three city administrators began singing "New York, New York." She covered her other ear.

"I hear from Paul there was a mixup. That you've been waiting at my office."

"That's right. I hope you weren't waiting for me somewhere else."

"Actually, I was." He sounded edgy, annoyed. "Miss Lawson, it's been a very long day. And this place is damn loud and crowded."

Anna gazed down at the sisal rug. How was she supposed to make this right? She could grovel but that still wouldn't get him the numbers. Damn loud and crowded? She felt a tap on her shoulder and looked up. William Johnson, in jeans, brown leather jacket, and phone in hand, looked back.

"Your hotel is dreadful, Miss Lawson." He snapped off his phone and reached for her coat. "I've got an hour before my next meeting. Let's get a drink."

## 38 • CINDERELLA

THE BAR WAS small, a long corridor of burnished mahogany booths, dim lights, and rectangular beveled windows. It was the type of bar she'd go to every once in a while with her parents as a teenager. They would order Old Fashions or Manhattans. She would have something clear and bubbling like tonic to appear sophisticated and assured. Would that it were so easy now. Tonight, at forty-four, with a grown-up vodka martini, she felt reduced to drivel because of William Johnson sitting across the table drinking Glenfiddich. Though lacking a border collie, he seemed like someone who should drink Glenfiddich: the hanks of heavy black hair, steady voice, knowing gaze, and hands, large, calloused, and workmanlike, just inches from hers. Why the hell was he here? A courtesy to Paul's wife? An apology for the mix up? Why hadn't he just taken the envelope, thanked her kindly, and stepped out into the night?

She took a salmon crust from the plate of smoked fish and kalamatas that sat inauspiciously closer to her than Johnson. So far the conversation had somehow been all about her: growing up, moving to the city, college, the MFA, Jed, Paul, moving to Onasego, Marty's offer. Almost everything but the important stuff: her pact with God, Molly's anger, the Derek mess, Joe being bullied, and Paul in general. Throughout the conversation, she'd found Johnson to be pretty much as he'd been at the board dinner:

informed, courtly, and direct. He was also, however, self deprecating, wry, and disconcertingly attentive. Then there was the ongoing fact that he was gorgeous. Every few sentences she remembered to breathe.

"So, how are things in Onasego now that you've been there a while?"

She sighed. "Recently I called 911 on a skunk. Then I called 911 on the animal control officer who was trying to trap the skunk."

"You mean Ellis?"

No getting away from Onasego tonight. "Yes, I mean Ellis. And, just tonight, I managed to forget my first meeting as recording secretary for the Friends of Catskill."

"Sounds like material for your column."

"You read my column?"

"Yep."

She pushed the plate of food toward him. "Name one."

"'Mea Culpa Mr. Moose.' What about being back in the city?"

"I'm rusty. I smiled at someone in an intersection today."

He grinned and reached for the olives, "Yeah, when I'm in Onasego, I have to remember not to flip people off in traffic."

Anna recalled the visit to Libby's house, the cashmere coat, her improbable suspicion that Johnson might be Libby's lover. Dawn's father. "I've gotten to know Libby Holmes a bit, and she's always talking about your mother. Mumma this, and Mumma that. You must spend a great deal of time together."

Johnson finished the scotch then glanced at his watch. "We do."

No help there. Anyway, the prince obviously had other obligations. Cinderella should be going. "I really want to thank you for the drink. And I apologize. I've been doing all the talking."

Johnson shrugged. "Because I've been doing all the asking. How about another drink?"

"Your meeting?"

"I can miss it." He raised his glass, beckoning the bartender. "You?"

One martini hadn't been the best idea. Two could be tragic. She shook her head and started to stand.

He looked up at her. "Please, stay. I won't be long."

*Please stay.* Those words might have to be tattooed on her body somewhere as a souvenir. She sat back in her chair. "Do you always do all the asking? At the board dinner you quizzed everyone but never mentioned yourself."

"Not too much to tell."

She picked the swizzle stick out of her martini, a tiny Statue of Liberty, and raised an eyebrow.

Johnson spread his hands, "All right, ask me anything."

Like what happened to his engagement? Probably not. The manila folder lay on the table between them. "Can you guys save Catskill?"

He thought for a moment. "Maybe. Phil Coxe, in particular, has some ideas."

Kind of cryptic. She decided on something a little closer to home. "Why did you choose real estate?"

A half smile lit his face. "Because it's real."

"To what do you attribute your success?"

He waited until the waiter placed a shot glass on the table and walked away. "Really good instincts."

"I saw you on the highway the day the police officer was killed."

"I remember it well."

It? Writing 101: no indefinite pronouns. Did he remember the day, well? Her, well? The check point, well? "What were you doing there?"

"Soccer. I coached his team."

She pointed the swizzle stick at him. "Why'd you leave Onasego?"

"Upstate can be tough. A story for another time."

She let the swizzle stick clatter to the table. "You said, ask anything."

Johnson tossed back the shot. "I've got one for you. Why did I ask you out tonight?"

Anna propped her chin in the palm of her hand. "I was sort of curious about that myself."

He set the glass down and folded his arms on the table. "I wanted to get to know you."

Her reply slithered out in two perplexed syllables. "Why-y?"

"Can't somebody just be interested? Maybe you can't explain it. So, I'm thinking dinner at my house."

His words seemed caught in the space between them. Suddenly she got it. An elaborate, Onasego prank.

"Somebody put you up to this, didn't they?" She gazed about the bar for a familiar face.

Johnson leaned in across the table. "I don't get put up to things. The mix up this afternoon was my plan to see you. I just never thought you'd wait at my office for so long."

Anna raised up on the arms of her chair to see better. But no Pug or Jamie or Deedee appeared. No cameras flashed. She sat back down. Then she pulled up the cloth and looked under the table.

Johnson raised his hand for the bill. "This isn't a joke. I'm interested. I think you're interested. Now back to dinner. How about pasta and salad?"

With the creeping sensation that she was starring in her own episode of *Fantasy Island*, she watched him take out his wallet. "Why would you think I'm interested? You know I'm married."

He reached for the bill from the waiter. "As I said, really good instincts. It's only dinner. Let's go."

Anna made another sweep of the bar for people doubled over in laughter, then picked her coat up from the back of the chair. William Johnson was interested. He wanted to have dinner. Never doubt? She pulled her phone from the coat pocket with a missed call from Molly. She looked up at Johnson. "If some old guy wrote a suggestive letter to a young girl, what would you do about it?"

Johnson threw a hundred on the table and picked up her suitcase. "Try not to beat his head in before I called the police."

She slipped the swizzle stick into her coat pocket with the phone. Cinderella would treasure it later on.

Outside the bar, the night was clear. They walked silently at first. Anna thought they must look so incongruous, like James Bond, especially as played by Pierce Brosnan, taking Ethel Mertz out for a stroll. Or maybe people would think they were brother and sister, adopted separately, of course.

Against the blazing Manhattan stage of shops, restaurants, hotels and office buildings, the Friday exodus inched along beside them. A stream of headlights, shiny metal, and insistent horns. Late-model cars, lots of cabs, a smattering of limousines, a few panel trucks. No upstate pickups that she could see. Suddenly the familiar brass and glass of her hotel loomed across the street. She tried to envision herself with Johnson in an *Architectural Digest* brownstone.

"You look alarmed. Are you?"

She searched for words, "Maybe like a trainee...sky diver."

He stopped and looked down at her. "Look, we've got an opportunity to get to know one another. Let's not pass that up." The mischievous smile from the pumpkin-pulling day played over his face. "Tell you what, while we cook, I'll tell you deep dark secrets about Onasego for your column. Now, go drop your stuff. I'll find a cab."

Over his shoulder she could see the friendly doorman still on his shift. She had to cook?

The lobby was more crowded than when she'd left. Brighter too. But reception was almost empty. She checked in quickly, crossed to the elevator and pressed the up button. If she hurried she could wash her face and redo her makeup before meeting William outside. William. She closed her eyes. Treasure every moment. Never doubt. A little adultery would have to be okay. The evening had the potential of becoming one of her great life events.

"Anna."

She wheeled around to see an agitated Jed. Tweed jacket, Lacoste shirt, khakis, Asics. "Where have you been?"

"Out for a drink. What are you doing here?"

Jed pointed to a couch near the concierge. There, Molly half sat, half lay, pale against the burgundy and green stripes. Her coat draped over her like a blanket. "We've been waiting for you. Molly's got something. They wouldn't let her in your room even though she keeps running into the ladies' room to vomit."

Anna turned to Jed, incredulous. "She couldn't throw up at your house?"

Jed looked around the lobby, then lowered his voice. "Ava's got a big presentation on Monday. She can't get sick right now."

"So it's okay to drag Molly, who is sick, over here." She looked toward the revolving door. "Jed, I have plans."

He rocked back and forth in his running shoes. "I didn't know what else to do."

Anna looked out over the lobby. She was a mother. Mothers took care of their sick children. There it was, maternal seppuku. She waited for the lightness of just seconds earlier to ooze away, then walked over to the couch and bent down. "Hey, honey. Your dad says you're not feeling so great. I'm sorry."

Molly opened her eyes. "It's that shitty food you made me eat."

Anna willed herself to remember her daughter was ill. "I didn't make you eat anything. Anyway, we've eaten vendor food a million times and never gotten sick."

"God, Mom, don't talk. Just get me to a bathroom and a shower."

"Look, I've got to go." Jed said, with his collar turned up and valet parking ticket in hand. We've been here almost an hour. Ava's waiting for me at home."

"Jed, my plans. What about me?"

"Look, maybe I panicked, but Molly's here now. It needs to be this way." He bent down and rustled Molly's hair. "You get better. We'll talk, Anna."

She watched silently as Jed stormed through the lobby, passing right by William standing in front of the concierge's desk. Beside her Molly struggled up off the couch.

"Mom, bathroom, now."

Anna woke to the phone ringing. In the dark she tried to figure out where she was, then the vomit smell hit her. The hotel. She looked at the bedside clock: the red numbers beamed eleven o'clock.

"Hello," she whispered.

"It's William. How's your daughter?"

She looked at Molly lying beside her. "Asleep. She has a stomach bug. I called home. My son has it too."

"What about you?"

"I'm figuring it's inevitable, probably on the GW Bridge." She heard ice cubes and glasses clinking over the line. "More scotch?"

"Cointreau. Regrets for our non dinner."

Molly muttered something in her sleep Anna couldn't understand. "It was probably for the best."

There was a pause, the city sounds drifting in, comforting, familiar, then: "Not to me, but look, I have to tell you something."

What could he tell her? It was all really a joke? "Okay."

"As a Catskill trustee, I made some inquiries on my own about the candidates for the development job. So I found out how good Paul is at fundraising. But I also found out about his reputation with women. You deserve better."

She sat up against the headboard. How was it that Onasego managed to expose the raw, messy corners of her life over and over again?

"Anna, are you there?"

Molly grabbed for the sheet. "Mom! For Christ's sake!"

Anna glanced around the corporate rate, generic bedroom. "Go back to sleep, honey. I'll be off in a minute."

"I'll say goodnight," William whispered, "but, look out in the hall."

A surprising wave of calm slid over her. Slipping out of the bed, she tiptoed to the door. Just outside, a miniature of Cointreau along with a crystal snifter waited on a room service cart. She lifted the business card taped to the bottle. On the front, William had circled his email and phone numbers and drawn an arrow to the back. She flipped the card over and read the scrawl. *To Skydiving WJ*

## 39 • COMMUNITY TURKEY DAY

POPS CLAMPED THE gas nozzle, leaned against the BMW, and peered first at Joe and Dawn in the back seat, then at Anna in the driver's seat. "Have these two been good? Cause if they've been good they get an ice cream. But if they've been bad…" he let the question hang there. Anna played along, stroking her chin, scratching her temple, eying the two in the rear-view mirror. Then, with a dramatic jab of her index finger, she clicked open the rear door locks, proclaimed, "Good!" and the two hurtled out of the car. Hmm, she thought. Some things are so easy.

"You want an ice cream?" Pops asked, wiping his hands against a paper towel.

She shook her head and watched as the old man followed the children inside. Toast and tea had been her diet for the past three days. While she made it out of Manhattan and all the way to Walton before the bug hit, the next forty-eight hours were absolute hell. Actually, the hell started Saturday morning in the hotel when Molly felt well enough to complain: complain about getting sick and about Ava wanting to spend all their time in a baby store.

But today was glorious. She looked across Main Street to the hills in the east, shimmering and green against a cloudless sky and, according to the bike shop, forty-one degrees, both the sunshine and heat welcome aberrations from the gray, freezing Onasego weather of the past month. Today she would drive into those hills to drop Dawn at Libby's, pick up her reserved turkey at Angus's Community Turkey Day, score material for a feel-good, folksy column about Onasego supporting its local farms, and possibly, just possibly run into William Johnson on the road to Libby's. Didn't most sons visit their mothers for holidays? She thought about asking Paul if William might be coming to town, but couldn't figure out a way to broach the subject. Since her return from NYC with the stomach bug, they'd talked very little.

"So," Pops said, opening the car door for Joe and Dawn, "these guys tell me you're heading out to get a turkey at Angus Lynch's farm. What's wrong with the grocery store?"

Anna waited to hear the click, click of Joe's and Dawn's seat belts. "Isn't getting back to nature part of upstate New York? What about you? What are you doing for the holiday?"

Pops lifted the nozzle from the gas tank, screwed on the cap, and handed her a receipt.

"I'll head over to the free dinner at St. Teresa's. They got those Butterballs; that's enough nature for me."

She switched on the ignition. "Oh, now, Pops. I can live without a Butterball. You have a good holiday, okay?"

Anna eased off Turnpike Road onto a sand and gravel shoulder behind Ray's turquoise Honda. Had she not been looking, the small wooden sign tacked onto a fencepost advertising Angus Lynch, Organic Meat and Produce would have been easy to miss. Across the road, fifteen or so cars and trucks filled the clearing beside the gray wooden Greek revival-style farmhouse while several more sat pulled off on either side of the road. On the hill behind the house, near a faded red barn, several clusters of people stood around what seemed to be smoking vats. The ride out had been, as she'd imagined, a scenic glory: evergreens splashed with snow, golden winter grass bent under azure skies, a doe and her fawn disappearing over the ridge turning onto Kelso Road. She should work photos into her column. This Community Turkey Day article would be a hit. She could feel it.

"So," she asked Joe and Dawn, "you guys want to stay in the car or go with me to pick up the turkey?" Joe and Dawn looked at each other. Decision making time. Across the road, Angus and Ray emerged from the house, spoke briefly with the golf coach and his wife whose names she simply could never remember, jumped into a dirt-spattered Jeep Cherokee, and spun out of the lot toward Delhi.

"Go," said Joe. He looked hopefully at Dawn.

From the side-view mirror, she caught sight of Victor of mobile slaughter house fame pulling in a few spaces behind her, followed by a Prius.

"Go," Dawn repeated in her slow staccato, "but you have to tell my mother you made me come here."

Anna looked down at her reward for "making" Dawn come, her new suede Clarks, already coated with mud. The error in footwear became apparent at Libby's where the house stood dark and the Windstar nowhere in sight. Although Dawn insisted that she stayed alone all the time, Anna still dutifully knocked on the door and walked around back through the jumble of wet leaves, grass, and mud in search of Libby. Even with Mumma up the road and neighbors around somewhere, it bothered her to leave a young girl in those woods "home alone." Finally, over Dawn's protests, she brought the girl with them on the turkey errand. A car door closed. She looked in the side-view mirror again as Laurel Loomis stepped out of the Prius. Shit.

"Let's wait a minute, guys." She leaned over the seat pretending to look for something in the glove compartment, but heard the steps. Then the knock on the glass. She rose slowly, opening the window.

"Hello, Miss Lawson."

Today, Laurel's braid was wound milkmaid style into concentric circles about the crown of her head. A beige turtleneck, fisherman's sweater, mid-calf denim skirt, barn boots, and what looked to be a propane torch, completed the ensemble. "Just a very early reminder, our next Friends' meeting is on the sixteenth of January."

Anna smiled. "I'll see you there, Miss Loomis."

Laurel took a step into the street, then turned back. A hint of warmth lighting the stony face. "I must say I am surprised and pleased to see you here, Miss Lawson. Perhaps I've been mistaken about you. Your witness today honors the lives of these magnificent creatures. Happy Thanksgiving."

Anna sat, bewildered, while Laurel allowed several cars to exit and enter the parking lot, raising the torch briskly to each before crossing the highway. What was that about and what was she going to do with that torch? Have a barbeque?

When Laurel was safely across the parking lot and halfway up the hill, Anna swung her car door open, then Joe and Dawn's. "Okay everybody out. Dawn, we'll have you back home in a jiffy where I bet your mother will be waiting for you." And, she thought, ushering the two across the highway, if I am very, very, very lucky, my new friend William Johnson just might be, too.

"Hey! Wait for me!"

Angie, perched high in the driver's seat of a new Lexus, waved to Anna and the children, then slid into a free spot on the shoulder several cars ahead of the BMW. Though the sales specs were still attached to the side windows of the Lexus, a COEXIST sticker already adorned the rear bumper. Lights and motor shut off, Angie stepped out onto the highway dressed in overalls, barn boots, tan Carhartt, and carrying goggles along with her ever present canvas bag. As unlikely a looking member of the Susquehanna Realtors Million Dollar Sales Club as there ever was. And, Anna thought, an unlikely-looking wife of a possible pedophile... stalker... salacious middle aged pervert... whatever one would call Derek. She hadn't seen Angie since a couple of weeks before the letter incident as Angie, ever true to the cause, decided to combine her Fort Benning protest with a run to Cuba. Would Derek have told her about the sudden cancellation of Molly's tutorials?

"Hi, there," Anna offered weakly as Angie scurried across the road to the parking lot, arms out flung for a big All Paths style hug. "Welcome back. Great car."

"It's so good to be back," Angie gushed, moving on to grab Joe then Dawn. "Can you believe that thing? Derek got it for me while I was away. I wanted one forever. Can't imagine why he finally bought it."

Anna could. "Where *is* Derek?'

"He'll be out soon. He's doing," she pantomimed throwing a throttle wide open, "his *Easy Rider* thing. Hey," she glanced between Dawn and Joe, "I had this great idea in Cuba. I am so grateful for all we have and I want to have a big, I mean big, Thanksgiving dinner. We can all put our food together and play like Pilgrims and Indians. Maybe we'll do it at the church. What do you think?"

Joe folded his arms across his chest. "I'll be Deganawidah."

Dawn rocked back and forth. "We're eating with Mumma and William. Can they come?"

Anna felt the train leaving the station. "Paul's been working so hard... we were thinking a quiet little meal at home."

Angie guided the children into the yard as Angus and Ray backed the Jeep into the space beside them. "Don't be silly. You'll have the whole weekend. Maybe we can get Derek and Molly to read us some poems." She paused as the two men got out of the Jeep, goggles dangling around their necks. "Hi, guys. Sneaking out?"

Angus, walking more stiffly than Anna remembered, seemed to hesitate at the sight of the four of them. Then he sighed and rubbed his face. "My old bull got loose. Coach thought he saw him over near West Kortright, but I couldn't find him."

Ray squinted out at the open fields. "He'll get hungry and come home. You know he will."

"Mom," Joe tugged on Anna's coat, "are we going to get a turkey or not?"

She glared down at her son. "Angus, please excuse my very rude son, Joe, who I don't think you've met and," she turned to Dawn, "this is our friend Dawn, Libby Holmes's daughter."

With a sideways glance at Ray, Angus rubbed his hands on his jeans, then gingerly extended his hand to Dawn, withdrawing it quickly as she gripped her purse strap and twisted closer to Anna.

"Dawn..." Anna began....

"It's okay," Angus said softly, "I understand about this. I do." Turning to Joe, he adopted a voluble air, laying his palm out flat. "And what about you, young man? Shakes or high fives?"

Joe reared back and slapped the outstretched hand chanting, "Tur-key! Tur-key!"

Grateful, for once, for Joe's lack of social skills, Anna took up the cause. "You're right. This is Community Turkey Day, and we need to go up that hill and get our turkey. Hey, and you can write this up for your 'Where I Live' project." She turned back to Angus. "How much do I owe you?"

Angus's gaze suddenly cut between Anna, Joe, and Dawn. "Anna, you sure everyone is up for this?"

"What?"

Angus, with a slight flick of his head, pointed up the hill. "You know."

Anna surveyed the hill. Almost everyone standing there were dressed much like Angie, Angus, and Ray. Jeans, sweatshirts, Carhartts, and *goggles*. "No, I don't."

"What is your understanding of Community Turkey Day?" Angie asked, head down, digging through the canvas tote.

Anna tried to shine her best beaming smile at Angus. She needed a story out of this. "Just that everyone comes here to get their turkeys from Angus cause they're free range, grass fed—,"

"And fresh," Angie interrupted, looking up from the bag, "very fresh."

"Right," Anna agreed. "As I was saying just this morning, I can do without Butterballs." She took her wallet from her purse, "So, how much?"

"Here it is." Angie pulled a laminated printout from the bag. "Angus asked me to bring these instructions for people," she seemed to be choosing her words carefully, "picking out their turkeys for the first time. You should take a look."

She handed the sheet over Joe and Dawn's head to Anna. The paper had an Ask Jeeves logo with the headline WEARING WORK GLOVES AND SAFETY GOGGLES IS STRONGLY ADVISED in bold letters.

Anna eyed Angie, Angus, and Ray before continuing. Instructions to pick out a turkey? She looked down the sheet.

STEP 1. TO KILL THE TURKEY, HANG IT BY ITS FEET. HOLD THE HEAD AND BEAK WITH ONE HAND AS YOU CUT THE TURKEY'S THROAT WITH THE OTHER. GET BACK, THE BIRD WILL FLAP. THUS THE GOGGLES.

She looked up at the thirty or so people on the hill and then back at Angie. "Oh, no."

Angie held her hand, flat and horizontal, to her throat. "Oh, yes."

Anna watched Joe and Dawn, with cookies in hand, trail out the front door of the farmhouse after Angus: Joe, talking to Angus a mile a minute, Dawn, shuffling but from the blush in her cheeks, excited about the impromptu excursion to the sheep pen and the lamas standing guard there. The door banged behind them. She waited until the trio crossed the road before flourishing the print out at Angie and Ray standing with her in Angus's kitchen. She read aloud:

SEVER THE JUGULAR VEIN, TRACHEA AND CAROTID ARTERIES AS YOU PULL THE KNIFE QUICKLY ACROSS THE NECK. SINGE THE BIRD TO REMOVE THE PIN FEATHERS. THIS CAN BE DONE WITH A PROPANE OR BLOW TORCH. CUT THE GLAND OUT UNDER THE ANUS.

She scraped a bench back from the kitchen table and sat down. "I almost took those children up there. Hell, I almost went up there. I even told Joe to write a report about it."

Ray walked to the sink and poured a glass of water. "What did you think was going to happen out here?"

"Silly me," Anna glanced up the hill, "I thought a Community Turkey Day would be lots of people out here," she paused, looking for a term for the way turkeys appeared in the grocery store as opposed to walking about on a farm, "buying turkeys, you know, ready to cook." She waved the printout. "A Community Sever and Singe hadn't occurred to me."

Angie took a seat on the bench opposite Anna. "Maybe—"

"You know," Ray cut in, leaning back against the counter, and staring hard at Anna, "this community, the people who come out here, they think it's important, even if it's only once a year, to look a creature in the face, know that it's dying for you, and then do your own butchering." He raised the glass and took a slow drink.

Anna read from the instructions.

STEP FOUR. CUT BETWEEN THE JOINTS OF THE KNEES TO
REMOVE THE FEET.

"Yeah, right, I'm going to tell my son to do that."

Ray emptied his glass into an aloe by the stove. "Some can, some can't.
Lisa's up there right now. I couldn't be prouder of her." He paused by the
back door to pull on his boots. "You're in a rural world up here. Lots of
people butcher animals, hunt, dress their kill. That's how they live. But you
wait right here, Anna. I'll go get your, you know, ready-to-cook, turkey." He
slammed the door behind him.

Anna pulled the BMW keys from her pocket. "I didn't deserve that."

Angie placed her hand over Anna's. "Don't take Ray too seriously. He does
believe in this, but he's also just so tired. You know how he is; he's got his job,
the Council, Lisa's home. And, just like he tries to help everybody in town,
he comes out to help Angus every Thanksgiving with Ellis and Tim. And now
with Ellis doing community service from the thing at your house—"

"My fault, again."

"No, Ellis got drunk and made a scene. But, since Tim is overseeing Ellis
and with Angus needing more and more help out here, Ray has been kind
of on his own. Why don't I make us some tea?"

Despite the situation, Anna found herself reluctant to leave Angus's
kitchen, a warm mix of maple cabinets and soapstone counters. "Good idea."
She rested her chin in her palm. "It *was* my first slaughter."

While Angie put water on, found tea bags and lemon, Anna studied the
cinnamon glow of the cabinets, foot-wide pine plank flooring, and gleaming
black two-oven Aga. Besides the back door and the door to the hall, a third
door led to what she supposed was Angus's dining room. Unable to resist, she stood and, pushing open the door, glimpsed a veritable greenhouse.
Fluorescent lights, orderly rows of terracotta pots, bright green vegetation.

"Better stay out of there. Angus is mighty fussy about his plants," Angie
called from behind her, "Besides, tea's ready."

Anna let the door swing shut. "Wow, is this place magazine ready or
what?"

Angie let her gaze glide over the kitchen as she walked two mugs to the table. "A real gem. I think his grandfather built it." She paused while Anna slid back onto the bench. "But, topic change, we simply have to have Thanksgiving together. I am so grateful that you've come to Onasego, that you are my new very good friend, and that we have this long, wonderful relationship to look forward to. So!"

Anna looked into Angie's shining eyes. Why hadn't she left ten minutes ago? "Angie, I really don't think we can."

Angie smiled. "I didn't get into the Million Dollar Club by taking no for an answer. Now, if you make yams and brussel sprouts, I'll do a Waldorf salad and rolls."

"Angie, I can't."

Angie must have heard some tone in her voice. She rested an elbow on the table. "Why not?"

"Derek sent Molly inappropriate letters. Letters about worshiping her body, things like that."

A look of pure relief washed over Angie. "Oh, my word, Anna, that's just his tortured poetic wanderer motorcycle bullshit crap. It's not serious. Tell me you didn't say anything about this to anyone."

Anna took a deep breath. "Paul spoke to HR at Catskill in confidence. We had to do something."

Angie slapped the table. "In confidence? In Onasego? Did you ever think you could wait 'til I got back? Talked to me?"

The back door swung open. Ray, with eyes twinkling, carried a large white plastic bag over his shoulder. "I got a column title for you, Anna." He looked between the two women, his good spirits obviously restored. "Okay, here it is. 'Tom the Turkey: Before you eat him, try to meet him.' Hey, what do you think?"

He dropped the bag at Anna's feet.

Anna pulled into Libby's, cut the engine, and tried to make out which direction the sirens were coming from. She waited while Dawn and Joe piled out of the car and into the cabin, now lit against the black, five o'clock night. As she started toward the door, red whirling flashes streamed onto the ridge in the direction of Elk Creek Road. The direction she'd just come from.

Overhead, a helicopter swept the valley. Libby met her at the door, guitar in hand. "What the hell is that about?"

Anna shrugged. "I don't know."

"Want to come in? Have a glass of wine?"

After the Ray and Angie tongue lashings, a glass of wine, or four, was exactly what she wanted. But behind Libby, the interior of the cabin looked much as it had before, a depressing chaos of clutter. And there was no cashmere coat on the rack, much less a William Johnson. Dawn's and Joe's giggles wafted up the stairs. She shook her head. "I'm late already. We stopped by earlier but you weren't here so I took Dawn with us. We've been over at Angus Lynch's picking up our turkey. Then that turned into a sheep and llama tour…" She paused, interrupted by Libby's phone.

Libby lifted the phone then dropped it back in its cradle. "You took Dawn to Angus's?"

Anna nodded. "Such a beautiful place. Just stunning."

"I know," Libby answered. She dropped the guitar on the couch. "Can't believe you took Dawn there. She knows she's not allowed."

"She made me," Dawn yelled.

The phone jangled again. Libby pressed the off button. "Angus is my uncle. The one who threw us out."

Anna leaned against the door frame. "God, I didn't know."

"Seems like Dawn tried to tell you."

The phone rang again. This time Libby snatched it up. "Jesus Christ, what?"

Anna saw her face soften slightly as she listened to the caller. "Right, Mumma, I'll call if I find out anything." Libby held the phone to her chest and stared out the window. "Mumma heard on the radio that there's been an accident on Elk Creek. That's where the ambulances and medivac were going."

Anna thought of all the cars pulled off on the side of the road by Angus's. "I was just there. What happened?"

"Crazy shit," Libby answered, hanging up the phone. "A bull got loose and some guy on a Harley hit him." She shuffled to the staircase without looking back at Anna. "Dawn and I have things to do. It's late; you better go."

## 40 • MOBILE SLAUGHTER HOUSE

ANNA LOCKED THE powder room door behind her, took a crumpled typed sheet from her pants pocket and flattened it against the Vans' Carrara marble vanity.

She reread the page.

> *"Alone in Onasego"*
> *Title (you decide):*
> *"My First Slaughter"*
> *"The Community That Kills Together…"*
> *"Before You Eat Him, Try to Meet Him" (suggested by Councilman Ray Rubino)*

> *Some columns write themselves. Some columns make you plow the lower forty. But rare is the column (like this week's) where the writer's dilemma is an over-abundance of irresistible details just there for the taking. However, if you can imagine a community-get-together turkey slaughter, you can intuit my problem. But if imagination fails, just go to Ask Jeeves (How to Butcher A Turkey) and look it up.*

> *Now, to set the scene, on the Tuesday before Thanksgiving, a clear, sparkling, unseasonably warm day, I drove out of Onasego through some of the most beautiful countryside New York has to offer. My destination was an organic farm where I could pick up a turkey for the family feast. The type of turkey with no head, feet, or feathers and his little drum sticks tied together BUT who had, heretofore, enjoyed a grass fed, free range, upstate, bucolic existence.*

Someone knocked at the door.

"Just a minute," she yelled, scribbling. She had the next sentence.

> *How was I to know that at Community Turkey Day the timing and (pun alert!) execution of "heretofore" would literally be in my hands? And that, Dear Reader, is the (!) meat of this week's missive.*

Anna stuffed the paper and pen back into her pocket, a wave of relief washing over her. It was always the transitional sentences going from the subject to the details that held her up. "All right," she thought to herself, fluffing out her hair in the mirror, then turning the sleek Porcher faucet on and off for sound effects, "party time."

Outside, the hallway was a crush of noise and bodies. It seemed that the whole of Onasego plus Delhi and Walton were at Jamie and Gwen's home for what Anna now knew was an annual Saturday night after Thanksgiving party. And what a home it was. Daisy Buchanan would have adored it.

Situated about three miles out of town on North Street, the house was an early 1900s white clapboard replete with three field stone chimneys, slate patios bordering the entire southern exposure, floor to ceiling beveled windows, seven bedrooms, five baths, a mahogany-paneled foyer, and, of course, the Carrara marble powder room. The stables were somewhere behind the house, hidden from the road. Given a winning power ball ticket, about 20 servants, and her own private oil well, Anna might have been jealous. Otherwise, she wouldn't have had it on a bet.

Tonight, the crowd seemed to have segregated itself with Caroline and her friends on the lower level either playing pool or taking roles in an Improv group led by Peter. On the main floor, the grownups clustered around the fireplaces and buffet tables while the barely and almost grownups huddled about the bar. Lisa, Ray's daughter, was in thumb wrestling mode again, but tonight it looked like for shots. Her father would be along, Lisa said. She also wanted to know, lips quivering slightly, if Anna enjoyed her turkey. The scattering of younger children, Joe being the oldest, were in the home theatre on the second floor watching *Jungle 2 Jungle*. Scanning the house for Paul, Anna's gaze fell on the life-size portrait of Gwen hanging above the landing of the staircase. In the picture, Gwen, in a strapless lavender chiffon gown and diamond chandelier earrings, stood on an open terrace against a starry sky. Her half smile for the painter, and everyone else, was straight on.

"It wasn't my idea." Anna turned to Gwen standing behind her. "Jamie insisted." Tonight Gwen was dressed in black satin pants, a loose fitting gold metallic top with pushed up sleeves, and many bangles. "I guess in this mausoleum, though, it sort of fits." She must have sensed Anna's confusion. "Jamie's grandparents built this house. I hate it. Always have. Whenever

Jamie misbehaves I start packing for my house in Sarasota. It's open, airy, glass everywhere. Oh, there's Phil." She waved to Coxe hanging up his coat. "I should get him a drink. Hope your first Onasego Thanksgiving went well."

"It was…" Anna began but her hostess's departing back didn't require an answer. Her eyes returned to the portrait. It was mixed, she thought, like Gwen. Like, Onasego. First it had been the Community Turkey Day mess with Ray and Angus. Then the screw ups with Angie and Libby. Next, Derek, who everyone was saying was so lucky, with a broken leg and concussion after hitting the bull… and Angie not returning any of her calls. No word from Libby and Dawn either. And, no sightings of William Johnson. But there were good moments too: Joe coming downstairs for the big meal in his Deganawidah costume; Molly condescending to watch a rerun of *Gigi* with her; and Paul, who she spotted now with a Catskill group near an impressive baby grand, contrite, affectionate, even offering to walk Ralphie. She made her way toward him.

"So there you are," he reached an arm around her waist, pulling her into the circle that included Pug, The Niece, a Herbless Deedee, and an Erikaless Tom. "Pug was just telling us to have a very good time tonight because it's all work and no play from here on. Right, Pug?"

Pug, eyes resolute over what looked to be an industrial-sized scotch, nodded. "Next week it's fundraisers in Boston and Philadelphia, then the finance committee session, then the Winter Board meeting, community meetings, then, bam, winter holiday. Not for us but for everybody else."

"And, no Eleuthera for me," The Niece pouted, sticking out her lower lip. "Mean old Pug."

Pug rocked back on his heels, "Mean old Pug is trying to save Catskill, my dear. I think that takes precedence. But maybe if you go play something nice on the piano for us, I'll take you to dinner later on."

The Niece managed a dainty humph but beelined for the piano. Almost immediately the catchy strains of "Cabaret" floated over the conversational hum.

"Things must be dire if you're giving up… Eleuthera," Deedee said, pronouncing the island name with the syllable-by-syllable focus of the clearly intoxicated. "I know how much you like it there." Her ensemble for the night, aqua tunic top, and very skinny caramel leather pants, seemed to

Anna a fortyish "I'm still hot," gesture. "What was the name of that resort? The Winder something?"

Pug tossed down the rest of his drink. "Yeah. Hey, Paul, you set for Boston?" Without waiting for an answer, his eyes swept over to Tom, "How about you, okay for Philly?" Tom, seeming weary, nodded.

Across the room Anna saw Molly and Caroline descend on Jamie, both girls carrying themselves in the careless, self-important way they seemed to have perfected over the fall. The concert with Gwen in Manhattan was coming up in a month; the girls would probably only get more insufferable until then. A cheer rose from the bar as Lisa held her fighting thumb aloft while clutching a bottle of something or other to her chest.

Deedee turned to Tom. "Herb's home with the stomach bug. Where's Erika?"

"Wellesley," he said. "Her sister is there. She's staying on for a week or so."

"Oh," She glanced sideways at Pug, "I didn't know if you two went off to resorts like Pug does."

"Excuse me, got to go speak to Phil," Pug announced, striding away from the group.

"She's drunk," Paul whispered in Anna's ear.

Anna viewed the crowd. "Like about every other person here. We ought to find Joe and get going." The girls were headed their way now. They probably wanted to have a sleepover. She stepped toward them.

Molly, fitted out tonight in a miniscule denim skirt and cardigan, pointed both index fingers at her like little guns. "There's a band at Nora's and we're all going. Everybody else's parents said okay so you have to, too."

She should have known this wouldn't be simple. She looked between the girls. "You're underage. They won't let you in."

Caroline shook her head. "They just stamp you for no alcohol. My dad will tell you it's okay. Yo, Dad!" Caroline beckoned to Jamie, talking to Phil Coxe and Tim. "And see, they're all going." She pointed toward the bar where in fact it looked like the young ones were massing for an exit.

Anna looked at Paul, who shrugged while Tom slid toward the piano and Deedee seemed suddenly fascinated with a loose thread in her sweater.

"What's up, future babe?" Jamie threw an arm around Caroline. Tonight, he had the easy swagger of a successful host.

Caroline wriggled out of her father's arm. "Tell Molly's parents it's okay for us to go to Nora's tonight. That we're not too young. Peter said he'll drive us."

"She's right." Jamie said. "It is an Onasego Thanksgiving tradition. We'll probably head down ourselves so I can pick them up."

Molly hooked her arm through Caroline's. United they stand, Anna thought. She tried to wrap herself around her thirteen-year-old daughter headed to a bar. But, on the other hand, a whole town dance sounded like a lot of fun. "Well, okay." With a whoop, the girls tore out of the room. She looked at Jamie. "What time do you think she'll be home?"

"How about if we play that by ear?" Jamie said looking over at Pug and Phil. "Paul, we've got a question for you. Won't have him but a sec, Anna."

Suddenly, with all the young ones already gone or on their way out, it seemed to Anna the party vibe just died. White-jacketed waiters carrying trays began collecting glasses; The Niece hit the last chords of "Yesterday." Even the little ones were filing down the steps now. Joe, with a couple others, on their stomachs.

Anna turned to Deedee. "We're leaving in a minute. Need a ride?"

Deedee, with head arched back, surveyed the room. "Hard to believe how much some people have."

No way she was getting pulled into that. "Please tell Herb we missed him," Anna chirped brightly. "I hope he feels better."

Deedee's gaze caught on a massive oil of Franklin Mountain. "To never worry. To have trust funds and inheritances."

Anna veered again. "I didn't see Jen tonight. Is she already at Nora's?"

Deedee held herself steady against an armchair. "She's thirteen. I'd never let her near there."

Anna held her hands in front of the heater vent in the car; the car was taking forever to warm up. "Just one sec," Paul had said before loping back up the Van's winding driveway for a last thought to share with Phil, Jamie, and Pug. First Jamie's sec. Now Paul's. Hell, she still had Ralphie to walk.

"Joe, is that seat belt buckled?"

She heard a quick click.

"Hey, Mom," Joe called from the back seat, "what's a masec... tomy?"

Careful, Anna. "An operation. Where'd you hear about that?"

"Those kids."

The driver's side door swung open and Paul stepped in, strapping on his seat belt.

"And, Mom," Joe grabbed the seat back, "kids at that party are swimming in the Polar Plunge. I saw a sign at the Y for it. I want to do it."

Anna looked at Paul. They wouldn't be taking Joe to another party for a long time.

"Oh, honey, you'd have to be such a great swimmer."

"I'm a guppy."

Anna tried to recall the levels. Guppy was an advanced beginner, Minnow an intermediate, a Fish was advanced. Even with Joe taking lessons every day that had to be years away. "Sweetheart, you'd have to be at least a Fish to do something like that." She made a face at Paul. "Right, Paul?"

"For sure, maybe next year." He eased the car into gear and pulled out from the shoulder onto North Street, empty, silent, lit only by the BMW's high beams. Thin flurries floated by.

Anna nestled down into her coat. "All okay with the guys in there?"

Paul nodded. "Everybody's just trying to get ready for the December Board meeting. Jamie's deep into how Tim's land gift will work. Phil's on the cost of technology, and Pug's just trying to keep up with both of them."

"Why Tim's land deal?"

"Not sure. Just know that Jamie is all about land these days."

The entrance to Lebanon Hill Road passed on their left. She glanced right. The blood-red barn she adored was somewhere near here. Paul tapped the brakes at the deer crossing sign, then tapped them harder as the headlights caught a buck trotting across the road ahead. "Just get me home," he said.

"Mom, will that operation make somebody well?"

Who was he talking about? In a few minutes, they would be home. Maybe there was a kid's explanation on line. "Yes, usually it will. But let's talk about that later." The two new spec houses on the ridge right outside the city limits slid by. *The builder got a primo view of the valley*, Tim had pointed out. *Lower taxes, too.* Lights jumped below at the bottom of the hill while gravel kicked up against the undermount as they rounded the bend into Onasego. Our new car, she thought. Porch lights flashed on from a brick rambler beside the road.

"But not always?"

This time Paul stamped on the brakes. "What the hell?" On the opposite side of the road a boxy SUV, smoking from the hood, lay on its side in the gully. Not ten feet beyond that, Ray's Honda sat slightly upended, crushed against a snow-dusted pine.

Anna blew on her tea. Tim, sitting beside her, stared at the waiting room doors. Across the waiting room, still festooned in orange and brown crepe paper for Thanksgiving, Jamie and Gwen huddled with Pug. The Niece, unlikely to get her dinner now, had accepted a ride home with Paul and Joe on their way to pick up Molly and Caroline at Nora's. Most of the others in the waiting room were new faces to her. Friends and family of Ray and Lisa, she thought, as well as friends and family members of the older couple, the Hoopers, pulled from the ditch. Mrs. Hooper, dead. Mr. Hooper, unconscious. Two little boys in tee shirts with 4H logos hurled race cars over the shiny Formica floor, ignoring the occasional shushing of their parents. Grandchildren? As each newcomer staggered in, the same questions were asked, the same little-known facts, answered.

"Lisa? They had to sedate her."

"They think she just lost control going around that curve."

"Nope, no black ice. Some minor roadwork."

"Been in Onasego visiting their son and his family. Had an early dinner, on their way back to Cooperstown."

"She was coming back from a party. Been drinking."

"The poor Hoopers, talk about the wrong place at the wrong time."

"Drunk? Maybe. Somebody said she was on a cell phone with her father."

"Ray heard it?"

"Jesus."

"There he is," Tim murmured as Ray lumbered toward them in his trademark shorts, Woolrich shirt, and incongruously carrying a candy pink clutch bag. For all her life, Anna knew she would never forget seeing him run into the swarm of ambulances, fire trucks, squad cars, and flares, screaming for Lisa.

Tim stood and held out a covered cup of coffee to him. "How's she do-ing?" The Vans and Pug sidled up silently.

Ray ignored the coffee. "She'll be okay."

Tim put his free hand on Ray's shoulder. "That's real good news, buddy."

"The docs say she'd had a lot to drink."

The PA called Dr. Ortega to the OR. Gwen coughed.

"They say a whole lot."

Pug stepped forward into the circle. "Ray, you know how terrible we all feel about what's happened."

Howls of laughter erupted from the boys, the cars now plunging from steel handrails.

Ray stuck the purse under his arm and stared back at Pug. "You should. You should feel damn terrible. My daughter killed a person tonight. She may go to jail." Ray turned, letting his gaze fall on each one in the group. "You were all there. You could have taken her keys, done something."

A young female doctor in green scrubs walked wearily toward the boys and their parents.

"Look, buddy," Tim began, but Ray cut him off.

"No, you look. This is Onasego. We're supposed to take care of each other." He wrenched out from under Tim's hand. "But not one of you took care of my daughter. Not a single one."


## 41 • LONG NIGHTS

ANNA BENT OVER the porch railing and examined the skunk entry. Tracks. The Skunk Skrammer didn't seem to be working. Even though Joe, as a job in his new schedule, had begun regularly sprinkling it around the opening, tiny imprints in the snow were still a common occurence. Maybe she would drive out to the Feed and More tomorrow and investigate other options. A bundle of red branches on the porch next door caught her eye. Whether the branches were supposed to be a sign of deep winter or Christmas she wasn't sure, but they were as ubiquitous in Onasego as the fall's mums and cornstalks.

A salt-stained Jeep pulled into the driveway. Probably someone turning around she thought until the motor shut off and Angus Lynch stepped out with a plastic bag. From the way he was dressed, heavy corduroys, jacket, tie, and a tweed jacket, it appeared farm work was taking a back seat to something else today.

"Hi, Angus," she called. "What brings you here?" She held the door for him to come into the house.

He held up the bag. "Top sirloin. Where's your kitchen?"

She led him through to the back hall and pushed open the door to the kitchen where Joe and Dawn sat at the table decorating Christmas cookies. Libby had called, finally, about a week after Thanksgiving. She was still a little chilly but okay about Dawn having some time with Joe.

"Hey, Mr. Lynch," Joe called.

"Hi, there." Angus set the bag on the counter. "Hello to you too, Dawn."

A smile flickered across Dawn's face. "Hello."

With mostly steady hands, Angus pulled four large packages wrapped in white butcher's paper from the plastic bag. "We need treats on these long winter nights. I know it's psychological but the solstice can't come soon enough." He looked up at Anna. "You do know what that is?"

She tried to do a good wry smile. "Laurel Loomis gave us a lecture on it last week at church. Besides being the longest, darkest night of the year, the winter solstice is a celebration of rebirth because beginning on the twenty-second, the darkness will be a little shorter, the light a little longer. Moreover," Anna dropped her voice mimicking Laurels somber tones, "the tasks for the season are concentration on one's spiritual path and reflection on what had been learned during the dark times. So there, Mr. Lynch."

Angus shrugged. "Sounds time consuming. Hey, what do we have here?" He pulled another, smaller package from the bag and slid it on the table toward Joe and Dawn. "Lookee there. Homemade fudge."

Joe snatched the package to his chest. "Mine!" Dawn giggled behind her hand.

"I'm afraid we can't have your lovely sirloin tonight," Anna said opening the freezer door. "Molly's in New York at a concert and an early Christmas with her dad, and Paul and I have the Catskill holiday party tonight."

"Why can't I eat it?" Joe whined.

She took out two ice trays. "Forget it. Your sitter's bringing Domino's."

Angus looked between Joe and Dawn. "You two having a pizza party?"

Joe licked green icing off his thumb. "Nope. She's got to sing."

"I have a rehearsal," Dawn said, dropping silver sprinkles on a snowman, "Mom, too. For the carol sing."

"That's right, your mother does like to sing," Anna added.

Angus leaned against the counter. "I thought the Catskill Board was in town this week, the big winter meeting everybody's on tenterhooks about."

Anna stacked the frozen vegetables on one side of the freezer. "They're here. They've been closeted since Wednesday afternoon trying to decide what to do about the financial..." she mimicked a teapot, "situation. Pug said there would be some kind of announcement today." She reached for the steak. "What do I owe this to, anyway?"

"The publicity you got me from the article about the Community Turkey Day." Angus tapped the wall phone. "I got people calling the farm from all over."

"I like your farm," Dawn interrupted, holding out a Christmas tree shaped cookie to Angus.

Anna watched Angus take the cookie from Dawn as though it were a ten carat diamond. How in the world could this man have thrown Libby and Dawn out of his house?

"Well, now, thank you, young lady. This looks like a very perfect cookie. Can I take it with me?"

"Mine's better," Joe sniggered.

Dawn stuck her knife in the bowl of frosting and picked up a stocking shape. "I'll make another one."

"And why don't I make us some tea?" Anna closed the refrigerator. She had never seen Dawn proud before.

"Wish I could," Angus said, his gaze fixed on Dawn swirling red icing. "But I've got to get to Cooperstown."

"Can we come back to your farm someday, Uncle Angus?"

Angus glanced at Anna and then back at Dawn. "Honey, that's up to your mother. But you know if she ever says it's okay, you just call me. I'll give you my number."

Reaching for his wallet, Angus pulled out a business card and laid it on the table. "There. Call me anytime. Day or night." He held out his hand for Dawn's second cookie. "Now, I have to be going."

Anna walked him to the front door. "I meant to compliment you on how elegant you look. Big doings in Cooperstown for the longest night?"

Angus reached for the knob. "In a manner of speaking, yes. I'm meeting Ray at the courthouse. Lisa's being arraigned today."

## 42 • A VERY LONG NIGHT

ANNA PUSHED OPEN the heavy glass and steel door to the foyer outside the Great Hall. A few steps away, through another set of glass doors, the low lights and voice of Brenda Lee singing "Rockin' a-*ROUND* the Christmas Tree" signaled the Catskill Christmas party in progress. In the foyer, however, under sharp fluorescent lights, four coat racks sat crammed with enough outer wear to rival an LL Bean outlet the day after Thanksgiving. With the temperature destined for single digits tonight, these northerners knew their limits. And, Anna thought, pulling off her own down coat, scarf, and mittens, and substituting the strappy gold sandals she had brought in a RiteMarket bag for the now fully broken in Clarks, she was no exception.

"Hey, where have you been?" Paul held the door to the Great Hall open with one hand, a drink in the other.

"The sitter was late."

Anna slipped her coat along with the grocery bag onto a wire hanger and, holding back several coats with one hand, shoved her hanger onto the rack. "Plus, Joe thought he might be getting a stomach ache. But he didn't." She turned back to Paul thinking he might comment on her transformation from house frau writer in jeans and mules to the French twist (redone four times), loose fit of the emerald satin sheath from Saks she hadn't been able to get into for two years, and the gaudy but "great looking, you-know-what-me sandals," according to the sales clerk at Payless. Instead, he pointed to the other end of the coat rack.

"You just pushed that coat off."

And there it was. The white cashmere coat from Libby's lying on the floor.

Paul waved her toward the Great Hall. "I'll get that. I have to call Boston, anyway." He pulled his phone from his belt. "People have been asking for you. Especially William Johnson."

Inside the Great Hall, the dance floor was empty. Except for a few takers in the bar and buffet lines, people sat at round tables, bent toward the centers, talking in tight little clutches. Segregated clutches, she noted, like Libby in tee shirt and jeans with the maintenance staff; Angie, sitting in for Derek, she supposed, with the English department; and Tim, Deedee, and Herb, with what looked to be a Friends group. On the stage, Pug, The Niece in a scanty, pointy-toed elf outfit, Phil Coxe, and Jamie, stood behind a stack of gaily wrapped boxes. And everyone, except herself and The Niece, dressed in everyday work attire. If she didn't feel so ridiculous, she could have enjoyed knowing where her next column was coming from. She thought about the white coat back in the foyer. Those pockets might have revealed a lot.

She felt a hand at her back. "Sorry," Paul said, "had to get that out of the way. Let's get you a glass of wine."

Suddenly Anna knew what must be wrong with the party. "Paul, what did the board decide?"

He steered her toward the bar. "They're divided. But Phil Coxe made a strong case for transitioning to an on line school. And I think a lot of the board are with him. So—they'll be feasibility studies, recommendations floated. Then at the spring meeting, the board will vote. Regardless of what they decide though, the school will still need a boatload of cash."

"When did Pug tell everybody?"

"There was a special meeting at five. Chardonnay?" He pointed to the Kendall Jackson for the bartender. "Obviously, the on line concept has huge implications for a lot of the people here. Everybody's in shock."

"So, everyone's still up in the air?"

He handed her the wine. "Yeah."

She tried to make her voice businesslike. "You said William Johnson asked for me."

Paul took another glass for himself. "For some reason he thought you did skydiving or something. Wanted to ask you about it."

She squinted back at Paul, "How odd."

"He's out there. Trying to reassure people, I think."

Then she saw him stooped beside a table from the athletic department. Gray slacks, white open-necked shirt, camel jacket.

The microphone buzzed. People looked up toward the stage at Pug, now in Santa hat and beard.

"Okay, everyone. It's that special time of year when we recognize, drum roll please, service anniversaries. Our elf," he smiled back at The Niece, "has kindly agreed to hand out the small tokens of the college's appreciation. First, let me call up the people getting five-year awards. When these people started at Catskill, Bill Clinton was in office, our tuition was fourteen thousand, three hundred and fifty dollars, and the number one movie of that year was *Jurassic Park*."

Paul whispered in her ear. "Can you believe the timing? College future unknown, but let's do service awards."

As the first names were called Anna looked out over the room at the professors, custodians, nurses, cooks, IT geeks, librarians, clerks, coaches, mothers, and fathers assembled there. Each and every one certainly wondering whether this would be their last Christmas at Catskill College.

Paul reached for her hand. "Let's find a table."

The ten-year people left the stage amid applause. The tuition was down to ten thousand, two hundred. Reagan was finishing out his second term, and the number one movie had been *Rain Man*.

Paul put his glass down. "I have to introduce some people."

"Okay." Anna looked at her watch. Nine-thirty. How many more decades to go? Despite the board decision, or because of it, the crowd appeared engrossed in the reminiscences of Catskill and Onasego: glory soccer days, open dorms, political protests, security chasing an escaped emu through campus, and on and on and on.

"All right," Pug intoned. "The year is now 1978, the President is Jimmy Carter, and the hit movie is *Grease*. The tuition is two thousand nine hundred and seventeen dollars. Will our twenty-year people please come on up?" Anna watched as Angie and Deedee joined a group of about fifteen to mount the stage.

Tim bent beside her chair. "I just heard about Lisa."

"And?"

He stooped down and whispered. "they charged her with second degree vehicular manslaughter, driving while intoxicated, and driving with a blood-alcohol content above point zero eight. She could get seven years. I'm going over to Ray's now."

Anna felt slightly sick. Young, vibrant Lisa. She nodded.

Onstage, Deedee was finishing a story about her first job at Catskill as a residential advisor. "So now, when I see these same people all these years later at alumni events, because they know… what I know… I get the dough." She reached for the clock from The Niece and curtsied against a roar from the audience.

Libby scraped the chair out across from Anna, one hand gripping her cell phone, the other her coat. "Dawn just called from Angus's. She said she got scared being at home alone."

Libby's words had a hard, cutting edge.

"I asked her why she called Angus. She said she saw him at your house and he told her to."

"That's not—"

Libby stuck one arm into her coat and stood. "Thanks, Anna. Thanks so much."

Anna watched as Libby made her way to the kitchen and pushed through the swinging doors. Until that moment Anna would have thought Libby incapable of disgust. Around her, applause broke out for Victor, another twenty-year veteran. Next, somewhat funereally, Pug announced that due to Derek's recent accident, Angie would accept the award on his behalf with the twenty-year folks. Another round of applause, a little less enthusiastic, rippled through the Great Hall. William Johnson sat down beside her.

"You look lovely tonight."

Anna glanced down at the green satin. "Incredibly overdressed."

He shrugged. "I thought you might call, at least to say hello."

Anna kept her gaze on the stage. "That night seems so unreal."

Johnson sat back. "I seem to remember Cointreau, a note at your door. I thought that was real."

She let herself stare at the camel lapels of his jacket. "Hello, William, how are you?"

More applause followed the twenty-year recipients as they stepped down from the stage. Pug continued down the list. "In 1968, Lyndon Johnson was president, our tuition was somewhere around fifteen hundred, and the number one movie was *2001: A Space Odyssey*.

"We only have one thirty-year person tonight. Come on up, Alphonso."

Angie approached the table, wine in hand, her gaze settling squarely on Anna. "Because of that little confidential chat you told me about, Derek is leaving Catskill. Although the school will lose a remarkable teacher and an eminent scholar, I can only assume you're quite pleased with yourself. Merry Christmas."

With the quick little step Anna knew so well, Angie marched back to the English department and sat down. She felt the tears massing.

"What the hell was that about?"

"It's about I can't do anything right up here." She blinked furiously. "Not with my family. Not at Catskill. Not in Onasego."

William pressed his handkerchief into her hand under the table. "Talk to me."

"I can't."

"Why?"

"This whole Onasego thing. It's just too damn much."

Onstage, Alphonso, the archivist, sat in his gift, an oak rocker with Catskill stenciled on the back. Pug used the cue. "Okay, everyone, Alphonso's rocking, we should too." He gestured to the DJ and led The Niece toward the dance floor. Jamie, with a hand on Paul's shoulder, handed him his cell phone. Shannon, the bookstore manager motioned for William to come to her table.

He waved a "one minute," then turned back to Anna. "Look, it is hard up here. I know that." Something in his eyes told her he did know. What had happened to him? "If you can't talk to me, find a therapist. I know a good one."

"No. I'll find one."

"Promise?"

She nodded.

His hand swept across hers. "And if you're ever ready to give us a try, just call."

She watched as William resumed his table chats, his manner low-key, his smile so comforting. She pressed the handkerchief against her cheek.

Onstage, Paul turned away from the crowd for an instant, then with the cell still to his ear, strode down the steps toward her, clicking off the phone just as he reached the table."

"What?"

"That was Gwen on Jamie's phone. Molly called Jed when she got to the city and found out he and Ava are adopting a baby girl from China next fall. She got really upset. Now she's left the concert and they don't know where she is."

## 43 • DR. BADESCU

ANNA STUDIED THE quilts and beeswax candles in the window of the Cottage Boutique on Main Street. At least she hoped she looked like she was studying the quilts and beeswax. In her jacket pocket she held the scrap of paper with the directions to the office of Dr. D. Badescu. The same Dr. Badescu she rejected months ago as a therapist because of her location over a tattoo parlor. The same Dr. Badescu who agreed by email to an early morning appointment today after a somewhat hysterical plea that Anna called in the morning after the Catskill Holiday party. According to the recorded message on Dr. Badescu's phone, she was to enter the door east of U TATTOO, the shop a few doors from the Boutique, come up the steps to the second floor, and the suite would be on the left across from a defunct bookkeeping firm.

Turning, she glanced across the street where Deedee and another woman she'd seen at school meetings stood outside the Java Joint holding takeout coffee containers and chatting. The two exited the coffee shop just as she was about to open the door to Dr. Badescu's building, thus, the flight to her current spot here in front of the beeswax candles. Deedee knew enough about her life. She didn't need to see her walking into a therapist's office much less studying tattoo designs.

Anna turned up the collar on her jacket. A chilly wind had risen in just the few minutes since she dropped Joe with Tim for a meter reading session that Joe could use for his "Where I Live" project. Only twelve hours before she'd been ready to cancel the appointment and might now be enjoying an hour to herself somewhere warm, but then came the call with Molly.

Molly, who showed up back at Gwen's hotel shortly after her run from the concert, and gone on to spend the weekend plus Monday and Tuesday as planned for an early Christmas with her father and Ava. Molly, who she was desperate to talk to. So last night, gathering up her courage, Anna had tried her at Jed's house and been relieved to have her come to the phone, even with a dull "Yeah?" for a greeting. In her most even tone, Anna had said she was looking forward to picking her up at the airport in Albany and loved her very much. Molly's response? "Fuck that shit." What did that even mean? The downtown clock struck eight. With a wave of relief, she saw Deedee kiss her friend goodbye and reenter the Java Joint. Thank God for refills.

Slipping across to Dr. Badescu's door, Anna seized the brass handle and let herself in. Like so many of the downtown stairwells, this one was stained, scarred, and literally dirty beige. Unwilling to touch the handrail, she climbed the short staircase cautiously. Upstairs, turning left on a frayed burgundy runner, she came face to face with the therapist's office. A sign for Susquehanna Accounting pointed in the opposite direction toward a dark, empty glass office. The UU Health clinic, this was not.

Opening the door, Anna found herself in a comfortable but no-nonsense waiting room. A desk, the receptionist's she supposed, was empty, but a sign beside a closed door read, *Please wait to be called.* Taking a seat in one of the two armchairs, she picked up *The Onasegon* from the other chair and reread the headline she'd first seen over coffee two hours earlier. *Councilman Quits: Cites Anger with City.* In an open letter to Onasego, Ray not only quit his job on the Common Council but also removed himself from all civic commitments, current and future. If Onasego hadn't helped his daughter, then why should he help Onasego? His closing sentence: "Folks, it's that simple."

The door to the inner office creaked open and the lady of the lake appeared in the doorway: black pleated trousers, ivory silk blouse, red belt and pumps, conservative gold jewelry.

"Miss Lawson." The voice was as she remembered, low and gravelly. "It's so very nice to see you again."

"Dr. Badescu? Domnica?"

"So you made promises to God, then you felt one of the panels at Catskill was sending you a reminder of that."

Anna nodded over a shredded Kleenex. "Right. Because of what Ellis, the guy I thought would murder me, said. It was like he and the panel were saying the same thing."

"Then you felt you had to come to Onasego. But once you got here, you say everything went… badly."

"No, I said, *to hell.*"

Domnica slid a box of tissues across her desk. "Please, give yourself a moment."

Anna, burrowed into a corner of a chocolate leather sofa, took another handful and mopped her face. Like a programmed sprinkler system, the crying jag erupted within seconds of entering the pale butter walls and lush Persian carpet of Domnica's office. Between sobs she sputtered and whimpered her way through murderers, predators, bullies, the weather, unmarked roads, small town intrigues, and skunks.

"And there's more. People here, they hate me. Think I'm crazy."

The therapist looked relieved. "Let's start there. Who thinks you're crazy? And, why?"

Anna reached for more tissues. "My daughter for one. I think because I'm alive. And according to Paul and my daughter's friend's parents, I'm hysterical and over protective. Even the family therapist I went to about Molly earlier this year said it was about me. That I needed to relax. I wanted to strangle him."

Domnica picked up her tablet. "And the ones that hate you?"

"There's Ellis. He blames me for getting him in trouble with his parole officer. And the woman who asked you to hold the dog at the regatta, that's Libby. She thinks I got her daughter to betray her. Another woman, Angie, a sort of friend, believes I got her husband fired from his job. I'm also one of the people Ray Rubino, the Councilman who is in the paper for quitting today, thinks could have stopped his daughter from getting in that accident. Then there's this other woman, Laurel Loomis. She hates me kind of like my daughter… because I breathe. And she says I'm always running down Onasego."

"Did you do these things?"

Anna looked out the window at the steely, heavy clouds over Franklin Mountain. "There were reasons."

"Maybe they're right then."

She stared back at Domnica. "You're not helping."

"Tell me," Domnica looked up from her notes, "when do you feel good about yourself?"

There was a question. "When the magazine is happy with the column. When I come home and the dog wags his tail. And there's a man," she looked sheepishly at Domnica, "not my husband, who makes me feel..." Anna searched for a way to describe the effect William had on her, "...that I'm fine, just as I am."

"You know... your first therapist was right. It is all about you."

"No, it's *not*!"

Domnica folded her hands on the desk. "It's about you because we can't do anything about those other people now, can we? Our time is getting short. Do you take yourself seriously?"

"Yes! Yes, I do."

"How?"

A few lacey flakes floated by the window. "I just do."

"What about other people? Do you take other people seriously?"

"Yes!"

"How?"

"Like I said, I just do."

Domnica stood. "Your assignment for our next meeting, January fifteenth, same time as today, is to observe how you take people seriously. And that includes you." Leaning over, she kissed Anna on both cheeks. "Merry Christmas. Happy New Year. Our time is up."

For once in her life, Anna was grateful for a Bekins moving van. The gray, corrugated giant in whose ruts she was driving was the tenuous link keeping her on Highway 88 and not in a field by the side of the road. She had heard of whiteouts before; this was her first time to be in one. Beside her in the passenger seat Molly dozed with her Walkman, oblivious to the snow-encased world, the wipers crunching ice with every back-and-forth sweep, the impassable exit ramps, or the mental struggle to tap, not slam, the brakes, as chunks of ice and snow from the eighteen wheeler's caked mud flaps exploded against the BMW's windshield.

"Mom," Molly slipped off the ear buds, "Pull off. Gotta pee."

Anna switched on her caution lights. "Can't. The weather's too bad."

"You want me to pee in the car? Dad would pull off."

Gray slush splattered across the windshield. Anna swore.

"God, you're hysterical."

A spasm seared through Anna's lower back. She hunched over the wheel trying to see. "Shut up, Molly. Just shut the goddamn hell up."

## 44 • O LITTLE TOWN

ANNA MADE A face at the computer screen and the lame attempts at a column there. She swiveled in her chair and gazed around the office hoping for inspiration to bubble up. Instead, she found herself staring at the sayings from Catskill she'd put on her bulletin board in September. They were so poignant, so weighty. By all rights, she should have had a personality change by now. Most of them were also straightforward too, like the one from the book of the Maya:

> The Mark
> you make
> upon the world
> is measured by God.

That kept her up at night. But there was one she could not get, again from the book of the Maya.

> Let there be light
> Let dawn break in the Heaven and the earth
> There will be neither greatness nor glory
> Till the human creature exist the created man.

What in the world would be a created man? Her eyes continued down the bulletin board to her list of to-do's. On the first to-do, TREASURE EVERY MOMENT, she'd give herself about a one out of five. Next, NEVER

DOUBTING, again a one. TAKE MOLLY AND JOE TO CHURCH, her only five. And DO UNTO OTHERS? That would be negative territory. And now this thing about taking people seriously. Yes, people should be taken seriously, but so should snow storms, murderers, old guys preying on young girls, and children getting bullied. And, if she went to her appointment after Christmas, that's what she'd tell Domnica Badescu.

"Mom!"

Joe ran into the study and threw himself onto her lap. "It's time. Come on."

She glanced at her computer screen: four-thirty. The bell-ringing and caroling at the Onasego Arts Center started at five. Another check on the "Where I Live" project. "You're right. I guess your dad and Molly still don't want to go." For most of the afternoon, Paul, Molly, and Joe had camped out in front of the TV watching ice skating. Paul taking advantage of the eve before Christmas Eve break in fundraising, except for a long call from Boston; Molly ignoring her and sulking because the Vans were en route to a ranch in Texas; and Joe just thrilled to have his father and sister around.

She, on the other hand, blew the afternoon trying to come up with a funny angle on wearing exactly the wrong clothes to the Christmas party—and failed. Like her titles. "Fashion Flub in O'town—Dressing Up." "Upstate Holiday Style—Reward Offered." Terrible. Horrible.

"And Mom, I saw the skunk run under the garage. I think Ralphie scared him."

Damn. She would have to leave a message for Ellis again. At least this time she had done every last thing he had told her including multiple applications of Skunk Skrammer.

"That skunk is tough. But," she hugged Joe, "so are we. Go get your coat and boots."

From her seat beside Joe on the fifth pew back from the front, Anna decided the Arts Center, a former Congregationalist Church, was nothing short of majestic. The place was all about height, with walls four or five stories high, a second-story choir loft, second-story lecterns. She massaged a pinch in her neck. Joe, craning straight up, might be crippled for life.

And the place was packed. Not only was the Children's Bell Corp performing but also the Onasego Girls Choir and the Onasego Choral Society.

Following those performances there would be a community carol sing, followed by a soloist performing, "O Holy Night," and the final entry that read simply *Messiah, Handel*. An organ piece, she assumed. With any luck, she and Joe could slip out after the bell ringing.

She felt a tap on her shoulder. The large man beside her in a royal blue New York Giants sweatshirt and jeans, pointed to the end of the pew where Mrs. Wimbish, her head covered in a bright paisley scarf pulled snug around her scalp line, stood waving. So there the reason was for Joe's question, also for the wig from the day of the meeting at school. A wig she chalked up to vanity. The woman was teaching right through chemotherapy. Jesus.

Anna nodded and punched Joe who proudly waved back. His night was made. She looked behind her at the entrance where ushers were placing folding chairs in the aisle to accommodate the steady stream still pushing in from the outside. So many of the faces seemed vaguely familiar. Had she seen them at RiteMarket? Downtown? In the middle-school parking lot? Then there were the people she knew: Angie sitting near the back; Ellis and Tim two rows ahead; Ray, alone, across the aisle; Pug and The Niece on the front row with Alphonso the archivist; and Deedee and Herb in line. Even though she had Joe's warm body pressed up next to her, she felt oddly alone.

Mrs. Wimbish continued to the front where the bell ringers sat in the first three rows dressed in black pants, white shirts, red bow ties, and white gloves. At her signal, a slight upward motion with an open palm, they stood in a group and with surprisingly little giggling or snickering, took their places around a table set with two rows of gleaming brass bells. At her next signal, gloved hands reached for each brass bell. The lights dimmed.

Anna looked at her watch. 6:00 o'clock. At the front of the church, the black and white outfitted ensemble of bell ringers, choir girls, and Onasego Chorale Society members, bowed first by order of appearance and then as one, as they had performed the last selection, "Go Tell It on the Mountain." The flourishy *Go tell it on the mountain that Je-e-sus Chri-ist is born!* was the rousing, perfect ending to an unexpectedly professional program by the one hundred or more performers. And, if she was mightily impressed, Joe had sat mesmerized for the hour, particularly after Anna pointed out Libby and Dawn with the Chorale Society on the top riser in the soprano section.

Anna could guess what his next great idea was going to be. Maybe she could get him in the bell ringers.

The first bars of "Joy to the World" filled the hall while, at Mrs. Wimbish's cue, the bell ringers filed back into their seats followed by the girls' choir. Around her, everyone held song sheets. Where had they come from, and how had she missed getting one? Alphonso rose and walked to the lectern holding up a baton and a songbook. Joe poked her, "Mom!" She shrugged helplessly. Another tap. The Giants' fan passed her his copy.

Four verses later, on the second *and wonders of his love*, Ray struggled past the family at the end of his pew and raced out of the building.

⚶

*We hear the Christmas angels*
*The great glad tidings tell*
*O come to us, abide with us,*
*Our Lord Emmanuel.*

Anna, glancing down at Joe, closed the song book after the last verse of "O Little Town of Bethlehem." Midway through the carol a column idea hit her, something about being in Onasego that gave much new meaning to phrases like *the silent stars go by* and *yet in thy dark streets shineth*. A stretch maybe, but doable. She looked down at her watch. Six-twenty. Would Paul even think about starting dinner? The soloist was next. Then Handel. Could she be anymore astonished? Beside her Joe chatted with his new friend, Mr. Giant.

After giving the audience a very few minutes to take their seats and settle down, Alphonso tapped the microphone. "That was nice singing everyone. Quite impressive." He reached for a violin from The Niece. "And now for a very special part of our program," he looked over his shoulder at the Choral Society, "I have the great honor of introducing our soloist. As many of you know, she is a mezzo soprano who combines faultless technique with God-given talent. Ladies and Gentlemen, it is with immense pleasure that I give you a true Onasego treasure, Miss Libby Holmes, performing 'O Holy Night.'" Joe looked up at Anna in confusion. She fidgeted for his hand. Libby's CD. Never, not even for an instant, did she consider playing it.

Once again, the lights dimmed and the church became silent. Members of the Choral Society shuffled apart, creating a path for Libby to descend the risers and join Alphonso at the microphone. While Alphonso's bow slid through the introductory chords, Libby gazed about the sanctuary, smiling softly. Then in slow, crystalline tones she filled all four stories of the Onasego Arts Center with the soaring, shimmering account of a night divine.

Six thirty pm. Once again, Alphonso, holding up a stack of sheet music, called for quiet. Then in a hearty, happy voice he announced that tradition would continue this year and welcomed any of the audience who would like to join the Choral Society for the "Hallelujah Chorus" to please come forward. At once, a wave of men, women, children, parts of families, whole families, gay couples, elderly, and one teenager in a wheelchair, at least a third of the crowd it seemed to Anna, left their seats to stand in front of the risers. And, Mr. Giant, taking Joe by the hand, led him to the front as well.

## 45 • MERRY CHRISTMAS

ANNA CUPPED HER hands over her cheeks while she waited on the sidewalk for Libby and Dawn. She didn't have a clue what she would say to Libby, but she had to say something. Light snow was falling and, according to the clock on the bike shop next door, the temperature was nineteen degrees. The stream of carolers plunging from the light and warmth of the Arts Center into the frigid, black night had thinned considerably, the heavy wooden doors opening and closing intermittently for stragglers. A few feet away, Joe, hands on hips, stood deep in conversation with his new friend, Bruce. So far she'd heard Joe say something about Deganawidah, Ralphie, and home schooling. For his part, Bruce seemed to nod a lot.

The doors opened again. Dawn stepped out first, laughing with her hand over her mouth, and Libby following right behind. Anna heard her shout something about a triple-decker chili burger. Both wore calf-length puffy pink down coats and moon boots. Anna met them on the sidewalk.

"What a lovely performance. Libby, your solo was magnificent."

Libby's ebullience vanished. She pulled up her hood. "Great."

"Really, what a gift."

"Really?"

Dawn pulled on her mother's arm. "I want Joe to come to The Pantry too."

Libby looked over at Joe in conversation with Bruce. "He can if he wants to. And if his mother says it's okay."

His mother. Anna pulled out her wallet from her pocket and took out a ten-dollar bill. "He'll want to. Thanks."

Anna and Libby watched while Dawn marched over to Joe and tapped his shoulder. Joe, in predictable form, tried to high five her while Dawn, also in predictable form, stood rigidly clutching her purse. Bruce smacked Joe's hand instead, waved goodbye, and walked toward the parking lot.

Anna made one last attempt. "I'm very, very serious, Libby. You were wonderful tonight."

Libby looked back at the church door where Pug and The Niece were helping Alphonso down the stairs, then back at Anna. "I tried."

Anna watched from the sidewalk as Joe duck-walked and Dawn strode beside Libby, shapeless in the pink coat, toward the Windstar parked across Aspen Street at the strip-mall there. Later, she knew, Joe would be dropped off quietly, sans escort. The bike shop temp flashed fifteen degrees. Without Joe's running commentary, the cold walk home would be colder. But that was all right. She could use every step to hate herself with no diversions. She pulled the backup mittens from her coat pocket, tugged them over her gloves, and started up Aspen, waving at Joe before he climbed into the Windstar. Besides Libby's van, two pickups and a black Suburban sat parked in a row, all three idling beneath the floodlights in front of a closed Block Buster, CVS, and Onasego Wine and Liquors. A block further on, Aspen became residential, the blackness dotted by occasional Christmas decorations, the blue glow of TVs, and curtained house lights. She walked slowly. It was the terrible day after the All Paths concert and her grotesque fight with Molly that Libby had handed her the CD. The time Pop told her to watch after her son. She felt tears beginning but willed them away. No crying. Crying might make her feel better. Her job right now was to feel profound self-disgust, shame, to feel loathsome.

An engine purred behind her. The black Suburban pulled up to the curb; the driver waved. She stared straight ahead, picking up her pace. Libby offered her a cup of tea that she'd turned down, lying about having to go to the dentist. A big lie that caused her to miss a chance to talk with William Johnson. The light on Green Street blinked from red to green, she crossed the street but then cut left, leaving the Suburban at the light. Why had it never occurred to her to listen to Libby's CD?

Steps tapped on the sidewalk behind her. Why had she never invited Libby to dinner? In for a glass of wine? To take a seat on the porch? She knew why. Because Libby was sort of shapeless and frumpy. Because she wore a uniform. Because she was a janitor. The footsteps grew closer. She walked faster. The Green Street Market was only a couple of blocks up; she would duck in there. Suddenly the footsteps were right behind her. She could feel the presence of another body, a hand on her sleeve. She whirled around. "Angie!"

The realtor grabbed both her shoulders. "Derek shouldn't have written those letters." Angie paused trying to catch her breath. "It's just that for the longest time he's been in this midlife crisis crap. You know how some men are. And the wreck's done something to him. He's like a child."

Anna looked away; the light had turned. She hated Derek for those letters. As far as she was concerned, the wreck with the bull had been pure poetic justice. "What do you mean he's like a child? Wasn't it just a concussion?"

Angie backed off a step. "That's what the doctors thought. But something else is happening. He's at the hospital for tests." She pulled a Kleenex out of her pocket. "God, the things I said to you, and I called myself a friend."

Anna hesitated. Angie looked as wretched as she, Anna, felt. "You are a friend. But, what's with this, 'you know how some men are'? Were you waiting for the thing with Derek to just go away?"

Angie gazed up at the snowflakes swirling through the streetlight's halo, then at Anna. "Isn't that what you're doing with Paul? Waiting it out?"

"Waiting what out?"

The Suburban pulled up beside them. Ric Anunzio slid across the seat and let the window down. He held out Anna's wallet. "I think you dropped this back near the Arts Center."

Anna ripped off her mittens and felt in the coat pocket. Air where the bulky mittens and wallet had all been crammed together. She reached for the wallet. "Mr. Anunzio, I am so embarrassed. Thank you so much."

The window started back up. "Think nothing of it. Merry Christmas."

Anna waited for Mr. Anunzio to pull away before turning back to Angie. "Waiting out what?"

Angie sighed. "I really am your friend. Paul has been everywhere with Erika, mostly in Boston, but around here too. Everyone knows. Everyone thought you did too."

A few hours later, Anna said goodnight to her family and closed the door to her office. Tomorrow would be all about Christmas Eve, cooking, last-minute present wrapping, *Miracle on Thirty-Fourth Street*, church, late-night stocking stuffing. But just now, she had two very important personal objectives to accomplish. First, she slipped Libby's CD in her computer and waited until a scratchy but pure "God Bless the Child" filled the room. Next she opened the desk drawer, pulled out the swizzle stick and business card from New York, and dialed the phone number. A recorded greeting clicked on immediately. *Merry Christmas. I'm away skiing for a few days. Please leave a message.* She waited for the beep. "Hello, William, Merry Christmas. Please call."

## 46 • I SEE

DOMNICA LOOKED UP from her notes. "Now, I want to ask about your little assignment, about how you take others, and yourself, seriously." Today the therapist had on camel pants and an aubergine cowl-necked sweater. The jewelry was beaten silver bangles.

Anna held a cappuccino from the Java Joint to her lips. Getting dragged by wild dogs to Unadilla would be preferable to discussing her little assignment. So far she had talked about the plans for handling Joe's home schooling situation, Molly and the A team theory, and Paul, but only that he was traveling a great deal. Nothing about Erika. And nothing about the call to William. The call thus far unanswered.

"I didn't interfere with your holidays, I hope," Domnica continued.

Anna took a sip. Christmas Day had passed uneventfully. No tirades from Molly, no marathon phone calls from "Boston," and no stomach aches from Joe. *And* the snow shoes she bought everyone had been a huge hit. In the days after, however, Molly returned all too quickly to fighting mode, and Paul, after a quick kiss for all, escaped for a frantic round of fundraising in the Philadelphia area... he said. She hadn't taken him on about Angie's news. There were the holidays to think about... and, of course, this was not the first time. For New Year's Molly partied at Caroline's, Paul stayed over in Philadelphia... he said, and she and Joe watched *The Black Stallion* parts one and two, after Joe passed his Minnow test, swimming the length of the pool, technically becoming a Fish, and one level away from the Polar Plunge. Adding to the discomfort was his swimming instructor on the subject: "Couldn't be safer. Hundreds of eyes on him."

"No, my Christmas was fine. I hope yours was."

"Quite nice. A few days in Vermont." She tapped the desk with her pen. "So, any observations?"

"My daughter asked me to stop the car in the middle of a whiteout so she could go to the bathroom and I told her to shut the goddamn hell up. I guess that wasn't taking her seriously."

"Would it have been dangerous to stop?"

"I thought so."

"Then you did just fine. Anything else?"

Anna looked out at the wooly blanket of sky. Forecasts called for six inches before midnight and another six to eight before daybreak. Though this would be her first major storm, there was a silver lining... the Friends meeting scheduled for tomorrow night would have to be cancelled. "Remember the Libby person I told you about? Well, she told me she was working at her music, but I entirely blew her off. She even gave me a CD I never listened to. Now I find out she's a very talented singer."

"Why didn't you listen to the CD?"

Anna rocked forward on the couch. Ruthless honesty... a pledge to herself. "I think because she's a janitor. And she doesn't look like a singer."

"I see."

Either there was a prick in that "I see," or her accent made it seem so.

"Is this one of the people," Domnica looked at her notes, "that thinks you are crazy or hates you?"

"Yes, but for another reason."

"What is that?"

Anna sighed. "Somehow I've gotten in the middle of something between Libby and her uncle. I don't really understand it at all."

"Have you tried to ask her about it?"

"Well, she's not really a friend. It's more like her daughter is a friend of my son."

"Is she not your friend because she's a janitor?"

Anna nodded. "Probably."

"Hmmm." Domnica paused and scribbled a note. "Have you ever talked to her about being a janitor?"

"No."

"Why not?"

"Because I assume no one would want to talk about having to be a janitor."

In an elegant gesture Anna now knew meant, "you think so, huh?" Domnica tilted her face ever so slightly to the side. "I would take care with assumptions. Furthermore, I suggest you find out what you're in the middle of with Libby and her uncle." She pointed her pen at Anna, "Now, the second part of your assignment, did you see anything about yourself since we talked last?"

"Wasn't the Libby thing enough to have to see?"

Domnica snapped Anna's file closed with a low, throaty laugh. "Oh, my dear, no. Not nearly at all. Continue with this... yes?"

## 47 • FRIENDS

ANNA GLANCED DOWN at her phone. No messages. With a sigh, she stepped out of the elevator onto the second floor mezzanine of the student center. Being dinnertime, the hall outside the commons was filled with students going in and coming out as well as huddling in small groups, no doubt planning their evenings. She gave a quick wave to the two students she shared the elevator with. Between them they used the word "like" eleven times in the one-floor journey. And that was after she started counting.

Next to the bathrooms. That's where the Founders Lounge, her destination, was supposed to be. She stepped around a trio with hockey sticks toward the restroom sign and, like death and taxes, her eyes met Laurel Loomis's as the latter taped newsprint to a swinging door.

"Miss Lawson, you remembered. How good of you. Give me just one moment."

Pulling a blue magic marker from her pocket, Laurel Loomis scrawled *Reserved—Friends of Catskill College—January 16, 6-8 pm.* After a second's perusal of her work, she stepped back to the door and converted the dots over the i's in Friends and Meeting to snowflakes. "Much better. Now," she held the door for Anna, "you may assume your duties."

Remembering her CALM training, Anna took a deep breath. That afternoon, after finding out the meeting really was on, despite six inches of snow, she held a confidence-building session with herself. Three empowering mental notes resulted. One: All she really had to do was be an observant and dispassionate recorder. Two: If she could write for *Manhattan Living,* she could take minutes for the Friends of Catskill College. Three: This was not her first time taking minutes. As secretary to the powwow at Camp Yonahlossee she took minutes lots of times, albeit mostly about trash patrol and snack shack hours. She pulled off her hat and gloves and followed Laurel Loomis through the door.

Not two steps inside, the Christmas party atmosphere hit her all over again. Heavy and funereal. Deedee, uncharacteristically dressed in navy sweats, and Ellis, probably dragged to the meeting by Tim, hovered beside a counter with coffee and cookies while maybe two dozen faces sat bunched listlessly around folding tables. At the front of the room, Tim stared out at the night through a side window. The Niece, the lone energetic vibe, sat in an armchair filing a fingernail.

Anna was surprised. Twenty people max, a far cry from the hundred or more at the opening cocktail party. And it wasn't the weather keeping people away. To give the city of Onasego its due, the streets were completely clear. At five that morning, the plows had revved up and kept on right through the day. With more snow forecasted for tonight, she had, on a whim, called the city, gotten the Deb person again, and asked if she could interview somebody on one of the crews. After putting Anna on hold for ten minutes, the answer came back as a yes, for noon on the fourth, weather permitting. Anna got off the phone, psyched. Something like "In Praise of the Plow" would be a good blue-collar contrast to her last column, "Alone in a Party Dress," detailing her sartorial screw-up at the Catskill Christmas bash.

"Okay, everybody," Tim turned from the window, the good soldier back on the job, "let's get started."

Anna slipped off her coat and bag and took a seat at a table near the back. Ellis, with a cup of coffee and a napkin of cookies, sat down beside her.

"So you still got that skunk."

She looked over at him. Cookie crumbs lined the ever present sneer. She hadn't seen him since the day in her front yard. "The Skunk Skrammer didn't work. And I used a lot."

Ellis stacked his cookies one by one, like poker chips. "Poor, poor, Alma."

This was one of the people who hated her. She had to do something. "The day you brought the cage, the thing with the police was a misunderstanding."

"Maybe for you."

"Look, I'm sorry."

"Remember, ten feet, real accurate."

"Ellis, I really am very, very sorry."

Ellis ran an index finger down his cheek, tear like, then topped the tower with an Oreo. Giving up, she rummaged through her bag for a tablet and pen.

"First off," Tim began, but then paused as the door swung open and a lone male student walked in. He waited for him to gather cookies and take a seat. "Okay, starting tonight, Anna Lawson," he pointed at Anna, "will take over minutes from Laurel. Thank you, Laurel, and welcome, Anna."

Anna smiled earnestly and made her first entry. *opening-Tim,

Tim continued. "Before we get into OLD BUSINESS, Denise has asked to say a word from Pug."

With an enthusiastic smile The Niece stowed her file and scampered to the podium. "Hello everyone, Dr. Wenley wanted me to tell you he appreciates the support of the Friends now more than ever. Finally, he wants you to know that you will be fully informed throughout any decision-making process. Thank you."

Anna half expected her to curtsey before heading back to her seat. Was speaker for Pug a new job duty?

Tim stepped back in front of the podium. "Onto Old Business. The only item I have is that nobody's volunteered for the Catskill fundraiser in April, the Forget Me Not."

Angie's hand shot up. "Forget it. We have to talk about Catskill and the on line school mess. I think we need a protest."

"Angie, that's new business."

A small, balding man sprang up, "Motion to skip old business. Second?"

"Second," an insurance guy Anna recognized yelled from one of the tables.

Tim leaned heavily, Anna thought wearily, on the podium. "Okay. So the board is trying to figure the best way out Catskill's financial problems. One idea is to make Catskill into an on line school for distance learning. But a lot of people's jobs would be affected, also Onasego's economy."

A heavy-set man in a Catskill fleece spoke up. "That's bullshit. We want a real college, real kids, real teams. Maybe we *should* protest."

"Yes, we want a real college," a nurse from UU Health shot back. "But I'd rather have an on line Catskill with some jobs than no Catskill at all."

Angie, with the fire in the belly look she usually saved for Cuba, interrupted. "I heard the Chairman of the Board say he's convinced distance learning is the future."

From the corner of her eye, Anna saw Laurel Loomis watching her.

A petite elderly woman held up her hand. "I don't even know what a distance learning school is."

"Hey, talk to *us*!"

Anna looked across the room to the couch where the student had settled. It was the same kid, Jason, who'd gone on at length at the cocktail party about students' contributions to Onasego's economy. "On line schools are cra…"

At *cra…* her pen ran out. She shook the pen and tried again. More white space. Digging into her purse, she prayed for a spare. At the front of the room, Tim pulled out a chair and sat down. She couldn't even begin to imagine how tired someone who walked all day for a living would have to be. And on days like today, through snow.

"Look," he said, "sure, we want Catskill to stay like it is. But the fact is the school's in trouble. These guys on the board, we gotta trust them; that they'll do the best they can for everybody."

Two pens rolled onto the table in front of Anna. She looked up at Ellis, who pointed across the room. At Laurel.

"Trust them to work things out the best for whom exactly?"

Anna looked up from her scrawls to see Deedee rise from her seat. She had seen Deedee in hyper mode, in soccer-mom mode, in sycophantic-employee mode, and drunk. This was the first time seeing Deedee cornered.

"Why should we trust them? Whether Catskill goes on line or closes altogether, the board won't suffer. Neither will the top guys at the school. They can just walk away, get great severance deals. It's us, the natives, who'll watch the shops close, take minimum wage jobs, have our children move away."

All around the room, people nodded in agreement, some reaching for their coats.

"What about the captain of the ship?" Angie said. "You think Pug would walk away?"

"Why don't you should ask," Deedee pointed to The Niece, "*her.*"

The Niece glared back at Deedee. "Pug loves Catskill. He loves Onasego. He wouldn't leave." Rising to the occasion, she looked around the room. "And it's not true that you don't have any influence. As Pug has said on many occasions, he sleeps so much better knowing the Friends are behind the college."

Deedee, with perfect timing, waited for the oratorical beat to pass. "And you would know."

Against a stunned hush, The Niece grabbed her coat from the back of the chair and stamped toward the door, pausing for a second to flick a quick glance back at Deedee. "*Et tu?*"

Comprehension flashed through Anna's brain. With the delicate wrist of a concert pianist, she lifted her pen into the air. That exchange would not make it into the minutes. Twenty minutes later, despite Tim's pleas for more discussion and trust in the board, the meeting adjourned. Actually it didn't adjourn so much as people just started leaving. Sadly, silently and, most of all, it seemed to Anna, hopelessly.

## 48 • EPIPHANY

DIRTY WHITE, THAT was the color of Onasego the next day. Dirty white sky, dirty white ground, dirty white cars coated in a mix of snow and salt. And if dirty white was the color, then the brawny roar of snow blowers up and down Summit Avenue was the sound. The snow blower was an Ayn Rand-type tool Anna had decided: grinding, pulsating, chewing, and spitting its way down sidewalks, driveways, and parking lots. A tool everyone in Onasego seemed to own except her.

Leaning against the handle of her snow shovel, she surveyed the broad, flat swath of virgin snow blanketing the driveway. At least five more inches fell between the time she'd gotten home from the Friends meeting the night before and lunchtime today, when the snow dwindled off to flurries. And it wasn't five inches of puffy, powdery snow but heavy, wet, and backbreaking. The kind of snow a guy should have to get rid of. Like Paul, still in Boston, not due back until her birthday, almost two weeks away. To be fair, Joe and Molly helped with the sidewalks, a little, before taking off for the pleasures of a snow day: Molly to the movie with Caroline and Joe to meet Dawn at the library and write a report for his project. So now, after finishing the sidewalks, she was alone with her own little piece of Siberia and a plastic shovel to clear it with before the temperatures started to fall again and the whole thing became one huge sheet of ice.

The phone buzzed from her slacks pocket underneath her snow pants underneath her knee-length down coat. Plunging the snow shovel in a drift, she pulled off her mittens and dug through the layers of clothes. She glanced at the display. William Johnson. At last. "Hi."

"Hello. I'm returning your call." His voice exuded all the warmth of a debt collector.

"Give me a minute to get inside." Holding the phone to her chest, she took the porch stairs two at a time, yanked open the door, and with the side of her foot, barred Ralphie from bolting outside. She sank into the couch.

"I'm back now. Where are you?" The words came out in broken patches. "Where... are... you?"

"At the office. I assume you want to talk about the condo for your friend." Anna could hear desk drawers opening and closing, papers rustling.

"What condo?"

"I've told her all I can do is make referrals to our realtors. Maybe you can get her to quit calling me."

"Who?"

"I've got to say you've surprised me, Anna. I never thought you'd use our relationship this way."

"What are you talking about?"

"Your friend. Ava Arnaut Oliphant. She's driving me crazy."

"Your ex-husband's wife? I got back from skiing and I bet she'd left a hundred messages here. All saying she's a friend of yours and I needed to call her."

Anna struggled to get out of her coat. "I know nothing about this condo thing. She recognized your name on the envelope I brought from Paul that day, but that was it. I am so sorry. She's kind of a bulldog."

A long pause followed with muted office sounds in the background. She tried to envision William in his office surrounded by whatever real estate magnates were surrounded by, but all she could bring to mind was how he had looked on the road that first day.

"So why did you want me to call?"

"Because of what you said at the Christmas party."

She waited. And waited. Then.

"You mean about giving us a try?"

Anna kicked off her boots. "Yeah."

"Why now?"

She decided against details. "Let's just say there's no reason not to. And I want to."

"Hold on, let me close the door."

She closed her eyes and curled up in the corner of the couch. She heard a door click.

"Then why don't you come down here for a few days so we can do that?"

The warm, molasses William feeling shot through her. "Getting away isn't so easy."

"You work for *Manhattan Living*. How hard could it be for you to think up an excuse?"

She sighed. "It wouldn't be hard except for the dog, the teenager, and the highly energetic, home-schooled little boy."

Silence.

"William, are you still there?"

"Your children do have a father."

Anna smiled to herself. And their father has a mistress. Maybe Erika could babysit. "You know as well as I do that he's pretty engaged right now."

A siren wailed from somewhere in New York City. "So, how about Albany? I've got to be up there on February tenth. We could meet somewhere near the airport. Spend the afternoon together."

The molasses was sinking lower.

The doorbell screech sliced through the house. Ralphie, snarling and growling, charged the door. Anna stood and saw Ellis peering in through the glass panel at her. "Ellis's at the door. I have to call you back."

"Wait, what about Albany? Will you come?"

She waved at Ellis. "Of course I will."

"Ellis, come in."

Ellis flicked his cigarette butt into the snow. "You still got that skunk. Tracks all over."

Anna stepped back from the door. She got off the phone with William for this? "I know that. Remember?"

"I'm gonna get him."

Now that was news. She stepped back from the door, waving him in. "Please, all the heat's leaving the house."

With a trapped look all his own, Ellis stepped over the threshold. Today, his one concession to the cold was a stained, red and black wool shirt over the customary black jeans and tee shirt.

"Come in the living room. Have a seat."

Ellis crossed his arms over his chest instead. "I said, I'll get him."

"That's great, but why? You weren't in a mood to help last night."

Ellis squinted at her. "People change their minds. All right? And no calling the cops while I'm around, not for nothing. One tiny thing and my ass'll be back in jail."

Ralphie's sudden whine filled the front hall followed by clomping boots on the porch stairs, then the front door swinging open with a rush of cold air. Joe came in first, his eyes wide with hurt or confusion, Anna wasn't sure. Behind Joe, Angus, with Dawn pressed against his coat, sobbing, shuffled into the foyer. Angus's gaze fell heavily on Ellis.

Anna grabbed Joe's shoulders. "What?"

Joe looked back at Dawn. "Pops."

She bent to look him in the face. "Pops, like have a blessed day, Pops?"

Joe nodded. "And free ice cream, Pops."

"Jesus Christ!" Ellis's face curled in disbelief. "You let them kids near Pops… alone?"

A car door slammed and Libby raced into the house. "What happened?"

Anna tried to keep her voice steady. "I don't know. They just got here. Something about Pops."

Angus looked over Dawn's head to Libby. "I was making a delivery on Main Street and found them running down the sidewalk."

Ellis slouched against the door frame to the foyer, "Don't you people know nothing?"

Libby stooped in front of Dawn. "Tell me, Dawnie. What happened?"

Dawn turned sideways to face Libby. "I didn't steal anything!"

"Who said," Libby began, but Dawn burrowed her face back in Angus's coat.

Everyone turned to Joe. Anna unzipped his jacket. "Joe, honey, you were supposed to be at the library. How come you went to Pops?"

Joe blinked back tears, his lips quivering. "I went to the library. But then I wanted a Choco Taco."

Anna pulled back the hood on Joe's parka and smoothed his hair. "So you walked from the library to Pops. What happened next?"

"Pops was outside doing something. I asked if we could have some free ice cream. He said sure." Joe paused while Anna eased his coat off. "But he said we had to go in one at a time so if a car came the other one could tell them just to wait a minute. So I went first. There weren't any Choco Tacos but I got a Nutty Buddy."

Anna glanced at Libby. "Then what?"

"I went outside and Dawn went in. It took a long time, and I was getting cold. Then a car came. So I went to get Pops, but nobody was there. I yelled, 'Pops, there's a car!'" Then Dawn came running out from behind this door. She was crying. She said we had to run. So we ran out of Pops and up Main Street."

Ellis slapped the wall with the flat of his hand. "You don't never go to Pops. Never!" He yanked the front door open and stamped out, the door slamming behind him.

Libby held her hand to her chest, then to Dawn.

"Dawnie, I think we should go upstairs. Just you and me for a little while. We'll put some warm water on your face. Talk a little more. Maybe Anna will make us some hot chocolate."

Anna forced herself to smile. "Sure, I will. Why don't you go in my bedroom? First one on the left. Fresh towels in the linen closet."

Reluctantly, it seemed to Anna, Dawn let go of Angus and took Libby's hand, letting her mother lead her out of the room and up the stairs. Once Anna heard the bedroom door shut, she turned back to Joe. 'You okay, JoJo?"

Joe grabbed his belly. "Mama, what's happening?"

Anna pointed to the couch. "I'm not sure. Pops upset Dawn. You go lie down for a minute while I make the hot chocolate. Mr. Lynch will sit with you."

Angus looked out toward Summit. "I should find Ellis."

"You can't leave *now*." Anna gestured upstairs.

"I'm just afraid that boy'll do something real stupid."

Anna glanced toward Joe sprawled out on the couch. "Tell me what's going on. From the moment Pops' name was mentioned, Ellis just went crazy. Why?"

"I guess no one told you." Angus pulled off his coat. "Pops is Ellis's father."

An hour later, Libby pulled out a chair at the kitchen table where Anna and Angus sat drinking coffee. From the living room, the familiar staccato sound track signaled the beginning of an old *I LOVE LUCY* episode for Joe and Dawn, underneath blankets on the couch.

"They all set in there?" Anna asked.

"Yeah. I called Mama Nells's for a pizza." Libby looked at Angus. "Why are you still here?"

"Because I asked him to," Anna broke in. "I thought we might need another adult. Now, how about some coffee for you, or maybe a big glass of wine?"

Libby managed a faint smile. "I wish, but I need a real clear head right now. Just coffee. Black."

Anna stood up and reached for a mug. "Is Dawn... okay?"

"I think so," Libby shrugged, "she wanted to watch TV with Joe."

Anna poured coffee for Libby, refilled her own cup and Angus's, and sat back down. From the living room, Ricky shouted that Lucy had some 'splaining' to do.

Angus folded his hands over the table. The tremors looked to Anna to have worsened steadily since Dawn's, Joe's and Angus's arrival. "So what did Pops do?"

Libby gazed down at the table, running her fingers along the edge. "He called her into his office. Said he wanted to hug her because she had been good. Then," Libby paused, her voice breaking, "then the bastard tried to feel her up. When she told him to stop, he said if she didn't let him he'd tell everybody she was stealing ice cream. Next he tried for her pants. That's when Joe screamed." She looked up at Anna and Angus. "Thank God for Joe."

Angus glanced toward Anna's wall phone. "I'm calling the police right now."

"No," Libby pushed up the sleeves of her Catskill sweatshirt and picked up the coffee, "you're not. Dawn went hysterical when I brought the police up. She'll talk to Mumma. That's it. Period."

Angus hunched forward over the table. "For God's sake, Libby, you can't leave somebody like Pops out on the street."

Libby shot Angus a look of pure hatred. "Not your call. And don't even think about going to the police on your own."

"She's my niece."

"She's my daughter."

"So show some responsibility."

"So shut the fuck up."

Listening to the two of them go at it Anna knew she was hearing some well-rehearsed lines. She interrupted. "But Libby, if you don't go to the authorities, Pops might try it with some other young girl."

Libby set the coffee down hard, splashing it across the table. "Both of you listen. I won't make Dawnie talk to anyone she doesn't want to. Besides, it's not like everybody in town doesn't know how horrible Pops is."

Anna grabbed a dish towel and handed it to Libby. "I didn't know one thing about Pops. I thought he was this sweet old guy who counted his blessings every day."

"Right," Angus said, dropping his hands to his lap. "A sweet old guy who'd have a few and beat his wife unconscious."

"What about Ellis?"

"Same."

Anna tried to picture Ellis as a kid beside Pops. "Why didn't somebody go to the authorities?"

Angus shrugged. "Neither Ellis or his mother ever pressed charges. So he just got away with it. And now," he let his gaze travel over to Libby, "you're going to let him get away again?"

Libby looked over her shoulder toward the living room and Joe's and Dawn's raucous giggles and then back at Angus. "Right. And don't you dare forget it."

## 49 • IMBOLC / GROUNDHOG DAY

ANNA PUSHED OPEN the heavy wooden door to La Taverna. Although the temperature outside hovered at fourteen, the crowded foyer was toasty warm with low lights, many candles, soft violin music, and walls painted Tuscan yellow. Between many episodes of calming Joe after the Pops debacle, and day-in day-out life with Molly, plus endless snow, she was desperate for at least an hour AWAY. And it was her birthday.

"Hi. Lawson for two at eight."

The receptionist, Janine, a fashionable twenty something, scanned her list. "Lawson, here you are. Will the other party be joining you soon?"

None of your business was what Anna wanted to say. She was still fuming from Paul's call over lunch. A Boston-area donor, yeah, right, just had to see him early tomorrow morning. How about if they did her birthday dinner on Sunday instead of tonight? "How about because it's not my birthday," was her prim response, followed by, "You think sitters grow on trees?" Then she hung up on him.

"No. My husband was detained out of town. I'll be eating alone."

Janine looked around the dining room and then back at the line. "I need to ask a really big favor. Tonight is scaloppini night and we're mobbed. Since you're alone could I seat you at the bar or with one of our other singles?"

Anna felt a reach out and strangle somebody moment coming on. First Paul. Now, Janine. Goddammit, it was her birthday. She looked into the bar. Not so crowded but in one corner, hunkered over cocktails were Pug, Phil Coxe on a cell phone staring right at her, and Jamie in what appeared to be a weighty, principals-only conversation. She gave a tiny wave in their direction. No way she wanted any part of that. "Okay. But not the bar, I'll share a table."

Janine beamed, delighted, beckoning Anna through the main dining room and past two smaller party spaces. The receptionist paused outside a small alcove. "Here we are. One of our best spots. Ms. Loomis always requests it."

And there she was. Laurel Loomis studying a menu at a table for two in front of a tiled fireplace. Three other small tables nestled together for what looked like a family birthday at the far end of the room. Janine placed a menu at the vacant seat. "Thank you again. *Buon appetito!*"

Laurel's gaze drifted up to Anna. "Ah, Ms. Lawson. My goodness, we're seeing a lot of each other. Were you stood up also?"

Anna pulled out the chair and envisioned her bulletin board. Treasure every moment. Never doubting. And now, take yourself seriously.

"My husband was caught in Boston. You?"

Laurel nodded. "My friend fell ill, such a shame it being Imbolc and all. Did you get my email? The one with the Friends 'distribution list?'"

Anna sighed. It might be scaloppini night, but the first course would be crow. The night before, Tim called asking for the minutes. My minutes? she asked. According to Tim, even with the way the meeting ended, the minutes still needed to be written up formally and distributed. Enter Laurel's list, preceded by a groveling plea from Anna. "I did, thank you. Hard to send out the minutes when you don't know where to send them."

"Quite hard."

The waiter, a long, thin college student Anna guessed, breezed in to the alcove. "I'm Ken. What can I get you ladies to drink?"

Laurel closed her menu. "Pellegrino."

Quite hard, indeed. "Scotch. A double."

Tonight, Laurel looked all wise womany with a severe gray bun, long black dress, and the ever-present pentacle. Not for the first time Anna considered the fact that the woman across from her was a self-identified witch. Dinner was a ways off and they had to talk about something. "So Imbolc... at church you said it was a time when our path becomes more fixed, seeds begin to stir. I'm curious, Laurel. How did you get involved with Wicca?"

"Oh, probably the lure of newts' eyes and frogs' toes, Miss Lawson."

"Anna, please. And I'd really like to know. Really."

A faraway look came over Laurel's face. "My father was a corporate executive, a company called CDG,"

"CDG?" Anna fluffed out her napkin. "That's who the head of the Catskill Board works for."

"Miss Lawson, do you want to hear this story or not?"

"Sorry."

Laurel returned to her reverie. "Father was a workaholic type who left family matters to mother, and despite my many efforts, that included me. As we moved every year or two for his job, I had many nannies and very few friends. But in the summers, so my parents could travel together, I was sent to this idyllic, pastoral spot." She paused for Ken to set two napkins, the scotch, Pellegrino, and a dish of peanuts on the table. He looked over the table at the two closed menus.

"Guess you'll need another minute."

Anna took a sip of the scotch. Her mind was already going for a column: "One Woman's Way to Wicca."

Laurel relaxed back in her chair. "I looked so forward to those summers. That's when it started."

Anna pushed the peanuts toward Laurel. "Were you staying with a Wicca group?"

"Heavens, no. We didn't know the word."

"Who then? Relatives? Family friends?"

Laurel's fingers strayed up to the pentacle. "No, Mother sent me to a girl's camp. A gorgeous spot," her fingers twined around the cord, "in North Carolina."

Impossibility tapped Anna on the shoulder. "I went to a girl's camp in North Carolina."

"Really?" Laurel dropped the pentacle and reached for her menu. "That young man will be back soon. We should probably decide." She held up the page of specials. "My camp was in the mountains. It had all the usual camp-type activities, an incredible staff, plus it was wonderfully ecumenical."

Anna gripped her scotch with two hands. There were hundreds of camps in the North Carolina mountains. "Mine, too."

Laurel ran her finger down the entrees. "Dairy is recommended for Imbolc and I've heard the cheese cannelloni is very good here. I think I'll have that." She peered over the top of the menu at Anna, a half smile lighting her face. "My camp had the loveliest name, from an Indian term."

Anna closed her eyes. Every camp she'd ever heard of had an Indian name except one Paul went to named for a section of Newark. "Tonawanda?" she murmured hopefully, the camp Barbara attended.

"No," Laurel squeezed a lemon slice into her Pellegrino, "I remember now, it was from the Tuscaroran. It meant trail of …"

Anna knew when she was beaten. She held her hand to her chest in the camp gesture used to bring quiet to the powwow. "Trail of the bear. Camp Yonahlossee."

"You went to Yonahlossee?" Laurel's air of disbelief reminded Anna of the day she read Walt Disney was afraid of mice. Impossible! No way! Was not!

"From age eight to eighteen."

"Ladies, what's your pleasure?" Anna and Laurel looked up at Ken, all business with pen and tablet in hand.

Anna considered the very odd situation she was in and the very small amount of scotch in her glass. "Wine."

Ken tapped the tablet with his pen. "Any specifics?"

"House red."

Laurel pushed the peanuts and Pellegrino aside. "Make it two."

Ken eyed them warily. "And dinner?"

Laurel glared back. "Later." She folded her hands on the table. "Truly, Ms. Lawson, I'm astonished. We are two people who can barely tolerate one another, and now we discover a much valued mutual heritage. Whatever are we to do?"

Anna threw back the last of the scotch. Domnica would be in pig heaven with this story. "Maybe, for starters, we should dial back the bare toleration part… at least for a while. Concentrate on the mutual heritage."

"I suppose that's reasonable," Laurel said. "You begin."

Anna decided to stick with Laurel as witch. "OKAY, the Yonahlossee Wicca connection. How did that work?"

"How could it not?" Laurel said, her hand once again clutched around the pentacle. "Every day hiking around those mountains, sleeping underneath the stars, mucking out the stables, it was all there, the sacredness and wisdom of nature, the interconnectedness behind all things. Surely camp gave you those impressions too?"

Not quite, Anna thought. Her impressions had run more to the delight of short sheeting someone… over and over again; fooling around on a sunfish for entire afternoons; and smacking a tennis ball so hard you could hurt somebody. And then there was the lightness and power she felt each day at camp being away from Sybil. "My impressions were not quite so lofty."

"Do you know why it closed?"

"Liability protection. Insurance rates sky rocketed, drove it out of existence."

"I think we call that extinction, Ms. Lawson. Akin to what might happen at Catskill."

Anna didn't say anything. Paul, probably screwing Erika about now, wouldn't want her to. But she had a question. "Were you ever able to get your father's attention?"

"I'm not one for idle sentiment, Ms. Lawson. Why do you ask?"

"Because my daughter wants to live with my ex-husband. But, like your father, he's quite driven, also remarried, expecting a baby, and doesn't want her there."

Laurel glanced at the fire, then at Anna. "I say let her try. If he's like most fathers, he'll end up adoring her, a good thing before other men come along."

Anna recalled the scene of Jed and Molly in the hotel lobby. "But this father—"

"If," Laurel interrupted, "he's cold to her then you'll be there. I didn't have anyone to do that for me and it took many years to understand this was my father's problem, not mine."

Anna nodded thinking about her mother. Camp had given her the first inkling that, like Laurel, the problem wasn't hers. Glasses clinked behind her. Ken, with corkscrew and cradling a Ruffino Chianti Clasico, approached the table.

"Mr. Coxe, in the bar, wishes you a very happy birthday."

Laurel gaped, "Your birthday? On Imbolc?"

Anna nodded. Imbolc had kind of a ring to it, certainly better than Groundhog Day. But why was Phil Coxe sending wine? It took her a moment to put the pieces together. Paul must not be screwing Erika tonight, at least not yet. He was probably the one Phil Coxe was on the phone with. Phil Coxe would have mentioned seeing her in the restaurant and Paul would have brought up her birthday. Small town. Damn small town.

"Thank him for me."

After Ken filled each glass about a third, Laurel raised hers in a toast. "Many happy returns, Ms. Lawson. And to the path ahead."

Anna checked to see that no one from the birthday party was watching. She tilted her glass and whispered, "To the path ahead."

Beneath Ken's grass-is-greener gaze into the larger dining room, the two women clinked glasses. He licked the tip of his pencil taking a stand. "Might you ladies be ready for dinner… *now?*"

A revised title for the column suddenly occurred to Anna: "From Arts and Crafts to Witchcraft: One Woman's Way to Wicca." Awkward but maybe. "Yes. Two cheese cannellonis please."


By the time Anna got the babysitter home, heard a long account from Joe about Ellis capturing the skunk in a Have A Heart cage, and pried details from Molly about her plans for a skiing trip with the Vans the next day, it was eleven p.m., the thermometer by the kitchen door read five degrees, and she still needed to get Ralphie around the block. Whisking her "seriously cold who cares what I look like coat, hat, and muffler" from their hook, she snapped Ralphie's leash on and stepped out into biting air and flurries falling from a black velvet sky. After a first breath, she pulled the muffler up over her nose and mouth and set off down Summit.

While Ralphie sniffed assorted pee-mails, Anna considered Laurel's advice about Molly. "Let her try." But try how? How could narcissistic, unpleasant teenage Molly wrangle her way into Jed and Ava's obsessive-compulsive routine of work, gym, and social circuit? And then there would be the blessed arrival in the fall. Molly had no idea of the immediate dominance of babies. Maybe she should take the path of least resistance and assume they all deserved each other.

Rounding the corner at Summit and Branch, Anna pulled the muffler back up over her nose and paused, struck by the snowflakes caught on the sleeve of her coat. She could see the points. All the points. Looking up through the street lights the flurries turned from lacy white particulates to showers of diamonds streaming lightly down to earth. The extreme cold was keeping the flakes intact. With each street light, the drifting diamond shower replayed over and over again. Reaching home, she felt like Newton getting bumped on the head.

She'd gotten her nightgown on when the first siren shrieked down Summit. Two more quickly followed. By the time she had her teeth brushed, sirens seemed to be traveling from all over the city. Creeping through Joe's room she pulled the curtains open to black sky and flurries toward North Street. It was when she looked west out the guest room windows that she could see the flames and smoke billowing high above the tree line between Catskill and Main Street.

"Wow, cool." Molly in PJs and Walkman joined her at the window.

"That is not cool. It may be some family's house. Or a student house."

Her daughter shrugged.

Anna felt the tears starting. "This isn't you. I know this isn't you. We need to talk…"

With a wry, half grin, Molly adjusted her headphones, turned, and swept out of the room.

## 50 • MORE PLEASURES, MORE PROBLEMS

"I'VE GOT ONE."

Joe leaped up from his seat, his hand in the air, while Anna glanced nervously around the sanctuary at all the familiar characters plus many more. Maybe cabin fever was at play, as the church was packed this Sunday, or maybe the special talk on THE ETHICALITY OF EATING was just too tantalizing to pass up. All the way to church Joe had babbled about how he had a really cool idea, while carrying a RiteMarket bag. This must be it.

Joe turned to face the crowd. "I passed my Fish test at the Y."

Polite applause rippled across the room. Hands shot back up. Anna gasped. "And SO," Joe broke in over the clapping, "My mom said if I passed the test I could do the Polar Plunge Jump."

She grabbed the boy around the shoulders. "When?"

Joe grinned impishly at her then turned back to the congregation. "Okay, guys, to be in the Polar Plunge I have to collect money. So today I'm starting the Jump With Joe Fund." He held up the RiteMarket bag. "Into the water I'll dash, if you give me some cash. You'll be a real honey, if you give me some money… at coffee hour." When he sat down, it was to yet another round of applause. Anna could have cried at the forbearance of the All Paths.

She leaned over and whispered in his ear. "You've got some splainin' to do."

Angie rose next. "I have a sort of pleasure and a big problem. My sort of pleasure is that the doctors think a stroke after the accident caused Derek's problems, not something worse like a tumor. For the problem, I don't know how many of you have heard but there was a big fire at Pops Exxon last night."

A reflexive buzz swept over the room. Anna looked back at Dawn and Libby sitting near the entrance. Dawn sat, wide eyed, her hands covering her mouth; Libby seemed equally shocked.

"The police think a skunk may have started it. Some wires near the ice cream stand had definitely been chewed and earlier that same night Ellis Utt and Angus Lynch caught a skunk right outside a broken window at the station."

Joe's eyes grew huge as he looked up at Anna. "Ellis's got TWO skunks now."

Angie shifted her weight. "So the concern is this. While we are grateful to Ellis and Angus for catching the skunk," she paused to let the congregation take that in, "unfortunately they were both totally stoned at the time. The police searched Angus's home, found the medicinal garden in the dining room, and confiscated it all. So the upshot of this is that Angus may go to jail for distribution, and since Ellis broke parole, he'll have to finish up his term and maybe some extra."

"What about Pops?"

"He was at home passed out when the police went to find him. Seems he has no insurance, so he won't be rebuilding."

A companionable quiet fell over the church, then pockets of low clapping. How did everyone know about Pops except her? Was there an insiders' guide to small towns somewhere?

Deedee, in jeans, hoody, and worst of all to Anna, bed head, rose next. "I have a problem," she said flatly. "As everyone in town knows, Catskill is in financial trouble and the board is supposedly deciding whether to remake the school into a distance learning school or leave it as it is. My concern is that the decision has already been made to go for distance learning. First, a consortium headed by Jamie Van has offered two million dollars to Catskill for property donated to the school for a sustainability center." Deedee shot a nervous glance at Tim before continuing. "The offer is contingent on Catskill going on line and the land would be used for a state-of-the-art baseball camp. Last night, the offer was taken under consideration by the board as a means of *sustaining* Catskill through its financial problems. Second, the board chair, Phil Coxe, actually asked what an on line school would do with it, anyway?"

"They can't sell it!" Tim shouted. "That land's not for a goddamn baseball field!"

Silence fell over the sanctuary. No squirming, no rustling, no nervous coughs. No sound at all until the scrape of a metal chair from the rear of the congregation where Dawn stood, clutching her purse, tears running down her cheeks, and Libby staring hard at the floor. The words as always came out in Dawn's halting way. "I... love... my... Uncle... Angus. He... can't... go... to... jail."

## 51 • PAUL

"Hi, you guys." Paul held the front door open for Anna and Joe. "I've missed you."

Anna swept past Paul, determined to avoid any obligatory welcome home affection. Joe, on the other hand, threw himself at his father, wrapping his arms around his waist. "Dad!"

Paul swooped the boy up and onto his shoulders. "How's the big D doing?"

Anna gave Paul a long look. "You should be glad he remembers you."

Paul gazed up at Joe. "Could Mommy be angry at Daddy?"

Joe seemed genuinely confused. "I don't think so. Dad, I started the Jump With Joe Fund at church and people gave me lots of money."

Paul knocked Joe's sneakers together. "I thought I was the fundraiser in the family. What's the Jump With Joe Fund about?"

"The Polar Plunge!"

Paul lowered Joe to the floor. "I'm sorry, Joe, I don't know what you're talking about."

Anna took off her coat and waited for Joe to hand her his. "Hard to keep up when you're not here and too busy to call." She opened the front closet door. "Joe, why don't you go work on a thank you note to the people who donated to your fund. I'll explain everything to your dad."

"Okay," Joe said, picking up the RiteMarket bag and heading for the stairs. "Dad, can we do something this afternoon?"

Paul scratched his head. "You mean before I take you out for any kind of ice cream you want?" The look of pure joy that came over Joe's face made Anna want to cry. Joe ran back to Paul, hugged him furiously again, and then tore up the steps screaming "YES!" They heard his footsteps on the hall overhead and the mighty clunk when he jumped on his bed. Without Joe to bridge the divide, Anna found herself in a wary face-off with Paul. He looked strained.

Paul blinked first. "Where's Molly?"

"With the Vans. Skiing." She turned toward the kitchen. "I should start lunch."

"I'll help." Paul pulled the kitchen door open for her, pausing while she took in the florist's box tied in red ribbon on the table. "Sorry about the birthday date. Maybe we could all go out to eat somewhere tonight. I've got to head back to Boston tomorrow."

And there it was. Paul's charm offensive. She slipped the ribbon off and opened the box to see lillies lying against lavender tissue paper. Lillies. The flowers he brought on their first date.

"Thanks," she murmured. "But I think we better pass on tonight. Molly has a test tomorrow." She took a china vase of Sybil's from the dish cabinet while Paul pulled a beer from the refrigerator.

"So, what's this thing Joe's doing?"

She ran cold water for the flowers. "Jumping through the ice into Spruce Lake. Remember, the fundraiser for sick kids? We told him he could do it if he passed the Fish test. Seems he passed the test. I don't know how to get out of this. Plus, he needs a service project for school."

Paul arched an eyebrow. "Is it safe?"

Anna raised an eyebrow right back and set the vase on the table. "His swimming instructor says it's completely safe. But, if you're really worried, you could always do it with him."

He peeled back the aluminum tab, settling that topic. "What else has been going on?"

"A lot," she answered, opening the refrigerator and studying the possibilities. Deciding on sandwiches, she reached for mayo, lettuce, and leftover chicken, and began carving. "Pops tried to molest Dawn, then a skunk-induced electrical fire burned down his gas station, the Friends of Catskill have probably gone defunct, Ellis and Angus got caught with drugs, and Laurel Loomis went to Yonahlossee. But," she paused and pointed the knife at him, "the big news, somehow Deedee found out, is that Catskill's Board is considering selling Tim's land to Jamie for twice what it's worth. And, oh yeah, Jamie's offer is only good if the college goes on line. But you already know about that, don't you?"

Paul leaned back against the counter. "Pug sent Deedee a tape of a conference call to write up. He wanted a feel for the community blowback and knew she'd leak it. The board will take a formal vote at the May meeting."

"Tim thinks it can't be sold. Because it was given for a sustainability center."

"It's an asset of the college at a critical time. And fundraising is not going all that well."

"Is it already decided?"

"The math is pretty convincing. Why so interested?"

"Because it's a big deal for this little town if Catskill converts to distance learning." She took a tomato from the windowsill, slicing it alongside the pile of chicken. "What about you? For or against?"

"Me?" Paul set his beer down. "I'm for whatever the board tells me. Right now we need this job; you know that."

She twisted open the mayonnaise jar. What she knew was that Paul was back for one afternoon, offering lillies and ice cream. That her son was thrilled. And that despite any lillies she was meeting William one week from today in Albany. "I don't know if we're even still a 'we.'"

Before she could stop him, his arms wound around her waist. "Of course we are."

## 52 • SYBIL

"So, ANNA, MAKE me understand, your husband has affair after affair and yet you do not confront him? You must be furious." Domnica squinted at the windows and stood. "Is it because of that other man who makes you feel good?"

Anna watched as the therapist walked over to the windows and fiddled with the blinds. In light of the current situation with Paul, today seemed like a good day to get into the whole Paul and his affairs conversation. Past and present.

"I don't get furious. Even very mad. I don't know why. But, it's not because of the other man." She suddenly felt flushed. The other man, Albany, just three more days.

Domnica clamped the cords on the blinds and sat back down. "Do you get upset?"

Anna studied the ceiling. "Molly can get to me in a second."

"What do you do when that happens?"

"I take the dog out A LOT," Anna said hoping the emphasis on "a lot" might inject a bit of humor. But Domnica wasn't buying.

"When you were little, did you get mad?"

When she was little... home with Sybil and Barbara. Daddy away on business. "Domnica, I was too scared to be mad when I was little. I feel kind of stupid about it now, but that's the way it was."

Domnica tapped her pencil against the desk. "Explain."

The picture of herself and Barbara as Indian princesses came to Anna's mind. "My mother was complicated. She could be great, unbelievable Halloween costumes, lessons, all that. But she always told me how stupid I was, and I believed her. But the main thing was these rages she'd get. It was just like wham! Fury coming right at you."

Tap. Tap. "Describe one of these rages."

Anna sat back in her chair; there were so many Sybil rage stories. "When I was six, we moved to a new town. On the first day of school, I got lost walking home. I think Mother must have been following me in the car to see if I knew the way. Anyway, she drove up beside me and just went nuts."

"And another?"

Anna thought for a second, then remembered one that had come to mind recently while she was cooking dinner for Molly and Joe. "One night, probably in fourth or fifth grade, I was carrying my plate with a hamburger to the table and somehow the hamburger slid onto the floor. Mother locked herself in the bathroom after that one. I didn't see her again 'til the next day."

"And why in the world," Domnica paused for a second then let her gaze fall on Anna, "do you now think it was stupid of you to have been afraid of these rages?"

Anna took a deep breath. She really hadn't figured this out until her thirties. "Because, at some point after she died, I realized that was *all* she did... go into these rages, scream and yell, and then close herself in some room. I was never abused or hit or punished or any of those things. So see, she was sort of right... I was stupid, I couldn't figure that out. But my sister Barbara did. She'd give it right back."

"What would your mother do when Barbara would, as you say, give it right back?"

Anna could see her eight-year-old self peering around the corner from the hall into the living room where her mother sat in the armchair in a nightgown, head down, sobbing, beseeching Anna's father to *do something* about Barbara. She remembered feeling shocked and kind of disgusted that her mother would switch to this helpless female act. But then she saw it was for real.

"That was the thing. When someone did give it back, she'd turn all weepy and pathetic."

No taps, just a gentle prod. "And?"

"Well, that would be scary too."

Domnica set her notes aside. "Why?"

Anna remembered the morning after that fight: Sybil in her long navy robe with red piping, pressed against Barbara's closed bedroom door, whimpering and begging Barbara to come down for breakfast.

"Because... she was so easily broken."

Later, standing in the deli line at RiteMarket for some cold cuts she could offer the plow guy the next day, Anna replayed the end of the session with Domnica. The Lady of the Lake came out swinging.

"As a child you believed that you were not only stupid but also that you could, unpredictably, enrage your mother or emasculate her. I am right, yes?"

Anna nodded.

"Then, with those fears, you sought safety and stepped back from feelings and action. Right again, yes?"

Anna blinked. She'd have to think about that one.

"So," Domnica rose, came around the desk, and took a seat on the couch, "feel sorry for your mother and her psychological agony. Feel sorry for yourself as a little girl." Her eyes bore into Anna. "But take confidence from your forty-four years, your knowledge, wisdom, and ability to gain more. And, for God's sake, take yourself seriously!"

"What about Paul?" she heard herself ask in a tremulous voice.

"Paul! My dear, have you heard nothing?"

## 53 • THE PLOW GUY

AT THE JANGLE, Anna peered down at the caller ID. Eleven forty-five a.m. Fifteen minutes until the plow guy's arrival. Why was Onasego Middle School calling? "Hello."

"Mom, it's me, I'm on the school phone. Caroline wants to sleep over tonight. Her dad's not coming back from Texas 'til late and her mom's having a bridge party. I told her it's fine. Okay?"

As usual, no "hi" or "hello" or any other basic telephone politeness. "Aren't you supposed to be in English right now?"

"We've got a sub. She's clueless. Look, Caroline can stay over, right?"

What fun. An evening with Molly's and Caroline's self importance. But it was the weekend. "Do you two have plans?"

"Mom, do you remember nothing? Like party, or Peter's new CD, perhaps?"

Peter's new CD. Actually she did have a vague memory of Molly mentioning something about a CD titled *MY LOVE* after the song from the slam. He'd probably make a fortune selling it at one of the middle school girls' games. "Where and when?"

She heard muffled back-and-forth discussion. "The church. Eight to eleven."

There had been a time not so long ago when Anna looked forward to Friday nights. A family movie, pizza. No prolonged negotiations. No sparring. No slashes to the gut. "Ten o'clock. I go to bed at eleven."

Molly's response, a disgusted, "Mom!" was so pro forma Anna could have said it for her.

"Take it or leave it."

"Trying to talk tough, Mom?"

Anna checked the impulse to hang up. "You know what? Let me think about it. We'll talk later. I've got an interview now."

"No!"

"Seriously, got to go. Talk to you later."

And that was that, another ambush by Molly and Caroline. Feeling weary she hung up the phone and yelled a pre-lunch alert up to Joe. Their agreement was that he could listen in on the interview with the plow guy as part of the "Where I Live" project. The only rule was that he had to be absolutely quiet. She surveyed her lunch preparations. The cold cuts from RiteMarket were already out on a platter, chips in a bowl, and various sodas in the fridge. Maybe if the interview went well, he would take her on a shift with him.

Joe, in full Deganawidah regalia of blanket and headdress, dragged in from the hall and leaned against the frame of the kitchen door. Anna took in the narrowed eyes, pursed lips, and generally brooding nature of the pint-sized pontiff. "What's up, Big D?"

"You know the letter we got this morning from the Polar Plunge?"

Anna nodded.

"Well, it says there are two new teams, Dive With Daniel and Cannonball With Casey." Joe kicked the shoe molding. "Now, Daniel and Casey have teams. It's not fair. It was my idea."

Anna rummaged among the table linens for three matching mats, a lovely thought cropping up. "Honey, why don't you just skip the Polar Plunge if you're not happy about what those boys are doing. Just hand in your money."

Joe glared at her. "No way, Mom."

She shrugged. At least she'd given it a shot "Well, the truth is that ideas, especially good ideas, get used by other people all the time."

"Stolen!" Joe yelped and pushed the construction paper band back from his forehead. "When's that guy coming, anyway?"

Anna checked the clock on the microwave. Eleven fifty-five. "He should be here any minute. Why don't you set the table for the three of us? Okay?"

He eyed her stonily. "Okay."

"Bruce!" Joe shrieked.

Anna held the door for Ralphie to come in from the backyard. By the time she got to the front hall, the plow guy was inside and taking off his boots. Joe, with one hand over his mouth, pointed at the back of the plow guy with the other.

Anna glanced between her son and the plow guy. "Joe?" She lifted Joe's hand from his mouth.

Joe looked up at her, stupefied. "It's Bruce! Don't you remember? He took me up front at the church to sing that hallelujah song."

"Yeah," the plow guy added in a distinct Long Island accent.

It took Anna a moment to put together that the plow guy filling the front hall was Mr. Giant from the bell-ringing/carol sing. That night she'd simply seen a large man in a Giants' sweatshirt. Now she saw a roly-polyish, mid-forties guy, completely bald, with twinkling eyes and a goofy grin. Not exactly the tough, gritty type she was expecting.

"Forgive me." She stuck out her hand. "Anna Lawson."

Bruce's handshake was two-handed and firm. "Bruce O'Malley."

"Thanks for coming by. I have some lunch for us while we talk."

"Supa." Bruce studied Joe's costume. "Might you be that Indian you told me about, Little Buddy?"

Joe looked up at Anna. "Mom?"

Anna quickly explained her deal with Joe for the interview to Bruce. Then she turned to Joe. "How about you and Bruce talk after our interview. I'll try to save some time."

Joe placed his hand back over his mouth and nodded.

Hanging his coat on the front peg, Bruce followed Anna and Joe to the kitchen table where Joe pointed to a chair for Bruce. The phone blared again.

"Please help yourself to lunch," Anna said glancing at the ID, not at all surprised to see Onasego Middle School again. She pressed the message button. "What can I get you to drink? Coffee? A soda?"

"Coffee, I think." Bruce pulled out the chair and peered up at Anna. "So, why write about plow drivers?"

Anna leaned back against the kitchen counter. "Keeping the roads plowed is such an essential service. But as a job, it must be so hard. I'm thinking a lot of people might be interested in reading about that."

Joe, eyes darting between the two of them, wrapped a pickle in turkey.

"Why a hard job?" Bruce, unscrewing the top from the mustard bottle, shot Joe a disbelieving look.

Anna turned back to the sink to fill the coffee carafe. "I'm thinking about things like dangerous driving conditions, bitter cold, the dark. And I would think the work must get really monotonous."

"What does mono... mean?" Joe began.

Anna held her hand over her mouth.

Bruce spread the mustard on a slice of rye bread with slow measured strokes, then rested the knife at the rim of the platter. He gazed up at her. "You got it all wrong." The *all* becoming a thick Long Island *awl*. "I got the best job in the world."

## 54 • THE BEST JOB IN THE WORLD

"OKAY." ANNA SAT down at the table with her legal pad. "Let's back up. How did you start driving a plow?"

"I used to drink," Bruce said, spearing a slice of cheese followed by two slices of roast beef, "a lot." He winked at Joe. "Not good, little buddy. So one night I was up here visiting and crashed my car. My best friend in the car with me almost died. But, for some reason, the judge who got the case took pity on me. No time, just probation, rehab, and community service. In my case, driving a plow."

Great angle, Anna thought, jotting down notes. Wreck leads to community service leads to career. "Is that why you say it's the best job in the world, because you liked driving the plow?"

"Hated it. Got some salt? Maybe a little pepper?"

Anna put the tablet down and retrieved the salt and pepper from the stove. Bruce took lettuce leaves and laid them gently across the bread covered with mustard. Joe, watching carefully, quickly spread mustard on a slice of bread before reaching for some lettuce of his own.

"Just moving snow from here to there over and over," Bruce said, sprinkling salt and pepper over the lettuce, "but, I came around."

Anna watched as he handed the salt and pepper to Joe, then cut the cheese and beef into long strips, alternating them in slow layers over the lettuce, while Joe followed along. "What happened?"

Bruce gazed at his creation. "Horse radish?"

Horse radish? Anna shook her head, then pushed back her chair as the phone rang again. "Excuse me, just one moment."

Bruce shrugged as she rose for the phone. "It's okay, hard to get good horse radish, anyway."

She lifted the receiver.

"Mom, Caroline has to know now."

"I'm in an interview. Goodbye." Anna hung up and turned back to Bruce in the process of cutting a pickle into paper-thin slices. "Sorry about that. Okay, so what made you come around?"

Bruce paused, knife in midair. "One morning I saw the sun come up over the mountains onto those snow-covered hills. I hadn't seen that since I'd gone camping with my dad as a kid. It just hit me that I couldn't think of a prettier sight."

Okay, she could write about the plow driver alone in the early morning. Sort of a "Lineman for the County" spin. She wrote down Glenn Campbell, Lineman. "So you came around because you got to work outdoors?"

"It helped." Bruce placed half of the pickle slices across the meat and cheese and slid the rest over to Joe.

Anna looked at her notes. "But it would still be real cold, lonely, and," she glanced at Joe, "samey, doing the same thing over and over."

Bruce rolled his eyes at her. "Real cold? That's what heaters and thermoses are for. How about capers?"

What next, watercress? "Sorry, again. What about lonely?"

"Nah. Gave me a lot of time to think. Olive oil maybe?"

That she had. The phone rang the same moment she stood. She pressed the call to message again before pulling the oil out from the cabinet beside the stove. "Is it okay to ask what you were thinking about out there?"

Bruce's eyes roamed over the shelf. "Maybe some vinegar, too. Well, I thought about why I did all that drinking. And what was important and what wasn't."

Anna placed both bottles on the table in front of him. Nix "Lineman for the County." "And your conclusions?"

Bruce sprinkled a little of both the oil and vinegar on the roast beef then pushed them to Joe. "Well, it hit me that there sure are a lot of us humans down here just sort of... existing. Living, dying, working, all that, but there must be some big job we're supposed to do. You know, like sharks don't just swim in the ocean, they clean them out. Bees don't just fly around, they pollinate flowers. So, that's what I want to know. What we're supposed to be doing."

Anna scribbled furiously. "In Praise of the Plow," this was not.

Bruce inspected his sandwich and Joe's, then proudly, it seemed to Anna, reached for two slices of bread and the mayonnaise. "Looking good, little buddy, now just a bit of mayo to finish it up." He peered up at Anna over the phone's newest incursion. "Still want to know about about… samey?"

"Hold on a moment." She picked up the phone.

"Okay," Molly hissed.

Anna turned her back to Bruce and Joe. "Okay, what?"

"Okay, eight to ten."

"All right. But ten on the nose." She lowered the phone and focused on Bruce. "So, samey?"

Bruce picked up the knife. "Here's the thing. It all fits together. If I screw up, people will be in danger." While he talked, he spread a thin coat on both pieces of bread in the steady slow sweeps he'd done with the mustard. "And to not screw up, I have to be real attentive to what I'm doing, you know, to what's going on around me, to what I'm thinking." He placed one of the bread slices on top of Joe's sandwich and the second on his own. "So, if the job makes me do all that, then it's sure not samey. Capish? And that's why it's the best job in the world… it gives me this big chance." He eyed Joe and with a dramatic swipe, first cut his sandwich in two and then Joe's. "That's darn close to a Long Island hero, little buddy. Best food in the world."

Joe stared at Bruce like a dog waiting for a bone to drop.

Anna leaned back in her chair. "You've lost me. A big chance for what?"

Bruce picked up his sandwich. "To figure it out," he nodded to Joe to do the same, "that big job."

Forty-five minutes later, Anna heard Bruce's heavy footsteps coming down the stairs. With becoming gravitas, he had accepted Joe's request for his own interview.

"About what, little buddy?"

"Mean kids. Bullies. Kids who steal ideas. And I'll tell you about Deganawidah."

"So," she said, walking Bruce to the front door, "many thanks for all your time. You and Joe get things talked out?"

Bruce reached for his coat. "Yeah. I think we got a plan. By the way, we looked him up, that D… guy. You never say his name."

"Why?"

"Respect, I think." With a quick bow, Bruce raised clasped hands to his forehead. "Hey, Joe wants to ride with me sometime. I think the city will okay it, but if not, maybe he can go this summer."

Yeah, and maybe Joe could get the details for the gears and asphalt column of her imagining. "Thank you again. Either one. What kind of route does the city do in the summer?"

Bruce pulled his knitted hat snug down over his ears. "That's my own business."

She opened the door and noticed the familiar big yellow van parked in front of the house. "You're..."

Bruce's face lit into his big toothy grin. "Mr. Ding A Ling! That's me, awlright!"

## 55 • TAILS OF THE CURVE

RALPHIE'S BARK SNAPPED Anna out of a deep sleep. She glanced at the lighted bedside clock, two-thirty. Usually at this time of night, the objects of Ralphie's attention were skunks, deer, or college students. She hoped it was deer; they didn't emit scents or throw up in the front yard. Wide awake, she flipped over on her side and remembering a recent resolution, inched toward the center of the bed. Going down the checkout line at RiteMarket, she read an article about recent divorcees trying to learn to sleep in the middle of the bed, freeing themselves from allocated sides and symbolically from marital confines in general. There and then she'd vowed to get a jump on things and practice. She pulled the covers up to her chin and wondered which side of the bed William preferred. And what about Paul when he was with Erika? Did he have to yield to her preferences? She hoped so. Then it hit her: a great idea for a column. "Dilemmas of Adultery: Your Side or Mine."

This time it was a yip followed by a plaintive whine. While Joe could sleep through a tsunami, she wasn't so sure about Molly and Caroline, for whom she had unexpectedly, warm feelings. They had arrived home on time, actually about fifteen minutes early, eager to chat and "share." Sitting around the kitchen table over hot chocolate, the girls described the minutiae of the CD party for her: who was there, who was not, the clothes that rocked, the clothes that should never have seen the light of day, the high school kids making a presence, the strangers that might have been agents, and, of course, the musical genius of Peter. Things got so friendly, Anna found herself proposing a spring trip to Greenwich Village for vintage clothes. She left them ensconced under blankets in the living room with a copy of *South Pacific* Caroline brought from the school library. With the strains of "One Hundred and One Pounds of Fun" wafting through the house, she half-hoped they would invite her to join them. But a little wiser now to the ways of teenagers she'd gone upstairs at eleven o'clock, draped herself in a new pink rosebud granny gown, guaranteed against the northern night from Chauncey's, and despite a very good book, shut off her light at eleven-thirty.

With another whine from the front of the house and a surge of willpower, Anna switched on the bedside lamp and threw back the comforter. Stepping out into the hall, she gave her eyes a moment to adjust to the darkness before tiptoeing past Molly's and Joe's rooms. Then, with one hand on the wall for balance and the other on the wooden rail, she crept down the stairs. Finally, at the bottom of the steps, she turned on the first-floor hall light and peered along the corridor to the front door. There, in coat, hat, and gloves, a tear-stained Molly clutched Ralphie to her chest.

"Are you okay?"

A nod.

"Is Caroline okay?"

"Another nod."

"Is Caroline here?"

A quick shake of the head.

"Where is Caroline?"

Silence.

"Honey, you need to tell me what is going on."

Molly buried her face in Ralphie's neck. More silence.

Anna pulled her robe tight. What was basic here? What would Domnica say? She suddenly thought of Sybil at Barbara's door. "Okay, Molly, you can tell me or you can tell the police. You've got one minute to decide."

❧

The story came out in pieces.

"So the whole overnight was about going to Peter's? And the movie was just a pretext to stay up late." She studied her daughter. "Why didn't you think I would hear you?"

Molly, crumpled against the armchair, shrugged. "You never have before."

Never have before? "How often have you done this?"

"Oh, Mom, lots of times."

"Where to?"

Molly burrowed into the chair, tucking her feet up under her. "Sometimes to Visionary Fields… with high school kids. But mostly, to Peter's. It's just down the street. We'd talk, listen to music. It's a place to go."

"What happened tonight?"

"*Tonight*," Molly's voice broke into a sob, "when I said we had to leave, Caroline told me she wasn't going to. She'd be in later. I said, no, that wasn't part of our deal." Molly paused, hurt contorting her features. "So then she said, 'tough,' and that she only pretended to be my friend so we could sneak over to Peter's."

Anna inhaled, C for calm. "What did Peter say?"

"He wasn't there. He was out."

"Doing what?"

"Getting beer."

Another BIG C. "For all of you?"

Molly nodded, brushing away tears. "Sure."

"Is that where she is now?"

"I guess so."

Anna considered her options: Walk over to Peter's and demand that Caroline come back to the house? Call the police and have them go to Peter's? She looked out at the black, still night. "What's the Van's home number?"

Molly's eyes grew huge and round. "Mom, you can't! It'll get all over school."

"Great. Now, what is it?"

⸙

"You know, Anna, you could have just called Caroline at Peter's and told her to get her ass back here. Not made such a big deal out of this."

Anna gazed up at Jamie standing by the front door. Even at three-thirty in the morning, and after being plucked, she assumed, from deep sleep, Jamie was perfectly occasion-appropriate: North Face jacket, jeans, chamois shirt, and hair tousled in a becomingly masculine way. Caroline, thank the universe, was outside in Jamie's Jag, idling in the driveway.

"You don't think it's a big deal that the girls lied to me, snuck out, and went to the home of a thirty-year-old guy who gives them beer?" Anna wished she'd changed clothes before Jamie's arrival. This idea of drawing a line in the sand wasn't easy, drawing it in pink rose buds didn't help.

Jamie reached for Caroline's overnight bag. "Actually, I don't. They're red-blooded American teenagers. And for Christ's sake, Anna, it was Peter. He's their youth group leader. It's like they snuck out to the babysitter's."

She gripped the collar of her granny gown. "So why didn't this babysitter just turn them around and walk them home. They're thirteen. Think about it. They were in sixth grade last year."

"Come on, Anna. It's called rebellion. It's what kids do."

She thought about that for a moment. Wasn't Jamie saying what lots of parents would say? What Dr. Young said was the A team. She pulled herself back from the brink. "It's also called dishonesty, it's called taking advantage, it's called underage drinking, and it's also called real damn illegal on Peter's part."

Jamie slung the bag over one shoulder. "You want them climbing in a car with a pair of sixteen-year-olds and some beer, Anna? I'll take Peter anytime. I talked to him tonight, something I guess you couldn't be bothered with. He said if these girls are going to be out late and drink, then he wants to be there for them."

Be there for them. Gag. "But these girls shouldn't be out late or drinking. We're the parents, not Peter. We make the rules."

"Oh, Jesus," Jamie's sigh was as disgusted as Anna felt, "Peter works with teenagers a lot. He gets them."

She knew fighting words when she heard them. "You're saying I don't?"

Jamie took a couple of steps toward her. "Look, Peter saw a situation where he believed he knew best and needed to take things into his own hands. And I get that! Happens all the time. I call it being responsible."

Anna felt the first waves pulsing at the base of her neck. She stood up. "Well, I don't. Molly, Caroline, and I had an agreement. They broke it. And Peter, he broke laws."

Jamie gazed down at her. "The world doesn't always run on the straight and narrow. I thought you and Paul were the type of people who understood that." He looked around the living room. "Where is Paul? Sleeping?"

Jamie talked to Paul every day. Most days more than once. He knew where he was. "Boston, as I think you know."

"Oh, right, Boston." He opened the oak door, letting in an icy blast of cold air. "Let tonight go, Anna. You know how to do that. Just let it go."

## 56 • JUST LETTING IT GO

*The Ding and Dao of the Plow*

*Warm winter wishes to you, Manhattan Living Readers. Having just checked national weather statistics, I see that you can look for average lows above freezing in just one month. While I, your intrepid Onasego reporter, will not encounter the same balmy temps UNTIL MAY. So, as I am embedded in winter for at least three more months, I hatched an idea for a somewhat different type of column for you this week. I just never had a clue how different. My original plan was to document, in gritty but grateful detail, the frigid, lonely, monotonous but absolutely essential world of a plow driver in upstate New York. And with help from the always helpful Onasego city clerk, I was supplied an actual plow driver in the form of Bruce O'Malley. But there my plan ended. Why? Because where I see frigid, he sees hot coffee, where I see lonely, he sees time to think, and where I see monotonous attention to detail, he sees a way to care for his community and A PATH toward wisdom. I should also mention that in good weather Mr. O'Malley drives a banana yellow ice cream truck and goes by the dubious title of Mr. Ding-A-Ling.*

*And, in yet another twist, my interview with a plow driver turned out to be an utterly gripping "what if" story. Because if it were not for a very wise judge who took a chance on a very foolish young man, Bruce O'Malley might still be in prison today for a drunken crash and the near death of a best friend. But this judge did take a chance, and I am absolutely sure the world is better for it.*

Anna reread the beginning. Good, but in need of polish.

"Mom!" Joe exploded into Anna's study, "I have a great idea and people can steal it."

Anna swiveled her chair and grabbed Joe onto her lap. "Hey, Big D, glad somebody woke up around here. I've been lonely."

Joe wrinkled up his nose. "You don't smell so good."

"I've been up all night. I need a shower."

He nestled against her. "Why'd you do that?"

Why indeed? Anna stared out the window over Joe's head and mentally ran through the list. Because of two arrogant bastards named Jamie and Peter. Because after last night it was so crystal clear she had to get Molly into some new situation, because she was intensely interested in a man who wasn't her husband, because Tim emailed at three a.m. with a REQUIRED Friends meeting for Monday night. And because of people with problems like Ellis, Lisa, Angus, Libby, Dawn and, not at all least, this precious little boy. She smoothed Joe's hair. "I was thinking, Joe, and working on my column a little bit. Sounds like you've been thinking too. What's your great idea?"

Joe sat up in her lap. "You know I told Bruce about those boys, how mean they were, and how they stole my idea about the Jump With Joe Fund. He said the real D would know that the boys are mean because they are sad about something. And, he said the real D would figure out a way for everyone to make a lot of money for the Polar Plunge without it being like a fight, so then the boys could be happy about something. So, I thought, and I thought. And then I got it! Instead of a Jump With Joe Fund and a Dive With Daniel Fund where people just give money to kids they know, we could just have a Kids For Kids Fund. Kids For Kids because we're kids and we're raising money for sick kids. And if it's just the Kids For Kids Fund, then all sorts of people would give any kid money instead of just to a kid they know. Isn't that neat?"

She kissed his forehead. "It sure is. But what if the boys don't want to do it? And what if they're mean to you again?"

Joe grinned. "I have an idea for that too. I'm going to ask Bruce if we could all ride in the ice cream truck. Then I bet those kids would do it."

She gazed at her son, genuinely impressed. "You are a genius. A certified genius."

"But I have to call Bruce, those kids, make signs. This is kind of what Dad does, right?"

"Right." She stared into the gray-blue eyes, so like Paul's. How could she even consider taking him from his father?

"Will you help?"

Anna glanced at the unfinished column. "I have to finish this first, cause I can't do it tomorrow. Maybe you could get your own cereal? Because the sooner I get this done, the sooner I can help you."

Joe's eyes grew huge. "Now I've got *another* idea. I'll do all kinds of stuff so you can work. I'll get my cereal. I'll get the paper. I'll take Ralphie for a walk. I'll take the sheets off my bed. I'll put newspapers in the recycling." He grabbed her shoulders. "Mom! I'll make you lunch."

The possibility of peanut butter and ketchup hovered. "Like what?"

"A herrrro," he purred. "And I'll be real quiet. Deal?"

She held up her hand for a high five. "Deal!"

He slid off her lap and headed for the door. "You want some cereal, too?"

Anna nodded, marveling at the world swinging around on a dime. Now if Molly's situation could be so easy.

Turned out it was. At least, potentially.

"Joe made that?"

Molly, still in her pajamas and robe, sat down at the kitchen table. Anna, with her mouth full of Joe's hero, nodded.

"It almost looks good."

Joe leaned forward over the table. "It's a hero. Want me to make you one sometime?"

Molly looked back at her mother. "Do I?"

"See for yourself." Anna cut off a corner of the sub and handed it to Molly.

In a Mikey moment, Anna and Joe watched Molly sniff and nibble around the edges before polishing off the rest. "That's awesome. Where'd you learn to do that?"

Joe shrugged. "This guy. Mom, I'll get the sheets off my bed. Then I'll take Ralphie."

Anna and Molly watched as Joe skipped out the door.

"What's with him?" Molly asked standing up and going to the refrigerator.

"Joe wants help with a project today, but since I'm on deadline he's doing some of my chores so, when I get finished, I'll have more time to help him."

Molly poured a glass of orange juice. "What did you and Jamie talk about last night?"

"I think we agreed to disagree."

"What does that mean?"

"He seems to think you and Caroline were just showing some teenage rebellion. I, on the other hand, feel that the two of you were dishonest, reckless, and with the beer, illegal."

Molly sat back down slowly, her expression troubled, vulnerable. "I don't even like beer."

Anna decided a half a hero was plenty. "You want the rest of this? What about vodka? You like that?"

Molly pulled the plate over. "How'd you find out?"

"Paul found the bottle in the trash where you and Caroline left it. Did you steal the twenty dollars from me too?"

Molly pulled a wad of Kleenex from her robe pocket, lips quivering. "Yes."

"Why?"

"Because I didn't want to come up here. And I want to go live with Dad."

Anna sat back, almost afraid to breathe. This had to be a mother of Domnica's taking someone seriously moments.

"I don't know why Dad wants another little girl. But he does; he is so excited. I know when they get the new baby, I'll never see him." Molly propped an elbow on the table, pressing back tears with the tissue. "I mean, I love you all, I do, but I have to go live with Dad for a while right now. And I really want to go back to my old school." She raised her eyes to Anna. "Please."

If only. "When we decided to come up here, I thought you might want to stay with your dad so I asked him. But he didn't think it would work, because he and Ava are so busy. I'm sorry."

Silence. Then the kitchen door popped open followed by Joe's head.

"Mom, the sheets are in the hall." He took in Molly's blotched, puffy face. "What's wrong with her?"

Anna motioned for him to close the door. "Molly and I are being private. You run on now."

The door banged shut behind him. Anna and Molly sat silently during Ralphie's delighted yelp, Joe's crooning, "good dog, you're a good dog," then the front door closing.

Molly wiped her nose with a bitter laugh, "Maybe if they had a dog I could walk, they'd let me live there." She pulled more Kleenex from her robe, "Or, maybe Joe could teach me to make hero sandwiches. Maybe they'd like that."

Laurel, not Domnica, now hissed in Anna's ear. *Let her try... you'll be there to help.* Then Joe's observation from early morning replayed, "I'll do all sorts of stuff so you can work." Slowly, slowly the outlines of an idea seeped into Anna's brain.

"Molly, how are you with babies?"

"Mom, what are you talking about?"

Anna folded her napkin and stood. "As we know, your dad and Ava really are very busy people. They'll probably get a nanny, but still, everybody with a baby needs a lot of help. Maybe you could convince them you could be of real assistance around the house, cooking sometimes, babysitting, even doing some chores like Joe is doing today. You have no idea how much people appreciate even a little help."

"You mean... like a maid?"

"No, honey," Anna opened the pantry, "like a big sister to little whoever will arrive, and a helpful daughter to your dad and Ava." She pushed a box of garbage bags aside and pulled out the saran wrap. "You can't expect people to do things for you without doing something for them."

A light entered Molly's eyes. "You really think if I could cook and stuff they might take me?"

Anna looked out through the kitchen window. She should have told Joe just to go around the block. "Well, for sure they won't be jumping up and down about a teenager who sneaks out, steals money, and does absolutely nothing around the house. Oh," she slapped her forehead, "and drinks at thirteen. I forgot."

"But, Mom," Molly raked her fingers through her hair, "I've never cooked. And babies, that means changing diapers. I don't know how to do any of that."

Anna leaned against the counter. "Believe me, you can learn diapers in about three minutes. And cooking... that's what cookbooks are for. I would even be willing to show you the subtleties of a vacuum cleaner."

"Would you talk to Dad?"

"Show me you're serious."

"How?"

For once Anna had a ready answer. "Clean up your room and keep it that way. Find something you want to cook and make dinner one night a week. If someone else cooks dinner, you clean up the dishes. Arrange some babysitting jobs." She dropped the saran on the table. "And, if you're not going to eat that sub right now, then wrap it up and put it in the fridge for later."

"That's all?"

Anna peeked out the window again. Joe was dragging Ralphie up the sidewalk. "That's a lot, actually. But there is more."

"What else?"

"You'll need to be kind to some people you haven't been particularly kind to, like me and Paul, and your brother."

"Sure" Molly reached for the plastic wrap and tore off several inches.

"And to one other. One who really needs a friend."

Molly eyed her mother cautiously. "Who's that?"

"Dawn."

## 57 • WILLIAM

"WILLIAM, CALL BACK in five minutes; there's a policeman coming up behind me." Anna lowered the cell onto her lap and slid into the right-hand lane on I 87 north. According to the MapQuest directions taped to the dashboard, she should be within a few miles of the exit for the airport and the hotel complex where she would meet William Johnson for, at the very least, lunch. She glanced at herself in the rear-view mirror. Maybe she'd add a little more eyeliner in the hotel parking lot. She peered again, maybe more mascara too. To her right, the road marker announced the exit for Wolf Road and Albany International Airport, a quarter mile ahead. When her phone buzzed next the New York state trooper was a safe several car lengths ahead. She raised the phone jubilantly to her ear. "Hi again. I should be at the Desmond in a few minutes. What's your room number?"

There was a pause, then, "Anna, it's Jed. You left a message for me to call."

The familiarity of his slightly arrogant, slightly irritated tone washed over her. "Jed, I asked you to call tonight."

"We have opera tickets tonight, so I took a chance. You said it was important."

A sign with THE DESMOND in large brown letters pointed left at the light. She switched on the blinker. "Look, I can't talk right now. I'm in traffic. And I have an interview in a few minutes."

His low laugh flowed through the phone. "Yeah. I caught that."

She wanted to scream with an overwhelming hatred for technology... and herself. She pulled through the light and turned into the Desmond lot. Amid the urban sprawl of Albany, the Desmond, a brick, colonialish structure, gave off a welcoming vibe, even with gray piles of snow stacked up along its perimeter. She threw the shift into park. "Jed, I gotta get off. When's a good time to talk?"

Another pause. She'd bet a lot of money that her ex was staring at the ceiling which was what he always did when mulling things over. She heard him sigh. A sigh she remembered well. Then: "Can't you just tell me the gist of it now? Surely, your, ah, interview can wait two minutes. And you know I don't have time for a lot of chitchat."

Her, ah, interview? No time for... chitchat? Just the gist. Well, all right. She switched the car off. "Onasego isn't working for Molly and she needs to come live with you. Soon." She eyed herself in the rearview mirror and decided against more eye makeup. "So, if you *do* find time for some, ah, chitchat," she looked up toward the windows of the Desmond, William was on the third floor, "give a call." And with that she clicked off her phone, locked the car door, and headed toward the hotel.

The door swung open and William, holding a phone with one hand, pulled her into the room. "Right, the meeting's at six. I'll see you there." With his free hand he helped her off with her coat and motioned toward the table by the window, set with linen, silver, plates under stainless domes, goblets, and a bottle of some type of red. The phone rang again. "Hello—hello—hm, nobody there. Just one more," he said punching in another number. "Hi, this is William Johnson in 311. Hold my calls, okay?" He listened, then added. "'Til five, thanks."

She settled into one of the club chairs and watched as he walked the phone back over to the nightstand beside the canopied double bed. In charcoal slacks and a black V-neck sweater, cashmere she was sure, he was altogether gorgeous. She glanced down ruefully at her own camel cords and turtle neck. What would the fiance have worn?

"So," William said, sitting down across the table from her, "you're here. Hungry?"

"I am." Her eyes roamed over the hotel room. A pleasant chintz and Queen Anne décor. Everything was perfect. Her phone buzzed. Molly.

"I'm on an interview."

"Just two minutes, Mom. You know how Dad likes Thai food, so I need *nam pla* for a practice recipe. They sell it at Crossgates at the Asian market, and since you're in Albany... Oh, and Joe's Polar Plunge team is coming over for cocoa tonight. He wanted me to tell you. Thanks, you're a gem, see you later."

Anna clicked the phone off. A gem.

"Your drive, okay?"

She nodded.

"Want some wine?"

"I do."

He reached for the bottle of burgundy and a glass. "I ordered an omelet for us. Hope that's all right."

She propped an elbow on the table trying to appear at ease. For months she'd fantasized about a meeting like this with William: a continuation of the night stolen by Jed and Ava because they couldn't handle a little vomit.

Loose, sexy, uninhibited. Possibly searing, rapturous, even life altering. "Omelets are great."

He handed her the wine. "What time do you have to head back?"

She took the glass and waited while he poured a glass for himself. And there it was, the gist of it, as Jed might say. "Four, four thirty."

He reached over and took her hand, running his thumb over her palm. "So how do you see our time going this afternoon, after lunch that is?"

She let herself focus in on the V at the base of his neck framed by the sweater. That bit of flesh, so exposed, so impossibly erotic. Did he have a clue what just his presence alone could do to her? But she was Anna Lawson, frumpy person, married, who'd just managed to all but tell her ex she was going to cheat on her current. A mother who now had to find *nam pla* and host little boys for cocoa tonight. "Not exactly as I hoped."

"Is this the Onasego thing you were worried about at Christmas?"

She took a sip of wine. "No. Just my life."

"Like what?"

"Like my son is having some kids over tonight for a Polar Plunge meeting and my daughter needs my help with a cooking project. Both things for them are critical right now."

He lifted the domes from the plates. "So, how about us?"

Anna gazed at the tiny new potatoes and spinach omelets that room service had so obligingly whipped up. Since misery never trumped good food, she took a bite. Perfect, fluffy, cheesy. And someone else had cooked it. Looking up from the plate, William's dark eyes, intent now and troubled, met hers. She leaned forward over the table.

"Do you know what I see when I see us together? If I'm honest?" She didn't give him a chance to answer. "I see an incredible mismatch, like James Bond and Ethel Mertz out on a date. Or Elizabeth Taylor and..." she hesitated, trying to remember the last husband's name, "...that Larry, somebody. Everyone knew at some point the scales would fall from Elizabeth Taylor's eyes and the same will happen with us. But worse." She pointed her fork at William, "cause I'm not just Ethel but Ethel with an ex husband, a current husband, and two children. So... when *your* scales fall..." There was no need for her to finish the thought. Instead, she gazed back down at the plate and speared a potato.

⁂

The rest of the meal passed quietly. Despite William's many protests, assurances, and endearing attempts at humor, including a wicked, "Bond, James Bond," moment, Anna knew she was right. She was in one life and he, another.

After a time, they politely moved to neutral topics: his new hotel project near the canal in Albany; Marty emailing back in the middle of the night to say he was running "The Ding and the Dao of the Plow" this week; William's belief that Catskill should absolutely go on line, the only practical approach; Joe's fundraising scheme; and Molly's plan to worm her way into Jed and Ava's house. Then the meal was finished.

"So," Anna said placing her napkin on the table, "I guess I'll be leaving."

William pushed back from the table. "You're really going back now?"

Anna stood. "I really am."

William made a show of looking at his watch. "Nothing I can say?"

"Maybe someday." She scooped her coat and purse off the bed. "But not right now."

He shrugged and walked toward her, taking the coat and holding it for her. "Why can't we just be together? Even for one afternoon."

Anna didn't trust herself to speak. She slipped into her coat and let herself out.

She made it down the hall to the elevator and pushed the button before tearing up. Beside the elevator, photos of the Desmond's atrium, billiards room, indoor swimming pools, conference rooms, and fancy restaurants beckoned. A thirtyish couple joined her at the elevator, all whispery giggles and light touches. From their conversation it sounded like an afternoon workout was planned, followed by swimming, dinner, and a raised eyebrow from him and more giggles from her. At last the elevator arrived. Next the long walk through the lobby, the parking lot, and back to her car that she'd so recently left with such enormous expectations.

She turned the key and waited for the heater to kick in. This was her life in Onasego. One moment, up. The next, a crashing fall. Why would life send William Johnson her way when a relationship was so clearly impossible?

Why? Why had she even agreed to come to Onasego? The first warm waves from the heater spread through the car. Then she remembered. She agreed to come to Onasego because of her promises to God, promises like never doubting, and treasuring every moment. And now there was even Domnica with her take-yourself-seriously assignment. A complete and perfect trifecta. Yanking the key from the ignition, she shoved the car door open and raced back into the Desmond.

## 58 • NO MORE MR. NICE GUY

ANNA SAT QUIETLY waiting for the meeting to start. Beside her tablet, three pens lay lined up like little soldiers on the desk. Laurel, from several seats away, had taken note and nodded approvingly. Maybe it was out of respect for Tim, or more cabin fever, but a respectable turnout of thirty-five or forty sat chatting around her in the Founders lounge waiting for Tim's REQUIRED meeting of the Friends to begin. All the usual characters plus a few, like the golf coach and his wife, and lacking a few, like Ellis, biding his time waiting for his hearing. Even Jason from Greek Life was there with a somewhat familiar-looking, henna-haired girl, both gorging on bundt cake brought by the elderly lady who didn't know what an on line school was at the last meeting. Note to self, Anna thought, get people who speak to identify themselves. The only names she knew in the entire group were Angie, Laurel, Denise, Deedee, Tim, and the ever-hungry Jason.

Anna was actually glad for this meeting tonight as an excuse to be out of the house. Since the kickoff meeting early Sunday evening of the Kids For Kids campaign, Joe had been in full obsessive-compulsive fundraising mode. The meeting started off ominously enough with Daniel and Casey swaggering around like little pains in asses, until the doorbell rang a third time, and Joe announced the arrival of a mystery guest. Outswaggering the other two boys, Joe opened the door to reveal Bruce and his ice cream truck idling in the driveway. After a quick turnaround the block and a promise for more from Bruce should the group together raise three hundred dollars for the Polar Plunge, the three boys became Kids For Kids with enough energy bouncing around to power a small country.

Likewise, with Molly's intensity level. If she could do Thai, then why not Tandoori? Cajun? Pacific fusion? Anna feared carpel tunnel from spice grinding.

But most of all the meeting gave her something to do until she could call William around eleven. She felt flushed just thinking about dialing the phone, waiting through the rings, feeling his voice wash over her. From the moment he opened the door assuming it was room service collecting the lunch plates, to the moment two hours later when she'd stumbled out of the Desmond remembering she had to buy *nam pla*, whatever *nam pla* was at the Asian market for Molly, she'd felt herself transform into another Anna. An honest and assured Anna about what was at stake in taking this step with William. And a radiant Anna who wasn't looking back for a second. Her only "Anna as usual" moment came when she asked him what side of the bed he preferred.

The door swung open, and Tim strode into the room. "Okay, everybody, come to order. Now!"

Stunned to be ordered around by Tim, the room quieted down instantly.

Throwing his coat on a front-row seat, Tim looked around the room. "The last time we met I said I trusted the corporate guys to work things out the best they could for everybody. Well, I don't believe that anymore."

In the pause while Tim walked over to the food table and poured a cup of coffee, one could have heard the veritable pin drop. Clenching the Styrofoam cup, Tim continued. "We know the chairman of Catskill's board is behind the distance learning idea. Now, suddenly, Jamie Van is trying to buy my land from the school for twice what it's worth for a fancy baseball camp. And he's saying he'll only buy it if the school goes on line, and we all know that'll be a knife straight through Onasego's heart. So what's going on here? What happened to open-mindedness, feasibility studies, and 'we'll keep you informed?'" He paused, maybe to let his words settle in with people or maybe to just keep his thoughts straight. Either way, Anna had never seen Tim angry before. She didn't know he had it in him. "Onasego and Catskill have always been a team. But now the board is all about this on line idea, using my land to help do it, and not saying one word about Onasego and our future. So two reasons I called this meeting: The first is my father didn't give me that land to make some rich people a whole lot richer. The second, and by far more important reason though, is if the board won't look out for Onasego, then we have to. And I think we're all agreed that means keeping Catskill the way it is. But, the thing is, I don't have a clue how."

With a shrug Tim left the podium to stand by the windows. Anna remembered him in the exact same spot at the previous meeting. But that night Tim had been all Mr. Nice Guy trying to protect the big guys.

After a few minutes, the nurse from UU Health stood. "My name's Joanne. So the board thinks it can convert to distance learning with money from Tim's land and, I guess, fundraise the rest. Can they do that… raise the rest?"

Everyone's gaze drifted over to The Niece. She sat up in her chair with a sort of "who me?" expression. "Well, I sure don't know, but there are some mighty good fundraisers on the board. And they've got Paul."

Anna stared down at her notes.

The little lady of the bundt cake stood. "I went to the library and looked up these distance learning, on line, whatever you call them schools. They don't seem fun or interesting to me at all." She sat down then stood back up. "Sorry, Peg, here. And, one more thing, why does this consortium need all that land for a baseball field?"

Anna jotted down Peg's comments. Peg of the bright crimson maple bough at Pleasures and Problems.

"But they make sense," a man Anna didn't know blurted out from the corner. "They save people a lot of money."

Laurel glared at Anna.

Anna jolted to attention. "Name?"

The man rolled his eyes. "Charlie Robbins. I'm sorry about your land, Tim, but at least if the school goes on line, some people will have jobs. That's important."

The quiet was awkward in Robbins's wake until Denise shrugged dramatically and stood. "I better run. I'll let Pug know what went on here tonight. Tim, I'm sure he'll call you. I know he'll want to explain."

For the first time since entering the room, a faint semblance of humor crossed Tim's face. "Explain, Denise? What could Pug possibly explain?"

It took Angie to state the obvious. "That's it? Not even a protest?"

Weak laughter rippled across the room.

Peg at the food table held up the bundt cake. "Please, everyone have some. I don't want to take any home."

Anna put away her pens and tablet. She waved at Peg and held up two fingers in the air. "For my kids," she mouthed.

From the back of the room, Jason raised his hand. "Okay if I say something?"

Tim nodded. "Sure."

With the easy saunter of the very arrogant, Jason approached the lectern. "I have to say this about the Catskill Board of Directors and everyone here with the one exception of Peg. You don't know shit."

## 59 • A PLAN

WITH HANDS ON hips and eyes narrowed, it seemed to Anna that Deedee looked like her old self for the first time in a very long time. "What do you mean we don't know shit?"

Jason shrugged, "Cause Peg's right. Kids don't want an on line school up here. Look," he lowered himself onto the corner of the desk beside the lectern, "kids like Catskill because it's built into the side of a mountain and got very cool classes and professors. But *also* because it's in Onasego. We like the way it is," he gestured toward the windows, "out there. It's kind of old timey. Not all suburbs and office buildings. You go out in the country and cow manure gets up your nose. There are about four bars. People play soccer in the friggin' ice and snow. But when it gets to be spring, it's like nirvana. Get it? It's a package, Catskill and Onasego.

Tim slid the lectern back against the wall. "But Jason, it's Jason right, you don't get it. Catskill still needs money. Lots of money. That's why the board came up with this other idea."

"But who does the board think they'll get all that money from? The alums, right? You think alums care about an on line school? You pitch saving the old Catskill right here in the old Onasego and then you're onto something."

Peg held up a knife triumphantly. "More cake, young man?" Scooping up a large piece onto a paper plate, Peg continued. "So, are you saying that it's good that Onasego never got developed?"

Jason beamed at her like a proud parent. "Yes! Exactly! People want to come up here and have things like they remember it."

Tim dropped back into a chair near the door. "But the board, they're all smart guys. Why would they miss this?"

Jason reached for the plate passed from Peg. "Beats me."

"So we have to get to the alums," Laurel announced, connecting up the next dot. "Let them know there's another proposal."

The henna-haired girl glanced up from a massive paperback entitled, *I AM THAT*. "Particularly the rich ones around Manhattan."

Now Anna remembered who the young woman with Jason was: the waitress at the first Friends meeting.

"And another thing," Jason added, "If the trustees vote on this at the May meeting, you've got 'til then to get the word out."

Dan, the golf coach, rocked back in his chair. "How do you do that?"

"EASY!" Angie, the Susquehanna Realtors Million Dollar Sales Club member, marched to the blackboard at the front of the room, picked up a piece of chalk, and scrawled:

ACTION ITEMS

#1. Develop Message to alums.

#2. Appeal to target population. Emails? Personal calls? Ads in local newspapers?

#3. Follow-up. Get alums to stop the board.

She wheeled around to face the crowd. "The message needs to be short and pithy, something you could fit on a bumper sticker. Don't over analyze. Come on, think!"

The room went deadly quiet.

"Think!" Angie shrieked.

"SAVE... THE OLD CATSKILL," Dan stammered with a flash of bravado.

Angie rolled her hand in a 'keep it coming' gesture.

"How about," Deedee studied the board. "IT'S YOUR CATSKILL. STOP CHANGE."

"Good!" Angie scanned the room. "Let's have some more."

Peg put a hand to her heart. "NO ON LINE. CATSKILL IS FINE."

"Good, again." Angie cried, adding to the list on the blackboard. "We're getting there."

"RIGHT HERE IN ONASEGO, YOUR CATSKILL. SAVE IT." A deep voice from behind Anna yelled.

"Better," Angie shouted, "keep going!"

"Okay," a redhead from the back volunteered, "try this, "YOUR CATSKILL AND ONASEGO… WHERE DEVELOPMENT PASSED RIGHT BY."

"Almost, we're almost there." The chalk against the board made little rat, tat, tats.

Anna felt a silent momentum take over the room, like a wave getting ready to break. Then an exuberant "I've got it!" from two rows over near Laurel. A newcomer jabbed the air in front of him. "In big letters write, CATSKILL… JUST LIKE WHEN YOU LEFT. Then in little letters underneath write, *Act Now. Stop Change.*"

Against an outbreak of spontaneous applause, Angie added the last suggestion to the board in big loopy letters. "GREAT! I LOVE IT!!"

Laurel clambered out of her seat toward Angie and the blackboard, her mouth in an O of astonishment. "Here's another idea! We could move our spring fundraiser to the weekend of the May board meeting. We'll ask the alums to attend and lobby the board. And it already has a perfect name, Catskill, Forget Me Not."

Tim, fixated on the blackboard, began nodding ever so slightly. "Okay, but what about number two? Somebody can set up a website, but how do we get people to it? We don't have money for phone time or mass mailings. We don't even have an alumni list we can legally use."

Peg ripped off a sheet of foil, molding it around a huge slice of cake. "How about a telephone tree? That's what we did in my day." She lowered her voice to a whisper, "Anna, for your children." Then she handed the package down the row in Anna's direction.

Laurel picked up a piece of chalk and put a question mark by Action Item #2, Appeal to Target Population. "If we could only find someone to mention our campaign in say, regional newspapers, or better yet, some popular magazine in the northeast, or even in Manhattan where, as Morgan pointed out, so many of Catskill's rich alums live, then we wouldn't have to use phones or mass mailings. If only we could think of someone." She pursed her lips. "Hmmm."

The aluminum foil crackled as Anna took the cake from the person in front of her and stuffed it in her canvas carryall. At the food table, Peg clapped her hands. "But, Laurel, it's wonderful, we do have someone! And she even writes about Onasego!"

This time, Tim grinned.


## 60 • NEVER DOUBTING (2)

"So the Friends tried to reel you in."

For midnight, William sounded way too alert. Anna pulled her feet up onto the kitchen chair, catching her white down robe over her toes. She felt like a big marshmallow: bright white, pliable, and slightly toasted after a fair amount of wine on only a small, but wonderfully crisp, *pakora*, Molly's latest creation, for dinner. In the two hours since the end of the Friends meeting, she'd walked the dog, had an excruciating phone call with Jed over exactly why Molly needed to come live with him, hence the fair amount of wine, and folded three loads of laundry.

"Yes, Laurel, especially, tried to make it sound like it was my duty as a member of the Friends to write columns basically addressed to Catskill alums."

"But you resisted."

"I did. But it was hard." From underneath the table Ralphie snored in low, shuddering waves. She slipped her foot out from under her robe and nudged him. "This Jason kid did quite a sales job. People are really excited about his idea. Why don't you think it will work?"

"I'll tell you exactly why," his voice was bordering on stern, "but, hang on a minute; I just got an email I need to answer."

She glanced at the clock. Twelve-fifteen. In six and a half hours Molly would be getting up for school and, judging from the folded stack of Kids For Kids flyers on the table, Joe was planning an early fundraising day. She got a happy glow thinking of her boy. During her absence not only had he folded flyers, but mounted a cardboard thermometer with gradations up to $400 on the refrigerator with magnets. Blue squiggles, representing water she assumed, reached to the one hundred and fifty dollar mark.

"Okay, I'm back."

She caught her breath at the perfect, deep William tone. The man could make millions with voice recordings. But then he probably already had millions.

"The kid's idea is all about nostalgia... not about the best way to save the school going forward. The distance learning concept and Jamie's land offer are compelling. Very compelling. Remember, people's livelihoods are at stake."

"But," she tried to think of a way to describe the enthusiasm, the hopefulness of the meeting, "other people think it will work. Like Tim and Deedee. Angie, too."

"Look," she heard soft tapping in the background; William was still on email, "it would take a massive infusion to get the school, as it is, back on solid ground. And, there's no easy way to say this, but people like Tim and Deedee, even Angie, they haven't lived anywhere except Onasego. Honestly, they don't see the real world."

Anna stared at the phone. This was not the romantic call she had been waiting for and planning all day. She wanted to tell him of her transformation because of their encounter and how the demanding therapist was going to paste a gold star on her forehead. She wanted to tell him she now knew she had a modicum of self discipline because she had walked out of the Desmond last Sunday afternoon instead of calling Social Services to pick up her kids. And she wanted, desperately, to arrange a date for their next meeting. Instead, he was emailing, and she now had to ask him an altogether unexpected but very important question. "You think Manhattan is more real than Onasego?"

Ralphie yipped. Joe stood in the door in his Ninja Turtles pajamas. "Mom, I need to sleep with you."

She lowered the phone to the table. "It's midnight. Why are you awake?"

He squinted at her. "I dreamed I couldn't swim. Is that Dad? Can I talk to him?"

Anna sighed, sensing a comeuppance moment from the universe. *Nana*

*nana boo boo, Anna Lawson. Treasure every moment.* "No, honey, it's not. You run back upstairs. I'll be right there."

With a yawn, Joe turned slowly and headed toward the stairs. Ralphie staggered behind him.

She picked the phone back up. "Ethel, here."

William's low laugh helped… a little. "One last thing. I'd be careful about including any reference to Catskill in your columns. Could be misconstrued."

"Mom!" The hall lights blinked off, then on, then off again.

Anna stood and flipped the deadbolt on the back door. Something felt left out. "How? Am I missing code here?"

There was no more tapping in the background. She poured a glass of water, shut off the overhead light, then leaned against the counter watching the hall light go on and off. Finally, at the count of thirty alligators, "Anna, I'm talking about Paul. People could wonder what side he's really on."


## 61 • SERIOUSLY

DOMNICA, SEVERE IN black sweater-dress and tortoiseshell reading glasses, peered over the top of a manila file folder at Anna. "Just one moment, my dear. Something I need to check from our last session. Yes?"

Anna nodded from the corner of the couch, comfy and warm after the chill both from outside and from the pool at the Y where she'd left Joe. With two weeks left until the Polar Plunge, today's dilemma was whether to full- or half-cannonball his way into the lake on the big day. For herself, she was eager to start this appointment. After weeks of agonized, soul-bearing and loathsome self observation, she finally had her triumphal run back into the Desmond to report. And while she didn't really want to admit she'd like to have Domnica's approval, she did, desperately.

Giving herself a moment of anticipatory smugness, Anna let her gaze travel over Domnica's office, a gem of understated, cultured decorating. What she wouldn't give to know Domnica's story. How did this aristocrat end up in Onasego? Why did she become a therapist? Was she married? Widowed? The plain gold band didn't answer that. She was certain a lot of people around Onasego must know Domnica Badescu's background, but how to ask without admitting she was seeing her as a therapist? And if she fessed up to seeing a therapist then she might be asked the critical question "Why?" And there was no way in hell she was going there with anyone in this town.

"So, my dear," Domnica lowered the file. "Have you given any thought to my speculation from our last meeting?"

Finally! Anna leaned forward. "You said that at an early age I sought safety and stepped back from feelings and action. But guess what I did two weeks ago? I had the opportunity to get together with, you know, that man I told you about. Well, I almost let the opportunity slip right by because of being married and the children and all that, but at the last minute, actually I was in the hotel parking lot about to leave, when I thought—*what am I doing?*—and I ran back in." Anna felt herself glowing. "How about that!"

"By getting together with, you mean….?"

Did she really have to explain? "Biblically."

"Ah, I see." Domnica pulled off her glasses and propped her chin in the palm of her hand. "Did you see this as taking yourself seriously?"

What was that about? "You bet!"

"And this man?" The therapist's eyes bore into Anna. "Did it feel as though you were taking him seriously?"

Anna sat back, frustrated. "You bet I took him *seriously*. And I can tell you, he took me pretty seriously, too."

"That's not what I meant." Domnica pointed the glasses at Anna. "As you mentioned, you are married. And you have children. What is his role to be?"

Anna wanted to throw her hands in the air. Where were the congratulations? The gold star? The pat on the back? "Hey, he's a grownup. I thought you wanted me to be brave. To take confidence from my experience, to not just seek safety. To try to get past my mother. And, damn it, I promised myself to treasure every moment."

"Is that what your husband is doing when he has affairs?" There was no easing up of the jaw. No sideward glance. And definitely no approval. Just Domnica rocking back in her chair staring at her. Well, she could do that too, Anna thought, smoothing her skirt and staring back. For about a minute that was, before a traitorous tear slipped out.

Domnica handed her the Kleenex box. "Treasuring every moment can get complicated. We'll address that next time. Let's turn to your mother. I've been giving her some thought."

Anna took a tissue. "Me too, for about forty-four years."

Domnica's gaze drifted to the window and then back at Anna. "From what you say about your mother, the rage, the fragility, it seems her portfolio for dealing with life was tragically slim. But *yours* is not. *This*," Domnica held up the manila folder, "was what I was trying to say to you at the end of last week. Pity that little girl, but take this grown up Anna seriously. You need to be her. The world needs you to be her."

"The world? Oh, please."

The jaw eased upward. "I mean every word."

So much for mascara. Anna blotted each eye. "Why?"

Cue the sideward glance. "My dear, have you not read this morning's *Onasegon?*"

☙

### IN SURPRISE DECISION, JUDGE CITES CHANGE IN NY LAW AND "ALONE IN ONASEGO" COLUMN

*Yesterday, in Otsego County Court, an Onasego woman pled guilty to second degree vehicular manslaughter. Lisa Rubino admitted to driving under the influence of alcohol over the Thanksgiving weekend, which led to a motor vehicle accident and the death of a Milford woman and serious injury to her husband. Under the terms of the agreement, Ms. Rubino will attend a 28-day alcohol rehabilitation inpatient program followed by two years of probation.*

*In accepting the plea agreement, Judge Rosen surprised many in the community as the penalty for the felony charge can extend from 2 1/2 to a maximum of seven years in prison. Describing his decision, Judge Rosen said that after speaking with Ms. Rubino, he believes she is sincerely ashamed and remorseful over her actions, is an excellent candidate for rehabilitation, and will be supported by her family's deep roots in Onasego. Judge Rosen also said his decision was heavily influenced by the spate of recent decisions favoring treatment over incarceration in drug-related cases and by an "Alone in Onasego" column, entitled "The Ding and Dao of the Plow." In that column an Onasego man recounts how the unexpected leniency of a judge following his youthful, but serious, alcohol violation led to a life of genuine introspection, service to his community, and, eventually, joy. "The article inspired me," Judge Rosen said. "If I could ever do that for another human being, I will consider my own life well lived."*

Anna looked up from the paper. "Holy…."

Now the nod of approval. "Indeed."

## 62 • A BAD CONFIGURATION

ANNA CLOSED THE kitchen door behind her and unclipped Ralphie's leash. Joe held the phone, scowling. "Five dollars? That's all?" He stuck his tongue out at the phone. "Mom, it's Jed." Joe handed her the phone and pointed toward the front hall. "Church, can't be late."

Anna cradled the phone against her shoulder. "Right. Go tell Molly five minutes."

She peeled off her gloves. "Hi, Jed."

Car horns blared over the phone. Jed's muffled, "Chinatown," followed by a car door slamming. "Anna?"

Anna closed her eyes and tried to summon Bruce's therapeutic vision of clear, sparkling snow. "Yes, Jed, how are you?"

"We need to talk."

Footsteps tramped in the hall overhead. Joe was making his last big pitch at church today for the Kids For Kids. She wanted to get good seats. "Jed, I'm on my way to church. Could we do this later?"

"I'll be quick. We're on our way to Mandarin."

Anna pulled out the coffeepot. Mandarin. "Okay."

"Ava and I have carefully considered your request to have Molly live with us."

Your request? She added azure sky above the snow. "Jed, it's what Molly wants."

More city sounds. The click of the cab's meter. Jed had rehearsed all this. "Anna, we would love to have her, but there simply isn't room. That's our conclusion."

The fifteen hundred square feet of primo Manhattan real estate appeared in Anna's mind. "You have a loft, Jed. A very big loft."

"Yeah, but the configuration is bad. So, here's the thing. Ava's sure one of William Johnson's four bedrooms would work for us to take Molly. And because they're near the park, it would be good for the baby. So maybe you could help us with that."

Anna swapped out the snow and sky image to one of herself mooning Jed. "And why would you think that?"

Her ex laughed. "We're good with numbers, Anna. And this was barely two and two. It's not amazing that you can call the Desmond and ask for anyone's room."

Vaguely she remembered a call to William's room with no caller. "Is this blackmail, Jed?"

She heard brakes and car doors opening. "We're at our class. Hey, could you give Joe five bucks for me? He hit me up for some swimming fund-raiser."

"This is really low, Jed."

"What? Five bucks?"

Anna let go of the vision. "No, Molly for Ava."

## 63 • YOU GUESSED IT... MORE PLEASURES, MORE PROBLEMS

JOE WAVED THE blue-and-white thermometer in the air. "My problem is that Kids For Kids needs forty dollars, well," he rolled his eyes, "thirty-five more dollars, before the Polar Plunge next Saturday. So," he held up the cookie jar that, the last time Anna checked, held Molly's homemade ginger snaps, and chanted,

> *Okay All Paths*
> *Don't you be greedy*
> *Give a little bit more*
> *For sick kids who are needy... at Coffee Hour!*

"Good thing the Polar Plunge is next week," Anna whispered to Angie, sitting beside her. "I think he's hitting the wall on rhymes." While Joe took his seat, several hands shot up.

Gail Somebody overseeing Pleasures and Problems today pointed at the crowd. "Deedee."

On the other side of the aisle Deedee pulled a petite blonde-haired woman up with her. Anna had been studying this woman through a lot of the service because, once again, while she was sure she had seen her somewhere before she couldn't place where. Not RiteMarket, not the library, not Catskill, not Penny's. Maybe not even Onasego.

"Hi, everyone. I have a pleasure today because I'm here with my sister, Deb. And she would like a word with you… especially after our last speaker's remarks."

Joe grabbed Anna's shoulder and hissed in her ear. "Me?" Anna shrugged, pondering the parents who would name their children, Deb and Deedee, and the fact she never knew Deedee had a sister.

Deb, more dressed than most of the congregation in a blue jacket and black skirt, looked around at the crowd and then at Joe. "I'm here as a co-chair of the Polar Plunge. I want to thank this young man and any of the rest of you who are supporting the event through your donations."

Joe pumped his fist. Anna closed her eyes to concentrate. She knew the voice…and face.

"We have ten young people in our community whose families desperately need the money this event raises, for help with medical issues. I'm making the rounds of the churches to encourage any of you who can, to contribute to one of the teams and to be sure and come out to Spruce Lake to support our jumpers. You can send in contributions through our website or, if you're downtown, you can drop them off with me at City Hall. Thank you."

The lights went on. City Hall. Deb, the ever-helpful city clerk who Anna had never taken the time to call and thank for now numerous favors. And the person at the hotel at the conference of City Administrators who tried to talk to her but she, Anna, had been too otherwise involved. Deb, the co-chair of the Polar Plunge, taking her Sunday morning to make the rounds of the churches to drum up support. Jeez.

More hands shot up. And one of them was Molly's sitting several rows up. Since the debacle with Caroline, Molly had deserted the youth group, either staying home from church all together or attending the main service with Anna and Joe. So what was this about?

"Hi, everyone." Molly pushed her hair back in the familiar nervous gesture. "This is kind of a pleasure-problem. The pleasure is that some of us are starting babysitting classes at UU Health. And the problem is that we need experience. So, if you need a babysitter, please keep us in mind. We are me, Molly Parish, Jen Molina, and," Molly turned to look behind her, "Dawn Holmes. Thank you. And, oh, yeah, any money we make this week will go to the Polar Plunge." Molly sat down and with a sideward glance at Anna, and smiled. Anna felt her heart literally start thumping. A miracle right here in Onasego; Molly was back.

Angie looked over the crowd, "Denise."

The Niece hauled herself up from the piano bench wearily. "I'm sorry but someone else will need to take over music for the Easter service and choir practices. I'm just too busy." Anna tried not to stare. The Niece looked terrible. Like she was coming back from a long illness. And The Niece never, ever passed up an opportunity to play in public. Something was up. She nudged Angie, who nodded knowingly.

"Pug dumped her. She's not taking it well."

By The Niece's appearance, Angie could be making the understatement of the year.

"Gwen."

Anna looked over at Molly and wondered if she'd had any contact with Gwen since the night at Peter's. Gwen was her idol. The mother she really wanted.

Gwen, with messy bun and sculpted jeans, faced the congregation from a few rows back. She took a long moment to begin and when she did speak, her voice was low, tremulous. "I have a long-standing problem I want to discuss. It has impacted my life daily and has gotten to be much too much to bear." People rustled in their chairs. The sanctuary grew still. There were only so many possibilities. Personal weakness? Addiction? Disease? Molly looked at Anna with puzzlement. Gwen took a deep breath, her eyes swept the congregation, then: "Gotcha!" She held up a stack of brochures and spread them like a fan. "These are pictures of my in-laws' furniture. My long-standing problem is that for most of my married life I have had to live with this stuff. But, finally, dear Jamie," she beamed down at her husband seated beside her, "has given me the green light to sell it *all*. So, my actual pleasure is that next Sunday afternoon, one to five, the Van family is having an estate sale at the house with half the proceeds going to Catskill, that is, *if* the school adopts a plan to transition to the distance learning concept. We think the donation will be some icing on the cake for securing Catskill's future in Onasego. Thanks and hope to see you there."

Anna jotted down Gwen's turn of phrase, *icing on the cake for securing Catskill's future in Onasego.* Smooth. Very smooth spin for the on line school side. Suggestive that both the campaign was about wrapped up, and no need to worry, Catskill and Onasego were going to be just fine. She wondered if Paul had written it.

"Tim."

Tim strode to the front of the church. Something was happening with Tim. Anna could see it in his walk, the steady intent of his expression. The total absence of the old "hail fellow well met-ness" everyone had taken for granted for so long. He scanned the crowd. "You know the problem. The Friends of Catskill College are fighting desperately to save Catskill as it is. Not," he acknowledged Jamie and Gwen with a slight nod, "as some others would have it. But we need help." Now Tim was looking right at her. "So, for any of you who are also so inclined, please come to our next meeting, a week from today, at three o'clock in the Founders Lounge at Catskill."

While Tim walked back to his seat, Laurel raised her hand and got the nod from Angie. She rose and positioned herself directly in a sunbeam coming through one of the stained-glass windows. "I'm Laurel Loomis representing Country Covens." Staring directly at Anna, she continued. "With the spring equinox just a little over a month away, it is a good time to reflect on our lessons from the cold and dark of winter. Warmth and light are coming and bringing to us the possibility of rebirth and growth. We should ponder on how we might use this possibility for ourselves and others."

During the ticklish lull that seemed to follow all of Laurel's pronouncements, Anna made sure to avoid any chance eye contact with either Tim or Laurel. Instead, she gazed at her children: Molly, jotting notes on a pocket calendar, and Joe, rocking back and forth, thoughts, like March clouds, flitting across his face.

Anna took the two cookies Joe was holding. Tim and Laurel were walking straight toward her.

"Hey, Joe, collected enough money?"

"Yeah, I got forty-five dollars."

"Great. You're hungry, right?"

Joe looked at the cookies and nodded.

"Okay, go find Molly and tell her we have to leave. Then come right back and tell me how you are starving and have to go home to eat. Got it?"

"Why?"

"Just do it. I'll give you a dollar."

Joe sped off.

Laurel stepped in front of her. "We need you."

Tim loosened his tie. "She's right."

But Anna was ready for them. Logic dictated only one answer. On the far side of the room Joe ran up to Molly talking to Jen and Dawn. "Look, Catskill trustees have a lot to say about whether my husband has a job and the majority of the trustees are for distance learning. That's a fact of life I need to live with for my family's welfare. So using my column for the Friends wouldn't be real smart. Also," from the corner of her eye, Anna could see Joe whispering in Molly's ear, "while I'm not a savvy businessperson, the people I know who are, say on line really is the future. So maybe that's a safer direction for Catskill after all."

Tim and Laurel stood silent.

"I'm sure you understand," she added weakly.

Laurel gripped her pentagram. "Think of Yonahlossee, Anna. An entity that gave life and meaning to hundreds, if not thousands, died. And we didn't stop it. Are you prepared to play that part again?"

"I didn't play any part. They couldn't get insurance!"

Tim glanced between them, stumped.

"Mom!" With pinpoint timing Joe slid in front of Anna. "I told Molly. I'm starving. We have to go home and eat." He held out a hand. "Do I get my dollar now?"

## 64 • POLAR PLUNGE

PAUL PULLED INTO the lot of the Spruce Lake Motel. "That has to be it," he said, pointing to a crowd of maybe a hundred standing on Spruce Lake.

ANNA LOOKED IN the backseat at Joe. Outside the sky was deep blue, the sun blinding on the snow, and the temperature at the bank read sixteen degrees. If life had been left up to her, she would be on the couch at home under a blanket watching a movie or wrapped in a blanket, working on a column in her cozy office with Ralphie. But, no. On this sparkling, crystalline, glacial day, she would observe teams of volunteers, including her very tiny son, jump through eight inches of ice to swim in Spruce Lake. She looked back at Paul with gratitude. On Tuesday he returned home three days early from a fundraising trip in the city. Since then he'd been to swim practice every day with Joe, watched *The Black Stallion* twice, and listened to Joe prattle on endlessly about what he was going to wear, the type of jump, and any and all things Polar Plunge. At night, after Joe went to bed, he paced, stewed, found reasons to call the Polar Plunge organizers with increasingly detailed questions, and generally fretted. For the first time in months Anna cared.

She swiveled around to face her son. "What are you thinking, my Joe?"

Joe clutched the solid blue thermometer to his chest. "I wish Molly was here."

"I know she wishes that too. But she got that big babysitting job." Anna forced herself to smile. "So, you ready?"

He squinted out at the lake. "Got to find Daniel and Casey. Get in line."

"And you'll keep that rope on no matter what... right?" Paul said referring to the rope that all children jumping would have tied around their waist in case they needed to be hauled out.

"You already asked me that a million times, Dad."

"Well, make me feel better, say it for a million and one times."

Anna squeezed Paul's shoulder. This was harder for him than for her.

"Okay, okay, I'll have the stupid rope on. Now, let's go!"

Paul sighed and shut off the car. "Okay, okay."

꙰

Of all the things she had done in her life, this had to rank as one of the stupidest, Anna decided as she and Paul joined the enthusiastically boisterous, or perhaps enthusiastically freezing, crowd of plungers and plunge supporters standing on Spruce Lake waiting for the event to begin. She studied the plunge area, a rectangle perhaps thirty by twenty feet with blocks for diving or jumping at one end and ladders for escape at the other. In between, exposed lake water, choppy and a dull black, lapped noisily over the rough-cut ice walls. Several snowmobiles stood parked off to one side. If standing around this hole in the ice seemed stupid, then suddenly the idea that she was allowing her son to throw himself into that water was criminal.

A human in polar bear garb and a bull horn ascended one of the blocks. "Okay, everybody, listen up."

The crowd bunched more closely together, a sea of snow pants, parkas, boots, scarves, knit caps, hoods, blankets, dark glasses, and goggles. The line of jumpers, many doing jumping jacks and jogging in place, gathered behind the blocks. Daniel and Casey stood next to Joe, but with their arms wrapped around each other's shoulders. Little pricks, Anna thought.

The Polar Bear took off his bear head. It was Mr. Anunzio.

"Hi, everyone. I'm Ric Anunzio, and welcome to the Fourth Annual Polar Plunge. Today we have fifty jumpers ready to freeze for the very good cause of helping some in our community who are in need. And just to let you know, so far these jumpers have raised forty-five hundred dollars."

Mittens muted the applause, but the vocal roar from the spectators more than compensated. In response, the jumpers in line bowed, curtsied, and pumped their arms Rocky like.

"I'll be introducing each jumper as they mount the blocks. While everyone's cheers will be appreciated, please take care not to get in the way of the volunteers helping out with the jump logistics. This is going to go real quick, so get ready for some fast, freezing, fun." He held up a clipboard.

"First off, the Davis Family making their third Polar Plunge appearance."

Anna watched fascinated as five figures shrugged off coats and hats and ran toward the blocks. At the edge of the pool, the mother, father, a boy and two girls, all in gym shorts and matching red tee shirts printed with The Dunking Davises, stopped for a quick huddle. Then, with a scream, the littlest, maybe an eight-year-old to Anna's eyes, pulled on a rope, climbed the block, and jumped. In an instant, the two other children and parents followed. It seemed only seconds before all five were clambering up the ladders and running for their towels and blankets, all to raucous cheers and clapping from the crowd, Anna and Paul included.

"Next up," Mr. Anunzio shouted, "representing our Unified Fire Departments, Ben Anderson and Jim Beatty." Two burly men in fire helmets and jams with red hearts ran for the blocks and jumped. Not any jump, but the fireman's jump from life saving. Once again, the crowd erupted.

Anna felt Paul's arm go around her. He leaned in close and yelled, "I wouldn't have missed this for anything."

"Me, neither," she yelled back, already trying to think up a first line for a column.

The next few minutes were a blur of bodies rushing the pool, signs and banners waving for the teams, and wild appreciation from the onlookers. Suddenly, Joe, Daniel, and Casey were only three teams back and dropping their clothes into piles. Yanking out the banner reading KIDS FOR KIDS in bright blue letters that Molly had made the night before, Anna handed one end to Paul, then pushed toward the front of the crowd. Three teams, then two teams, then it was Joe, Daniel, and Casey standing in front of the blocks.

Ric Anunzio spread an arm around all three. "And here is my favorite team, KIDS FOR KIDS. These boys have raised four hundred dollars for other kids. Let's give Joe Lawson, Daniel Stone, and Casey Brown a huge hand." Suddenly Anna was aware of a swarm crowding up behind the banner. In the blur of arctic outerwear she picked out Bruce, Ellis, Miss Wimbish, Angie, Deedee, Deb, Tim, Dawn and Libby, members of the Y class, and a dozen or more, suddenly deeply beloved, All Paths. Almost everyone hoisting homemade Kids For Kids signs.

With a high five to each other, Daniel and Casey pulled on ropes, climbed the blocks, and back flipped into the water. Clearly, a planned presentation. Joe, clearly *not* a party to the plan, scrambled up the block and half canon balled, half belly flopped in as fast as he could behind them, ignoring the "ROPE! ROPE!" yell from Ric Anunzio. In the longest five seconds to date in Anna's life, there was no sign of Joe. Just opaque, sinister, choppy black water. She wasn't sure who got their coat off first to jump in after him, herself or Paul, when suddenly, like some river creature, her boy burst up from the water, stroking and splashing full out to the ladders, where he pulled himself onto the edge of the pool and into Ric Anunzio's waiting blanket. All to frenzied screams and whistles from the gathered crowd. After a long hug from the principal, Joe spun around and found her eye, a victimized, awkward child, triumphant, at last.

Anna watched Joe, running and sliding on cloud nine, and Paul just running, make their way toward the car. The plan was for Paul to hustle Joe into a hot shower and dry clothes at home and then join her for the post Polar Plunge soiree at the Arts Center. She would ride with Angie and help serve food prepared by eager Polar Plunge volunteers the night before. Although she was mostly frozen, Anna let her gaze roam over the crowd. This would have to go down as one of the happiest days in the Lawson family household, and it was due to these other frozen humans around her. All these people here, who worked so hard for other people, had made it possible for Joe to have his day. A day he would remember all his life. She wanted to just run around and hug people. Maybe she'd write a letter of appreciation to *The Onasegon*, give her tax refund to next year's Polar Plunge, or heck, start a team herself.

"That was your boy out there, right?"

Anna peered at the mystery white cashmere coat—on Pug, alone, a wool cap pulled down low over his ears, walking hurriedly.

"Yes, it was. He started that team."

"Well done," Pug called over his shoulder, "tell him I said well done."

Anna watched his departing back. That was the coat for sure. Why did Libby have Pug's coat? Did she do mending on the side? Suddenly realizing she couldn't move her right foot, Anna hobbled into the crowd streaming off the ice to find Angie. And find her she did, almost immediately, right beside Derek, in his wheelchair, and Peter.

"Great swim by Joe," Angie said, pulling Derek's blanket up around his neck. "Peter's taking Derek home. I just need to get the key to the Arts Center from Ric. I'll be right back."

Anna, reluctant to face Peter and Derek, much less talk to them, watched Angie barrel into the crowd.

"That was some jump Joe made," Peter offered in the sudden silence.

Derek nodded. "That boy has really made a mark on this community."

Anna pondered what to say. There was only so much hypocrisy she was capable of.

Peter tucked his hands under his arms. "We haven't seen Molly at youth group lately. I had hoped everyone would just let bygones be bygones."

"I hoped for that, too, Anna." Derek said.

Let bygones be bygones? Anna sized up the two men and decided this was a "seize the moment" moment if there ever was one. "Well, guys, you hoped wrong. In my book, you're both nothing more than perverts. You can explain that to each other. If I ever so much as see you approach a young girl again you can expect to show up in one of my columns in explicit detail. And I don't think you want that." She saw Angie returning behind Derek. "Are we clear?"

"Got it." Angie called holding up what Anna supposed was a key.

Moving as quickly as she could with one useless foot, Anna turned back to the land. She was not going to let those two ruin her day. For a second she took herself back to Joe's face as he stood in Mr. Anunzio's arms. She had seen pure joy there. Nothing less.

Five minutes later, she sat in the passenger seat in Angie's SUV, waiting for the traffic to clear. Her foot stung as it began to thaw. She jumped in her seat at the knock on the car window where two people bent, faces peering in. It was Ray and Lisa wrapped in blankets. Anna let the window down.

Ray put his arm around Lisa. "Your article. Thank you."

Lisa burrowed against her father. "I swear… I will do something good."

Anna could not find a word. Not one. All she could do was wave as Ray and Lisa backed away from the car.

"Look," Angie murmured, "they're going back out there." And sure enough, Ray and Lisa turned toward the lake, so recently filled with bodies and jump paraphernalia, but now just an empty white expanse with a ladder. They walked slowly, deliberately, toward the pool. The one, bearded and portly, the other trim with long black hair whipping in the wind. Another figure trailed some ten feet behind.

"Tim," Anna whispered, finally finding her voice.

Angie and Anna sat spellbound as Ray and Lisa walked to the edge of the ice, slowly unwound their blankets, and handed them to Tim, now at their side. With no warm up jumping jacks, frenzied screams, or Rocky antics, the father and daughter simply nodded at one another, clasped hands and jumped.

## 65 • THE MARK YOU MAKE (1)

ANNA PAUSED AT the top of the steps and surveyed the banner, thermometer, and many Kids For Kids signs, most autographed by their owners, littering the front hall. While a trophy would have been easier to store, Joe, thank God, had this tangible Polar Plunge debris from the day before. She would have to think long and hard how best to organize it into a scrapbook or decoupage. With a beer in one hand and cocoa in the other, Paul emerged from the kitchen into the hall. From the living room, an announcer called a foul against the Knicks.

"I need to talk to you for a minute, Paul."

He looked toward the living room. "Right now? It's fourth quarter."

"Kind of important."

"Then, sure," he held up the cocoa. "I'll just give Joe this."

Anna gripped the manila folder with the article she had spent half the night on and started down the steps. "Meet you in the kitchen."

"Trying to have your way with me again?" he called back lightly.

She picked up one of Ralphie's chew toys from the landing. Having sex with Paul the night before probably hadn't been the best idea. However, explaining that they might be separating didn't seem to fit in with the celebratory atmosphere in the Lawson household either. Joe, still on a high from the Arts Center bash, seized Molly's return from babysitting as an excuse to relive the glory in exacting detail: the scary waiting in line, climbing up on the blocks, the jump, the applause and, of course, the party. Throughout the recitation, Paul and Anna provided elucidatory spectator gasps, applause, and lively whoo hoos. The exciting reenactment led to drinks, order out, Molly's announcement that someday she would like to be in the Polar Plunge, and ultimately, Paul seeing an opportunity.

"Heading over to Gwen's sale?" Paul said following her into the kitchen.

Anna picked up her purse and rummaged for her keys. "No, I've got a meeting. Maybe a long meeting. That's what I have to talk to you about."

Paul pulled out a chair. "Okay, shoot. Remember, I have to leave for the airport at four."

Loose change clunked against tile as Anna turned her purse upside down on the kitchen counter. Amid receipts, tic tacs, and other purse detritus, the keys sat tucked in the middle of the checkbook. "Molly will be here. She's making dinner."

Paul set the beer on the table. "You won't be back?"

Why did being honest and acting courageously have to be so hard? She caught herself. Last night's sex hadn't been too honest. More a sentimental coward's way out. "It's a meeting of the Friends of Catskill. There is a core group still fighting the on line school idea. They want me to help."

Paul eyed her warily. "Help, how?"

"To get their message out. Write some columns about Catskill and Onasego that alums in New York might read."

"Like what?"

Anna held up the manila folder. "I wrote one last night called 'The Town That Astounds.' It describes how this area has so much going for it. All the cultural and educational opportunities, the rural beauty, the depth of the charitable work, the history."

"You wrote this last night?"

She shrugged. "Later, last night."

"How would that help the Friends?"

Anna stashed the keys in her pocket and began separating the coins on the counter. "It would just be a beginning piece, landscape sort of, before going into the debate over Catskill converting to distance learning."

Paul hesitated, "And you really think Marty will go for this? Doesn't sound much like one of your typical columns."

Anna stacked up five dimes and four quarters. "I just heard back from him. He likes the underdog angle, a small town fighting dubious progress."

"Will there be good guys and bad guys?"

"I suppose."

There was quiet, the Knicks made a big score, then the expected explosion.

"What about my job? Remember? The job we moved here for."

She pushed nickels one way and pennies another. "I didn't plan this."

Paul scraped the chair back, standing. "I know the whole on line issue backward and forward. You don't."

"But," she uncrumpled a receipt from RiteMarket then held it up for Paul to see, "you don't know this town. You go on fundraising trips while I stay here and do the schools, the grocery story, the Y, the volunteer stuff, the church thing. I'm the one out shoveling."

"And in case *you* forgot," he said snatching the receipt and ripping it up, "that's our agreement. You run the house and I make the money." He waved the checkbook in her face. "And I currently make money at the pleasure of the Catskill Board of Directors."

Anna scooped the remains from the counter back in her purse. "But having a real, living, breathing Catskill is essential for Onasego. If Catskill goes on line, people will lose their jobs. Businesses will shut down. Maybe no more Fun and Fabulous. Maybe no more Polar Plunge. Think about yesterday. I've never seen that much heart on display in my life."

Paul took her shoulders. "This feels like betrayal."

Another seize the moment, moment. "How many times have you betrayed me, Paul?"

He pulled her in close. "Oh, hell, Anna, you know none of it was serious."

"Not even Erika?"

She felt the flinch run down his body. "No, certainly not Erika."

"So why do you do it?"

The steam from just seconds earlier vanished. "Cause I can't seem to stop. But you know that."

She ran her hand over the contours of the boyish face. "You have to go soon, Paul."

He took a long moment. "Are we talking about a business trip?"

"Nope."

"Separation or divorce?"

Her mind played over Joe and Paul trash talking, running over the ice, duck walking. "I'm not sure."

"Why now?"

"It should have been a while ago."

You've never strayed, Anna?"

Shit. Honesty. Domnica. "Only once."

"So you should understand," he smoothed her hair back, "it doesn't really matter."

Joe's whoop from the living room signaled a Knicks' win.

She laid her face against his shoulder. "No, Paul, it mattered very much."

## 66 • COMPLICATED

"WILLIAM, IT'S ME. Just wanted to hear your voice. I'll try again later."

Anna clicked off her phone and sat back in one of the new super-sized comfy chairs that were supposed to transform the cold, empty Great Hall into a warm and inviting place for students to gather. But as the lone inhabitant of the new furniture, the plan didn't seem to be working. Which was fine, as she needed some time before the meeting. The scene in the kitchen had been a lot tougher than she'd expected. Kind of like ripping off an arm.

The thing was…. Paul had it right. If she was really, really honest, somewhere in her mitochondria she'd known from the get go that he would be a hard guy to keep on the farm. But she'd buried that little instinctive nugget under the vanity that she was THE ONE to make him change his ways. Well, that, and maybe the fact that Paul, bad boy flirt and all, was such a gift after Jed and his billable hours. On point two, her support of the Friends, true again. What did she know about the future of higher education? And then there was the whole separation thing. Anna from Paul. And Paul from Joe. She'd taken Molly from Jed and hadn't that worked out so well. And where the hell was William?

"You here for the Friends' meeting?"

Anna looked up to see Ray in shorts and an O Yanks tee-shirt walking in with Tim and Laurel.

"I am." She threw her phone in her purse. "All the way."

"Me too," Ray said, motioning toward the elevator. "So, come on. We've got work to do."

Ray pondered the flip chart. CATSKILL… JUST LIKE WHEN YOU LEFT. *Act Now. Stop Change.*, and Angie's action items from the last meeting. People from that meeting, plus Deb, Ellis, released temporarily into Tim's care, and several new student faces brought in by Jason and Morgan, watched him ponder while munching on chocolate torte, freshly baked by Peg. Anna, in the midst of writing instructions to Molly on how to julienne, felt a punch to the shoulder. She looked at Deedee, the puncher, sitting beside her who pointed to Laurel who pointed at her watch, then held up a pencil and made a drawing in the air.

"Minutes," Ellis, sitting at Anna's left, drawled.

Anna resisted the urge to stick out her tongue.

"Okay, everybody," Ray announced from the front. "I see where this is going. You have to get alums to lobby the board against the on line college idea. And you have to get them here in May so there won't be any wriggle room when the board votes. But how are you going to get them to drive up here?"

Deedee pointed at Jason. "This was your idea. So what, exactly, besides the campus, would get you to drive four hours from Manhattan to come back to?"

"Easy. Downtown. The bars, Mama Nells's, Sid's."

"But suppose you're forty-four years old with three kids. What are you going to do with them that weekend?"

Jason slunk back in his seat. "Ask me when I'm forty-four."

Amid the groans Tim raised his hand. "Angus said that he got calls from all over after Anna wrote about his farm. People wanting to bring their families. Kids could do that."

Ellis turned an exasperated eye to Tim. "Hey, kids, meet a pot farmer. Great idea."

Deedee waved off Ellis. "But meet *a* farmer *is* a great idea. How many city kids get to visit a real farm? We could make a map."

"Okay," Angie said walking to the front. She turned the page on the flip chart and wrote *Alum Family activities, # 1: Farm tour.* What else?"

Coach Dan held up a hand. "How about the O Yanks? And the Baseball and Soccer Halls of Fame? They're all near here."

"Certainly," Angie answered, adding #2 and #3.

"Sometimes the Glimmerglass opera has children's productions," Peg offered.

"What about activities right here in Onasego?" Ray asked.

The question brought a momentary pause, then from Morgan a rapid, "Canoeing and kayaking on the Susquehanna."

Jason's hand shot up. "Okay, I've got this now. What about a whole day camp on the campus for kids? Track, swimming, gymnastics? Then their parents can schmooze around."

"And talk to the board," Ray said.

"And talk to the board," Angie repeated. "Fabulous idea. What else?"

"Downtown there's the Farmers' Market and a band every Saturday," a man sitting behind Laurel shouted. "How about the Red Neck Mothers, Ellis?"

Ellis cracked his knuckles. "I'll be in jail."

Deb waved both hands. "How about this? We get the city to close traffic to downtown that Saturday. The restaurants and hotels could do special alum deals. Same with the merchants and sidewalk sales. We could get a banner made to go across Main Street, **CATSKILL AND ONASEGO... Just Like When You Left.** And we print bumper stickers, storefront signs, maybe tee shirts."

Ray bowed to the group. "And it all fits right in the Forget Me Not theme. Perfect!"

Laurel raised her hand. "Wait! I think we should expand on the Meet A Farmer idea for the children. Like, Meet An Ice Fisherman or Meet A Wild Bird Rehabilitator. There are so many people we could contact."

Anna looked up from her minutes, opportunity knocking. "You know, my article about Country Covens got a lot of calls. Laurel, you could talk to the children, too."

"Meet a Witch!" Peg chirped.

Anna turned to meet Laurel's smoldering gaze and smiled.

Anna pulled into the driveway behind Paul's car. The dashboard clock read four-thirty. Maybe he'd gotten a ride with Pug or somebody to the airport. The phone in her coat pocket buzzed. Looking at the caller ID, she felt herself relax for the first time in hours. William.

"Hey, I tried you earlier."

"I know. My mother was in town. We had a long lunch and a walk. She just left."

Anna tried to visualize the grainy, tiny figure in Libby's van the day of the regatta sitting in a shi-shi restaurant with William. Or perhaps they didn't do things like that. Maybe Mumma loaded up some of her canned goods for a semi home cooked meal before bumping down the seasonal road to Manhattan.

"Well, I have two news items here. The first thing is I told Paul we should separate."

Long pause. Then, "You sure?"

She stared at the phone. Not quite the expected response. "I thought you'd be glad."

Another pause. "Would you be doing this if I wasn't around? And what about your children?"

What the hell was this about? Who had he been talking to? "Look, I can't say I've thought through every detail. I've procrastinated for so long about this separation, but then, you know, after the Desmond."

"What's the second piece of news?" His voice sounded weary.

The notebook with today's minutes stuck out of her purse. This was supposed to be the hard part. "I've just come from a Friends' meeting. I'm going to help them. I think they have a shot at changing your—I mean, the board's—mind."

Very, very, very long pause. "Anna, I think we need to not see each other for a while."

Light snow dusted the windshield. He had been talking to his mother, that's who, over a long lunch. "Why?"

The velvet voice was devastating. "Two reasons. First off, it doesn't sound like you've thought this separation all the way through. Especially where your children and I are concerned. Second, I'm a member of the Board of Directors of Catskill. Your husband, even estranged, works as our point-man to raise money to save the school. Now you, a known journalist, are siding with the opposition. It's all too complicated."

She wanted to hit something. "You mean it wouldn't look right for me to be with you and have my own opinion?"

"No, I said complicated. Like we shouldn't let our personal situation muddy matters when the college and the town situation are at such odds."

Anna shut off the car. "Okay, gotta go."

"Come on, Anna. I'm trying to think for both of us."

She pushed open the car door. The snow was sticking to the driveway now. "Well, don't."

Paul met her at the front door. "Hi."

She took in the jeans and tee shirt. "Why are you here?"

"I should shovel the driveway soon. And, Molly's got that stir-fry for dinner."

"What about your work trip?"

"Cancelled it."

She scanned the living room and hall. No Molly or Joe. "I thought I was clear. You need to leave."

"Oh, you were clear," he reached up to help her with her coat, "but, I don't want to."

## 67 • DO(ING) UNTO OTHERS

"Mom!"

Anna slid the article she was reading into her top desk drawer. "Joe, I'm kind of busy."

Joe, dressed as Deganawidah, entered the office solemnly and sat cross-legged on the floor. "Why is Dad staying in the guest room?"

She glanced at the clock. In eight minutes, Jed would be waiting for her call. "We told you. We need a little break from each other. And shouldn't you be downstairs? He'll be here any minute to pick you up to go back to the Long House."

Puzzled green eyes looked up from the floor. "Sometimes Molly and I need a break. But Dad and I don't ever. And you and me don't."

"Wait 'til you're a teenager."

Joe propped his elbow on his knee and put his chin in his hand. "How long will the break be?"

"Don't know." Actually, she did sort of know. While she was baiting Laurel at the Friends meeting, Paul, like any development guy worth his salt, had come up with a pithy proposal very quickly. He would move into the guest room. He would also pitch in with Joe's schedule, help clean, shop, and limit business trips to three days a week. The major provision of the plan, however, was more of a bet: If Paul made it to the end of the school year without showing any interest in another woman, she would, at least, consider family counseling. She'd agreed in about two minutes because it made no sense not to. She didn't have all the details of a separation thought out yet, but having Paul around helping was way better than being a single mom and doing everything. So the agreement could last for almost three months or, depending on his libido, tomorrow. A horn blared from the driveway.

"That's your dad."

Joe jumped up. "Sure you don't want to go?"

And deprive Paul of his first foray alone into the wide world of home schooling? No way. She smiled, "Oh honey, I've got work to do. And you know I've already been."

The horn blared again and Joe ran for the door.

"Don't forget your notebook!" Anna yelled after him. "You have to write a 'Where I Live' report."

She waited for the door to slam and opened her desk drawer. The article she had been reading was gold, pure gold for her call to Jed. For herself, pure guilt. She circled a paragraph, set the phone on speaker option, dialed and waited. One ring, two rings, three rings. Surely Jed's phone at the ever-so-upscale offices of Hardin and Hardin had caller ID. Four rings. Five rings. Click.

"Yeah, Anna, I'm here."

She donned her cheery voice. "Hi, Jed. How are you?"

"Busy, not much time."

Big surprise there. "How's Ava?"

The vibe softened immediately. "All baby, all the time. What do you think of the name, Pemberley? You know, from Jane Austen."

Pemberley Parish, Chinese baby girl. "Perfect. I love it."

"So what's up?"

She focused on the photo of Molly pinned to her bulletin board. "I wanted to talk more about the condo question and Molly coming to live with you. You think I have influence with William Johnson, but I don't."

A pause then *whomp* back to business. "Too bad. I was hoping we could do a deal."

Downstairs Ralphie started barking. She got up and looked out the window. Nobody. "So the only way Molly can come live with you is if you get one of William Johnson's condos?"

"Yup."

No more cheer. She walked over and closed the door to muffle Ralphie. "Come on, Jed. You're not like this. I know you're not. This is your daughter, Molly, who wants to come live you. She's been killing herself learning how to cook and babysit. You'd love having her."

"Not if we're tripping over each other."

"There are other condos in Manhattan."

"Not the ones Ava wants."

She sat back at her desk. "Jed, I can't get you a William Johnson condo. Believe me."

"I don't."

The barking stopped. She hesitated, pulled up the mental image of Ray and Lisa taking the plunge, and plunged in herself. "Well, in that case, I've got a deal for you."

"You do, do you?"

His sarcasm was helpful. She sat back in her chair, calm, cool, and furious. "I do. I've been considering a column on fathers."

"So?"

"Absentee fathers actually. It's a big problem." She picked up an article from the *Star Ledger*. "Here's some research: 'The absence of a father has been linked to risky behavior in youth like dropping out of school, early sexuality, substance abuse, criminal behavior, and acting out.'"

"We're divorced, Anna, ergo I'm absent. Nolo contendere."

"There's more," she flipped the page. "'And, generally speaking, any man in the home will not do. Children with a step-father do not fare as well, and those who share a home with the mother's boyfriend do even worse.'"

"Where's this going?" His voice was flat, Dirty Harryish.

"You know how I like my columns to be authentic. If you can't find a way to let Molly live with you for a while, then our situation will personify the prevalence of the absentee father phenomenon. My own daughter's father, partner in a mega successful law firm, healthy and able, won't let her come live with him, even temporarily. Even as he is awaiting a new child.... a new daughter." She waited, forcing herself to breathe. This was her best shot. Really, her only shot."

"A lot of people know we were married once," he said at last.

"Right. It's sort of an ace in the hole. Deal metaphor and all."

"You wouldn't."

"Wouldn't what?"

"Write this column."

She propped her feet on an open drawer. "You want to find out?"

## 68 • UH-OH

"So, Anna, it has been some time since we talked. What is going on with you?"

Domnica looked like an elegant sign of spring today in a sunny yellow silk shirtdress, nude heels, and delicate gold bangles. And, as usual, she exuded that quality Anna had only ever picked up from select European women, of being more stylish than anyone in the room and, seemingly indifferent to it.

"I feel like I'm out on an enormous limb."

"How is that?"

Let me count the ways, Anna thought, brushing dog hair off her jeans. "I've demanded a sort of trial separation from my husband. Not exactly the best move for someone with a low paying part-time job. I've threatened my extremely legalistic ex husband with some very bad PR in my column if he doesn't let our daughter come live with him. I've signed up with the Friends of Catskill to help them fight the on line school concept, and therefore I'm also effectively fighting my husband, the other guy I'm interested in, and possibly common sense. Plus, I have no idea what should happen with Joe's future. All I'm sure of is that he had the best day of his life when he swam in the Polar Plunge."

"I read about his Kids For Kids team in *The Onasegon*. You must be proud." Domnica smiled briefly, then pointed her pen at Anna signaling back to work. "Let's break down your big limb; start with the separation. Why now?"

"I think my time, you know, with the man I spoke to you of, pushed me to it."

"The biblical man?" Domnica asked dryly.

Anna recalled Domnica's low estimate of that relationship. "Yes, but as I told you, this separation was also way overdue. I knew that."

"And your help for the Friends group?"

"I think what they're trying to do is extremely worthwhile. And I agree with them."

"So on these two issues you are sure of your purpose, if not the outcome?"

Anna felt a warm ray of confidence. "I guess I am."

"And if the Polar Plunge was the best day of your son's life, why not try to seek something similar? You should trust yourself to find a way for him."

Easier said than done, Anna thought. "I can't keep home schooling him. With this separation I have to get a real job."

Domnica shrugged. "You're a writer, my dear. Write."

Another easier said than done. "What about maligning my ex husband in a column?"

Domnica stared at Anna, her chin edged to the forty-five degree mark. "I think you know the correct way forward on that issue as well."

Anna sighed. "Well, maybe. I do know one thing for sure: I'm not treasuring every moment like I promised myself I would."

Domnica flipped back a page in her notes. "Ah, yes. Why did you make this promise?"

"I thought I was going to die. So, among a few other things, I promised God that if I could live, I would never doubt him and I'd treasure every moment."

"Never doubt... God? Treasure every moment? My dear, I may have some land in—is it Florida?—for you. And what does treasuring every moment even mean?"

Anna thought for a second. "I guess finding enjoyment in every moment. Not taking time for granted."

"Those are two very different things. How can one enjoy every moment? Could you ever have enjoyed your mother's rages?"

"No."

"Could you have enjoyed learning of your husband's affairs?"

"No."

"But you learned from your mother's rages. They helped form who you are. The latter you seemed to have pushed aside until recently."

Anna suddenly felt exhausted. "I can't learn from every moment."

"Goodness, no. But you can try to be present enough to realize what's happening. Or store the moment away until you can make some sense of it."

The scene of herself lying in front of Molly's door rose up in Anna's mind. "That even sounds way too hard."

"It is hard," Domnica nodded. "Just this past weekend I found myself listening to my son describing a situation with a woman. I wanted so to push it all aside and just watch the tourists out the window, enjoy a very good lunch."

"Same here. For months now I've wanted to run every time my daughter opened her..." Anna stopped, her synapses firing a profound uh-oh. She gripped the couch arm. "You saw tourists out of a window around here?"

"Oh no. In Manhattan where my son lives."

"You have a son?"

Domnica glanced down at a photo frame on her desk. "Why, yes. His name is William."

Anna studied the photo of William in cap and gown standing with his mother and an older man outside Hardy Hall.

"Such an attractive family."

"That picture is old," Domnica said. "My son is now 48 and my husband died in a hunting accident some years ago."

William was a near perfect mix of both parents. Dark and intense like Domnica. Tall and lanky like his dad. She remembered the Christmas party. "I know one," he'd said about a therapist. "Where did you and your husband meet?"

"I came to study at Columbia after the war. He was a law student there."

Anna couldn't stop herself. "And, Onasego?"

"Bill was from here. I followed along. But," Domnica picked up her file again, "enough of this. We have to get back to treasuring moments and your big limb."

Anna watched the therapist shuffling papers, inserting notes here and there, and tried to superimpose this personage onto the tiny figure in the van, the hardy farm lady canning and preserving, the little old lady up the rutted road from Libby's, the mother who had talked her son into calling off a relationship.

"Mumma?"

Domnica looked up. "How do you know that?"

"From Libby and Dawn."

She lowered the file. "Why are you just mentioning this now? We've spoken of Libby and Dawn before."

"I didn't put it all together until just now. They only call you 'Mumma.' Or, William's mother 'Mumma.'" Anna gazed around the office, the serene escape from Onasego. She would miss this. "I also know William. But I never put Johnson with Badescu."

Domnica shook her head. "Sometimes I forget what a small place Onasego is. How do you know William?"

Anna picked up her purse and coat to leave. "Biblically."


## 69 • ANOTHER EQUINOX

ANNA READ DOWN Laurel's Wicca Wire mass email detailing upcoming holidays:

> March 20: Spring Equinox. A time of growth and possibility. A good time to start new ventures.
> April 30: The Great Beltane. A time of love and union from which comes creation, growth, and harmony. A time to work in the garden or some activity which will help nature grow.

Below the write up, Laurel had thoughtfully attached a picture of herself waving from a tractor.

Anna picked up the front page of *The Onasegon*, scanning down to weather. *March 17. Sunrise 7:09. Sunset 7:06.* Almost an equinox. She thought back to the fall equinox, the beginning of so much of the Molly trouble, Joe jumping in the lake, Paul slipping off with Erika. Maybe she should just ignore this one. But! Was she not in the midst of a new venture? She clicked out of Laurel's email and went back to the one she had composed to Marty. She considered the subject line, A PROPOSAL, then deleted it. What to title a plea for a full-time job, with a livable wage and benefits? She thought of Domnica's note, a thoughtful two-page, single-space document closing out their therapist/client relationship, in her center desk drawer. In the note, Domnica reiterated, among several other thoughts, her "You're a writer. Write!" admonition. Anna stared at the screen. William and Domnica, handed to her like gifts, then jerked away. Why? Was it her perfect ability to screw up? Or was it the universe butting in again? She shook herself and banged out, MARTY, I NEED A JOB! That was clear. Then added SOON! Downstairs Ralphie barked, and she heard the front door open, followed by "MOM!" and "We're back, Babe!" and, the perennial, "Jeez, Joe, gross!"

By the time she spell-checked the email and pushed SEND, Joe, Paul, Molly and Ralphie were crowded into her office, all sporting some green nod-to-the-Irish including Ralphie, with the "Kiss Me I'm Irish" button Paul pinned to his collar that morning.

"Hi, how was it?" Anna asked, referring to the St. Patrick's Day Cabaret with the Onasego Symphony that Paul had come home with tickets for.

Joe climbed into her lap. "Mom, all these drunk kids are walking around everywhere yelling and screaming. Dad says they've got green beer!"

Paul pulled off his tie. "The cabaret was packed. I knew there was symphony up here but I had no idea they were so good." He looked at Joe. "I think I'll have a green beer."

Awe spread over Joe's face. "You have green beer?"

"Yeah, it's called Heineken. Want some?"

Joe leapt out of Anna's lap and ran to the door. "Beat you down there!"

"No way," Paul yelled, catching Joe by the shirt and racing past him down the hall.

In the relative quiet that followed, Anna marveled at how gorgeous Molly looked in an emerald green sweater-dress and boots. "What did you think?"

"It was all right." Molly reached around and pulled the door closed. "Mom, we have to talk."

## 70 • KIND OF CRAZED

MOLLY STUCK HER head around Anna's office door. "Has Dad called yet?"

Anna looked up from Joe's report on the Long House and shook her head. She didn't know who was more nervous about this expected call from Jed, herself or Molly. Returning to Joe's report, she circled *bos* and *aros* in red. The boy got the spelling for Deganawidah right every time. So why were bows and arrows so hard? Her eyes traveled back over to the computer screen and Marty's email.

*"Town That Astounds"—Great! Based on response considering possible series on Upstate Towns for weekend getaways. Ideas? Also, working on job specs. Need your CV ASAP. Marty.*

She looked over at Ralphie sleeping in front of the space heater. She should be thrilled with that email but instead felt oddly removed. And what was the difference between a CV and a resume, anyway? She jumped at the phone's sudden brrrring.

"Hello?" She heard papers rustling, a TV in the background. "Jed?"

"Yeah."

Anna tried to breathe a calm C at the anger in that "yeah." She had to get this right on two counts. One, because Molly asked her to call him. And, two, because she had to somehow make Jed understand, without putting it into words, that what Molly wanted her to say was exactly opposite of how Molly really felt.

"Thank you for agreeing to a call." She mentally pushed aside the fact that he had needed a week to work her into his schedule. "We really need to talk."

"Why? You want to threaten me some more? Tape me for the cops or something?"

Anna gazed at her bulletin board and the *speak evil of no one* admonition from Handsome Lake. "No, I want to apologize."

That was a conversation pauser. The TV voices disappeared.

"I'm listening."

She took a deep breath. "First off, I was wrong. I knew it and I was going to call you. I am kind of crazed that you won't take Molly, but libel probably isn't the best way to make that happen."

"You got that right."

"But more importantly, I didn't know it, but Molly heard parts of my conversation with you."

"How did you not know that?"

"Molly came back to the house to pick up something. I heard the dog bark but didn't hear her. Anyway, she told me in no uncertain terms that she considers you a great dad and if it doesn't work for her to come and live with you and Ava and… Pemberley, then she understands completely. And I was to call and let you know that. Furthermore, I should stay out of her business."

She waited. And waited. "Jed, you there?"

"Give me a minute. I'll call back."

"She really said that? You didn't make it up?"

Anna's shoulders slipped down a notch. Jed's voice had lost some of the growl. "Yes, to the first. And, no, to the second."

Another long pause. She scratched Ralphie, now lying on her lap, under his collar. Then…

"Look, Molly is a great girl. A super girl. Can't believe she learned to cook. But I just can't do it without that condo."

Wrong answer. According to her plan and the tenets of reverse psychology, Jed should be calling the moving van after hearing Molly's complimentary and gracious statement of understanding regarding the living situation. Shoulders back up. "Why?"

"Because Ava thinks if she has to be a full-time stepmother she should get something out of the deal. And she thinks you can get it for her."

Anna felt sick. Her eyes strayed to Molly's most recent recipe for *pupusas* tacked to her bulletin board. "But I can't." She heard the TV click back on, a chair swiveling, the office revving up again.

"Then, and this may be counterintuitive," Jed said in his best I'm-the-brilliant-lawyer-listen-to-me tone, "I have to conclude that everything is fine. Molly can't come live with us because you can't get the condo. But, according to you, Molly understands if she can't come live with us and is fine with that. So, you see, everyone is fine."

Did she also hear relief in his voice? Why not? With that logic he didn't have to deal with Ava, Molly, or a new condo. She had not only given him an out, but he could also pin it all on her!

"Jed, this is so unfair. You're denying Molly her deepest wish and blaming me for it. You call her and tell her exactly what this is about!" She gripped the receiver, astonished by the sudden whine of the dial tone. Ralphie, still snuggled in her lap, turned and stared, his brown eyes searching hers.

The door creaked open. Molly slipped through, Bennie Bear in hand, and stood beside her desk. "That was Dad, right?"

Anna tried to gin up the MOM smile. "Yep. I apologized and told him what you said. He really appreciated it."

"And..."

Anna sighed. Why did she have to lie for Jed and Ava? "Your dad said they don't have enough room for you to live there."

Molly's gaze cut to the window.

"He said they would have to get a new condo."

"That's all he said?"

Anna wanted to scream. Not so long ago, she could have pulled Molly onto her lap. Now she couldn't even reach for her hand. All she could do was *not* tell her what Jed really said. So she smiled the fake smile again. "Your dad thinks you are, and I quote, such a great girl. And he can't believe you learned to cook."

Bennie Bear smashed to the floor. "He can't believe I learned to cook?" The sullen edge so recently lost settled back over Molly's features. "Well, I fucking can't either."

## 71 • APRIL FOOLS

RAY CLICKED ON the overhead projector. The lead article of *The Onasegon* filled the screen at the front of Founders Lounge.

*April 1, 1998*
*Trustees Believe Anti-On Line Stance by Friends of Catskill College Well-Intentioned but Misguided.*

*By Mac Bruny*
*The Onasegon*

*In a wide-ranging interview with The Onasegon, Catskill College's top trustee Phil Coxe stated that the school's future viability lies in remodeling itself on a distance learning (on line) concept recommended by several members of the Catskill Board of Directors. He went on to say that the anti-on line position of the Friends of Catskill reflects the membership's inadequate understanding of the challenges facing higher education. Referring to the Friends' efforts to preserve the school as a traditional four-year liberal arts institution, Coxe quipped, "Strategic vision, not bake sales, will save Catskill College." Moreover, Coxe elaborated, the Friends' apparent willingness to pass up two million dollars to underwrite the school's transition to distance learning would be viewed by any business person as "gross financial naivety."*

*The two million dollars that Cox referred to is the price offered by the Van Consortium, led by Jamie Van for undeveloped, wholly owned Catskill property, should the school obligate itself to the distance learning concept. In calls with The Onasegon, Van stated that the consortium's premium offer "is a visionary stroke that allows for development of the local baseball camp market opportunity, while at the same time, providing corporate philanthropy in support of Catskill's organic positioning for the twenty-first century."*

Anna scanned down the screen. Since early morning, emails had passed fast and furiously among the Friends questioning the timing and motivation of the article.

"So, what are we going to do?" Ray asked, switching the lights back on. The Niece, Anna was surprised to see, had slipped in during the brief darkness.

"I think Jamie Van needs an organically positioned visionary stroke crammed right up his," Angie hesitated, "you know."

Over the titters the golf coach chimed in from the back corner. "We've got a plan; we stick to it. Keep on keeping on."

To Anna's right, Jason punched Morgan, hissing, "Right on!"

"We have a plan," Ray said, massaging his temples, "but this article makes us sound like a bunch of country bumpkins."

Angie threw up her hands up in despair. "It's kind of like Jamie Van is king and he's decided what should happen around here. Gotta have an on line school. Gotta have all that property for baseball."

Anna didn't dare look up from the minutes and possibly see Tim's face.

Deedee took up the cause. "Well, he is like a king, with the banks, the restaurants, all the horses."

"No more horses." Everyone turned to look at Ellis, pointing at himself. "Remember me? Animal official? The missus trucked them off. Too cold."

"Whatever," Deedee allowed, "so just banks and restaurants; Jamie still throws a lot of weight up here."

"Look, everyone," Ray broke in, "we need to stay on point. And that point is that somehow we have to convince a majority of the board to vote our way. Eleven trustees. We need six."

"What about Pug?" The Niece asked.

The Niece's question caused a momentary hush before Deedee explained, "Pug only votes in a tie. We need to keep him out of it."

"Could Pug, Jamie, and Phil Coxe be right?" There it was. The thought that Anna couldn't let go of. But why had she said it out loud? She studied her minutes.

In a slow regal movement, Laurel pulled herself to full height and walked to the front of the room. "Mrs. Lawson raises a good point. Moreover, it is the same point that Ray referred to earlier when he asked how to combat the inference of *The Onasegon* article that we are quaint yet clueless meddlers in affairs, such as strategic visions, that are beyond our limited faculties to comprehend. And, because we must deal with this question, I will tell you the answer."

Scribbling furiously, Anna felt the room collectively lean toward the podium.

"Jamie Van, Phil Coxe, and perhaps even Pug," Laurel began, then paused for dramatic effect, gazing around the room, "fail to understand that any plan for the future of Catskill College..." she paused again to raise an eyebrow, "must recognize that we are all participants in the great interdependence of life."

Ellis slapped his forehead. "Aw, jeez, stop her. Come on somebody. Stop her right now." Even Ray looked pained.

"Don't laugh, gentleman," Laurel continued, "there is good news. Our plan demonstrates this relationship. Our plan supports life. The plan of Misters Van and Coxe does neither. And now, excuse me, I must go." With a nod to the room, Laurel turned and strode out of the lounge.

Ellis counted out loud to five before banging his head on the desk.

"So what do we do now, Ray?" Anna was surprised to hear Libby finally get involved.

Ray gave her a wry smile. "I guess, unless someone gets a better idea, we do as Dan said. We keep on."

Angie caught up with Anna in the parking lot. "Got a minute? Two things."

Anna nodded. She really wasn't looking forward to going home. Since the Jed call, sharing a house with Molly was really just self abuse. Either she was contemptuous to the point of cruelty or, even worse, locked in her room in the dark.

Angie pushed the ever-present tote over her shoulder. "Ray wondered if you could go back through the minutes starting in November—see if we're overlooking something. And number two, now don't worry because financing's impossible, there's an offer on your house."

Instantly Anna saw herself, Molly, and Joe camped out in a high-school gym. "Who?"

"I can't tell. It's confidential."

The vision expanded to Ralphie pawing at the gym door under a NO PETS ALLOWED sign. "Nothing is confidential in Onasego. You told me that. And you're supposed to be my friend."

"I am."

"Well, prove it."

Angie peered off into the night, then glanced toward the hill leading down from the Great Hall. Nodding to herself, she scanned the parking lot in a three-hundred and sixty degree circle before leaning up to whisper in Anna's ear. "Peter."

## 72 • MORE APRIL FOOLS

ANNA WALKED INTO the kitchen from the meeting to find Joe, in his paja-mas, cutting pictures out of magazines, and Paul, hovering over his com-puter. She sat down beside Joe. "What are you doing still up?"

"Working on my project report. Dad said he'd help me."

She turned to Paul. "Thought you were frantically getting ready to go to Philly tomorrow."

"Not so frantic." The look he gave her was soft. Easy.

Joe gazed up at her. "Mom, what's on your nose?"

Anna slapped a hand over her face and turned to Paul for help.

Paul squinted at her. "Wow, kinda gross."

She was half out of her seat headed for the powder room mirror when Joe collapsed over his cutouts, cackling.

Paul smiled gamely up at her. "April Fools. Okay, Joe, say goodnight."

Anna, chastened at having fallen for the grade-school trick, pointed to her cheek, "Kiss."

Still smirking at the prank, Joe stacked up his scissors and pictures before rounding the table, giving her a noisy kiss, followed by a second one for Paul. They waited to hear his footsteps on the hall upstairs. Paul stood and opened the refrigerator. "Wine?"

"Um, sure." She pulled off her coat and gloves. "Where's Molly?"

"Upstairs. She's been on the phone a lot tonight."

"Wonder if that's good or bad."

"Don't know. How was the meeting?"

"Everyone is pretty bummed by that article in the paper this morning." She took the glass he offered her. "Was that your idea?"

"Not the wording, just the interview." He settled back in behind his com-puter.

Anna held her glass up to him; underestimating his professional abilities would be very foolish. "You suits are tough."

"One suit thinks you are, too. You really got to Jamie."

"I did?" She tried for a Julia Roberts sized grin. "Great! How?"

"Jamie was annoyed by 'The Town That Astounds.' He thinks thousands of cramped Manhattanites will come running up here to buy property and drive up land prices."

"Why wouldn't a banker like that?"

"Maybe because it might get in the way of more baseball camps. *His* baseball camps." He ran his forefinger around the rim of the wineglass, an old nervous habit. "Kind of weird, isn't it? We've become the Carville and Matalin of Onasego."

"We've…" A sudden elephant in the room. She propped an elbow on the table and tried to push by. "Hey, guess what, Peter made an offer on the house."

"This house?"

"Yeah, but Angie doesn't think he'll get financing."

Paul's hand crept over hers. "You know, everything is so uncertain: my job, your maybe job, Catskill, Molly, Joe, now this thing with the house. And then there's us." He traced the outline of her fingers. "We've been in this new arrangement for exactly thirty-nine days now. Any thoughts?"

Any thoughts? She studied Paul, leaving her hand where it was. Sure she had thoughts, thoughts like… what to do with this hugely flawed, impressive, needy, but ultimately good man. Also, her son's father. Should she comment on that? Or on Joe's delight having his dad in the house to plan an April's Fool's trick with? Now that would be a conversation. And then there was William. Her attraction to him. Basic, simple, essential. Should she share that?

"No. Not really."

## 73 • SYBIL

ANNA LOOKED AT the computer screen. Eleven-fifteen p.m. Molly should have been back from her babysitting gig by ten-thirty. At eleven-thirty she would call.

Pulling her robe tighter, she willed herself back into the stack of Friends' minutes. Reliving her few meetings as secretary just brought back all the emotion, the divisiveness, the sense of helplessness, the David and Goliath of it all. Ray wanted outstanding details, something overlooked. But what could they have overlooked? The situation seemed straight forward. Catskill was in financial trouble. Phil Coxe and Jamie Van, convinced that going on line was the future-oriented way out of trouble, convinced others of same. Jamie Van then figured out a funding scheme by acquiring Tim's land bequest to underwrite the transition. On the other side, the Friends of Catskill wanted to maintain the status quo, and had bet/hoped/prayed that alums would feel likewise and support that vision of Catskill and Onasego's future with their pocketbooks. Clear cut. End of case. Looking back through the notes, the only outstanding issues seemed to be nailing down all the "meet a blank" people and getting someone to explain to Peg why Jamie would need so much land for his baseball complex. Baseball diamonds are BIG, Peg; ditto the parking lots around them. Since she, herself, had no idea how big an acre was, good city girl that she was, maybe she should look that up, maybe Ask Jeeves. Downstairs the front door creaked open, followed by light steps toward the kitchen. Finally.

She clicked back into her emails one last time before bed. Two new ones. The first one was from Ray with the subject: Ellis Farewell:

*Dear friends of Ellis, please join us for a farewell to Ellis at the Friends meeting scheduled for April 29th... As Ellis must report for his incarceration on May 3rd, this will be our last chance to say goodbye. With respect for Ellis's love of food, a potluck appears to be in order, so please bring your favorite Ellis-inspired dish. RSVPs to Ray or Tim. No gifts, please. Prison rules.*

Anna laughed out loud. You had to love a small town. And talk about columns writing themselves.

She looked down the hall again. No Molly yet. The second email was entitled FYI from Deedee. The address list included all the Friends members. She read:

*Now the board is hosting a huge cocktail party for alums in NYC on April 15th. The board is planning to use the event to get ahead of the Forget Me Not. Do their selling, conveniently, in the city. This is terrible news.*

Anna clicked out. Bad news it was, and probably another of Paul's ideas. Why drive to Onasego when Onasego is coming to you. Lights snapped off in the hall. Molly appeared at the top of the steps.

"Hey, Molly," Anna whispered.

"Night."

"Come talk for a minute."

"Too late. Going to bed."

She heard the slur before she saw Molly lean against her bedroom door, catching her balance.

"Molly, where have you been?"

Manic laugh. "Babysitting."

Anna made it down the hall just as Molly slammed the bedroom door in her face. The alcohol scent lingered in the doorway. "Molly, open this door."

Silence.

Anna tried to make her voice sound reasonable. "Come on, Molly, talk to me."

"No! Go 'way! Now!"

Anna gripped the knob. "Molly, please! Please, come on, open the door!"

"Mom?" Joe, his face wedged between the door and doorway to his room, peeked out. "What's wrong? What are you doing?"

Anna turned from Molly's door suddenly, seeing herself as Joe did. As she'd seen Sybil so many years before.

Anna opened the kitchen door, let Ralphie out, and sat down at the kitchen table, suddenly calmed by the vision of herself as Sybil, pleading at a daughter's locked door. Pleading, screaming, demanding, all tools in Sybil's sad quiver that never really worked. She felt oddly appreciative of her mother to know that. For the first time in twenty years a cigarette sounded like a good idea. She held her index and third fingers in a smoker's v and inhaled. No nicotine rush, but a slight uptick in steadiness. Just like Dr. Young's C for Calm.

Up, and down, her life in Onasego, just like the hills around the city. From glee over an endangered small town's fete for an admired arsonist to despair over her wounded, frighteningly vulnerable daughter. From the life-lifting Polar Plunge to self-proclaimed strategic visionaries pushing Catskill and Onasego to, what? She inhaled again and Laurel whispered, "extinction, like Yonahlossee." Anna stared at her two fingers, exhaling, this time pretend smoke rings. Okay, but the big question: What to do about these situations: Molly's dilemma? Onasego and Catskill versus so-called progress? Ralphie scratched at the door at the same instant Domnica's portfolio comment descended, or possibly ascended. Again, like answers to a prayer... but so direct! "Yes, right, thank you," Anna murmured. She rose to let the dog in, confident about what had to be done. And, finally, to get some sleep.

## 74 • THE MARK YOU MAKE (2)

*April 4, 1998 9:00 am.*
*JParrish@aol.com*
*Subject: Column*

*Jed,*

*Molly didn't take your decision well. She is angry and hurt and taking it out on Joe, Paul, and me, but more importantly on herself with risky behavior.*
*Therefore, I've decided to reactivate my plan to write a column about the devastating effects of absent fathers because I believe it is true and I will use the example of my own family. This will not be slander because what I am seeing is in line with the research on children of absent fathers. If you would like to reconsider your position and attempt to remediate the situation, you have a week. I need a call from you with plans for her to live with you by April eleventh or I will write said column, or possibly a feature entitled "JED: The True Story of an Absent Father."*

*Please don't think I am kidding. Feel free to forward this email as you wish.*

*Anna*

*PS Baby pixs of Molly are in the mail to you. Maybe they will help you in your decision.*

*APRIL 5. 2:00 AM*
*Editor@ manhattanliving.com*
*Subject: "Alone in Onasego"*

*MARTY: The Catskill Board will be in NYC on 4/15 to lobby alums. The column below needs to run as soon as possible after 4/15.*

*"Alone in Onasego"*

*Reader Alert: This special installment of "Alone in Onasego" is an appeal to alumni and friends of Catskill College and Onasego, NY. The column is also highly biased.*

*Right now, a battle is being waged for the heart and soul of Catskill College and Onasego, NY. For those who have followed my columns this year, you know that I moved here in September for my husband's employment. What I found was a smart, vibrant, opinionated, stubborn, and idiosyncratic small town where the person beside me at the checkout could as easily be a dairy farmer as a physics professor, where the symphony is as fully supported as soccer; where families go snowboarding in the park after church; and where modern development in all its certain repetition, fortuitously, passed right by.*

*What I also found was an inextricable tie between Catskill College and Onasego. A tie going far beyond the usual reciprocity between student-driven commerce and municipally funded police, fire, bus, and medical services.*

*In recent years, Catskill College has suffered financial challenges such that now a massive capital infusion is necessary to keep the school in operation. Opinions, however, differ on the way Catskill should operate going forward. One side believes the best-case scenario for Catskill and its future is to transition to an on line institution because of the school's remote location and the inevitable growth and convenience of distance learning. This position, championed by Phil Coxe and Jamie Van, two Catskill trustees, would effectively make the brick and mortar halls atop College Hill into an on line educational store and could be a death blow to the city of Onasego as we know it. This position would be semi-funded by selling land donated to Catskill as a nature sustainability study center to Jamie Van of the Van Consortium for a baseball camp complex.*

*The other side in the debate for Catskill's future holds that support from Onasego and Catskill alums/supporters can save the school in its traditional, dynamic form for students, alums, and the community, to enjoy and benefit from for decades to come. This view is held by the Friends of Catskill College, an Onasego volunteer organization whose sole purpose is to support the school. This dedicated group of people, composed of Onasego residents, and Catskill employees and students, has spent countless hours trying to educate and rally friends and supporters of Catskill and Onasego to the absolute criticality of what is being debated.*

*The Catskill Board of Directors will vote between these two positions on Friday, May first, at noon. Beginning on Thursday, April thirtieth, the Friends will hold its annual "Catskill: Forget Me Not" campaign with a huge lineup of activities and events. For anyone who believes in Catskill College as more than a system of computer lines and telephones, who believes in the future of small towns and Onasego in particular, who believes in the preservation of our open and rural spaces over baseball camps, COME TO ONASEGO FOR THE FORGET ME NOT WEEKEND! MAKE YOUR VOICES HEARD TO THE BOARD OF TRUSTEES! BRING YOUR FAMILIES AND FRIENDS FOR THE CATSKILL/ONASEGO EXPERIENCE! CLIMB COLLEGE HILL AGAIN! (Or vans will be provided) THINK ABOUT THIS: CATSKILL AND ONASEGO: ONCE LOST, LOST FOREVER. GO TO www.SaveCatskillandOnasego.org FOR ALL DETAILS.*

*Next Week: A Chicken Health Handbook (sold at the Feed and More Store)*

## 75 • A THAW

ANNA PULLED INTO the parking lot at Visionary Fields, cut the motor, and took in the roof of the world view before her, somewhat amazed. By God, it was happening.

Underneath a cloudless azure sky, the mountains, woods, and fields encircling her for miles and miles were... green. Just the week before on a drive to Cooperstown, the countryside lay blanketed in snow, white and dazzling. How had the change happened so fast? "Joe, look. There's grass everywhere. I think it's spring."

In the back seat, Joe, riding high, gripped Ralphie like a big pillow against his good clothes. An hour earlier, her boy presented his "Where I Live" report to great critical acclaim from Mrs. Wimbish, Mr. Anuncio, Paul, Bruce and her. During the congratulatory group chit chat that followed, Mrs. Wimbish slipped Anna a post-it with the name of a school to check out for Joe in Manhattan. Anna's complete bewilderment must have shown as Mrs. Wimbish added, "Well, dear, with your separation, everyone in town just assumes…" Your separation? Everyone in town? Was there a mic hooked up to the kitchen?

"Me and Ralphie don't like spring. We like snow. Is Dawn here?"

Anna checked the rearview mirror where Libby's Windstar was just pulling in the lot. On the front bumper was a brand spanking new sticker: **CATSKILL AND ONASEGO… JUST LIKE WHEN YOU LEFT. ACT NOW. STOP CHANGE.** While more and more of the bumper stickers were showing up around town, she hadn't had the nerve to put one on the BMW. Seemed like doing so would be a) the finger in Paul's face and/or b) a blight on the new car if they had to sell it. "Here she comes. Zip up, it's still cold out there. Hey, brush off the dog hair first." Seemingly on cue, Ralphie began whining and pawing the window.

Anna took a deep breath. She was nervous, unsure what to expect. Libby's call to arrange a get together, a chance for Dawn to see if her allergy shots were working with Ralphie, was completely understandable. The doctor wanted Dawn to start slowly, a first visit outside, then fifteen minutes indoors, gradually ratcheting up to full time. But Libby also referred, obliquely and curtly, to a need for talk. Anna opened the door for herself and then for Joe still clutching Ralphie. "Joe! You didn't have on your seat belt. You've been so good for so long."

The side door of the Windstar slid open and Dawn stepped out, bundled in the ever-present puffy pink down and purse. Joe pulled at her hand, "Don't get mad, Mom. I won't do it again. Ever."

With an effort, Anna tried to lighten up. "Hi, Dawn, how are you?"

"Good," Dawn answered in the automaton voice Anna knew so well. But rather than the wide eyed, slightly baffled expression the girl usually walked around the world with, her gaze was set squarely on Ralphie, and she carried a tennis ball and bag of mini milk bones.

Libby, in square black sunglasses and a Catskill stocking cap, rolled down her window. "Dawn, remember what the doctor said. Just pet him at first."

But Dawn, shuffling up to Joe, pitched her purse behind her back and held her arms out for the dog. In response, Joe, either peevishly or in a misguided attempt at humor, held fast to Ralphie, turning his back on Dawn. In a flash, Dawn reached out and grabbed hold of Joe's ear. Within seconds,

Ralphie was streaking across the field with Dawn and Joe screaming and running after him.

"This might take a while," Libby called out to Anna. "We can wait in the van… if you want to."

Anna nodded, unsure of Libby's tone, and walked to the Windstar. As she climbed into the bucket seat, Libby picked up a box of bumper stickers from the floor of the passenger side and threw it onto the back seat that more than a little resembled her living room. She pointed to a cup of coffee in the drink holder. "I brought one for you. Hope cream and sugar are ok."

"Great, thanks," Anna said. For conversation's sake, she pointed back to the bumper stickers. "You're working on that committee?"

Libby nodded. "Yeah, thought I could put a bunch around the dorms and things. Get them on more student cars."

After a moment or so of silence, Anna tried again. "Can't believe how fast the snow melted."

"Might be floods," Libby said reaching for her coffee. "Upstate, you never know."

Anna picked up the Styrofoam cup. Near the far end of the field Ralphie loped about in circles while Dawn and Joe held out what she supposed were the milk bones.

"I need to get something off my chest." Libby clicked the heater down to a manageable hum. "You were right."

Anna hesitated, "About what?"

"About how Dawn shouldn't have been left alone at night and how she should have been seeing Angus all along."

Anna stared at Libby trying to figure out something gracious to say, and then decided, what the hell. "Why'd you change your mind? And, for the record, I never tried to get her with Angus. It just happened."

"Whatever," Libby said, her gaze locked straight ahead, "he's good for her."

Anna peeled back the tab on the coffee lid. "I'm glad."

Libby took a moment. Then: "You and Angus were right about something else. Pops. He went after another young girl."

"God, no!"

"It's my fault. If I had done something, told the police about what he tried to do to Dawnie—it wouldn't have happened."

"Maybe, maybe not."

Libby swatted at a tear seeping beneath the dark glasses. "No maybe. Angus and Ellis knew that, and they did something. I should have been the one to burn his place down."

Across the field, Joe held up the tennis ball, then threw it to Dawn. Ralphie lay down in the grass, watching. "You said 'went after.' Who? How?"

Libby eased back against the seat. "After the fire, he started going to church over near Morris. Got in with the pastor there and his family. The Gleasons. Anyway, seems they kept a rein too tight on their daughter and he saw an opportunity, said he'd take her to Hershey Park. I heard about it at RiteMarket."

Anna knew that name. "Somebody Gleason wrote a letter to the editor about one of my columns, something about God and Dean and Deluca. So what happened?"

"They didn't get too far. A motel clerk in Binghamton turned them in."

Anna caught her breath at the thought of a young girl and Pops in a motel room. "Are you going to the police now?"

"Already have."

"Libby, I'm so sorry. I really am."

Libby pulled out a Kleenex from her pocket. "Pops is evil. And there are a lot of Pops in the world. I don't know what in the world I was thinking."

"Hey," Anna interrupted, "tell me, ace reporter, about it. I'm the one who thought he was the nicest guy in town."

A companionable quiet of self recrimination fell over the car. They watched Dawn and Joe becoming more and more frustrated with Ralphie's antics: throw the ball to Ralphie, wait for Ralphie to bring it back, wait for Ralphie to run away again. When Joe held up the milk bone bag, pulled one out and ate it, the faintest smile crossed Libby's face. She glanced at Anna.

"You know how surprised you were when you found out I could sing?"

Anna nodded. "Never opened the CD. Assumed you were just somebody messing around. Another great journalistic trait, assuming."

"Well," Libby finally turned Anna's way, "I didn't think you could write. Not until I saw the article that got Lisa off. Although," she pointed at Anna, "I did like 'Alone in a Party Dress' That broke me up."

"Me too." Anna said. About once a month, the specter of herself proudly entering the Great Hall in the emerald satin sheath and gold sandals would appear, snickering at her. "Speaking of Angus, how is he?"

Libby pulled off her cap and ran a hand through the frizz. "Okay, I think. They finally dropped all the charges against him, so that's big. Mainly, I just take Dawn over there and pick her up. Since she did those babysitting lessons with Molly, she got good with him." Libby dropped her voice. "Dawn hasn't heard from Molly in a while."

Anna shrugged. "Molly wants to go live with her father, it's not working out, and Molly is taking it out on everyone. Everyone!"

Libby cranked the heater back up to a dull roar. "I never thought about that. That Molly might want to live with her dad."

And Anna realized she had never drawn the parallel between Molly, Dawn, and absentee fathers. Could she get any stupider? "Does Dawn ever? You know, want to live with her dad?"

Libby seemed suddenly fascinated with the steering column. "He's never been in the picture. Maybe he should have, but he's not. Another time I should have done something."

Subject closed. Couldn't be clearer. Anna drained her coffee. Down the field, Joe and Dawn turned and started back to the car with Ralphie trotting right behind. That was the trick all along. They only needed to walk away for him to come back. Kind of like Paul, actually. Scanning the view again, she wondered why in the world she hadn't been back up here since her Maria, goldenrod and asters... and William, day. Then a terrible thought crossed her mind "It's so beautiful up here. What will happen to all of this if the school goes on line?"

Libby pulled off the glasses. Her eyes were puffy and tired. "With no real school here, it'll be cheap. Somebody will buy it. Maybe Jamie. More camps." Then she held out the label on her uniform shirt. "It's what will happen to all the rest of us that keeps me up at night."

Anna stared out on the field, overcome with the enormity of Libby's situation. Libby could lose everything. On impulse, she reached for a handful of bumper stickers from the back seat. "Hey, we're trying, right?"

Libby crushed her empty cup and pitched it onto the back seat. "You still don't get Onasego, do you? Right, we're trying. But we're up against

Pug and Jamie and that crowd. Guys who call the shots." She looked out at Dawn kissing Ralphie beside the van. "And they always have."


## 76 • A DEAL

ANNA PICKED UP the phone—the call she had been frantic for and dreading. "Hi, Jed."

"Got your email."

His voice was nondescript. She scanned her various bulletin-board notices for courage. "You did?" Like Mr. Detail would miss an email.

"I really am a bastard, aren't I?"

Come again? Jed had just called himself a bastard and asked her to agree with him. "Is this a trick?"

"No, it's not a trick. You want me to say it again?"

She considered to err on the side of caution. "I think so, yes."

"No problemo. Listen to me. I-AM-A-BASTARD. Okay?"

There was even a lilt to his voice. Like bubbling water over stones. "Okay."

"Sending me those baby pictures of Molly was genius. We had just gotten some pictures of Pemberley and it hit me like a rock. Molly's my baby, too. When can she come?"

This was way too much, too soon. "Don't toy with us, Jed."

She heard a laugh from the Jed of long ago. "Look, Ava and I started this whole thing because we thought you could get us one of Johnson's condos. Have to say we were pretty impressed when you threatened me with that column the first time. Then when you came roaring back with a feature… by God, we were bowing at your feet."

Anna reached for her tablet. Tactics, strategy, gamesmanship. Why hadn't she played to this before? Jed and Ava lived for this stuff. The thought gave her cold chills.

"And you're right." His voice turned soft. "I've been rotten to Molly for a while now. Kind of caught up in my own affairs."

She closed her eyes and willed herself not to say anything smart. Jed had just said something fairly human. "Can't say I've been at my best either."

"Have you got some time now? Maybe we could figure out the school schedule and all."

Anna looked at the clock. Fifteen minutes until Joe's swim practice. "Jed, I've got all the time in the world."

Twenty minutes later they were about at a deal. Molly would go down for some weekends soon and then move in for the summer and through the next school year. Anna was ecstatic, even feeling a ray of near warmth toward her ex. "Molly'll be home about six. You'll call her and tell her?"

"Yeah, sure," Jed sounded positively ebullient.

"Great. I better get off. Joe's late for swim practice."

"Okay, just one more thing."

One more thing? The ray of warmth wavered.

"Your last column, 'The Town That Astounds' about Onasego was really good. Sounds like a super place."

Now she was entering the Twilight Zone. Anna nudged a reluctant Ralphie off her lap. "You don't read my columns."

"But Ava does. She wants to drive up there. Check it out as investment property."

Anna gave a mental tip of the hat to Jamie Van's prognostic abilities. "Tell her to come soon. A local guy, Jamie Van, is leading a consortium to probably drive Catskill out of business and put up a huge baseball complex on college-owned land. And, as Catskill goes, so goes Onasego." A towel flicked in front of her eyes. At the other end of the towel Joe stood in his swim trunks and Polar Plunge tee shirt. She mouthed, two minutes and reached for her phone and reading glasses. "A lot of us are fighting the plan tooth and nail. Except we don't have very many tooths or nails. Check my next column, or get Ava to. It'll have all the details."

There was a pause, then: "Will William Johnson be up for this fight?"

Aha. The sucker punch she had half been waiting for. "Why?"

"Because," Jed lowered his voice to a whisper, "Ava still wants one of those condos. And I'm trying really hard in this second marriage to change my ways from the bastard you know and used to love. So if there is any way you can help, even put in a word for us, I'll do your taxes, I'll get you free legal help, I'll do whatever."

Joe stuck his fingers in the corners of his mouth making fish faces.

Anna stood and switched off her desk light. "Jed, now you listen to me, I–CAN'T–GET–YOU–A–CONDO!" She lowered her voice. "Paul does the taxes and I don't need any legal help. Sorry, gotta go." She hung up the phone, blissfully content. A good day in Onasego. Molly was going to Jed's.

## 77 • NEVER DOUBTING (3)

WITH ONE HAND on the gas pump, Anna pulled the buzzing phone from her blazer pocket with the other. "Hi, Marty," she shouted. "What's up?" Marty's voice was garbled. Complicating matters were the ambulance and fire truck racing up Main across from the QuikGo station. "Column" and "sixteenth" came through. "Marty, it's hard to hear you," she shouted again. "Did you say you'd run the column on the sixteenth?" She heard "Okay, right?" She jammed the phone against her ear. "It's perfect, cause the alumni thing is on the fifteenth." Marty went off on something ending in "on line." She could only guess. "Right, on line, only." Another ambulance blared down the street. She heard something about "interview," and "thirtieth." The job? Was that what he was getting at? She needed deep quiet for those details. "Hey, it's really too tough to hear. I'll call back in a minute from home." Then she added quickly, "Hope you heard that," and clicked off. Resolving to learn how to text message as well as put the pump on automatic, Anna watched the price climb until it finally stopped at nineteen dollars. Time to get a compact, she thought. Somebody on TV had forecast one-fifty a gallon soon.

"Well, hello, Anna," an assured female voice called.

Anna looked across the island where Jamie and Gwen, all tight jeans and nubby sweaters, stood by the open trunk of Jamie's gleaming black Jaguar, precision packed with Louis Vuitton luggage. Jamie seemed to be searching for something while Gwen lounged against the car. Conde Nast couldn't have posed them better.

"Jamie's going to *kill* me," Gwen said. "Somehow I packed my books on tape. And I can't possibly travel without them. I'm so addicted." Peeling herself off the Jaguar, she strolled over to the BMW. "I couldn't help overhearing you on the phone. Something about the city and an alumni event on the fifteenth. Would that be *our* Catskill event?"

Anna looked into the enormous gray eyes so perfectly made up. "Yeah."

"How interesting." Gwen tossed her hair back. "That's where we're off to today. Going down a little early to check on details."

Anna couldn't resist. "I thought Deedee was the alumni coordinator. Doesn't she do the details?"

"This is a board-sponsored get-together, a bit over Deedee's head." Gwen's tone implied that Anna must certainly agree. "So, your column for the sixteenth, are you writing about *our* little affair when it hasn't even happened?"

"No," Anna said. And that was the truth. The column was about an alumni event on the thirtieth. She pulled the receipt from the console and stuffed it into the pocket of her cords.

"Here it is, Hon." Jamie held up a small valise probably worth, Anna guessed, a month's rent.

"Jamie, come over here. Anna is writing a column that has to come out right after the board-alumni meeting." Gwen swung back to Anna. "Well, what's this column about?"

"Like all my columns, Onasego."

Jamie slammed the Jag's trunk closed. "I just hope that when you write your next columns, you write them responsibly."

Anna decided it would be a good time to clean the windshield for the first time in her life. "Maybe you could explain that." She lifted a brush from the water pail.

"Columns like the one you wrote, 'The Town that Astounds,' you're going to get city people up here swarming for land." Jamie stepped across the island and handed Gwen the valise.

Anna recalled her question to Paul. "Why wouldn't you, a banker, want people up here swarming for land?"

"Because I really do have Onasego's interest at heart. We both do," Jamie said, circling an arm around Gwen's shoulder. "The baseball camps will keep it rural up here. Uncluttered. Clean. And except for the summer, mostly quiet."

Anna tried to straighten out her swipes across the windshield. "But what about Catskill, all those jobs…"

"Catskill, except maybe as an on line school, isn't feasible." Jamie lifted one of Gwen's curls, running it between his fingers. "I wish you—the Friends that is—would get that."

"You're so sure?" She bore down on the passenger side window.

"I am so sure. You're still very new up here. It's a complex situation." He hesitated, "And you can't think you're doing Paul any good."

Anna rubbed at an imaginary spot on the side mirror. She knew conde-scension when she heard it, even without a rosebud nightgown on. But was he right? Pug, Phil Coxe, William, and Paul all thought he was. And like Libby said, he was very used to calling the shots. Could she be making a horrible mistake with the column? With Onasego? With Paul's job?

Gwen pushed back her sleeve. "Jesus, look at the time. Seems we'll just have to wait and read the column." She reached out and put a light hand on Anna's shoulder.

"Jamie told me he gave you some friendly advice about letting the people who know about things take care of them. Think about it." Then, with a quick wave, the two swept around the island and into their car.

Anna watched while they drove out of the gas station, chatting, adjusting the visors, turning onto Main, presumably toward Franklin, and the shortcut across the mountains to 17, the Thruway, then, finally the Parkway into the city. A city that was, at least for her, so far less complicated than Onasego. A city where she was confident and assured. A city where many people called the shots. She looked at her reflection in the spotless side window; Marty was waiting.

## 78 • NITTY-GRITTY DETAILS

ANNA SHOOK THE rain off her umbrella and pushed open the door to Nora's. Having vowed after the poetry slam never to enter the restaurant again, she was surprised to feel a comforting, homey vibe inside. She glanced around the open room, searching for the Friends group she was meeting for a work-ing lunch. Instead, she saw William and Domnica sitting at a small table for two by the window, William staring at her and Domnica choosing from the tea selection. She hesitated just a second, then ever so slightly ruffled her fingers in his direction. He nodded. And for an instant, they were back in the bar in Manhattan. Alone and easy.

"Anna!"

She looked back over her shoulder, then walked the few steps to where Tim, Ray, and Deb sat at a table for six. She pulled out a chair. "Hope I'm not late."

"Nope," Ray said. "We just ordered soup and salad for everybody. And there are Deedee and Angie coming in now. Good timing."

Like Anna, Deedee and Angie brushed off umbrellas and shook out raincoats. Unlike Anna, they both took a few minutes to speak to various friends around the restaurant.

"Wow, that's a lot of rain," Deedee said, taking the seat next to Ray. "Everything's just saturated."

"One of the wettest seasons on record," Tim added. "A lot of snow, a lot of rain, bad mix."

"Guys, I'm sorry," Deb said, "but I've only got an hour. Can we get started?"

Ray held up an agenda. "Good idea. First up, anyone hear how the board's cocktail party went?" Everyone's eyes drifted to Anna.

"Paul said it was very well attended, about three hundred people," she glanced around the table hating to tell the rest, "that Jamie gave an extremely convincing talk about the logic of transitioning to distance learning, the timetable, the logistics," she made herself look Tim in the eye, "also, the critical role of the consortium money."

"That's about the same as what I heard," said Deedee. "Some reliable alums called in."

"Do we know how much money they've raised?" Deb asked. Again, eyes focused on Anna.

"I didn't ask. It wouldn't be right." Despite the deep emotions around the table, Anna knew that these people would accept that answer. She wondered how many others would.

"Okay, Deedee, maybe you can find out," Ray said. "Let's move on to Anna's column. Any impact?"

"Laurel got gushy about you nailing the interdependence of things," Angie offered. "That's all I know."

"Where is Laurel?" Tim asked. "I thought she'd be here."

Angie looked at him like he had two heads. "She's doing all this *and* you know Beltane's coming up. Huge time for her."

Ray tapped his spoon on the table. "Back to the column, did we get any results? Maybe more inquiries? Reservations?"

There seemed to be a collective shrug at the table.

"No real change," Deb said finally. "But, hey, Anna, I liked it all right."

"Yeah," Ray added, "a little long, but okay."

While the others tried to come up with something complimentary, Anna felt punched. She had been so sure of that column. What did she miss?

"Nitty-gritty details next," Ray said, "like when the banner's going up, Jason's kids' camp, and, here's a new one, how to get Libby to sing. But, under the 'thank heaven for small favors' heading, a few free minutes first. Here comes lunch."

As the waitress placed soup and salad at each place, Anna let herself turn back to William and Domnica. But they were gone.

Once again all eyes were on Anna. "What do you mean you won't be here for the Forget Me Not?" Deedee was incredulous. "We need you."

In the midst of the after-lunch nitty-gritty details, the schedule of who would oversee what at the Forget Me Not figured prominently. And figuring almost as prominently was the blank beside Anna's name, making it obvious she wasn't signed up for anything.

Anna poured a packet of Half and Half into her coffee. "I have a job interview in Manhattan that day. Also, I need to check out a school for Joe."

"A job interview?" Deedee repeated.

"Just found out last week. I begged for another date, but that's when their board meets. I'm sorry."

Deedee's gaze darted around the table. "So you're leaving."

Anna felt like she was the chew toy and Deedee was the dog shaking her back and forth. "I don't know. I do know I need a full-time job and there may be one at the magazine. And, big, there might be a good school for Joe in the city."

"Then the rumors are true? You and Paul separated?"

No wonder there was such a homey vibe in Nora's, Anna thought. Everyone in here knows everything about everyone else in here. Except for her. "Whatever Paul's and my relationship is, it's our private business." She reached for the sugar. "What's next, Ray?"

Twenty-five minutes later, the group broke up. Deb, Tim, and Ray leaving together, Angie at the bar getting change for a twenty, and Anna paying the bill with her credit card because she had no cash. She was also trying very hard to ignore Deedee across the table glaring at her. But Deedee won.

Anna looked up at her. "What?"

"Were you just not going to tell us?"

"About what?"

"Your plans to go back to the city."

Anna added a tip and shoved the bill in the leatherette holder. "I don't know what I'm doing yet. But I'm sure you can understand that if I need a job, I need a job."

"Yes, I understand that."

"Then why are you so upset?" Anna held up the bill for the waitress.

Deedee reached for her purse hanging from the chair back. "Let me ask you one thing."

"Sure."

"Did you even think about looking around here?" Deedee fished in her wallet and pulled out two fives.

That caught Anna off guard. The answer was no. Not for a minute. She shook her head.

Deedee stood and pulled on her coat. "Thought so. It's like I told you once. When things get hard around here, some people can just walk away. Most others can't." She dropped the money on the table.

"Okay, here's what I owe," Angie announced, arriving at the table and waving a ten.

Anna watched Deedee thread her way through the tables and out the door.

"That's for the tip," Angie said, adding two ones to the ten. She sat down beside Anna. "I've got some news for you. I thought it was bad news, but, with you going back to the city and all," she scrapped her chair closer, "it's probably not."

⁂

"Paul, Peter got financing. He's buying the house."

Anna hunkered back against the car seat listening to Paul's short, crispy questions against the engine idle.

"How? When? Which bank?"

She gazed around the parking garage. "I don't know. I didn't want to talk about it in Nora's. Angie's coming over later."

She heard crackling, then airport announcements.

"Look, my flight's boarding. Find out all you can. I'll call you tonight."

She lowered the phone and shut her eyes. A possible job. A possible school for Joe. Molly going to Jed's. Now the house getting bought. Even Ralphie soon back with Dawn. Was the universe making decisions for her again? But what about Paul—and William? She dropped the phone at the knock on her window and slammed the door-lock down, a move she had practiced for months. Terrified to turn all the way around, she looked in the side mirror. Her fingers found the switch, the window slid open with a low hum. In one movement, William leaned in and kissed her. "Nine more days until the vote, Anna. Just nine more days."

## 79 • MODERN FAMILY

*FETE for a FELON: Recently, members of Onasego held a going away party for a very special arsonist. About twenty residents came together for a very special going away… to a nearby correctional facility for one of Onasego's very own felons.*

Anna studied the screen. Where was her brain? Two *going aways*? Two *very specials*? *Two felons*? She blocked everything but the title and hit delete.

"MOM," Molly's yell blared up the steps, "GET ON THE PHONE. DAD WANTS TO TALK TO YOU."

Paul, just back from ten days in Manhattan and Boston, appeared in the doorway to her office. He yanked at his tie. "You want a glass of wine?"

She nodded and reached for the phone. Details. Details. Details. A plan, not uncomplicated but a plan, had been reached for the next weekend. She, Molly, and Joe, would leave at the butt crack, Joe's words, of dawn on Friday the thirtieth, arrive in NYC in time to visit the school Mrs. Wimbish suggested, then on to drop Molly and Joe at Jed's office, and finally to her afternoon interview at *Manhattan Living*. Jed and Ava had kindly agreed to keep Joe until Saturday morning. Then on Saturday, Anna and Joe would return to Onasego. Molly would follow by bus on Sunday. Molly and the Port Authority. That should be a story.

"Hi, Jed. Everything still a go?"

"Yeah, think so. Thought I'd take Joe to see the Knicks Friday night. Molly and Ava are going to catch a show."

"Jed, that is so nice but you don't have to entertain Joe."

"Molly and Pemberley's brother? Sure, I do."

Pemberley's brother? She needed to have a serious talk with Joe about the modern family.

"One more thing," Jed continued, "I know you said you don't need any legal help—"

"And that I can't get you a condo," she interrupted.

"But—you know the Van Consortium you mentioned and wrote about in your column? I looked them up. There's only one in the country, out of Tampa, and it's in gas exploration. You might want to check on that."

Anna had a funny image of Jamie and Gwen in coveralls and hard hats getting into the Jaguar. "They must be named something slightly different then. These guys are all restaurants, banks, and, trying hard for baseball camps."

Paul reappeared with two wine glasses at the door. She waved him in.

"So, I'll see you around noon on the thirtieth. And, that really is so nice about the game and Joe." She was about to hang up when her modern family manners caught up with her. "And love to Ava, of course."

Paul handed her a wineglass, moved a stack of files from the ottoman, and settled across from her. "What am I disturbing?"

Anna looked at her "Fete for a Felon" title. "I was trying to get a jump on a column, but I think I'm dangerous. You must be tired. Long trip?"

Paul flexed his shoulders. "Yeah, it was. Lot of talking, lot of explaining. You guys are making my life kind of tough."

"We're trying." Anna reached into a desk drawer and pulled out a photo of the coach and The Niece standing on ladders hanging the banner across

Main Street. Deb had done a fantastic job getting it made, Catskill's own dark green lettering against a crisp white background. **CATSKILL (and ONASEGO)... JUST LIKE WHEN YOU LEFT. ACT NOW. STOP CHANGE.**

Paul studied the picture. "So The Niece is in with the opposition. Wonder if Pug knows that." He handed the photo back to her. "I read your column. Pretty good."

"That's right. Pretty good, not the best." She gazed sideways at him. "And up against *you guys*, we need the best."

Paul moved on. "So tell me about Peter buying the house."

"Angie said in the past few years people can get these crazy loans with almost nothing down and not much, if any, collateral. But she said, even given that, she's still amazed Peter got financing. He has no real income."

"Why would he want it?"

"He plans to live here and rent out rooms for the mortgage. He thinks he'll make money."

Paul leaned back against the wall. "So, we have decisions. Like what we're going to do."

She nodded. "Sort of looks like moving back to the city is shaping up. Molly at Jed's, this school possibility for Joe, a job at the magazine."

"What about us?"

And there was that elephant walking back into the room. She decided to try for light. "I have no idea how you've been behaving."

"I've been good. But Anna, I have to tell you. It's hard." He paused, then added, "Really hard. And something I've just started to think about, I have no idea why I'm like this."

She might be trying for light, but he was going for seriously honest. She knew it when she heard it. And she knew what she had to do.

"Paul, remember when you asked me if I had ever cheated on you. And I said, once. You should know that was recent."

His gaze dropped to the floor. "Is it still going on?"

"On hiatus."

"William Johnson?"

"How did you know?"

"Same way everyone knows everything around here." He grinned. "Guess we should put off the marriage counseling."

"Do you hate me?"

"How could I?" He looked back up at her. "What are you going to do about it?"

"Don't know." She smoothed out nonexistent wrinkles in her robe, a flannel she'd replaced the down one with in honor of the warmer weather. "It's so hard, like you said. There's us. We made vows. But I am enormously attracted to another man. And you have your wandering libido. Then there are the kids. They're front and center in all this. So what do we do?"

The Paul grin emerged. "Wish I knew. The world's a complicated place." He leaned over and pulled at his shoelaces.

"Not for those guys." Anna motioned toward the post-its on her bulletin board with the inscriptions from the library panels. "They make everything seem so clear, so straightforward."

Paul looked up from his wingtips. "It's true. Sometimes at work when I'm just sick of it all I go out and read over them. When I leave here, I'll miss that."

Anna recalled her shock at seeing them the first time. "I thought one of them was talking to me that day I agreed to come here."

Paul picked up his shoes and wineglass. "Maybe you could get one of them to tell us what to do. Speaking of which, I told Joe I'd watch twenty minutes of *The Black Stallion* with him. That's all I can take. Then I'm going to unpack. You?"

She glanced back at "Fete for a Felon." "Maybe I'll try the column for another bit. Hope something gives."

Paul stood up and stretched. "We have to make decisions, Anna."

"I know." She looked back at the post-its. "I know."

*80. APRIL 24... 3:00 AM*

*Marty, my column of 4/20 was lacking. Could you post one more? Please!*

*"Alone in Onasego"*
*A final appeal to alumni and friends of Catskill College and Onasego, NY.*

*As of today, April 24th, there will be just a few days for alums and supporters of Catskill College to try to save Catskill, and I believe Onasego. I wrote about this in an emotional, somewhat frantic post a week ago. Today, as my last appeal, I ask that you try to remember what it is like to stand in front of Catskill's library and look east across Onasego, the valley, the mountains, the sky, and the river. Then see yourself turning toward the front walls of the library... toward the following words for living:*

Let There Be Light
Let Dawn break in the Heaven and the earth!
There will be neither greatness nor glory
Till the human creature exist the created man. POPOL YUH

We should understand well that all things
Are the works of the Great Spirit. We should
Know that he is within all things: The trees, the grasses,
The rivers... We should understand that he is also above all
These things and peoples. BLACK ELK

I wipe away the tears from thy face
I make it daylight for thee
I beautify the sky
The land shall be beautiful
The river shall have no more waves
One may go everywhere without fear. DEGANAWIDAH

The Mark you make upon the world
Is measured by God. CHILAM BALAM

*And now consider your life without this view and without these words of eternal, if not easily understood, wisdom. Also consider the possibility that future students of Catskill College may never see this view or these words except on a website.*

*The future is in your hands.*
*www.SaveCatskillandOnasego.org*

Anna woke to a gentle hand on her shoulder.

"Don't you want to be in bed?" Paul whispered.

She blinked herself awake and checked the time on the computer screen. Five a.m. This was a first. Asleep at her desk.

"What were you doing?" Paul switched off the overhead light.

"I got an idea, one that might be better than pretty good." She stood up. Her neck hurt. She yawned. "See you in a couple of hours."

She was about at the door when he whispered again. "Can I read it?"

His request made her feel strong, useful. "Sure."

## 81 • IT BEGINS

PAUL WALKED INTO the kitchen, good black suit, pale blue tie, monogrammed cufflinks in hand. Battle gear for the opening reception of the Catskill Board of Directors' spring meeting.

"Wow," Anna said, turning from the oven. "Could you be going to a very upscale reception or something?"

Paul bowed. "And so it begins, the weekend we've all been waiting for."

Anna pulled a casserole from the oven. "Board Weekend and vote, Forget Me Not, school visit, and job interview. Sort of terrifying."

"Yes, it is." Paul looked at his watch "And, for me, right now is as good as it's going to get until Sunday. In forty minutes I need to be at Jamie and Gwen's for drinks and dinner, then meetings all day tomorrow and Saturday morning, followed by the vote at noon, and then, either way, the fallout. Hey, that smells great. What is it?"

"Chicken and artichoke hearts; no Oreos, so Ellis probably won't touch it."

"Right, his send off is tonight."

"It's just a few of us having a potluck for him," Anna said, peeling back a layer of tinfoil, "but, it's also kind of an opening reception for us. Everyone's worked so hard getting the Forget Me Not together. Tonight will be a little pause before it gets frantic." She reached for two plates from the china cabinet."

"For Molly and Joe?"

"Yep, they'll be back from walking Ralphie soon."

Paul held out the cufflinks. "You mind?"

Anna paused. Helping with cufflinks was very close to zipping up a dress, both date-night preludes. "Helpless male," she said finally.

Paul held out his wrist. "Why don't you come to the reception with me? You know you're invited. And if Molly is babysitting, we could go out for a drink or something afterward."

She put one cufflink on the counter, surprised that the offer was tempting. "Thanks, but no. Can you imagine how thrilled the Vans would be to see me after my last two columns? And last but not least, I expect to be sound asleep by nine."

He held out his other wrist. "Still leaving for the city at five?"

"That's the plan. Should be back mid-afternoon on Saturday." She threaded the second cufflink. "I have a question. Why is Gwen having this reception at her house? Not at Pug's, or at Catskill?"

"Control, I think. She's bringing in a trio from the city, chef from the Otesaga, you get the picture." Paul tugged at the jacket sleeves.

"A major impress and seduce."

"Right."

"And nothing from Catskill or Onasego." She reached for a serving spoon and began ladling the casserole out for Molly and Joe.

"Right again."

Anna shook her head. How many times had she'd been outmaneuvered by Jamie and Gwen. "Do we even have a chance?"

Paul leaned back against the counter. "Jamie is determined to get that land. Phil Coxe really believes distance learning is the right way to go, as does William," his voice faltered, "Johnson. Those are three very forceful people. They also have a plan and the consortium's money."

"And they have you." She covered Molly's and Joe's plates in plastic. "You, who probably could have thought of a plan for us."

Paul's face softened. "Maybe. I learned a lot these past couple of months, taking Joe around. But the on line idea has merit; it really does. And Catskill needs that money."

Ralphie's bark mingled with the front door opening and Molly and Joe sniping at one another. "I guess it's time for you to make your way to the Vans and for me to head to Catskill. Wish you were on our side."

"Wish you were coming to the reception."

The reception with William, Paul, Jamie, Gwen, Pug, Phil. Even Erika, maybe. Thank you, Ellis. "Sorry. Got a fete for a felon." She patted his shoulder. "Good luck this weekend. I'll see you on Saturday."

"Good luck to you." He caught her hand. "Tonight, then just two more days."

Tonight and just two more days until what exactly? "Hey, take an umbrella. It's supposed to pour again."

## 82 • F--CKED

"ALL RIGHT EVERYBODY. For he's a jolly good fellow, on three," Ray and Tim stood on either side of Ellis at the front of the Founders Lounge with guitars poised. "Now, one and a, two and a—"

As the small group broke into song Anna eyed the assorted dinner items and wondered if the calorie count wasn't deeply symbolic of the edginess streaming from the assembled Forget Me Not organizers. The potluck table was knee deep in solid comfort food: chips and dips, chili, mac' n' cheese, beef stroganoff, enchiladas, shepherd's pie, fried chicken, potato salad, meatloaf, and twice-baked potatoes. The canned artichoke hearts in Anna's casserole were conspicuous for being green and from the vegetable group. The only other greenery, or fiber, were sprigs of cedar, Laurel's tip to the upcoming Beltane, interspersed among the dishes. At the end of the table, alongside an enormous cheesecake, sat Peg's masterwork: a white sheet cake featuring a smiling, waving, gingerbread man in an orange jumpsuit made from candy-corn bits behind black liquorish stick bars surrounded by pale blue frosting flowers under M&M script reading: *Farewell Ellis—We Will Forget You Not.* Gummy bears made up the border, while sprinkles clung to the sides.

And if there were not details a plenty to worry about for the next day and a half, a deep design flaw in the planning had emerged, leading to a pervasive case of gallows humor. While attendance indicators looked good based on reservations at the Holiday Inn, enrollment numbers for the kids sports classes, and requests for Meet A (Blank) schedules and maps, no one

knew if the alums making these reservations were pro or con Catskill going on line. The Friends' members just might have gone to heroic lengths
to entertain pro-distance learning people. Complete crapshoot as the golf
coach uncharacteristically called it. Only the next two days would tell.
They really could have used Paul on planning. Back up front, Ellis pirou-
etted and bowed to the very loud conclusion. "fel-el LO, which NOBODY
can deny."

Tim held up his guitar. "Thank you. Hope tomorrow everyone will be
at the plaza for the last concert by the Red Neck Mothers until our friend
here is a free man again. We have a very special set lined up beginning with
'Folsom Prison Blues' AND Ms. Libby Holmes will join us, a true honor, on
at least two of the numbers."

Ellis yanked Tim's arm down. "But now, seeing as I am the guest of honor,
we're going to eat. My last meal and all."

Ray pointed out the obvious. "You're not going to death row, Ellis."

"But," Ellis rocked back on his heels, thumbs hooked in his jeans pockets,
"it's my last meal today, see."

At the moment, Anna thought how much Ellis reminded her of Joe. Or
vice versa. And, how by driving to the city tomorrow, she would probably
miss out on some of the best columns of her life.


"So you came." Deedee's voice was frosty. She stood across the fried chicken
platter from Anna.

"Of course."

"Thought you might be at Gwen's with the rest of the bigwigs."

"Why would I?"

"Maybe because you'll be leaving our little group soon. Maybe because of
it being the last big bash at that house."

Anna squinted up at her. "What are you talking about?"

"The Vans," Angie said, reaching for a drumstick, "they're moving to
Florida."

Anna had a dim recollection of Gwen mentioning a house there. "Why?
They're an institution in Onasego."

"Gwen's sick of winter," Angie continued, "and Jamie wants to get more
and more into baseball camps around here which he sees as seasonal. So

they'll go down there and come up here for summers. He's looking for a condo in Cooperstown."

The Niece added a plate of sticky buns to the table. "Maybe that's why Gwen sold all that furniture."

Anna moved on to the potato salad. "When did you find out?"

"Just the other day," Deedee answered. "Seems Caroline blabbed at school a little prematurely." She speared two enchiladas. "So, they will continue to enjoy their very rich, very privileged, and now very warm life in Sarasota."

"Plus, they'll have great golf," the golf coach, a couple ahead in the line, said. "I took the team to Sarasota one year for practice. I remember flying out of Tampa and thinking, man, I could get used to this."

"Not me," Angie made a face, "Bugs and alligators."

Sarasota. Tampa. Anna looked down the line at the coach. "Is Tampa near Sarasota?"

"About an hour."

"And the heat," Angie shook her head, "my God, the heat."

"Is there any natural gas near Tampa?"

"No idea. Why?" The coach added shepherd's pie to his plate alongside mac' n' cheese.

"Someone recently told me about a Van Consortium out of Tampa, but it was involved in natural gas exploration."

"Hey, Vic," the coach shouted to Victor at the desserts, "is there any natural gas near Tampa?"

"Nope." Victor cut into the cheesecake.

The coach shrugged. "Must be some other Van."

Anna turned toward Deedee. "I heard it was the only Van Consortium in the country. I kind of blew it off."

Victor strolled toward Anna and the group at entrees. "If you're looking for natural gas, you're standing on one of the biggest deposits in the world. The Marcellus Shale Field."

Deedee's eyes narrowed over the table. "There's no gas drilling around here."

"Not now because it's been too pricey to get to. But there's this technique they've developed down in Texas at the Barnett Shale called hydrofracking that could change all that."

Anna glanced at Deedee, "Barnett... shale? Carolyn said Jamie travels to Barnett all the time. I thought it was a town."

Angie pushed back into the group. "I've even read about iguanas and pythons."

"Angie, please!" Anna's voice must have sounded as hysterical to everyone else as it did to her. A hush fell over the room. "Listen, everyone. There may be something huge happening. Victor says we are standing on a very large reserve of natural gas and..."

"Alma, we're standing," Ellis put his hands together prayer-like, "at a party. My party."

"Largest reserve in the country," Victor broke in.

"And," Anna tried to ignore Ellis dropping to his knees, "there's a process being developed in Texas that could be used to get to this gas."

"Alma, the skunk, remember the skunk?"

"Not now, Ellis! Victor, explain shale and this hydro thing, please!"

Victor stepped around Ellis, lowered his plate to the table, clasped his hands, and transformed into his professorial self. "Shale is a rock layer thousands of feet down that can contain natural gas. The Marcellus shale field, where we are, covers the southern tier and Finger Lakes area of New York, down through Pennsylvania, Ohio, Maryland, West Virginia, and Virginia. An enormous area." He spread his arms wide for emphasis. "And while geologists have known about the Marcellus since the forties, even mapped where the gas most likely is, it's not been economically viable to tap the gas. Til now." He paused, the academic formality sliding away, concern taking over. "A few years ago, a man named Mitchell in Texas came up with a new way to get into shale and make money. He realized he could horizontally inject millions of gallons of highly pressurized water and chemicals, some toxic, into the shale to release the gas. The technique is called slick water hydrofracking. Or fracking for short."

"But why isn't this fantastic?" the coach asked. "The country needs gas and everyone around here living on top of this thing needs money."

"I'm sure some people, many people, will think it is," answered Victor wearily.

Laurel walked toward him, visibly trembling. "Couldn't these toxic chemicals seep into the groundwater?"

"That's correct," Victor said. "However, it's not just the chemicals injected into the ground that are worrisome, but also the contaminated fluid that returns to the surface. Not only is it toxic, but potentially radioactive. And this water is usually stored in open lagoons until disposed of."

Libby held up a hand. "But if it's in open lagoons, what if it rains? Or there's a leak?"

Victor nodded. "More contamination."

"So all the water," Libby said, "underground and above ground, could get contaminated?"

"Absolutely. And the vegetation that water could come in contact with."

Ellis sat back on his heels. "And the animals?"

Victor's eyes swept the room "And the humans."

"Okay," Ray said, clanking a knife against a glass, "this fracking whatever it is, sounds like it could be really good news or really terrible. But how about we debate this maybe on Monday?"

"Ray, everybody, here's the thread," Deedee's face was ashen but her voice was strong. "Jamie and family are moving to Sarasota, an hour from Tampa. The only Van Consortium in the country is located out of Tampa, and it's involved in natural gas exploration. And Jamie's been traveling a lot to Texas where this hydrofracking was developed. Now it turns out we're sitting on a ton of natural gas and Jamie is in line to get control of more than a thousand acres of land through the school deal. Don't you see? We don't know what he might do with Tim's land. And to Onasego."

Out of the corner of her eye, Anna saw Tim stagger to his feet. "First, he steals the land... then he poisons it?"

Dinner was forgotten except by Ellis, who insisted that now, tonight might really be one of his last meals. The others, Ray, the Coach, Victor, Deedee, Laurel, Deb, The Niece, Peg, sat in a circle. Tim stood at his old place by the window while Anna repeatedly called Paul, with each call going to message.

"We have to stop that vote," Ray said flatly.

"I always wondered why he needed all that land for a baseball camp," Peg announced somewhat imperiously. "Three acres per field and a thousand acres. That's quite a number of fields, I believe."

"Three acres?" Angie looked around the group. "That's all? How do you know that?"

Peg glared at Angie, incredulous. "Twenty-five seasons with Onasego's farm teams."

Anna listened to them, humiliated. Peg's question had been right there in the minutes. Had she acted on it? Taken Peg seriously? No. She'd just written her off as a bundt-cake yapping old lady. Sort of like Jed. A guy who just wanted a condo."

"Also explains why Jamie would pay that kind of premium," Deedee said.

Deb joined in. "And why he was looking at these old geological survey maps in our office."

"We have to get to the board," Ray said. "The whole Consortium deal could be fraudulent."

"Could be," The Niece said. "That's right. We're not sure Jamie is involved in this fracking."

"He is. You know he is." The group turned to Tim, caught by the fury in his voice. "I'm going over there right now."

"No, you're not," Laurel announced. "You'd cause a scene."

"Think I care?"

Laurel gripped the pentacle. "You should. There are many influential people at the Vans right now. Besides, Mr. Van could buy the land but not act on it for years. We have to be very smart, here. Keep steady heads. Everyone breathe."

That idea lasted about twenty seconds. Ray spoke first. "We still have to get to the board. And we still need proof about Jamie."

Anna did, however, take a deep breath. And then another. The universe and Onasego were calling.

"Okay, this is what we're going to do," Anna pushed back her chair. "I'm going to the reception. I'll bring Paul back to listen to us."

Tim glanced at her. "Oh, *you* won't cause a scene?"

Anna brushed the comment aside. "No, I'm invited." She saw a knowing look pass over Deedee's face.

Angie grabbed her arm. "What about Jamie's consortium? The information we need?"

"That's a call I can make on the way to the Vans."

"Who to?"

Anna picked up her raincoat and purse. "A guy who really, really wants a condo."

## 83 • SPRING BOARD GAMES

ANNA TURNED RIGHT at the fork on North, phone in hand, and squinting through the rain. "Hey, Ray, information on the consortium is being sent to my home fax, so all of you go there; Molly will let you in. I'll try to round up Paul and join you as fast as I can." Next she phoned home. "Molly, about ten people are coming over. Offer them some tea and coffee, okay? Also, check my fax. Your dad is sending some information and I need for it not to jam."

"Way too busy, Mom, gotta pack."

Way too busy? "If you want a ride with me to your dad's tomorrow, you will do exactly as I asked. And, you'll get Joe packed. Clear?"

A mumbled "Okay" came back at her.

With a sigh, she clicked off and pulled into the driveway at the Vans. From the number of cars, Jamie and Gwen must have invited many more than the board for the reception. But who? The mayor? State representatives? The glitterati of Onasego and Cooperstown? Suddenly her courage failed. Was she about to humiliate herself for all time? The board members were smart people. Wouldn't they know if Jamie was going to build a baseball complex or not? Wouldn't they know about hydrofracking and leases? Wouldn't any Catskill property already be shielded with restricted-use clauses? She could end up looking so ridiculous that Marty and the magazine would wish they had never heard of her. Laying her head against the steering wheel, she shut her eyes, the thwack, thwack of the windshield wipers comforting against the downpour. If only she could go home, put on her very soft bathrobe, close the door, and go to bed. Suddenly Gwen's silvery laugh rang out across the open lawn, probably greeting someone at the door. "Friendly advice," Gwen said that day at the pump, "let the people who know about things take care of them." Anna sat up, switched the headlights off, the windshield wipers, and then the car itself. "Come on, Sybil. Let's go."

Anna shook out her umbrella under the portico and walked into the mahogany foyer she recalled so well from the Thanksgiving weekend party. To her right and left, clumps of people stood chatting while waiters passed drinks and appetizers. A quartet played on the landing under the blank wall where Gwen's portrait had hung before. Hands outstretched, a maid approached Anna for her wraps. Anna debated what to do. One way or another, she wouldn't be there for very long. She handed over the coat and umbrella. Perhaps people would be more receptive if she wasn't dripping on them.

"Anna," Tom walked up to her with a little hug, "haven't seen you in ages. How are you?"

"I'm good. Really good." Anna looked over his shoulder to see Erika a few steps away. Did she care? No, not really. "And how are you, Erika?" BUT, why not let her dangle for a minute? "Didn't Paul tell me you were in Boston a lot last year?"

Erika managed a crooked smile. "Near Boston—at my sister's."

"Well, it is lovely to see you two here tonight—" Anna leaned over and touched her arm, "together. Excuse me, I need to find Paul."

Anna cut through the living room, smiling at some familiar faces, trying to ignore the others. In jeans and a work shirt she wasn't exactly dressed for the occasion, an irony not lost on her, given the usual Onasego propensity for dressing down. After several minutes, she spotted Paul by the bar talking to a young blonde, complete with little black dress and slinky sandals. She sped over and tapped Paul on the shoulder. "Excuse me, Paul. I need to talk to you right away."

To his credit, Paul didn't skip a beat. "Lindy, could you please tell my wife we just met? And that you're Pug's date."

To her credit, Lindy looked only moderately appalled.

"That's not why I'm here." Anna smiled at the young woman, "Please excuse us," and pulled Paul into a corner. "I think Jamie is lying about why he wants Tim's land. I need for you to come with me and hear some information so you can explain it to the trustees. The Friends of Catskill people are at the house waiting for us."

"Whoa, why would he lie?"

"It's complicated. Very complicated. Will you just come?"

He looked around the room. She knew he was weighing his job against what she was asking him to do. "Okay. Let me get my coat."

"I need to get mine too."

Paul started for the foyer, then turned back to her. "Isn't there someone else here you should talk to?" She followed his gaze across the room to William and Domnica standing in front of the fireplace.

She looked back at him. "Thank you."

The walk across the living room took forever. William and Domnica stood by themselves, Domnica, quietly elegant in a simple garnet sheath and William in an ivory shirt and black suit.

"Hello, my dear," Domnica kissed her cheek. "So lovely to see you."

Anna felt surprised at how much she had missed the older woman. "I'm sorry to interrupt, but I wonder if I might speak to William for a moment."

William glanced between Anna and Domnica. "Anything you can say to me you can say in front of my mother."

Anna gave a quick look around before beginning. "I think Jamie is lying about what he'll do with the Catskill land once he buys it. We have reason to believe he wants to use a new technique to drill there for natural gas." When neither William nor Domnica said anything she floundered on. "Something called hydrofracking. It's used to get at gas in shale. I don't really understand it, but pressurized water and toxic chemicals are injected into the ground to release the gas."

William gazed down at her. "Where did you hear this?"

"From Victor, a geologist at Catskill, and from my ex husband."

"Paul?" Domnica asked.

In a "shoot me now moment" Anna shrugged. "The other one. He's sending information about it to my house right now. Some of the Friends of Catskill are also there who would like to talk to somebody, or bodies, from the Catskill Board."

"Now?" William asked.

"There's no other time." Anna soldiered on. "I'm hoping you will come with me. Paul's coming too."

"You know I'm for the on line proposal?" William countered.

"I do."

In a quiet motion Domnica turned toward the fire, taking herself at least figuratively out of the conversation. William studied Anna's face. "Let's go."

Anna was just about in the clear when she heard Gwen's voice call out for her. "Anna Lawson! Now this is a surprise." Anna turned to face Gwen strolling into the foyer with Phil Coxe on one arm and Pug on the other. Tonight, Gwen stunned in a teal tunic hitting just below the knee. "I didn't expect to see you here," Gwen said, dropping Pug's arm to beckon a waiter serving prosecco. "Are you leaving already?"

"I'm afraid I have to run," Anna murmured.

"Are you running with two of my guests?" Gwen asked innocently. "Seems Paul also had to run," she looked at William holding his coat and Anna's, "and now I see another guest is 'running.' Why the rush?"

"I have to leave very early tomorrow," Anna answered. "Appointments in the city." And that was true. Every word.

"What a shame," Pug offered in a tone signaling he'd be thrilled to bring her car around.

Phil Coxe handed his glass to the waiter. "I would welcome a chat about your last two columns, Ms. Lawson. Particularly the one where you portrayed me as a champion of Catskill's ruin."

Anna was going to let the comment go until she noticed Domnica peering in her direction, one eyebrow raised. The therapist might as well have been screaming, TAKE YOURSELF SERIOUSLY! "I stand by the column."

"We're trying to have a nice, sociable affair here, Anna," Jamie said breaking through the group to stand beside Gwen. "No partisan politics."

Anna took her coat from William standing oddly silent. Jamie and Gwen, so smooth. And such hypocrites. "Is that why there's no real sign of Catskill here? Except for the trustees, I mean."

"Whatever in the world are you talking about?" Gwen asked, innocent hand raised to chest.

"No students, no faculty, no Catskill jazz band, no Catskill choir. You wouldn't even know the school was out there."

"And no Friends of Catskill either," Jamie cut in. "Come on, Anna, you know you were invited only as a courtesy to Paul. You shouldn't be here."

And there it was, a glimpse of that other Jamie. Anna could have kissed the man. "I know. So I'm leaving."

Phil Coxe must have noticed the slip as well. "I'm curious, Anna. Why did you come tonight?"

Anna sized up Phil Coxe, remembering the way he had badgered her at the opening board dinner to come up with an idea to make Catskill better— and then to do something about it. A complete jerk? Yes. But a genuinely concerned one. She made a snap decision. "Gwen, I need to steal one more of your guests." She turned back to Coxe. "I know you can dish it out, but can you take it?"

The chief trustee folded his arms across his chest. "Try me."

At least she had his curiosity. "You probably don't remember, but not long after Paul and I moved here, you said something to me like, 'Isn't there some kind of Friends' Association?' Then you ordered me to 'Get involved!' Do you remember that?"

He shrugged. "Vaguely."

"Well, there is a Friends' group, and now you..." With a flourish she motioned to the door.


## 84 • A TIME OF LOVE AND UNION

"So this is what I did for the Polar Plunge. I came up with these rhymes to raise money, like, 'Don't be greedy, sick kids are needy.' Maybe you need a rhyme like that for Catskill."

Anna, collecting plates with Libby and Laurel, listened in amazement as her son, detouring from his job as cookie passer, lectured Phil Coxe on how to save Catskill. She reached for his shoulder. "Joe, honey, a lot of people want to talk to Mr. Coxe. Take the cookies around one more time, then Molly will go with you up to bed." As Tim and Ray swept in to take Joe's place on the couch, she mouthed "sorry" to Coxe, waved to Molly to come get Joe, then allowed herself a moment, exhausted but pleased.

After an initial awkward entry of herself and Paul, with William, and Coxe, Peg and Deedee saved the day by suggesting that everyone really should eat. The food from Ellis's going-away party, sans Ellis, thank God, had traveled to her dining room table accompanied by plates, silver, and napkins, as well glasses and coffee cups set out by Molly, in a show of more maturity than Anna would have imagined for many years. While everyone got a plate and settled in chairs, she'd run upstairs and found, another nod to Molly, a neat stack of fax pages on her desk. On the way to the Vans' she'd suggested some keywords to Jed, who, ever resourceful, turned up pure gold. Probably as foreplay, Jed and Ava even highlighted the relevant paragraphs. The reports left no doubt that Jamie was planning on gas exploration and drilling using hydraulic fracturing techniques, or fracking, as the reports called it, on Tim's land and "on land to be acquired in and about Onasego, New York." She'd made copies of the most damning pages on the fax for William, Paul, and "Phil," as he insisted she call him in the car on the way over. While the Friends members ate scattered around the living room, the three men set up temporary shop in the kitchen, with Joe, clearly not having gone upstairs, ferrying in plates prepared by Peg. After dinner, "Phil" addressed the group from the hallway. In clear terms he let the Friends know that he would share the information on the consortium with the full board at tomorrow's breakfast meeting. Then he asked that anyone else having an opinion on Catskill's future to please speak with him or William over coffee. Whether it was the soporific effect of the comfort food or simply good sense prevailing, the mood in the house was civil, business like and, at moments, friendly.

"So, ladies," Paul said, coming around to speak to Anna, Libby, and Laurel, "good work tonight."

"What happens next?" Anna asked.

"I want to hear this," said Deedee, waving a fresh pot of coffee.

Paul thought for a minute. "Can't say. But I won't be surprised if the land deal isn't dead. There's no way the trustees can vote on that now."

Laurel clasped her hands together, jubilant. "A reprieve."

"But," Paul added, "even with the consortium out of the picture, that doesn't mean the Board can't still vote on the big issue of transitioning to on line or not. Although where the money will come from now is beyond me."

Deedee sighed. "So we're still duking it out this weekend. And probably losing."

"I can't stand it," Libby said, her voice cracking. "After all this time, Catskill and Onasego."

"Don't jump to conclusions just yet," Paul said. "I have doubts about Jamie remaining as a voting member come tomorrow morning." He looked over at Phil Coxe, "or maybe by later tonight."

Anna looked at her watch. Ten-thirty. Five would come very early. "What does that mean?"

Paul glanced around the group. "That Pug would have to vote if there's a tie."

"But, Pug is for distance learning," Libby said.

"True," Paul answered, "unless there's a miracle or he gets converted before Saturday."

Anna scanned the room. Almost everything was picked up. Whatever was going to happen would have to happen without her. "I'm sorry, but I have to pack."

Libby jumped in. "We'll finish up. Come on, Deedee, I think there are some plates on the front porch."

"But nobody ate out there," Deedee said peering over at the closed front door.

"Yes, they did." Libby grabbed her arm. "Good night, Anna."

Making the universal sign for crazy, and pointing to Libby, Deedee set the coffee on a side table and followed Libby into the hall.

Anna picked up the coffeepot. One last round and she was out of here.

"Mr. Lawson," Laurel said, her voice crisp, precise, "your Mr. Coxe there, he is a high-ranking executive with CDG brands, correct?"

Anna paused. What was Laurel up to?

"Yes, he is, Ms. Loomis."

"I would like to speak with Mr. Coxe."

Paul motioned to the couch. "How about right after Tim and Ray?"

Laurel shook her head. "I'm hosting a small bonfire tomorrow, in celebration of Beltane, and as part of our 'meet a witch' program. I would like to invite Mr. Coxe."

The barest amusement played over Paul's face. Anna could almost imagine what he was thinking after her many stories from church. But ever the pro, he said, "I'm afraid Phil's completely booked with alumni and board events."

Laurel fingered the pentacle. "Ask him, Mr. Lawson. Tell him the daughter of Laurence Loomis is the host." She took the coffeepot from Anna. "I'll take care of this. Thank you for your work tonight, Ms. Lawson."

Anna and Paul watched Laurel make her way to where William Johnson, the coach, and Victor were seated and offer coffee. Paul put his hands on his hips. "What the hell was that about?"

"No idea," Anna said, "but I've got to get to bed. What about you?"

"I'm going back out. See you in the morning."

She looked at their living room, the Friends members still there, Phil Coxe on the couch. "Back out, where?"

Paul gestured to William Johnson holding his coffee cup up to Laurel. "We're getting a beer."

In the steady predawn rain, Paul leaned in through the back window of the BMW to give Joe a kiss. Molly, curled up in blankets and pillows, was already fast asleep. Anna hadn't really expected him to get up in time to say goodbye, especially as she had heard Ralphie growl around two and the front door close.

"Dad, I don't want to go," Joe whined. "I want to stay with you."

Paul huddled under his umbrella. "Buddy, I wish, but I'm so busy today. And you're checking out a new school."

Joe tried again. "I'll be good. You saw how much I helped last night."

"Tell you what," Paul pulled Joe's blanket up around his neck, "Monday we'll do something great. A day just for you. Okay?"

Joe kicked the back of Anna's seat. "Fine!"

Paul came around to Anna's open window, stooping down.

"Were you really out 'til two?" She blew on her hands, already anxious for a cup of coffee in Roscoe.

"Yeah."

"With William?"

"Um, hum."

As much as she wanted to know everything, she also knew this was not the time to ask. "Go back to bed. You've got a big day."

"You, too. And be careful. This weather's ridiculous. What time are you meeting Jed with Molly and Joe?"

"About one, after the school meeting. Then my interview starts at two. Jed will drop Joe off tomorrow at the hotel midmorning."

Paul looked over her into the front seat. "Got your phone?"

"Yep."

"Directions?"

She pointed to the glove compartment. "A map. I got lost before, remember?"

From the backseat Joe piped back up. "I'm going to the Knicks game, Dad. Look for me."

"I will, Big D. And you take care of your mom, okay?"

Paul leaned in and kissed Anna on the cheek. "However, this thing works out… we'll be okay."

## 85 • THE GREAT BELTANE AND MR. MURDERER

JOE, A BLUE and orange Knicks cap falling over his eyes, bolted across the hotel lobby to meet her. "Mom! I saw Patrick Ewing! I SAW HIM, MOM! He was so close."

Anna knelt on one knee for a hug. "You lucky boy! Wow!" She looked up at Jed, casual in chinos and golf shirt. "Thank you! Clearly, he had a wonderful time."

"We both did. Great game," he handed Anna Joe's backpack, "and a very late night. How did the interview go?"

Anna struggled to her feet. "It went all afternoon, then also very late, lots of people, drinks, dinner, after dinner. I mean, I'm exhausted. Overslept this morning. But—I got the job!"

"Congratulations! So you'll be moving back here?"

She looked at Joe. "TBD."

"What about the school? Good?"

"I liked it a lot." She looked down at Joe. "What did you think?"

"Good. But," he grabbed her around the waist, "I want to stay home with you."

"Oh, Joe," she felt in her pocket for the parking ticket, "got to go to school sometime."

"So," Jed gazed over Joe's head at her, "what's happening in Onasego?"

"Don't know and it's killing me. They're voting at noon today." She pulled out the cardboard stub and nudged Joe toward the lobby door. "Thank you again for all that you and Ava did. That information was nothing short of amazing."

Jed caught the door for them. "And?"

It took her a moment to catch his drift. "All right," she said as they squeezed under the canopy out of the drizzle with the rest of the hotel guests awaiting cars or taxis, "I'll ask about a condo. Want a lift somewhere?"

"No thanks, I'm meeting Molly and Ava just a couple of blocks over. Going shopping for Pemberley." He hailed the valet attendant and then faced Joe. "Come back. I need another guy around."

"Sure. I'll bring my dad. We'll all go to a game together!"

Jed flipped the brim down over Joe's eyes in what Anna was sure was a "modern family," moment of his own. "Great idea." Then, after a quick hug for Anna, "Molly's bus should get into Onasego tomorrow around five. You drive carefully, okay?"

"Okay, love to Molly and Ava." She turned and gave Joe the look.

And her son, with exquisite accuracy, gave it right back, before yelling, "Thank you, Jed."

With a hand in Joe's, she watched her ex-husband disappear into the swirl of cab drivers, shoppers, workmen, dog walkers, runners, and, she thought, somewhere out there, even Patrick Ewing—everyone, in their own way, navigating a rainy day. Joe tugged her forward; the valet guy was at the curb. Handing the attendant a five, Anna held the back door for Joe, then climbed in the front seat, and, spotting a break in the oncoming rush, pulled out into the traffic.

Two and a half hours out of the city, Anna switched the windshield wipers up a speed, the drizzle turning into a steady shower. Could it rain anymore? At least this last leg of the trip, the two-lane over the mountains, was all but deserted today—a welcome change from the congestion of 87 and 17.

In the back seat, swathed in blankets, buckled in, "Listen, Mom, click, click," head lolling against the window, Joe was finally asleep after delivering a coma-inducing account of the trip to Madison Square Garden: their seats, the warm up, courtside antics, the announcer, the hot dogs, and somewhere in there he even got into the game itself. But now, what about Onasego? She picked up her phone from the dashboard, half afraid to call. Punching in Paul's number, she listened to it go to message. No surprise there. She skipped over William. He'd be in the meeting with Paul. She tried Angie, who immediately picked up.

"Anna? Is that you, Anna? Everybody shut up, it's Anna."

She heard crowd buzz in the background. "What do you mean everybody? Where are you?"

"At Nora's. We're celebrating."

"Talk louder. Celebrating what?"

"Paul and William's plan. The board voted by acclamation last night. It's done."

"What plan?"

"A hybrid. Keep the school but add an on line option. Just a few courses at first. Then build up gradually. It's brilliant."

"How can they pay for it?"

"Here's Phil. He'll explain."

Phil? Feeling slightly ridiculous without another car in sight, she stopped for the red light at a one-lane bridge. Below, the water was churning, wild. As the light turned, Coxe came on, ecstatic. "Anna! Gotta hand it to you and this Friends group. Catskill and Onasego... Just Like When You Left. The alums came in droves. And we got the message. Don't fool around with tradition. Keep students on College Hill. Our challenge grant is already halfway done. Hey, here's Libby. She wants to talk."

Libby and Phil Coxe? Best new buds? A challenge grant? On her right a sign flashed by. Small, brown with white letters. Was this her turn?

"Hey, Anna. Angus came to hear me sing. It was like old times. So great! Dawn and I are moving in with him."

That was fast. "Super. What challenge grant is Phil Coxe talking about?"

"He and Laurel got together. Announced it last night."

"But the vote? What about Pug and…?" Ahead the road forked. Right or left? She glanced at the glove compartment, the map? then wheeled right. "And, Jamie, and the acclamation thing."

"Jamie didn't vote, and Pug supported the Friends all the way."

She flicked the wipers off, the shower now a sprinkle. "Why?"

Libby laughed. "Long story short— Deedee, The Niece, and I took care of that. Tell you about it sometime. Here's Ray."

"Anna… everything worked!" Ray voice was husky, the words coming out in rasping bits. "All of it… the meet a farmer, the kids' coaching lessons, the downtown activities—and we've got all sorts of ideas now to keep those alums coming back. Coupons to everything around here. A summer Elder hostel—they can audit courses, use sports facilities. But here's some-one else."

A pause and then, William. "Say you got the job."

Anna slowed, the road suddenly narrow and rocky, manifestly unfamiliar. Beside the road, a stream pocked with limbs and debris raced along. "I did. I got the job. But, William, I've made a wrong turn. There's a stream. It's very high."

"Do you have any idea where you are?" His voice was steady. She thought of him on the highway that first day with the young cop.

"Near the reservoir, I think."

"Stay on the line, Anna."

Ahead, Anna saw a low current break over the road.

"Now there's water crossing the road in front of me. It's moving so fast. William, I'm scared."

"Can you back up?" William must have gone outside. No more buzz.

She looked in the rear-view mirror at the blind curve behind her. "Not really."

"Can you turn around?"

Anna lowered the car windows. A foot-wide shoulder rested between the car and the rushing water. A rocky hill banked the opposite lane. "I think so. Hold on."

She dropped the phone in her lap, gently tapped the brakes, then slid the car into reverse, turning the rear of the car perpendicular to the hill.

William's voice called up to her. "Anna, are you there?"

"Couple more minutes." She wiped her hands on her slacks. The water gushing over the road was just feet away. "Two more turns." Shifting into drive, she wheeled the car to her right staying clear of the shoulder, now almost submerged. "One more." She lowered the car into reverse and straightened out. "Okay, I think we're all right." She sighed just as the car lifted left, gliding on its own toward the stream. She stomped on the brakes. Nothing. Outside, water covered the road in front, behind, on both sides. With a lurch the car dipped into the stream. "WILLIAM, WE'RE IN THE RIVER!"

Yanking off her seat belt, she twisted over the seat toward Joe, clawing at the blankets, digging for the metal clamp. "WAKE UP, JOE! WAKE UP! WAKE UP!" Once again the car lurched, rolling onto one side, knocking her back against the window, water flooding into the car.

## 86 • THIS SAME GROUND

ANNA WOKE FROM the terrible dream. She was warm and dry, well covered, not wet or freezing or reaching helplessly for Joe. But the room was dark, the bed not her own. Then she remembered: the interview, the magazine, the hotel. She closed her eyes again, still so sleepy. Such a horrible dream: the strange road; the out-of-control car; water everywhere; climbing out the window to find air and then trying to get back for Joe. William had been in the dream too, and many, many people she didn't know, screaming and shouting.

She wondered what time it was. Jed would be bringing Joe to meet her. She turned on her side, squinting through rails for the clock on the nightstand.

A light glared overhead. Why was housekeeping coming in now? But it was Paul who stood beside the bed, looking down at her. Paul, haggard, unkempt. He bent toward her. "How do you feel?"

Why was he here? "Tired. So tired. Paul, the bed has rails."

"You've been asleep for a long time."

Anna tried to process what he was saying. But why was he here saying anything? "What time is it, Paul? I have to meet Joe. Downstairs."

He pulled the sheet up around her neck. "Don't worry about that right now."

"Will you get him?"

"Why don't you sleep some more?"

"I had a terrible dream."

"I'll stay with you."

The next time Anna woke, Paul was sleeping in a recliner beside her. Even asleep he seemed exhausted, beaten. She focused on the room, institutionally medical: felt the bandage on her forehead; picked at the cotton gown covered in tiny blue squares. And she remembered, clearly this time: Joe bundled in the blankets, the road, the stream, the car slipping in the water, trying to wake Joe up, trying to breathe.

She fought against the fear seizing her chest and throat. How could she ask? Because then she'd know. "Paul."

Her husband opened his eyes.

"Where's Joe?"

## 87 • SIX WEEKS LATER

ANNA SLIPPED THE white leather album from her mail slot in the All Paths Church vestibule; the entries were complete, according to the church secretary. Outside, Onasego bustled in the June sun with summer activity; while inside, a soft midweek stillness suffused the church, muffled strains of classical music wafting down from the office upstairs. She tried to arrange her thoughts. Should she look at the book at home? Drive some place out in the country? Decisions were so hard. She peeked in the sanctuary. Empty. Most of the chairs stacked up along the walls. Out in front of the church, two mothers chatted over baby carriages, one stooping to retrieve a dropped bottle from the sidewalk.

With a light shove, she pushed through the swinging doors into the sanctuary, then dropped onto one of the unfolded metal chairs. Letting her gaze drift about the room, she took in the upgrades from the capital campaign: newly stained paneling; pearlescent white walls; and stained glass windows gleaming brilliantly red, gold, and green. The church must have looked about the same on the day of Joe's service, but she wasn't sure. All she remembered was that the room seemed crowded, Tim and Bruce officiated, and that someone, Paul or Molly probably, brought *The Black Stallion* and Joe's Big D headdress for the altar table. According to *The Onasegon*, various politicos and emergency personnel attended, some making comments for the media about record rain falls and the unseasonably late snow melt.

With a sigh, she lowered the album to her lap, swept past the CONDOLENCES in silver lettering, and opened it to the first page, a picture of Joe holding up his RiteMarket bag with donations for the Polar Plunge. Underneath the picture were names of the congregation already signed up for next year. These All Paths, could there be any better people? In a sympathy note, someone wrote there was debate over whether the team should be called Jump With Joe or Kids For Kids.

She turned the page. More pictures with a note from Libby and Dawn underneath. Pictures of Joe holding his George pumpkin at the regatta. Joe with his ribbon. The ribbon under her pillow now so that at the end of every day, she could climb into bed and hold it between her hands, hour after sleepless hour.

The next page was Joe's class with Mrs. Wimbish, new pixie, no scarf, and Mr. Anunzio. The two little pricks stood in the back row where you could barely make out their faces. She should probably think of a new name for them. Or no, maybe not.

She flipped through Tim's and Ray's entries. Later.

Familiar spidery cursive caught her eye a few pages on. "I can't be your therapist, my dear, but I can be your friend. Domnica." Next, pages from the swimming class, a formal condolence from Pug. "Thinking of you in your time of sorrow." And from Phil Coxe, "Someday we will talk about our sons, not that they died, but that they lived." Hmmm. Not likely.

Several pages over Anna found the double-page entry from Bruce, a score for the Hallelujah Chorus. The inscription read, "Joe Lawson, A Big Job Guy." Ellis's contribution was a coupon for Extra Strength Skunk Skrammer, taped in the book she assumed by the church secretary.

She skipped to the middle and landed on a page from the Vans. "Dear Anna, Paul, and Molly, Joe was a dear boy who brought humor and fresh thinking to all who knew him." Nice comment, and true. In a recent late-night talk, Paul explained that Jamie really believed that as fracking and natural gas would save Onasego, Catskill going on line would save the college. And, if by combining the two, he could free some very promising land, drill quietly to attract investors, and get into the Marcellus first, why that was just good planning. Locals, according to Jamie, would be thrilled to lease their land for two or three dollars an acre. A page over from the Vans, she found an old black and white photo of the valley, strangely affective in its simplicity, signed, With Deepest Sympathy, Laurel Loomis for Country Coven.

Deedee and Angie had lengthy entries. Again, she'd read those later. Since the accident, one of them or Libby, had stopped by the house every day for whatever: driving Molly to stay with Jed and Ava; stashing dinners in the refrigerator; coaxing her from bed; or, as the Forget-Me-Nots turned entire yards a delicate blue, out for a walk. On the days when anything but breathing was impossible, one of them sat nearby. And when those three weren't there, Paul or William tried to be. Paul, who, once assured Catskill was saved and on a good course for the future, finally went to sleep that Saturday morning, with his phone turned off. Paul, who now irrationally held himself responsible because he hadn't let Joe stay home. And William, who, after calling emergency responders in three counties, raced from Nora's and found her in the sheriff's van beside the river. William, now working from his mother's house, to be close by.

"Miss Lawson."

Anna looked up at Laurel holding a large vase in one hand and a plastic bag filled with pink peonies, still in bud, in the other.

"Pardon me. I can arrange these later."

Anna closed the book. "I have to go, anyway."

Laurel set the vase on the altar table. "Miss Lawson, I am so terribly sorry."

"I know."

Pulling scissors from her pocket, Laurel began clipping stems on the diagonal before plunging them in the vase. "You're leaving soon?"

"Yes, Peter wants to get into our house and—" She couldn't finish the thought. "—and there's no reason to linger."

Laurel stepped back from the arrangement then reached for the three longest stems. "This new job, you're certain?"

Laurel had never been good at subtlety. She was about to make A POINT. Anna eyed the door. "I really have to get going."

"Ms. Lawson, please!" Laurel held the flowers in front of Anna, "These peonies will be beautiful, won't they?"

The peonies beamed pink and satiny, the point was coming. "Laurel, I can't do this today."

"Do you see the ants?"

Anna peered at the flowers. Tiny ants, several of them, were crawling around the buds.

"Ms. Lawson, the ants eat away nectar that in turn allows the buds to open. It's a symbiotic relationship."

The POINT was in there somewhere. "Stop."

Laurel sat down beside Anna. "With your column and your following, you could be an ant. Help that Onasego will need."

Despite everything, Anna smiled. An ant. Joe would love that. "I have to go."

"Ms. Lawson! We know paradise can vanish; and this hydrofracking could do it. The money will be so huge, powerful people will say it's required, that jobs and families depend upon it, that regulation will make it safe enough when it can never be made safe enough. Solar and wind, much less simple economy, will be forgotten. And there will be thousands and thousands of Jamie Vans forming their companies, paying politicians and lobbyists." Laurel paused, trying to collect herself. "You do understand this."

Anna fished in her pocket for a Kleenex and handed it to the older woman. "I wrote about the day in, day out life in a small town. Bad clothes, people like you hiking after a moose. There's nothing I can do."

Laurel pressed the tissue against her eyes. "This will be an epic battle and IF you stay, you can keep our story alive."

Anna looked around the room. Since her first encounter with Laurel, the woman had been right. Every time. She respected her enormously. But. "Laurel, my entire life is an IF right now. What IF I hadn't taken Joe to the city? What IF I hadn't made him wear a seatbelt? What IF I hadn't gotten lost? And, most of all, what IF I had never moved here? I thought I was supposed to, so I did. And look what happened. I lost Joe and the one thing I know is that I can't be here without him."

Laurel gripped her hand. "Ms. Lawson, Anna, please. Our world might end."

Anna leaned in and kissed her softly on the cheek. "Mine already has."

## 88 • DEPARTURE

ANNA WAVED AT Bruce driving away and pulled the screen door shut.

"Who was that?" Paul asked, walking out of the kitchen. By a miracle he held the bag of dog food Anna had spent the past half hour looking for. He stashed it by the door.

Anna pulled a card from her capri pocket, a Zen raked sand and stones design on the front, and handed it to him. "Bruce said today is the forty-ninth day after—" she hesitated, "the accident. Seems in Buddhist circles this is a big day for Joe."

Paul threw the card on the front hall table. "Save us."

"He meant well." Anna scooped up Ralphie, whining near the door.

"So," Paul looked over the downstairs, "the movers are coming at one. We good to go?"

Anna nodded. Boxes were packed: Paul's to an apartment, Molly's to Jed's, her things, and Joe's, to storage. Paul would take the household goods for the time being. Throughout the packing process, they had been relentlessly kind to one another.

"Just about. I'm taking Ralphie for one last walk." She held her chin up for a lick. "Then it's back to Libby's for this little guy. At least until they move to Angus's."

"Where're you going?"

"The field by the middle school. Always meant to take him there and never did. You're staying at Kitt's tonight?"

"Yeah, I can get in the apartment tomorrow. You?"

Paul asked innocently enough, but she knew it was all about William. "I'll be at Libby's."

His hand rose to her hair, smoothing it back behind her ear. "How about breakfast tomorrow before you take off?"

"I'd like that. The Pantry? At eight?"

"Yeah," She heard the catch in his voice. "Anna, I brought us here. I cheated. I have no right to ask but can't we....?"

She edged back, let Ralphie jump to the floor. "Paul, as far as you and me, or William and me," she shrugged. "That's not something I can think about." Joe's blue-gray eyes gazed back at her. "I just can't."

Veterans Park was mostly empty except for the summer tennis program on the lower level. A turquoise Honda remarkably like Ray's wrecked one buzzed past, rounded the loop, and buzzed back again in the opposite direction. Ralphie, on some dog mission of his own, pulled and strained through the pink and blue phlox bordering the edge of the woods, tugging her along the road. Reaching the top of the path to the upper level, she saw the wire fence enclosing the middle school soccer field with a sign reading NO DOGS ALLOWED. With it being midmorning and only a dozen cars in the parking lot, she decided to risk it. What could happen? Detention? Swinging the gate open, she let Ralphie off the leash and marveled at the complete joy of a small dog racing toward a bird, barking frantically, and sending it skyward. Surely there was a friend in the city whose dog she could walk. Maybe she could help at a shelter.

Vowing to never take warmth and sunshine for granted again, she dropped Ralphie's leash in the grass, leaned against the fence, and stretched her arms out along the top of the wire. All the fields were empty today, not only the middle school field but also the two on the far side of the high school, mats of dense green under a blazing blue sky. In just a few short weeks, however, soccer season would gin up once more, these fields manicured, precision lined, with legions of uniformed, shin-guarded players appearing as predictably as the peepers in the Veterans Park stream. Molly never had a chance. Like Deedee said, the A's would get scholarships, while the B's, they'd get to play. That was the same day Deedee delivered her opinion about out-of-towners just leaving. Well, that would be her. Tomorrow. Back to the real world, and a skyscraper with her name on it, where she could spend many hours each day losing herself in puff pieces for *Manhattan Living* readers. Across the field Ralphie broke into another burst of delirious barking, bounding about in circles, and occasional leaps against the fence. For an instant, a vision of this same field punctured with drilling equipment wavered unbidden. She shook it off, turning away.

At the far end of the parking lot, what looked to be an Onasego patrol car eased in from the school's entrance, proceeding directly to the fence.

Grabbing the leash, she yelled for Ralphie while the uniformed officer, familiar and young, stepped out of the car, carrying a pole with a loop on the end. He opened the gate.

"Officer Taylor."

"Mrs. Lawson. I'm so sorry for your loss. I saw Joe at the Polar Plunge. He did great. "

"Thank you."

"That your dog, ma'am?"

As she was the only other human in sight, it was a fairly safe assumption. "Yes. I'll get him out of here right away." She yelled again, deepening her voice. "Ralphie, come!"

Ralphie lay down across the field in front of the fence.

"Ma'am, you're not supposed to be in here. If you can't get him, I'm afraid I'll have to. And that'll be a ticket. Plus the pound."

"I'll have him right away." This time she pulled out the big guns and clapped. When that didn't work she set off across the field, followed closely by Officer Taylor, gripping the pole.

"Come, Ralphie, come!"

Ralphie, tongue hanging out, panting, gazed over his shoulder at her affectionately.

Taylor stopped, shaded his eyes and pointed in Ralphie's direction. "Hey, would you look at that." On the ground in front of the fence a plump, orange and white bird with a brown and white chest stood stock still staring up at them with steady black eyes.

Anna flashed on the back road to Cooperstown

"I've never seen one around here before," Taylor said, leaning against the pole, "just up in the Adirondacks. Can't imagine how it got in here."

Willing the dog to be still, Anna crept up to Ralphie, and clipped on the leash. "That's a grouse, isn't it?"

Taylor got his phone out to take a picture. "A spruce grouse, to be exact. Almost extinct. And look, he's not moving."

Anna caught her breath, her eyes sweeping the fields, the hills behind the school, the stream, the woods. *I wipe the tears away from your face.* "JoJo?"

## 89 • EPILOGUE NOVEMBER 20, 2000

ANNA SMILED AT the ecstatic email: Pemberley Oliphant Parish, two years old today! In the picture, Molly held the toddler, outfitted in a pumpkin onesie, with Jed and Ava standing on either side in buckled Pilgrim hats, holding plush velveteen turkeys. Details of the new condo were hard to make out, but according to Molly, it was "amazing."

She clicked back on the inbox. A link from Paul to the write up about him in the *Chronicle of Higher Education*: "Administrator Steps WAY Out of the Box." An accompanying picture showed Phil Coxe, Laurel, Pug, and Paul, with a pair of giant scissors in front of the renovated space for the new Catskill On Line center. In the background, Lindy, she believed, held a champagne flute aloft. Pug, Pug, Pug.

And what was this? A reply to a very old email from her to Marty about the Chicken Health Handbook column. He still wanted it?

The last email was from BarbaraBrant@yahoo, confirming her flight into Albany, as well as a rental car. After Thanksgiving in Onasego, she would drive to visit friends in Poughkeepsie. The email ended with, *Hey, got some info on Sybil. Need clear instructions to your house.* As Barbara shared her directional dyslexia, she could only imagine her sister's terror reading a return email detailing unmarked dirt roads, doublewides, and prayer flags. Plus, there was the whole issue of the house itself, little more than a shed to most, but to others, like herself, an architectural gem. Anna sat back in the desk chair with a twinge of panic that she might have passed on living here.

Sure, purposeful, the veil ripped back, that was how she felt after the encounter with the grouse. Sitting on the couch with Libby that afternoon, finally having a glass of wine together, the decision was so crystal clear. But actually it was no decision at all, just a quiet inner voice announcing what would happen. "You're staying in Onasego."

"I'm staying in Onasego," Anna said to Libby and Dawn.

Libby offered her a bag of Goldfish. "Why?"

Anna shoved aside a stack of back issues of *Opera News* on the coffee table and put her feet up. "Joe."

No explanation asked. No explanation needed.

"But where will you work?" Libby asked. "Where will you live?"

Anna shrugged. "Don't know."

"We're moving in with Angus, you could live here!" Libby offered eagerly.

"And I would come over," Dawn giggled softly.

Live at Libby's? Anna began scratching under her shirt collar, then stopped when Libby mentioned the three hundred dollar monthly rent: cat food money in Manhattan. She stuck her hands in her pockets. "How about utilities, say in February?"

"Round a hundred," Libby answered passing the Goldfish to Dawn.

Even with the extraordinary events of that day, cold logic kicked in. Four hundred dollars for rent and utilities. While she had some savings, it wasn't a lot. She refilled her glass and forced herself to see the little house beyond the STUFF. After a few calibrated blinks, she liked what she saw. Sand colored stucco walls with dark wood trim. Broad plank floors. A huge window on the woods. Beside the central room, a tiny kitchen, bedroom and bath, what else in the world was needed? She remembered first driving up to the house all those months ago, seeing Joe lying in the leaves, ecstatic about being licked in the face by Ralphie, and how much she'd admired the spare, simple lines of the cottage from the outside. The inside could be the same. Perfect, announced the inner voice. That night, after a short dream about a rare species named house grouse, she slept deeply, continuously, for the first time since Joe's death.

And mostly, the new plan worked. Although not in one straight line.

Logistics had been easy. The owner of Libby's house, who built the house for his only child as a surprise (the surprise being on the owner as the child really wanted a condo in Binghamton), was delighted to have another renter handed to him on a plate. Transportation also worked out easily. After turning down Angie's offer of Derek's motorcycle, adding "thank you" after "no," she'd found a beat-up Subaru through *The Onasegon*. And Marty, after admitting initial bewilderment with her decision, came around with alacrity, using a print term he liked, to the idea of saving on a full-time salary and benefits while still having the column going. *Churning along nicely, actually.* Sometimes she took on stock topics, chicken health, for example, but just as often harder issues, like adult men preying on young girls, and the sudden interest in the Marcellus. That Jamie Van knew she was looking over his shoulder was a source of late-night contentment.

Molly was easy as well. She missed Joe, Anna knew she did, but at the same time she was having her long awaited "chance," reveling in her new role as Jed's teenage daughter, Ava's stepdaughter, and Pemberley's older sister. Moreover, the four-hour distance worked for both Molly and Anna. Molly freed from having a nagging mother, while Anna, with daily thanks to Jed and Ava, likewise freed from *being* the nagging mother.

Paul had not been easy, though. Not at all. Initially, he assumed that if she was going to be in Onasego, then they would "heal their pain" together by getting out in life, finding new hobbies, joining things, attending events. She was stunned. When she tried to explain about the grouse and Joe and the sudden gift of clarity about the need to stay in Onasego, he, not surprisingly, was the baffled one. When she'd added her belief that something far greater than she'd ever suspected was at work, something that the guys who wrote the library panels must have known about, Paul, constitutionally, couldn't hear any of it. In a compromise, they agreed to once-a-week dinners and liberal call privileges.

William was more oblique, accepting but never questioning her decision to stay in Onasego and live in the little house alone. On the weekends he came to visit, they drove to small restaurants and inns he knew of in places like Albany, the Hudson Valley, the area around Gloversville, nothing too far away. There was talk about longer trips in the spring, perhaps to the Finger Lakes, the Thousand Islands, and maybe Lake Placid. After many miles, and a few startling experiments with a global positioning system, she realized that the quiet driving and exploring was not just a diversion for her, but also meeting some need of his. A need somehow connected to his wary relation with upstate. Her only clue was the level of detail he'd given in an account of the Revolutionary War massacre at Cherry Valley. Perhaps one day he'd tell her.

Friends were also in her life: occasional lunches with Angie, some walks with Deedee and Libby. During one anguished patch around Joe's birthday, the trio tried to take her mind off things with an accounting of the Alum weekend beginning with Laurel's "offhand" comment to Phil Coxe about her father, Laurence Loomis, an early innovator at CDG and mentor to many. In an "amazing coincidence," Coxe turned out to be one of those mentored. When Laurel mentioned her intent to offer a considerable chunk of her inherited CDG stock to Catskill for a challenge grant in her father's memory, Coxe all but fell over himself to become the co-sponsor, promising an equal number of CDG shares. Next, after breaking out the wine, the ladies recounted the gritty details of Libby, Denise, and Deedee's "Come to Jesus" talk with Pug about his vote over taking the school on line. With Ralphie in a chair as Pug, and Angie as Denise, Libby and Deedee reenacted their threat to go public, if the vote didn't go the right way, with a common story about young girls being wooed by a well-known college president and the job offers extended to keep them quiet. With a sideward glance at Anna, Libby added, "Ellis and Angus, they led the way."

She'd also had a few beers with Ray, now considering a rerun for the city council. On a "can you believe this?" note, he dropped the news that Jason and Morgan also wanted seats at City Hall, as shadow candidates for students. "They say they're residents. I say residents pay taxes." Another time, Ray confided that Tim had been rocked to his considerable core by the whole land affair and what he saw as the duplicity of officials in high positions. Plain-speaking meters were the extent of what he wanted to handle for a long time, and she understood that.

Bruce showed up at her house now and then, a rare visitor. Once with an invitation to a zendo, another time offering to plow, and most recently with some Tibetan monks sightseeing in the Ding-A-Ling van. She'd thought long and hard about a column, The Dharmalings, disliking herself for wanting to write it, then writing it anyway. Bruce thought it was hilarious. Just wanted to know why there were no pictures.

Except for email articles regarding technical aspects of fracking, Laurel had been conspicuously quiet. Perhaps her new position on the Catskill Board left her little time? And, while Anna liked to think the fiery activist was still searching for ants during her Sunday manifestos at Pleasures and Problems, she couldn't say for sure, not having been to church since Joe's funeral. The thought of sitting there without her boy being entirely ridiculous.

Leaning back, Anna stretched her arms overhead, and looked out the window as she did every day, several times a day. It was a simple view, trees, fields, a peek at hills and mountains. There was something to be learned out there but she didn't know what and she didn't know how. One day a fox pup pranced up the driveway; another time a moose (she was willing to bet the very same one; how many could there be?) chewed on an aspen outside her door; and turkeys, looking like comical bad guys in black, lumbered through fairly regularly. She'd never seen another grouse, but that was all right. One had done the job. Mostly it was skunks, deer, lots of deer, and squirrels who turned up out front, well, along with Domnica and Dawn.

Domnica was a friend now, just as she'd promised, strolling down the lane for a quiet walk or cup of tea in front of the window. Domnica, who could talk about native herbs, troubleshooting propane tanks, or cleaning oriental rugs in the snow, along with evil, injury, goodness, loss, and the staggering ability of life to go on. It was to Domnica that Anna brought her thoughts about the pain of losing Joe, what Paul could not take in. How at certain times the pain felt like it might be an opening to something she needed to understand. Almost an opportunity. But like the view outside the window, she didn't know what, and she didn't know how. Domnica's reply? Kisses to both cheeks with the gentle admonishment to "Write about this pain. Let all this work on you." Then with a wave of her arm, she'd pointed out burdock, a helpful herb for kidney and skin complaints, and turned off toward home. Two topics stayed off the conversational table, however, the first being Domnica's life in Romania (a mere flutter of the therapist's hand silenced Anna's one and only inquiry); and the second, William's father.

And then there was Dawn, her true gift. Dawn, who visited often, always with Ralphie. Dawn, who should be arriving soon to spend the night. Libby had a gig at Nora's, and Angus was making a rare trip to watch. Anna stacked the papers in front of her. A progress report would be requested.

If anyone had taught her about being alone, it was Dawn. Dawn with her great eyes on the world, saying little, accepting her special vantage with maturity and innocence, all of a piece. Dawn, who loved Libby, Mumma, Ralphie, and now Angus boundlessly, but didn't mind eating lunch every day in the school lunchroom by herself. Dawn, who had her eye on a check-out job at RiteMarket, where she would get to wear a red tee shirt with RiteMarket written in white script, and maybe spike up her hair. Dawn, who admitted one night that of course she knew who her father was. Pointing to her eyes, she whispered, "the same, exactly the same." Dawn, who clung fiercely to "my friend Joe," talking about him in the constant and casual way

Anna craved. And Dawn, the only person who knew that she was working on a book. On her last visit, she begged Anna to tell her about it.

"But I don't know how it will work out, Dawnie. The plot is way up in the air."

Dawn gave her the bad eye at "plot."

"The story, what happens in the story."

"So," Dawn could do disgust as well as Molly, "you know some."

Anna looked down at the draft. "I know a lot, but I've only written the very beginning."

Dawn picked a burr from Ralphie's tail. "Read that."

Anna glanced at Dawn, sitting smugly with her purse strapped across her chest and Ralphie, his head at an angle, both fixed on her. Hmm. She held the page out in front of her and sat up straight, "Okay. Here goes."

*Most people have no idea of the beauty of upstate New York, or how a person can be shaped and claimed by living there.*

Her voice sounded reedy, thin. Outside, the sun dipped below the mountains; Ralphie lifted a leg, poised to scratch, while Dawn giggled behind her hand. A tough group, really. Anna took a breath, C for calm, and decided to go on.

*In the late 1990s, I was one.*

## NOTES AND ACKNOWLEDGEMENTS

I'VE HAD THE great pleasure of living large parts of my life in two small towns: Mt. Airy, NC and Oneonta, NY. Both towns have populations of around 10,000 and both are nestled in mountain foothills with breathtaking scenery. While I borrowed from both towns while writing *ALONE IN ONASEGO*, the fictional town of Onasego as well as the events I have happening there in the book, are just that, fiction. However, anyone who has been to Oneonta will recognize many familiar places and events in the book: Christopher's Restaurant and Country Lodge, (Christopher's Restaurant burned in 2017), the inscriptions on the library at Hartwick College, Downtown Oneonta, Wilber Park, the Unitarian Universalist Church, Southside, the Grand and Glorious Yard Sale, the Polar Bear Jump, and the Handbell Christmas Concert at the Methodist Church. Two tragedies in the book are also based on actual events that happened in and near Oneonta: the first, the murder of Ricky Parisian, an Oneonta native and New York State Police Investigator who, while off duty, heroically tried to break up a robbery and was shot in cold blood by the robber; and the second, the drowning deaths of members of a local family on a flooded road.

In other notes, the movie *Winged Migration* that I refer to in the book was filmed in 2001 while *ALONE IN ONASEGO* is set in the late 1990s. Likewise, *The Sopranos*, which I have being shown in 1998, did not air until 1999. Also, some may be surprised that I place early ideas of fracking in New York in the late 1990s, but, in fact, slick water fracking was successfully developed and proved in the Barnett Shale in 1997/1998 while leases for natural gas mineral rights in the Marcellus Shale were offered in Otsego County, NY in 2002.

I want to thank the following friends for reading various drafts, catching errors, being honest and making suggestions. They are Susan and Cary Brunswick, Naomi Fisch, Gail Henry, Jeff Hilliker, Ginnah Howard, Anne Murphy, Brandel France de Bravo, Mary McDowell, Gwen Verhoff and Linda Wilcox. Thanks also go to Ioana and Eggi Razi for help with Domnica's name. David Hutchison spoke with me about local fracking issues.

I also want to thank Valerie Haynes of Illume Writers and Artists, Cindy Dunne of Blue Farm Graphic Design, and my husband, David Bachner. Valerie and Cindy are total pros as well as insightful and patient. And then there is David, always helpful and almost always right.

## ABOUT THE AUTHOR

Forrest Bachner lives in Washington DC and Oneonta NY with her husband. She is the author of *The Colour of the Times: Margaret Shippen Arnold and the American Revolution—A Novel of Treason.*

www.ingramcontent.com/pod-product-compliance
Lightning Source LLC
Chambersburg PA
CBHW050917250626
47155CB00001B/272